## LOVE REMEMBERED

Ross took Emily by the shoulders. "It wasn't a mistake, Emily. Neither of us was ready for the consequences at the time, but I think it would have happened sooner or later."

Emily shook her head. "You can't know that."

He traced her jaw with one finger and bent his head closer. "Yes, I can," he said softly, "because I remember how right it felt."

Emily knew she should break away, but she couldn't. A tingling warmth was weakening her limbs, and she knew that time and experience had not changed her feelings for him at all. Ross pulled her tight against him and kissed her again, moving his warm, seeking mouth over hers so that her lips instantly parted.

Books by Donna Grove

*Broken Vows*
*A Touch of Camelot*
*Return to Camelot*
*Forever and Always*

Published by HarperPaperbacks

**Harper Monogram**

# Forever and Always

### ⇜ DONNA GROVE ⇝

**HarperPaperbacks**
*A Division of HarperCollinsPublishers*

# HarperPaperbacks
*A Division of* HarperCollins*Publishers*
10 East 53rd Street, New York, N.Y. 10022-5299

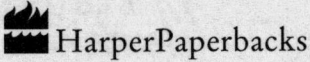

If you purchased this book without a cover, you should be aware that this book is stolen property. It was reported as "unsold and destroyed" to the publisher and neither the author nor the publisher has received any payment for this "stripped book."

This is a work of fiction. The characters, incidents, and dialogues are products of the author's imagination and are not to be construed as real. Any resemblance to actual events or persons, living or dead, is entirely coincidental.

Copyright © 1996 by Donna Grove
All rights reserved. No part of this book may be used or reproduced in any manner whatsoever without written permission of the publisher, except in the case of brief quotations embodied in critical articles and reviews. For information address HarperCollins*Publishers*, 10 East 53rd Street, New York, N.Y. 10022-5299.

ISBN 0-06-108404-2

HarperCollins®, ®, HarperPaperbacks™, and HarperMonogram® are trademarks of HarperCollins*Publishers*, Inc.

Cover illustration by Aleta Jenks

First printing: October 1996

Printed in the United States of America

Visit HarperPaperbacks on the World Wide Web at
http://www.harpercollins.com/paperbacks

❖ 10 9 8 7 6 5 4 3 2 1

# Forever and Always

# 1

## Lancaster, Pennsylvania, May 1865

*Aunt Essie was right.* Coming home again wasn't going to be easy.

Emily Winters was the last passenger to disembark from the train at the Pennsylvania Railroad Station. Behind her, the hulking black engine hissed and belched a last gasp of scalding steam. Before her, other passengers hurried on their way or stopped to greet family members who awaited their arrival. Emily had no family here to meet her. She hadn't bothered to telegraph ahead. She was too afraid that, in the end, she wouldn't be able to summon the courage to step down from that train after all.

Emily took a deep breath to clear her mind and steady her nerves. Nevertheless, when she turned to face the bustling street intersection that crossed outside the train shed, her heart seemed to lurch and tremble in her chest.

*Home.* It hadn't changed at all.

If she were a Southerner returning home after four

long years of war, it would be quite a different story, but this wasn't the South. This was Pennsylvania, once a part of the original thirteen colonies. Lancaster was an old town, a town that in accordance with its age, was slow to change. No, it hadn't changed in four years, but Emily sure had.

Her palms were sweating inside her white kid gloves and her mouth had gone dry as a bone, but she was careful to keep her chin up as she stepped out from beneath the train shed. In many ways, Lancaster was still a small town, and it was likely that she would run into someone she knew. Whether they would recognize her in passing, however, she didn't know.

Today she wore a demure navy blue day dress and a small velvet hat. Her jet black tresses were arranged in a tasteful chignon. The image she endeavored to present, that of a mature, self-possessed young woman of twenty-two, was a far cry from the confused, frightened eighteen-year-old who had so hastily departed this place.

She approached the corner of Queen and Chestnut Streets and waited as a host of open wagons, buggies, and other conveyances rattled through the busy intersection. In one hand she clutched a small carpetbag. That and a leather handbag were all she had brought with her. Immediately upon receiving her sister's telegram, she'd acted on impulse, leaving to catch the first train out of Calvert Station in Baltimore.

She was here to attend her father's funeral. That was bad enough. Why hadn't she been able to summon the courage to return before this? Why hadn't she been able to bring herself to come back six months ago when her sister Karen wrote to tell her that the newspaper had shut down its presses forever? Perhaps her father had needed her then. Despite their differences, she had been the only member of the family who had cared as deeply for the *Penn Gazette* as he had.

Knowing what she had to do now, Emily crossed the street and passed the public horsecar that would have taken her home. Instead, she headed south on the brick sidewalk. She didn't have to spare a thought as to where she was going; her feet remembered the way, and that was just as well. Her head filled with vivid memories as she passed a bookstore, tobacconist, drug store, confectionery, and several small hotels, all of them as sweetly familiar to her as the remembered aromas of her own mother's cooking.

She was aware that she garnered a few curious glances from other pedestrians. She supposed that most of them were taking note of a newcomer in town, as evidenced by the carpetbag she carried. Their glances were so brief, however, so perfunctory as they passed by on business of their own, that she doubted they recognized her. But she recognized them. Jack Martin, who ran a grocery on West King; the widow Herr, whose youngest daughter had attended grade school with Emily; Betty Stauffer, who worked behind the counter at the Hager & Brothers store. And there were others, of course, many, many familiar faces.

Emily avoided eye contact with all of them. She had no desire to draw attention to herself. They would hear later that Nathaniel Winters's daughter was in town, and then they might remember seeing her on the street. By that time, if she was lucky, she would already be gone. Back to Aunt Essie's in Baltimore.

Emily's pace slowed as she approached her father's print shop. There it was, just ahead, a narrow three-story, red brick building, squeezed between Wentz's Bee Hive Clothing Store and Wenger & Stewart's Dry Goods.

Shuttered windows, like sleeping eyes, faced the street. The window shade on the door glass was pulled down. Above the entrance, the large *Penn Gazette* sign had been replaced with a simple, dignified wooden plaque: *Nathaniel Winters, Printer*. Below this, a hand-printed sign: *Closed. Death in the family*. And under that, in the inside lower corner of the door frame, a message that caused Emily's heart to sink like a stone: *Property for Rent. Inquire at the office of Joshua S. Latham, Attorney at Law*.

Setting down her carpetbag, Emily cupped her hands around her face and peered through the shutter-slats of the front window. Fruitless. Dark as a tomb. All she could manage was a glimpse of the corner of one desk. What had she been hoping to find?

"Em? Emily?"

Her hands fell to her sides, her heart skipped a dreadful beat. She recognized that voice, but of course, it couldn't be him. Her imagination was playing cruel tricks. She'd been nervous about returning home, and naturally she had been thinking of him, and—

"Emily Winters! I'll be damned! It *is* you, isn't it?"

Emily didn't turn around. She couldn't. Her disbelieving gaze fixed on a blurred image in the window glass, the reflection of a young man standing behind her on the street. It couldn't be him.

She forced herself to turn, slowly, as if in a dream,

half expecting him not to be there, half expecting that the hazy, distorted image in the glass was the whole of him, the essence of a ghost long since dead. But he was there.

He had changed over the years. Gone was the boy she had known. His youthful features had been replaced by the rugged, hard-angled face of a man. And those shadows beneath his eyes. Could they be testimony to the suffering and tragedy he had witnessed in war?

"Emily! How long has it been?" He shook his head, looking as if he too could scarcely believe his eyes.

Emily opened her mouth to answer, but she made no sound. There was still much about him that hadn't changed. Those same deep, dark, shining brown eyes; his hair, the color of brown sugar, a lock of which always insisted on dropping across his forehead no matter how faithfully he combed it back. His smile. The same, always the same. One dimple becoming more profound whenever that smile broadened to a full-hearted grin, as it did now.

"Ross," she whispered.

"Emily, you look wonderful!" He apparently didn't notice that every drop of blood had drained from her face.

"I thought . . . I thought . . ." Her tongue felt as thick and heavy as a slab of granite. Her vision grew hazy around the edges.

His expression changed. He reached out for her just as she swayed on her feet. "Em? What's wrong? Are you all right?"

"They told me you were dead." Then the world seemed to lurch and blank out.

\* \* \*

Ross rose from his chair as Dr. Weaver, a stoop-shouldered, gray-haired gent in his early sixties, emerged from the examining room of his office and closed the connecting door behind him.

"Is she going to be all right?"

The older man offered a beleaguered smile and removed a stethoscope from around his neck. "Well, as far as I can see, she seems fine. Of course, she's got the wind back in her sails by now and won't let me near her. She's got a mind of her own, that one."

"Emily always did take after her father."

The physician chuckled amiably. "That is a fact."

"You know, she scared the hell out of me when she fainted like that."

The older man's hazel eyes sparkled. "I suppose it's not every day a fair young damsel swoons in your arms, is it?"

"No," Ross said. "Are you sure she's all right?"

"Well, physically she appears fine. My guess is it's emotional. This kind of thing happens with a lot of women when there's a death in the family. For one thing, she shouldn't have been traveling alone. You just make sure she gets home, then have her mother give her a good hot meal followed by some rest."

Ross threw a doubtful look at the door to the examining room. *Emotional. Happens with a lot of women.* But Emily wasn't a lot of women. Barring any physical reason for her fainting spell, Ross could already guess what had brought it on. Shock.

He had learned upon returning home three months before that he had been reported killed in the Wilderness campaign. The truth was that he had been very near death when he was wounded and captured by the rebs during that bloody battle. He spent over seven months in Confederate prisons before being paroled and returned to Harrisburg.

Ross had soon learned that prison was a fate much worse than death, with one exception. After his release, he'd been given a second chance at life. Upon returning to Lancaster and learning that he'd been reported killed rather than captured, he'd tracked down some of the men in his former regiment to find out what happened.

He now believed that the young man buried in his stead was a green recruit named Johnny Little. Ross had loaned Johnny his Saint Christopher medal shortly before closing with the enemy at Wilderness. Unlike Ross, Johnny had been a practicing Catholic. Going into his first battle, Johnny was grateful for Ross's small gesture. Ross learned later that it was the medal that caused Johnny's charred remains to be misidentified as his own.

But that had been cleared up months ago. The case of mistaken identity, which was the talk about town for weeks, was old news. Everyone knew the story by now, especially the Winters family. That was the thing. Ross's first stop after arriving in Lancaster had been at Nathaniel's print shop. Why hadn't Nathaniel or his wife or Emily's sister, Karen, written to tell Emily that Ross was still alive?

His musings were cut short as Emily appeared, the drawstrings of her handbag looped over one wrist as she adjusted her hat. Except for a slight pallor to her skin, she looked as if she were coming from a ladies' tea rather than from a doctor's examining room after collapsing on the sidewalk.

To Ross, she looked much the same as she always had—petite and delicate-featured, with hair the color of shining obsidian and astonishing sea blue eyes. Ross remembered how those eyes had a way of reflecting her moods. When she was happy, they could shine out from beneath those thick, sooty lashes as brilliantly as polished sapphires, but when she was angry, they seemed to turn dark and stormy to reflect that wicked temper of hers.

Those eyes turned on Ross now, locking with his own, and what he saw there was all stormy blue. "You needn't have waited."

"I wanted to make sure you were all right," Ross said, feeling suddenly awkward. Now that she had her bearings, she was treating him like a stranger.

Dr. Weaver interjected. "Take the horsecar home, and make sure you get some rest when you get there."

Emily turned on the doctor. "A horsecar? Why, my house is just down the road."

"I'll walk you, then." Ross scooped Emily's carpetbag from the floor where he'd dropped it upon their unceremonious arrival.

Before Emily could argue, the doctor joined ranks. "Why, that's a fine idea, Ross. I can trust you'll see to it she gets home without skinning her nose on the bricks."

Seeing that she was outnumbered, Emily tossed up her hands. "Oh, fine. Let's go."

Ross gave the older man a grateful wink. "Thanks, Doc. I'll come by to settle the bill tomorrow."

Emily interrupted before the good doctor could reply. "You won't settle any of my bills, Ross Gallagher. I can certainly take care of my own— "

Ross cut her off by snagging her elbow and propelling her to the door. "See you tomorrow, Doc!"

They came out into the deserted alley between the

doctor's office and the drug store next to it. As soon as the door slapped closed, Ross swung Emily around to face him. "You're all grown up, but you sure haven't changed much, have you, Em?"

"What are you talking about?"

"Still stubborn as a tick."

"I beg your pardon?"

Ross dropped her arm. "Come on." He started toward the back end of the alley, a shortcut they both knew well.

"I mean it, Ross," Emily said, following on his heels. "I'm grateful for your help, but you don't have to pay my bill. And you don't have to walk me home."

"I think I can afford a dollar for an office call, and knowing Doc Weaver, he won't even take that much seeing as he couldn't find anything wrong with you."

"That's what I've been trying to tell you both. I was just tired from the trip, and then when I saw you, I . . . I—"

She cut off sharply. Ross glanced back to find that she had stopped. Her head was bent, her face averted. She raised a hand and turned away, but not before he saw that she was trembling.

He hurried back to her, afraid she might faint again. "Em? Are you all right?"

She shook her head, refusing to look at him. "They told me you were dead."

Ross realized that she was on the verge of tears, and he was at a total loss as to what to do with her. Her anger and resentment he could handle, but this? He wanted to reach out to her but wasn't at all sure where he should touch her or even *if* he should touch her. Too much time had passed since they had parted, and the manner in which they had parted . . . Well, Ross knew from the way Emily had treated him in Doc Weaver's office that his greatest fear had come to pass. Nothing would ever be the same between them again.

"Everyone assumed I was killed in the battle at Wilderness," he began, "but I was wounded and captured by the rebs. I spent about seven months as a prisoner before I came back and found out there had been a mistake."

"How long have you been home?"

"I was released in December, then I passed some time with friends in Washington. I decided to come home about three months ago."

There was a long pause before she turned to fix him with moist, red-rimmed eyes. "Three *months?*"

Again, Ross felt an urge to reach out, to comfort her somehow, but his arms felt leaden and clumsy. "I went to see your father for a job. That's when I heard the newspaper shut down."

"Why didn't they tell me you were still alive?"

"I don't know."

"You could have written. Didn't you know where I was?"

"The day after I got back, I went to see you, but Karen told me you had moved to Baltimore to live with your aunt Esther. She gave me the impression that—" Ross stopped, reading her puzzled expression and beginning to get the idea that something was wrong.

"The impression that what?" The tremulous note in her voice was all but gone. She lifted her chin as she spoke, and Ross thought he saw the hint of storm clouds forming in the depths of those deep blue eyes.

"She gave me the impression you were going to be

married. I didn't think your fiancé would appreciate you hearing from me even if we are just . . . old friends."

Emily stared at him, betraying nothing that went on inside her head. Ross had no idea whether she was angry, hurt, or just surprised. "My sister told you I was getting married? That doesn't make any sense. You must have misunderstood her."

Ross's gaze dropped to Emily's bare left hand, confirming that she wore no betrothal or marriage ring. That sight filled him with a surprising sense of relief as well as a new suspicion. Oh, yes, there had been a misunderstanding, all right, but he was beginning to think that it was a misunderstanding deliberately created by Karen to keep him from contacting Emily.

He weighed whether or not he should pursue the subject. He had not misunderstood Karen. He recalled every word they exchanged on the front porch that day.

He'd gone to see Emily the day following his visit to Nathaniel at the shop, and so it hadn't come as a shock to Karen that Ross Gallagher was alive and standing on her doorstep. Her expression, however, made Ross feel about as welcome as a fox in a henhouse. There was no mistaking that look. She held a grudge against him, and that had come as a bewildering surprise. In all the years Ross had known the Winters family, Karen had never been standoffish.

Ross was even more surprised to learn that Emily was living in Baltimore. Nathaniel had made no mention of it the day before, and it only occurred to Ross later that Nathaniel had, in fact, been deliberately vague when he had inquired after Emily. Why hadn't he told Ross that Emily wasn't living at home? Ross could only surmise that Nathaniel and Emily might have had some sort of falling out. They were both hot-tempered and hardheaded, and if they'd had a serious quarrel, it would have been a snowy day in hell before either one of them admitted to being wrong.

Now, Ross looked away from Emily's upturned face. What had happened between her and her father was in the past. Nathaniel was dead, and this wasn't a good time to bring up Karen's odd behavior.

"Maybe you're right," he allowed. "Maybe I misunderstood Karen about you being engaged, but she made it clear that you had a life of your own. I figured that if you wanted to contact me, you would."

"You thought *I'd* contact *you?*" There was a short pause, then, "I certainly doubt that any proper young lady would take it upon herself to initiate correspondence with a gentleman."

Proper young lady? Since when did Emily Winters give a fig about propriety? When had she ever referred to him as a gentleman? Ross looked back at her. Just as he suspected, a teasing smile curved her lips.

"Miss Winters," he replied with mock formality, "I'm gratified to see that you have been studying your etiquette manuals with such obvious dedication while I've been gone."

"Indeed," she said. "I've studied them *devotedly*."

He raised a brow at her emphasis, not missing this pointed reference to the word games they used to play. "You were quite *zealous*, then, Miss Winters?"

"One might even say *assiduous*, Mr. Gallagher."

Assiduous. A tough one to beat. Ross smiled. "Well done, Miss Winters."

Their eyes held. For just a fleeting instant the

impenetrable barrier of time collapsed and things were as they used to be. Easy. Comfortable. Right. A faint voice, a voice from the distant past, sprang to life in his mind. That voice was his own. *I'll never betray you, Emily. From this moment on, you're my blood sister and I'm your blood brother. I'll stand by you and I'll never lie to you. Forever and always. Now, you say it, Em.*

Then, the moment was gone. Passed as quickly as it had come. Emily was the one to look away this time. "We should be getting along."

"You're right." Ross tried to inject into his voice a note of lightness he didn't feel as he gestured toward the south end of the alley. "You do remember the way, don't you?"

"Better than you, I'll bet."

Soon, they emerged onto the sunlit street. They turned west, walking in silence as they passed many familiar people. Ross nodded politely to some and waved to others, taking notice that Emily kept her attention focused ahead, acknowledging no one.

He soon became aware that heads turned to follow their progress down the street. As a boy, an Irish Catholic in a predominantly German Protestant community, he had learned to sense the subtle prejudice that followed in his wake. More recently, as a man risen from the dead, he had been quite an object of interest, but Ross wasn't the one people were staring at now. He had to assume their curiosity was directed at Emily.

Before long, the brick sidewalks, storefronts, and other business buildings were behind them. The landscape took on a rural character. Spreading young cornfields, verdant green meadows, sprinkles of butter yellow and soft lavender wildflowers, rolling hills and woodlands stretched as far as the eye could see.

Emily and Ross stayed to the side of the Columbia Pike as an occasional buggy, horsecar, or wagon rattled by, headed out of town. They turned onto a quiet dirt road. It was the same road they'd both taken home from school years ago.

The more he thought about it, the more curious Ross became about Emily. In order to elicit such interest from the townspeople that knew her, she must have left home not merely a few months ago, but years ago. Maybe that helped explain why she'd stopped answering his letters. But why had she left in the first place? And hadn't she come home to visit her family during that time?

"So," Emily chose that moment to shatter his train of thought. "How's the family?"

Ross was surprised at the question. He'd never been very close with the Pennsylvania Dutch farm family that had raised him. "Well, Sam died a couple years ago, you know."

Emily nodded but didn't say anything. Ross couldn't tell whether this was because she already knew or because she wasn't surprised. "But Alma's doing well enough," he added. "I visit her from time to time."

"Where are you living now?"

"I'm renting the old Hockstetter house. It's not that far down the pike from here. You remember it?"

"Of course I remember it. But it's an old farmhouse. Don't tell me you've taken to tilling the land at this late date."

"No, I never took to farming, much to my family's disappointment, but I do like living out in the country. It's quiet, and I have time to think, and . . . well, you know."

"Time for writing," she finished. Her attention was on the road ahead, but her mouth curved in a private little smile.

"You know me too well," he replied, thinking that no girl he had ever met, not even his beautiful fiancée, Johanna Davenport Butler, had ever been able to hold a candle to Emily Winters when she smiled.

"So, what are you doing for a living these days?"

Ross hesitated. He had anticipated this question, but he still wasn't sure how to answer. "Well, I'm writing for the newspaper," he said, opting for the truth.

"The newspaper? But . . ." Her voice faded as his meaning dawned on her. Emily stopped in her tracks.

Ross came to a halt two steps ahead of her. He didn't look back. He knew what was coming.

"I don't understand," she said. "The newspaper folded."

"The *Gazette* folded."

"But you just said— "

"I'm writing for the newspaper, Emily, the only newspaper left in town. The *Herald*."

Dead silence. Ross turned to meet her hard stare. The afternoon breeze loosened a wisp of dark hair from her chignon to stray across her face. She batted it away, not taking her eyes from him. "The *Herald*. You're working for that vile Malcolm Davenport. *Again*."

And so there it was, hanging in the air between them. As damning as if no time had passed at all. Betrayal.

"He offered me a job," Ross said evenly. "Your father wasn't in a position to do that."

"You didn't have to take it."

Ross felt his own anger stirring. "What was I supposed to do? Starve on principle?"

"That wouldn't have been a bad start. Many writers do."

"Your father understood my position, Emily. Why can't you?"

"I'm not my father."

Ross had to clench his jaw in order to hold his tongue. She was a woman now, full-grown, poised, and undeniably attractive, at that, but underneath it all lurked the same exasperating, mule-headed little girl in pigtails he had known so many years ago. There would be no changing her mind on this subject. Not today, anyway.

Emily held out her hand. "Could I have my bag, please?"

Ross gave it to her without a word.

"Thank you for seeing me home," she said, then continued up the road toward a red-painted covered bridge. Her family residence was less than a quarter mile distant.

As he looked after her, his anger began to fade, and he felt a painful stab of regret. The plain truth was, he had missed her. It didn't matter that she was impulsive and exasperating. It didn't matter that her passion for justice sometimes blinded her when it came to life's impossibilities. He missed her laugh and her enthusiasm and her imagination and her dreams. He missed her because a long time ago she had believed in him when few others had. He missed her friendship most of all.

"We sure did make our share of mistakes," he said under his breath. Their relationship had gotten off track a long time ago, but that didn't mean it had to stay that way. Whether she liked it or not, Ross vowed to do whatever it took to make up for what had happened in the past. He would make things right again.

# 2

*"I don't know what came over me. I've never fainted before in my life."*

Emily sat on her old bed, stripped down to her cotton chemise and drawers, two fat feather pillows stacked behind her. Through her childhood, she had shared this room with her sister, Karen. Now it belonged to Karen's daughter, but, much like the town that had greeted her upon disembarking from the train, it was the same as Emily had left it. The rose floral wallpaper, the white muslin summer curtains that billowed in the open window, the writing desk, the crazy-patchwork quilts on each of the beds. Even the pictures on the walls hadn't changed.

Karen perched on the edge of the bed, holding a soup bowl in one hand and a spoon in the other. "Don't be so hard on yourself, Em. What with Papa's death and that long train ride and—"

"And what with coming home and seeing Ross again, you mean," Emily interrupted pointedly.

Her sister merely frowned. Like their mother, Karen was a natural mediator, skilled at smoothing over arguments and upsets. Her troubled expression told Emily she perceived a disagreement on the horizon and would attempt to deflect it. "Here," she said, dipping the spoon into the bowl of chicken corn soup. "Have some more."

"I don't want it."

Karen lowered the spoon with a pained sigh. It wasn't only in temperament that they differed. A stranger would have been hard-pressed to tell they were sisters. With her generous, round face, her cafe-au-lait curls, and wide gray eyes, Karen took after their mother's side of the family. Emily, by contrast, had her father's narrow countenance, his coal black hair and piercing blue eyes. And there were those who also said she had inherited more than his physical traits. Nathaniel Winters had loved nothing more than a rousing good argument.

"You're just tired," Karen said.

"Embarrassed is what I am."

Karen dropped the spoon into the soup. "At least you woke up before he had to carry you all the way to the doctor's office."

"Well, maybe I wouldn't have fainted in the first place if I'd known Ross was still alive."

Karen shook her head wearily. "Oh, Em."

"Why didn't you tell me? You sure were quick enough to write when you heard he'd been killed."

Karen set the soup bowl on a tray on the night table, then rose from the bed and moved away. In profile, her five-month pregnancy was apparent, a slight swelling beneath the waistline of her black mourning dress. She was one of the lucky few. Her husband, Henry, had returned home from the war healthy and whole.

Bowing her head, Karen reached up to massage her temples. "I just thought it was better for everyone. What good would it have done?"

"It might have saved me from making a complete fool of myself in front of the whole town, for one thing."

"I would have written to you eventually. We had no way of knowing you'd be coming home."

"That shouldn't have had anything to do with it. Ross and I were friends."

Karen looked up, her uncharacteristically blunt words catching Emily off guard. "You were more than just friends, Em, and we both know it."

Emily couldn't quite bring herself to look away from her sister's pointed gaze. She realized now why Karen had delayed telling her of Ross's return. She was the only person in the world who knew the truth. She was trying to protect Emily from being hurt again, trying to maintain an uneasy peace with what was past. Swallowing hard, Emily started to ask, "You didn't tell—"

"No. You made me promise not to, remember?"

"Yes."

Emily was relieved when there came a knock at the door. Karen called out to grant admittance, but not before throwing Emily a look that indicated she was not through with all she had to say on the subject of Ross Gallagher.

Emily's mother appeared in the doorway. If anything had changed since Emily's hasty departure four years ago, it was her mother. Although she had visited Emily just five months before in Baltimore, it was only now that Emily noticed how much Marguerite Winters had aged. As always, her hair, a chestnut brown, was gathered into a loose chignon at the nape of her neck, but it had begun to surrender to the subtle gray invasion that had only sprinkled through it before. Her eyes, a sweet, soulful gray, still sparkled when she smiled, but she hadn't smiled much since Emily had arrived. She looked tired.

"I wanted to see how you were doing, dear," she said, pausing in the doorway. "Feeling any better?"

"I'm feeling fine, Mama. I don't know why you two are insisting I rest when there's nothing wrong with me."

Marguerite threw Karen a significant look. "Hasn't changed much, has she? Still disagreeable as a billy goat and thorny as a rosebush."

Karen merely rolled her eyes as she gathered up the soup tray.

From down the carpeted hall, they heard the patter of a child's feet. Karen's four-year-old daughter, Dorcas, appeared, hovering behind her grandmother's crepe skirts. The child had inherited Karen's crowning glory, her naturally curly hair, but her face, square-jawed and Germanic, was her father's through and through. "Mammy, I thought you got lost."

Marguerite patted her head. "It's been years and years since Mammy's gotten lost in this big old house, tulip."

As Marguerite spoke, Emily didn't miss the furtive yet curious looks she received from her little niece. Although disheartened by the child's wary manner, she wasn't surprised. Dorcas had accompanied Karen on her occasional visits to Baltimore only a few times, and that had been a while ago. The child had no memory of Emily, and it would take more than simply her mother's well-meaning assurances to convince her that the irascible dark-haired stranger who had commandeered her bedroom was indeed a blood relation.

Deciding to meet her niece's suspicions head-on, Emily offered an encouraging smile. "Hello, Dorcas."

"'Lo." The child's response was almost inaudible, muffled into her grandmother's skirts as she hid her face.

There was an awkward silence before Karen spoke, softly admonishing, "Dorcas, remember, this is your aunt Emily."

"That's quite all right." Emily brushed off the slight. She was determined to hold a smile. "It'll take some time for us to get acquainted."

From downstairs, they heard a knock at the front door. Whoever it was, the timing couldn't have been better.

"More callers," Marguerite said. She took Dorcas's hand. "Come, tulip. Let's see who's at the door."

Before they turned to leave, Marguerite addressed Emily. "You stay put and rest. Calling hours will be over soon, then we'll see about supper."

"I still say there's no reason to coddle me, Mama, I'm—"

"Fine," her mother finished for her, turning away. "You said that before. In that case, you can wash and wipe dishes after we eat. How's that?"

Emily gave up on arguing. Her mother had a soft-spoken manner, but when her mind was made up, there was little anyone could do to change it.

Karen was left standing in the middle of the room, resting the soup tray over the bulge of her waistline. "Give up the fight," she advised.

Emily sank back into her pillows. "It's so strange.

# FOREVER AND ALWAYS

Being home again, being in this room. It's as if I never left."

Karen's lips crooked into a sad little smile. "Yes. Having you here feels like that to me, too."

After a moment of melancholy silence, Emily scowled. "You can go now. I'll just lie here thinking dark and stormy thoughts until someone comes to release me."

"Well, if you find you absolutely can't sit still, maybe you can go through some of your old things."

"What old things?"

Karen inclined her head toward the closet. "In there's a whole crate of your old sketchbooks."

"My old sketchbooks? Really?"

Karen moved toward the door. "See you at supper."

As soon as her sister was gone, Emily threw back the sheet and climbed out of bed. She hadn't thought about those old sketchbooks in years, but now that Karen had mentioned them, she couldn't wait to get a look at them.

She pulled open the closet door. On the floor, a scarred wooden crate was crammed to overflowing with loose papers and sketchbooks. Emily felt a tiny thrill tickle through her. For the first time since stepping off the train, she was able to put her father's death and the shock of returning to find Ross alive out of her mind. She carried the crate over to the bed and set it down.

Digging through to the bottom layers, she searched for one sketchbook in particular. Then she saw its raw, dog-eared edge and pulled it out, baring it to the light of day for the first time in years. Settling back onto the bed, she pulled her legs up to sit cross-legged as she laid the sketchbook flat before her. It suddenly struck her that she hadn't sat in such an unladylike position in years, not since those days when she had worn her hair in braids. Since about the time she had made the drawings on these very pages.

## April 1855

*"Papa, that boy is back again.* He wants to speak with you." Emily stood in the open doorway to her father's office.

"What's that, Emily Elizabeth? What boy?" With his pen poised over a sheet of paper on his desk, Nathaniel Winters looked up with a frown. He still retained a full head of hair, but its color, once black as starless midnight, was now speckled with gray. Even his chin whiskers were giving in to these distinguished signs of age.

Accustomed to her father's crusty temperament, Emily tossed her head, flipping a braid over her shoulder. "It's that boy, Ross Gallagher. He was here yesterday and the day before and the day before that and—"

"Oh." Nathaniel raised his pen hand, nipping his daughter's recital in the bud. "I suppose he'll just keep coming back, won't he? Like some blasted housefly? Is that about the size of it?"

"Sure does seem like it."

"Well, go fetch him. Might as well get this over with."

Emily couldn't help a little scowl as she headed back toward the front of the shop. Along the way, she effortlessly skirted a pair of job presses and two tall composing desks where young men in aprons and rolled-up shirtsleeves stood setting type on composing sticks.

Emily knew the layout of her father's place of business so well she could have negotiated safely past desks, cabinets, worktables, and printing presses with her eyes shut. She even loved the smells. Printing inks, turpentine, new paper, and pipe tobacco.

This, the first floor, comprised the job printing department and front business office as well as her father's private office near the back. Adjoining his office was a small, windowless room with a washstand and a cot that was always kept stocked with fresh linens and clean towels. That was where Nathaniel stayed when he had to work into the wee hours of the morning. Since the *Penn Gazette* had become a morning daily, night work was not an unusual occurrence. The newspaper itself was printed on a new double-cylinder power press up on the second floor. Also located upstairs was the folding room, the composing department, and an office area for a news reporter and an assistant editor.

The boy who waited by the front door was familiar to Emily. Since he had moved in with a neighboring farm family in February, they took the same road into town for school. Rumor had it that he was from New York City and that his mother had died, leaving him orphaned. The Brenner family had taken him in after he was bounced back and forth among other relatives.

Aside from these rumors, Emily knew firsthand that Ross Gallagher had his share of problems with bullies in the schoolyard. His chief adversary was a boy named John Butler, whose family owned one of the biggest mills in town. John and his friends' constant name-calling—much of which Emily didn't understand—was nevertheless awful, and Ross often sported a black eye or a split lip after tangling with his tormenters. From what Emily could tell, the source of Ross's troubles with John seemed to be his half-Irish background and his Catholic religion. Emily has recently begun to notice that this second word, *Catholic*, was often pronounced in a derogatory whisper even by adults.

After observing this phenomenon, Emily had asked her father about it. He told her that Catholics differed from Episcopalians no more than one nest of skunks differed from another and that it was indeed an unfortunate thing that so many people were cursed with brains no bigger than a peanut. Then he had shooed her off, telling her to go play. While his answer had not cleared things up entirely, it had shed enough light for Emily to know that it was just as wrong for those boys at school to be making fun of Ross Gallagher as it was for them to tease the black or Jewish children.

While it was true that Ross Gallagher's life story had an undeniable heartrending quality, Emily was having a very hard time feeling sorry for him at the moment, and it had nothing to do with him being Irish or Catholic. He was here to get a job, and Emily didn't care for that idea at all. Whatever job a thirteen-year-old boy could do, Emily figured she could do just as well. But she hadn't convinced her father of that fact yet. And now, along came this boy, this *upstart*, ready to snatch opportunity right out from under her nose. No, she didn't like that idea one bit.

Ross's lanky adolescent frame snapped to attention as Emily approached. "So, uh, what did he say, Emily?"

Emily wrinkled her nose, annoyed that he was suddenly acting like they were friends. Jiminy pats! They weren't even in the same room at school. He was in the upper grade classroom with that snooty Johanna Davenport, whose father was an alderman at church and owned the competing daily newspaper in town. Ross had never even bothered to say hello to Emily until he came poking around her father's shop looking for a job.

"He said you can come on back, but . . ." Emily trailed off ominously.

Ross looked alarmed. "But what?"

"He's not in a very good mood."

Emily knew that her father's surly reputation often preceded him and was gratified to see it was true in this case. Ross's Adam's apple bobbed as he swallowed hard. "He isn't?"

Emily inclined her head toward the back of the print shop. "Come on."

"Uh, maybe it's not such a good time to bother him, Emily. Maybe I should come back later when he's not so busy."

Emily smirked to herself as she led Ross past the compositors, both of whom looked up sympathetically as the nervous lad passed.

"He's here, Papa!" Emily announced when they reached their destination.

She noted with satisfaction that her father appeared profoundly annoyed as he looked up, interrupted yet again in the middle of a heated sentence. His deep voice boomed so loudly, Emily imagined it shook the rafters overhead. "Well, dad blast it! What's he waiting for? Send him in!"

Emily stepped to one side and gestured for Ross to enter. "You heard him."

Ross's healthy, suntanned complexion had gone cotton white. The expression on his face told Emily that if he had a choice between entering the den of a disturbed grizzly and entering Nathaniel Winters's sanctified cubicle, he would most happily choose the grizzly.

Nathaniel's voice cracked the air like a bullwhip. "What's the matter, boy? Your shoes get stuck to the floor?"

Emily almost giggled as Ross actually looked down at his scuffed brown boots, but her glee fizzled when he looked up again. His expression had changed. Some color had returned to his cheeks. She saw something in those dark brown eyes that made her frown. It was the same look he wore when faced with John Butler's insults. Something in those eyes told Emily that it would take a lot more than a grouchy newspaper editor to make young Ross Gallagher turn tail and run.

He took a deep breath and stepped into the room. "Sorry to disturb you, sir. If this is a bad time, I—"

"Hold that thought!"

Emily stuck her head around the corner of the doorway to see her father scribbling furiously, ignoring the youth who stood before him. After a few moments, he tossed down his pen. "Well, what is it, young man? I haven't got all day."

"I heard you were looking for an errand boy."

Nathaniel's impatient gaze shifted to Emily, who still gaped around the corner of the doorway. "You need something, Emily Elizabeth?"

"No."

"Well, then, why don't you go put your head someplace where it'll do some good?"

Miffed, Emily pulled back out of sight and waited. There was a moment of silence inside the room.

"You still there, Emily Elizabeth?"

"No."

"Go on, now. Mind your own business."

Emily slinked past the archway, throwing a rebellious scowl at her father for good measure. What use was a newspaper reporter who minded her own business?

She passed by a towering black walnut cabinet, intending to head straight for the rear exit, but just as she glanced over her shoulder to see if anyone was watching, Billy O'Leary came thundering down the back staircase.

Billy was a jovial, redheaded Irishman and just about the biggest, handsomest man Emily had ever met. He sometimes let her help load fresh paper into the press for printing, and he never failed to acknowledge her presence, which was more than she could say for most adults.

Billy grinned and ruffled her hair as he passed. "Well-and-a-day! There she be! Me sweet *mavourneen*, Em-il-ee!"

Emily could muster little more than a tongue-tied gurgle in response. Billy addressed every female from the age of two to eighty-two in a similarly flattering manner, but that didn't squelch the flush of pleasure that rose to her cheeks when he called her his sweet *mavourneen*.

Emily waited until Billy stopped to talk to one of the compositors up front before making a break for the back door. Seconds later, she was safely outside and rounding the rear corner of the building to the brick alley between the print shop and the dry goods store next door. As she'd known it would be on a warm spring afternoon such as this, her father's office window was propped open. Pressing her shoulder blades against the brick wall next to it, Emily strained to hear the conversation passing within.

"What did you say your name was, son?"

"Ross Gallagher, sir."

"Gallagher, Gallagher... Wouldn't be related to the Gallaghers on Chestnut, would you?"

"No, sir. I live with Mr. and Mrs. Brenner west of town."

"The Brenners? Why, they're neighbors of ours."

"Yes, sir."

"How is it you came to live with them?"

"Well, uh, my ma died a year ago, sir. Mrs. Brenner was my ma's cousin."

"I see. They have a nice-sized farm. I reckon they could find plenty of work for a young fella like yourself."

"They have six boys of their own, all grown, and I've already talked with them about it, sir. Except for planting and harvest, I could work every day after school and most Saturdays."

"Uh-huh. How old are you, Mr. Gallagher?"

"Thirteen, sir."

"You have any experience in printing?"

"No, sir, but I sure would like to learn the business."

"What makes you think you want to learn the business, Mr. Gallagher?"

"Well, sir, I've always had a desire to write, and I

# FOREVER AND ALWAYS 31

know that the newspaper business is where many fine writers learn their craft. Besides, it seems like a good thing to spread the truth and speak out for what you believe is right, and . . . "

Emily's shoulders sagged. Jiminy pats! This was even worse than she had imagined. Ross Gallagher, in his own awkward, adolescent vernacular, was spouting the Gospel According to Nathaniel Winters. How often had her father waxed eloquent at the dinner table over freedom of the press and educating the public on the important moral issues of the day?

After Ross concluded his speech, there came a lengthy pause. A very bad sign.

"I like the way you think, Mr. Gallagher, but it's a long way from errand boy to editor."

"Yes, sir."

"Where are you from? Originally, I mean."

"New York City, sir."

"Is that right? You know, as a boy, I apprenticed for four years with the printing office of John T. West on Chatham Street in New York. You ever hear of them?"

"No, sir."

"I got to know a young journeyman printer while I was there. At that time, he was quite a bit older than you are, son, but you remind me of him. His name was Hod Greeley."

"Greeley? You can't mean Mr. Horace Greeley of the New York *Tribune*?"

Her father chuckled. "That's right. Well, I suppose you got yourself a job, Mr. Gallagher. You'll start out making deliveries, cleaning up, and running errands. Understand?"

"Yes, sir! Thank you, sir!"

Emily didn't need to hear any more. With a silent groan, she slid down the wall to her haunches, not giving a deuce about the dirt that smudged the short hem of her calico dress. She covered her ears and squeezed her eyes shut. *Dad blast it!*

Emily knew her father well enough to realize his outward bluster was just that. Outward bluster. Inside, he was really just as squashy as a big old mud pie. He had never had any sons of his own, and now that there would be an industrious, eager-to-learn youth on the premises, Nathaniel would take him under his wing and pass on what he knew of his beloved newspaper business. Emily had seen it happen often enough in years past, but it hadn't mattered to her back then. Now it mattered a lot. Now it was her turn!

Jealousy bloomed full and bright and green in her chest. She knew it wasn't right, but it was there just the same. And she knew that there was only one way to make that feeling go away. Make Ross Gallagher go away. If her father wouldn't do it, well, by darn, Emily would have to.

## 1865

*Remembering, Emily ran her* fingers over the cover of her old sketchbook. On impulse, she flipped it open to the middle and caught her breath. Before her was the face of the boy who had come to work in her father's shop all those years ago. If she had opened it to any other page, she might have found a landscape sketch or perhaps a rough, half-finished drawing of a squirrel.

The pencil sketch was crude, the work of a child's semiskilled hands, but it was impossible not to recognize Ross as he had looked to her then. The tousled, shaggy brown hair, those dark, shining eyes, that dimpled smile. Tentatively, Emily ran her index finger along the faded lines of his jaw. Her own childish scrawl trailed across the bottom of the page: *I love you, Ross Gallagher. I will love you forever.*

With tears burning her eyes, she flipped the sketchbook closed and flung it back into the wooden crate. Forever hadn't been such a long time, after all.

# 3

*It was hot and muggy,* the kind of day when the clouds are steel gray and hanging low. Not even the hint of a summer breeze tickled the oak trees that lined the city street next to the Episcopal church cemetery. Perfect day for a funeral, Ross thought. The only thing missing was the rain, and he reckoned that would come too before the day was done, but by then, Nathaniel Winters would be well and deeply buried in the welcoming brown earth.

The Reverend Mr. Carpenter, a tall gentleman of fifty-odd years, stood at the foot of the pinewood casket. "For as much as it hath pleased Almighty God, in his wise providence, to take out of this world the soul of our deceased brother. . ."

The sight of that casket brought upon Ross a profound, chest-constricting sense of loss. It was true that it was he who had allowed their correspondence to lapse during the war, but before that, Nathaniel had been more of a father to him than anyone, certainly more than Sam Brenner. Even though the Brenners were family, Ross had never

# FOREVER AND ALWAYS

felt like more than a hired hand growing up on their farm.

Ross didn't blame them. By the time he arrived on their doorstep, orphaned at thirteen, the Brenners were too old to take on raising another child. They'd already raised a brood of eleven of their own, but they were pure, down-to-the-bone Pennsylvania German stock. Their sense of Christian duty dictated that they take the half-Irish youngster into their home.

Ross tugged at the uncomfortably stiff choker collar of his shirt. He wore a somber suit and crepe armband in deference to the man who was being laid to rest today, but he'd spent almost four years in Union blue, much of that time with the uniform in tatters on his back. He was still having a hard time getting used to formal civilian dress.

His fiancée, Johanna, nudged him, a subtle cue that he was being impolite. Ross stopped tugging at his collar and gave her a sideways glance. Curvaceous, honey blond, and blue-eyed, Johanna Davenport Butler looked as lovely as ever. Her clear complexion shone radiantly from beneath the brim of her bonnet.

Ross shifted his attention, his gaze sweeping through the gathered mourners to find Emily. She stood between her mother and a close friend from childhood, Reverend Carpenter's daughter, Melissa. Emily's black veil was lifted, and her head was bent, her gloved hands clasped in prayer. She hadn't yet spared Ross a glance, even as she passed in the church aisle on her way to the front pew. And it wasn't because she was too immersed in her own grief to have noticed him. Ross knew this like he knew the beat of his own heart. He knew it because he knew Emily as well as he knew himself. Oh, yes. Emily was as aware of his presence as he was of hers. She was ignoring him on purpose.

Reverend Carpenter concluded the service, and, after a moment of respectful silence, the crowd began to disperse.

"Let's go," Johanna whispered, casting a discreet glance in the direction of the grieving family.

"No, wait. I think we should say something."

Johanna's reply was cut off as Ross felt a solid slap on his shoulder. "So, Gallagher, I heard you were back. You look pretty damn good for a dead man."

That singularly annoying voice from the past caused Ross to turn and face Karl Becker's lanky six-foot frame. He was golden blond and angular, and his hazel eyes glimmered with impudence. He wore a silk top hat and a stylish black frock coat over matching trousers. Except for a few lines around his mouth and eyes and the mahogany cane upon which he rested his weight, he hadn't changed from the devil-may-care rogue of their youth.

Ross knew that Karl had joined the Union army sometime after he had, but they hadn't fought in the same regiment. Now, it took great effort for him to muster a few polite words for his old friend. The last time they had seen each other, Karl had been nursing a broken nose, courtesy of Ross.

"Good to see you again, Karl. How have you been?"

With a nod of his head, Karl indicated the cane he carried. "Except for this bum leg, I'm doing quite well." His gaze shifted to Johanna. "And you, Mrs. Butler, are looking ravishing, as always." Without waiting for a reply, Karl looked back at Ross, his tone mocking. "You've done well for yourself, Rossy, but then, I never had any doubt you would."

As penniless youths, they had both had lofty ambitions. Judging by Karl's stylish attire, he looked well on his way to attaining them. Ross absorbed his old friend's candid observation dryly. "I'm surprised to see you here."

"Oh? Why?"

"I didn't realize you knew Nathaniel so well."

The corners of Karl's mouth lifted. "Oh, it's not Nathaniel I came for, it's Emily. I heard she was back in town."

Knowing that Karl was goading him, Ross didn't take the bait. Instead, he held his old friend's challenging gaze and forced an acidic smile. It had been over Emily that their boyhood friendship had disintegrated. Ross had suspected that Karl's intentions toward her were less than gentlemanly, and he wondered now if Karl intended to pick up with her where he'd left off.

"It was thoughtful of you to come," Ross said evenly. "I'm sure Emily will appreciate your support."

"I'm sure she will." Karl's smug tone was so teeming with innuendo it made Ross want to bust his nose all over again.

Flicking his gaze to Johanna, Karl lifted his top hat. "Good day, Mrs. Butler." To Ross, he winked. "See you around, Gallagher." And, with that, he ambled toward the line of mourners that had formed to offer condolences to the family.

"Son of a bitch," Ross muttered under his breath.

Johanna sounded awestruck. "Well, I'll be dipped. Imagine that. Karl Becker, of all people."

"I thought he moved away."

"Yes, but I heard he's back," Johanna replied. "He's gotten a clerkship to study law under David Stauffer on King Street."

Ross absorbed this grimly. If Karl was back in town, perhaps it was a good thing Emily was returning to Baltimore.

Johanna tugged on his arm. "Let's go."

Ross was reminded of the exchange Karl had interrupted. "No, I think we should say something."

"Most everyone else is just leaving, Ross."

"But there are some people stopping to say a few words. Probably those who haven't had a chance to pay their respects during the last two days." Ross gave her a pointed look. "I think we fall into that category."

Johanna straightened the black felt bow to her bonnet. An unnecessary gesture. Her bow was as elegant and perfect as everything else about her. "I don't know if it's the proper thing to do. You know how Nathaniel Winters felt about my father."

"And that's precisely why Malcolm sent you to represent him," Ross countered.

"I don't want to cause trouble."

"It's Emily, isn't it?"

"Don't be silly. Emily has nothing to do with it."

Deciding to end their impasse, Ross grasped her above the elbow and steered her toward the line of people by the closed casket. "It's the right thing to do."

Johanna was led without another word of protest, most likely because she could think of no way to disentangle herself from his firm hold without causing a scene.

The receiving line moved quickly, and it wasn't

long before Ross reached out to shake Henry Miller's beefy hand. Henry had married Karen Winters shortly before war broke out. While Ross had fought in Pennsylvania's Fiftieth Regiment, Henry had served three faithful years in the Seventy-ninth.

"How are you doing?" Ross asked.

Henry shrugged. "As well as can be expected. It'll take some time to get used to not having him around."

"That's true for a lot of us," Ross said.

Henry nodded politely at Johanna. "Nice of you to come, Miz Daven—uh, I mean, Miz Butler. Sorry." He'd caught his slip too late. He flushed with embarrassment.

Johanna smiled graciously. Technically, she was a war widow, having been married a scant month to John Butler, the spoiled son of a wealthy mill owner. The illustrious John had been an early casualty of war. Rumor had it that he'd accidentally shot himself in the foot, developed gangrene, and died before ever getting the chance to distinguish himself on the battlefield.

"That's quite all right, Mr. Miller," Johanna assured him. "By the end of June, my name will be Gallagher, and then we'll all have something new to get used to." She inclined her head to peer up at Ross. "Isn't that right?"

Ross gave her a warning look. This was not the place to discuss their impending nuptials.

As the woman in line ahead of Ross and Johanna moved on, Karen turned to see who was next. Her expression hardened. She uttered only one word. "Oh."

Once again, Ross got the message. Karen still held a mysterious grudge against him.

She gave him a short nod. "Ross."

"Karen. It's nice to see you again, although the circumstances are less than—"

"Yes," Karen interrupted, casting a cool eye over Johanna's impeccably dressed figure. "How nice of you to come, Johanna."

"I was so sorry to hear of your father's passing. It must have come as such a blow," Johanna said.

"Yes. It did."

"You must let me know if there's anything we can do."

"Yes. Thank you."

Ross was relieved to see the woman ahead of them finish speaking with Marguerite Winters and move on. Unlike her daughters, she had not lifted her mourning veil, and so when Marguerite looked to see Johanna standing before her, Ross couldn't read her expression. It was to her credit, however, that her kindly greeting came out smoothly and without hesitation.

The feud between Nathaniel Winters and Johanna's father was legendary. Although both men had been members of the same Episcopal congregation, they held vastly different political views. Later, when Nathaniel's weekly paper grew to become a daily, the *Gazette* came into direct competition with the only other daily newspaper in the county, the *Morning Herald*. The *Herald* was well established, having been founded by Malcolm Davenport's late father early in the century.

Johanna swept up the older woman's hand. "Mrs. Winters, I want you to know how very sorry I am at your husband's untimely passing."

"Why, uh, thank you, my dear."

"My father asked me to express his heartfelt condolences. Even though he and Mr. Winters failed to see eye to eye in business, he always had nothing but the utmost respect for your husband on a personal level."

"I'm sure Nathaniel would be, um, gratified to know that."

"He also said to tell you that if there's anything he can do for you or your family, you're to let him know."

"Thank you, but—"

"Anything at all. We're all members of the same congregation, and it's time to let bygones be—"

"So true, dear," Marguerite said, slipping her hand free.

Ross stepped forward. "I'm very sorry, Mrs. Winters. Nathaniel will be sorely missed in this community."

Whatever it was Karen held against him, Ross was glad Marguerite didn't seem to share her hostility. The older woman's embrace was warm and sincere. "Ross, it's so good to see you again. Thank you for coming."

"He was a good man," Ross said softly.

"Oh, yes," Marguerite agreed, breaking the embrace, her voice trembling with emotion. "He was rather set in his ways, but he *was* a good man, wasn't he?"

"The best."

"He was always especially fond of you, Ross. Please come by to visit."

As Marguerite proceeded to greet the next person in line, Ross held his breath. Johanna was just stepping up to address Emily. Those two had never gotten along.

"Oh, Emily, how awful it must be to have to return home under such dreadful circumstances."

"Yes." Emily's tone was not unlike her sister's only moments before.

"It's been so long since we've seen each other. What has it been, almost four years now?"

"Yes."

"You're looking well, despite all that's happened."

"Thank you, Johanna. So are you."

"Ross has been so dreadfully worried about you since yesterday. Mercy, he told me you fainted."

Emily looked at Ross with annoyance. "It wasn't anything."

"Are you feeling better?" Ross asked, catching and holding her gaze.

"Much."

"We didn't get to talk very long yesterday, Em. We should do some catching up."

"I'm not sure how long I'll be in town."

Ross tried to read the meaning behind her clipped words, but except for the darkening expression in her eyes, her thoughts were closed to him. He had to swallow hard to control a surge of raw frustration. Here they were, face to face, yet she was cutting him off as effectively as she had four years before when she'd refused to answer his letters.

Johanna was prattling on, ". . . must be going, but do come by for a visit before you leave town. As Ross said, it's been so long and we have so much to catch up on."

"I'll try to find time," Emily said, wearing an expression that said she would rather have her fingernails torn off.

Johanna tugged on Ross's arm. As there were still

more people waiting, he had no choice but to follow. "Good-bye, Em."

"Good-bye, Ross."

He forced himself not to look back as they crossed the cemetery to the city sidewalk. "Thank God that's over," Johanna said when they were out of earshot.

"It wasn't so bad," he said tightly.

Johanna sniffed. "I think Emily was always a little bit jealous. Of you and me, I mean."

"It wasn't like that with Emily and me," he said, though if he were pressed, he knew he wouldn't be able to put into words exactly how it *had* been between Emily and him. Especially toward the end. The word *disastrous* came to mind.

"Well, maybe not for you," Johanna said, "but for her it was different. Another woman can tell."

"You weren't a woman back then," he said, impatient to get her off the subject. "You were a girl. Both of you were girls."

"That's not the point," Johanna said as they crossed the street to the opposite sidewalk. "She was sweet on you, Ross. Maybe you didn't see it, but it was there, and when you started coming to call on me—"

"Can we please drop this subject? It's history."

"Fine."

A few moments of silence passed before Johanna couldn't resist speaking again. "She wasn't very friendly, was she?"

"Well, the two of you were never exactly friends."

"I hope she doesn't take me up on my offer to come visit."

This irked Ross. "What do you mean?"

"I mean, a woman like *that* coming into my home. It wouldn't look proper at all, would it?"

"What are you talking about? What's the matter with Emily?"

She gave him an odd look. "You mean, you don't know?"

"Know what, for chrissake?"

Her sumptuous lips thinned into a prudish line. "Oh, Ross, that language. You're not in the army anymore."

"It's going to get a lot worse unless you tell me what you're talking about."

"Well, I assumed you knew. Everyone does." Johanna lost the prudish frown and took on something close to a sly smile. "But I suppose you'd already left to join the army."

"Johanna," Ross warned, losing patience.

"All right, let's see. I suppose it was sometime during that winter after you joined up when Emily had to leave town. It was after the new year, the end of January, as I recall."

"Had to leave town?" Ross tried to remember the date he had received his last letter from Emily. He thought it had been close to the time Johanna was referring to. Four attempts to elicit correspondence from Emily after that had gone unanswered. "Is that when she moved to Baltimore?"

Johanna laughed. "To go 'visit' her aunt, they said. Mercy, there's only one reason a single girl suddenly up and leaves home for an extended visit with out-of-town relatives."

Ross stopped cold. He stared at Johanna. "What?"

Her arm was still wrapped possessively around his, and so she was forced to stop with him. "You heard me."

But he couldn't have heard her right. Emily would

# FOREVER AND ALWAYS 45

have told him. Ross had to struggle to breathe past a tightening knot in his chest. "Sounds like nasty gossip."

"Maybe," Johanna said in a tone that plainly said, maybe *not*.

Ross had to look away from his preening fiancée to think clearly for a moment. It wasn't true. It couldn't be true. Again, he tried to remember the date of the last letter he'd received from Emily. January. Had it been in January? "She would have told me," he muttered. He hadn't meant to speak his jumbled thoughts aloud, but Johanna didn't seem to notice his state of shock.

"Well, she didn't actually *tell* anyone that I know of, but she didn't need to. It was obvious. Everyone had it figured out by the time she left. She had gained some weight, and she had been spending time with that awful Karl Becker before he enlisted."

"Karl?" Ross asked, looking at Johanna hard. "Are you sure?"

"Of course I'm sure. Everyone saw them together over the holidays."

"Karl," Ross muttered again under his breath. Suddenly it all came clear. He remembered the gleam in his old friend's eye just a few minutes ago when he had spoken of Emily. During that last year before war broke out, Karl Becker had begun calling on her from time to time. Back then, much to Ross's relief, his womanizing friend had never seemed to interest Emily beyond the stage of idle flirtation, but now Ross had no way of knowing what might have happened between those two after Ross left in September to join the army.

"He was always so wild. It's surprising that he's

managed to make anything of himself," Johanna added.

"Damn it!" Ross barely registered Johanna's words. He had warned Emily about Karl. He had warned her at the very start, on the night of the chestnuting party when he'd first caught them together. Karl had lured her behind the Brenners' springhouse to steal a kiss. Looking back now, Ross knew he'd probably overreacted, pulling Karl away from Emily and throwing a punch that broke his former friend's nose. But he'd done it for all the right reasons. Karl was notorious for setting his sights on any engaging smile that caught his eye, whether it be that of an innocent farm girl barely out of braids or an attractive widow twice his age. Emily had been sixteen then and no match for Karl's slick charms.

"Ross, that language of yours," Johanna chided, "Won't you at least try to curb it in public?"

"It can't be true. It's an ugly rumor. It has to be."

Johanna urged him forward again. "Well, possibly, but I doubt it. Emily stayed away for almost four years. It took her father's death to bring her home. What does that tell you?"

"It tells me that she found a better life living in Baltimore than she did in this gossiping town, that's what."

"I can understand if you don't want to believe it. You're shocked, that's all. You've said often enough she was like a sister to you, and I suppose no big brother wants to believe the worst of his little sister."

"She *was* like a sister to me, and I know she wouldn't . . ." He trailed off. He didn't want to believe the rumors, but doubts were creeping in again. And guilt. What if . . . ? He pushed the doubts away. The rumors weren't true, he reminded himself. This wasn't the first time a young woman's reputation had been damaged by false, vicious gossip.

"I wonder what she did with the child," Johanna mused. "Probably gave it up for adoption. Or maybe she's even raising it herself down in Baltimore."

"What child?" Ross demanded. "Hell, there *is* no child! All this is the result of wagging tongues and small minds!"

Perhaps it was because of Ross's irascible mood that Johanna didn't chastise him for his foul language. Nevertheless, he was glad to see they were approaching the Davenport household, one of the finest in this upper-crust neighborhood.

When they stopped at the front gate, Ross disengaged from Johanna's possessive grip. "I don't want to hear another word about this, is that understood?"

"Certainly. I'm just telling you what I heard, but if it upsets you, then we'll leave it be."

"Fine. Enough said." Ross let out an aggravated breath and reminded himself that he had no reason to be so furious with Karl. The rumors simply weren't true. He refused to believe them, and that was that.

"I suppose I'll go finish out the afternoon at the newspaper," he said. "I've got a deadline to meet."

Johanna lifted a gloved index finger to touch his jaw, urging him to look at her. "Just so long as you don't forget supper tonight. Seven o'clock. Mother is expecting you."

She smiled then, tilting her chin up, her blue eyes sparkling. If Ross didn't know better, he would think she was setting up to kiss him. But Johanna was no more likely to commit the social faux pas of kissing a man, even her betrothed, in public on the street than she was to parade naked through Centre Square.

There was a time when Johanna's considerable feminine charms had driven him crazy with adolescent desire, and, indeed, she had led him a merry chase before her father had drawn the line and demanded that she marry within her own social circle. But that was years ago. Ross was older and wiser now and no longer idealistic. He was marrying her for a number of reasons, the least of which being that she was still quite pleasing to the eye.

"Seven o'clock," he said.

"Don't be late," she cooed, letting her finger slide down the line of his jaw before turning to open the gate and walk up the front steps. She tossed him a coy wave before disappearing in a swirl of dark silk and crinoline.

Feeling drained, Ross headed back toward the center of town. Luckily, the *Herald* office was a good ten-minute walk, time enough to clear his head. Now he knew why Emily had attracted such curiosity the day she'd come back to town. He remembered how she'd refused to make eye contact with the people they passed. It made him sick at heart, but he also knew Emily had enough gumption to face down the gossipmongers if she chose to. She was a fighter, and no one knew that better than Ross.

When Johanna had referred to Emily figuratively as Ross's little sister, she spoke the truth, but Johanna didn't even know the half of it. No one did. Neither Emily nor Ross had ever let on how close they had been as children. The schoolyard teasing would have been unbearable. Friendship between a boy and a girl was unheard of. But somehow it had happened. It happened during one unusually hot summer in 1855.

Even now, as a man, Ross could look back and admit that no matter what else they had been to each other, no matter all the heartache and troubles that plagued their relationship in later years, Emily Winters was probably the best friend he'd ever had.

But it hadn't started out that way.

# 4

## May 1855

*It was Saturday.* As Ross swept the floor around the job presses, he whistled a few bars of "Turkey in the Straw" and pretended not to notice as Emily Winters strutted by on her way to the front door. Once she was past him, however, he stopped his work and fixed her pointy shoulder blades with a narrow-eyed glare. The little weasel.

Like most Saturday mornings, she'd been hanging around the print shop since it had opened, poking into things and making a general nuisance of herself; and, like most Saturdays, at quarter to eleven, she was headed out the door with a burlap sack slung over one shoulder. Ross was always glad to see her go. Today, however, he was even happier to see her stay true to her usual Saturday routine. He had a plan.

Propping his broom against the wall, Ross pulled off his work apron and hung it on a peg in the rear of the job department. Yesterday, she'd nearly gotten him fired. After school, he'd carefully organized, bundled, and tied with twine several orders of sales circulars, menus, billheads, and carton labels for delivery. He'd made the mistake, however, of leaving the two tied bundles unattended on the worktable for ten minutes. When he'd returned and pulled them from the table, he'd realized immediately something was wrong, but it was too late. His meticulously packaged print orders burst loose from their tied bundles and spilled to the floor. Ross had stared at the paper disaster at his feet, then at the ropes that dangled from his fingers. They were still knotted at the top, but the bottoms had been cleanly sliced.

"This is the end of the road for you, little Miss Weasel," Ross muttered as he pulled open the front door and stepped out onto the busy sidewalk. He spotted Emily ahead and set out to follow her at a safe distance.

The cut twine incident had been only the latest in a series of suspicious mishaps since Ross had gotten his new job. Spilled ink. Lost orders. Ross had known it would do no good to tell Mr. Winters that his own daughter was behind these misadventures. At worst, it would have sounded like a lie, at best, petty. But yesterday, Mr. Winters had finally called Ross into his office, grimly shutting the door behind them, and Ross's heart had sunk into his shoes. He was sure that his new job and his entire future in newspapering were about to go up in smoke, but then Mr. Winters had fixed him with a gruff look. "My daughter, Emily Elizabeth, she wouldn't have some bone to pick with you, would she, son?"

It was then Ross realized that Mr. Winters knew the truth. But that alone, apparently, wasn't going to solve Ross's problem.

"I'm running a business here, Mr. Gallagher," he said sternly, "I do not have the time or money to afford such shenanigans."

Ross swallowed hard. "No, sir."

"A man is innocent until proven guilty. I assume you are aware of that tenet. It is the basis of the criminal justice system in these great United States of America."

"Yes, sir."

"But a business is not a democracy."

"No, sir."

"My father had an old saying, Mr. Gallagher. It's easier to catch flies with honey than vinegar."

Ross was confused at the sudden change in subject. "Flies, sir?"

But Mr. Winters opened his office door, effectively dismissing him. "And I believe it was Mr. Franklin who said, 'Time is money.' I suggest that you give both those old sayings some serious consideration."

Oh, Ross had given them some serious consideration, all right. Mr. Winters wasn't about to banish his own daughter, even if she was a spoiled, bratty nuisance. It was up to Ross to smooth things over with the little hoyden. And soon.

Ross continued to follow Emily as she headed out of town on the Columbia Pike. He felt sure she was on her way home. His plan was to wait until she turned off the pike to confront her, but when she did turn off, she surprised him by heading for the Brenners' woodlot instead of crossing the covered bridge that would have led her home. Where was she going?

When she disappeared into the woods, Ross followed, keeping her blue calico dress in sight through

# FOREVER AND ALWAYS 53

the trees. He stopped at a break in the thickest part of the woods to see her picking her way up a steep, rocky incline. By then, his curiosity was really up. The nimble manner in which she zigzagged up the hill told him she'd tested her best paths many times before.

Ross followed until he came to the top of the hill. The trees were scarcer down below and there was another rocky knoll across from him. A grassy creek bed nestled in the niche between the knolls. Ross guessed the little stream was an offshoot of Mowrer's Creek, which ran west of his family's farm.

Ross hunkered down to watch Emily down below. She'd dropped her burlap sack near the creek and now stood at the base of an old oak. Rubbing her hands together, she jumped to grasp the lowest limb and hung there, her stockinged legs swinging free above the ground. Then she did something Ross never expected. She skinned the cat.

Penduluming back and forth a few times to gain momentum, she swung her legs all the way up to push through the narrow space between her arms. For what seemed like a long time, her legs stayed that way, sticking straight out over her head at a perpendicular angle from the tree limb.

Ross had to clap a hand over his mouth to stifle a laugh. Her white drawers were in full view up to the waist, and her faded blue dress and white petticoat hung straight down like a tent. There was no sign of her head at all, just the tufted ends of two black braids pointing to the ground below the hem of her topsy-turvy dress. Like all boys, Ross had skinned the cat many times, but this was the first time he'd seen a girl do it.

Emily's legs started to wobble as she strained to

extend them farther, tipping downward as if trying to touch the ground behind her. Ross was sure she was going to break her neck, but then, with a jerk, she pushed her legs and hips the rest of the way through the space between her arms and flipped around, turning loose of the limb and landing on her feet. Her dress dropped down to her knees, and she brushed off her hands, shaking her braids back into place behind her shoulders.

Ross shook his head. So, all right. She was good. For a girl.

Emily strolled over to her burlap sack and pulled out what looked like a large journal. After spreading the empty sack out on the grass, she settled on the ground, crossing her legs into an eight beneath her skirt. For a long time, her head remained bent as she worked in her journal. At first, Ross assumed she was writing, maybe because he was a secret writer himself, but then he noticed her long, bold pencil strokes and realized she was drawing. It was time to approach.

Ross tried to be quiet as he started down the slope, but it was steep and there were loose rocks. He was about three-quarters of the way down when his heel jammed on some loose soil, sending a shower of pebbles down the slope, himself along with them.

"Whoa! Look out!" Ross called, losing his balance and regaining it again a split second before he would have landed on his behind at the bottom of the hill.

Emily was already on her feet, wielding a long, pointy stick. "What are you doing here?"

Ross grinned and brushed himself off. "A better question. What are *you* doing here?" He started toward her but stopped when she raised the stick.

# FOREVER AND ALWAYS

"Get away! You'd better leave me alone or I'll—"

"You'll what?" Ross challenged, then added smugly, "And anyhow, does your pa know you come here every Saturday?"

Emily's fierce expression faltered, but only for a split second. She didn't lower the stick. "Sure he knows. What business is it of yours?"

Ross snorted. "Why do I have the feeling that you're being less than completely truthful?"

"Why don't you just go away and leave me alone?"

"You can put the stick down. I'm not going to hurt you." Ross narrowed his eyes. "Although maybe I should, considering it's been you pulling those tricks on me at the shop."

She blinked. It was the only sign that she might be worried. "You don't have any proof of that."

"I don't need any. Your pa knows, too."

At this, her forehead crinkled, betraying her completely. "He does?"

"Put down the stick. You couldn't hurt a mouse with that thing."

Emily evaluated her meager weapon, then lowered it cautiously. "Did he say so?"

"Not in so many words, but he knows."

"You're lying. If he knew, he would have given me the dickens for it."

"I hope he does."

Emily threw down the stick. "Well, I'm his daughter, and you're just an errand boy. We'll just see which one of us lasts longer."

"A business needs an errand boy more than it needs a pesky little girl hanging around all the time," Ross retorted.

"Pesky?" Emily stiffened her spine indignantly.

"Papa lets me help out a lot. I even know how to set type. Do you?"

"Not yet, but I'll learn soon enough. I pick things up pretty quick."

"Ha! You're pretty full of yourself, I'd say. Why don't you go on home?"

"Because I don't feel like it." He glanced down where Emily's journal lay open on the grass. "So, what's this?" He bent to pick it up.

"No!"

Emily sprang, trying to snatch the journal. She was fast, but Ross was faster. He turned his back, raising it out of her reach. "Ooooh! What have we here?"

Emily grabbed at his arms. "You worm! You pig! It's mine!"

Ross laughed as he pulled loose from her scrambling fingers and dodged her next attack. "Such baaad words from such a nice little girl!"

She kept coming, her arms flailing. "Give it to me! It's mine!"

Ross eluded her and ran a short distance away, turning his back to steal a look at what she was so hell-bent on hiding. The journal was open to a pencil sketch of a rabbit. And it was good. Darn good. At first glance, he thought it looked more like the illustration in a real book than the work of a child.

There was a bloodcurdling holler. Before Ross could turn around, something huge struck him from behind. He staggered forward, a little stunned by such unexpected force and weight. He had been butted once by a billy goat. He had also been attacked by a shrieking, foul-tempered rooster. This was like a nightmarish combination of both.

She had jumped him and now had her spindly,

# FOREVER AND ALWAYS 57

bony legs wrapped tight around his middle. Her arms locked closed around his neck, and he had the fleeting thought that he'd never known a girl who acted like this before, either.

"Hey!" he exclaimed, "what are you do—*accckkk!*" She was squeezing his windpipe on purpose!

"Drop it, Ross Gallagher! You drop it right now!"

In an effort to shake her off, he started turning in circles, but she clung like a bloodsucking leech.

"Drop it!"

He didn't drop it. Darned if he was going to now! He hugged the journal to his chest, and with his free hand, reached up to wrest her arms from his neck.

She shrieked into his ear. "Let it go! Dad blast it!"

He was now half deaf, not to mention near choking, so he did the only thing he could do under the circumstances. He dropped to the ground and rolled onto his back, pinning her beneath him.

The air rushed from her lungs and her grip around his neck went limp. She was deathly still. Cold panic lanced through his middle. No! What if he'd squashed her? How would he explain it to Mr. Winters?

Alarmed, Ross rolled off of her. By the time he sat up to check if she was still alive, though, she was coming back at him. Ross raised both arms to ward her off. "Cut it out!" he yelled, but she didn't seem to notice that he'd dropped the journal to protect himself.

Ross collapsed onto his back, grabbing blindly for her arms, but she went for his face. Her fingers entangled in his hair. *"Ouch!"*

Well, she'd made one humdinger of a mistake that time. He would never stoop so low as to hit a girl, but two could play at this game. Ross tugged hard on the braid that hung above his face.

She screeched. *"Ouch!"*

Her nails scratched his scalp, her fingers tangling deeper into his hair.

He yelled, "Ouch! Darn it!"

He pulled again. Harder this time. Her eyelids clenched and her mouth pulled back into a grimace. "Stop it!"

"No, you stop it!"

Emily hesitated. It was her turn, yet she didn't move. A slow minute ticked by as they glared into each others' eyes, their faces mere inches apart, each held captive in a hopeless stalemate. Ross knew that she was trying to think her way out of this, but there *was* no way out of this. If she was smart, she would let go. If she was stupid, they could be here till dark.

She growled in disgust. "Aw, dad blast it!" Her fingers slipped from his hair, then she rolled off of him and collapsed onto her back in the grass.

Ross closed his eyes. His scalp tingled where she had pulled out a hank of hair. He tried to remember how all of this had started. The journal. The rabbit.

"You shouldn't have taken my sketchbook," she said.

Ross opened his eyes. Through the oak tree branches overhead, he could see puffy white Saturday afternoon clouds loitering in the bright blue sky. "I reckon I shouldn't have, but you shouldn't have played those tricks on me, either."

He heard a snort, then she giggled. He turned his head to see she had one hand clapped over her mouth.

"What's so funny?"

When she looked at him, her eyes glinted with mischief. "We're even."

"I guess so."

Sitting up, she shook her head to send loose dirt and grass blades flying. One of her braids, the one Ross had yanked, had lost its ribbon. Emily stood to frown down at her smudged and wrinkled dress. One of her stockings had sagged down to her ankles and the white drawers visible below her hem were grass-stained. "Dad blast it," she muttered. "My dress is ruined. My mama's going to kill me."

Ross pushed up to his feet. "Just tell her you fell on your way home."

She didn't answer but let out a disgusted sigh as she retrieved her sketchbook. She brushed dirt from the open pages and flipped it closed.

"It's really good," Ross said.

"What?"

"The rabbit. It's really good. I don't understand why you didn't want me to see it."

She hugged the book to her chest. "You think it's . . . good?"

"Yeah. It's as good as the illustrations in the books that I've seen. You ever read *The Pickwick Papers*?"

"Yes, I love Charles Dickens."

"Well, it reminds me of the drawings in that book. Not that there are any rabbits in it, but it shows the same exceptional attention to detail."

When her eyes widened, Ross noticed that they weren't so dark blue, after all. Once, when he was four, his mother took him to see the ships coming into New York harbor. Whenever he had looked out upon the same harbor after that, the water appeared to him unimpressive, a dank grayish kind of blue, but on that particular summer afternoon, the sky was clear and his outlook was bright.

Sunlight reflected white and silver off gentle ripples of water in the far-off distance. It was the sun or perhaps his own impressionable four-year-old perspective that colored the harbor an ever-rich, deep royal blue, a majestic, sparkling, life-giving blue that stole his breath away.

Ross thought Emily's eyes were the same sparkling blue of New York harbor on that one very special summer day so long ago.

"You really think my drawings are that good?" she asked.

"Yeah," he said, "I really do."

They stood there, not saying anything, for what seemed like forever. Finally, Ross cleared his throat. "Well, I gotta go." He started to turn away.

"You won't tell my papa, will you? About how I come here some Saturdays?"

Ross looked back at her. "No, I guess not."

She smiled, and he smiled back. He started to leave again, then stopped. "You know, this is really a nice spot. No one bothers you here, do they?"

"Not until you came along." Her tone held just a hint of dry sarcasm. She sounded much older than eleven at that moment.

That made Ross smile again. "I was thinking, maybe I could bring one of my journals down here some Saturday. Maybe you could do some illustrations to go along with one of my stories."

Her face brightened. "You write stories?"

"Well, some." Suddenly embarrassed, he looked down at the ground. "They're not that good, but I figure that if I practice long enough and keep up with school and everything, maybe I'll get better, and—"

"I'd love to hear some of your stories."

He looked up to see her hugging her sketchbook even tighter. "And it might be fun to do illustrations for them," she added.

Ross felt a combined rush of apprehension and anticipation at seeing her eager expression. He had never allowed anyone to read his stories before. His family, the Brenners, weren't very encouraging. Sam and Alma had always been perplexed over his odd habit of scribbling, as they called it, but Emily didn't seem to think it was odd at all.

He broke into a grin. "Maybe next Saturday morning after I get done with my chores and before I have to go to work."

"Nine o'clock?" Emily asked.

"Nine o'clock sounds good."

They stood in awkward silence for another interminable moment before Ross turned away for the last time. "I'll see you Monday, Emily."

## May 1865

*Ross stood before the imposing* King Street *Herald* office, a four-story red brick structure known as the Davenport Building. He barely remembered walking the last six blocks. What am I doing here? he thought.

He belonged here. He worked here.

But Ross hadn't returned home from that bloody war intending to work for Malcolm Davenport's newspaper. He'd returned to Lancaster for two reasons and two reasons only. To go back to work for the old *Gazette* and to mend fences with Emily. Except the *Gazette* had already gone out of business by the time he arrived, and Emily had started a new life down in Baltimore, a life that Karen had made perfectly clear didn't include him. Things hadn't worked out at all as he had planned.

But they'd worked out.

He'd always wanted to write for a living, and now he was doing just that. He was also set to marry the girl he'd always dreamed of marrying. Things had worked out fine.

But Ross didn't feel fine. Nathaniel was dead. The *Penn Gazette* was a thing of the past. And Emily was going back to Baltimore. No, Ross didn't feel fine at all.

# 5

*Two days later,* Karen opened the window shutters, allowing a stream of daylight to flood the deserted print shop. "I don't know why you insisted on coming here, Em." It had taken some doing, but Emily had talked her sister into stopping by on their way to market. Now they were confronted with the dispiriting sight of silent job presses, empty desks, and worktables still laden with stacks of paper.

As Emily moved through the shop, her footsteps on the hardwood floor sounded hollow and foreign. She had never known the place to be so infernally quiet. "I just wanted to see it one more time."

"I suppose I can understand that," Karen said. "You spent a lot of time here with Papa."

"This is where he loved to be."

"Not so much toward the end."

Emily turned around. "What do you mean? He loved it here."

"Papa just wasn't the same after the *Gazette* shut down, not his old fighting self. I can't help wondering if he could have fought off the pneumonia if—" Karen blinked back sudden tears. "Oh, well. There's no point in thinking that way."

"I'm not so sure. The paper was important to him. It gave him a reason to get up in the morning."

Karen pulled a black-bordered handkerchief from her handbag and dabbed at her eyes. "Well, he had us, didn't he? I'd say his family was worth getting up for in the morning."

"I'm not talking about family. You know what I mean."

"I suppose only you understood him that way, right, Em?"

Emily was surprised by the undercurrent of jealousy in her sister's words. "I never said that. I never said that at all."

Karen closed her eyes and struggled to rein in her emotions. "I'm sorry. But the paper folded. There was no way to avoid the inevitable."

"Inevitable? I refuse to believe that."

Karen opened her eyes, all signs of impending tears now vanished. "The paper was losing money. Very soon, we would have been penniless. If it weren't for Henry's job at the mill—"

"That's preposterous. How could he have gone bankrupt? The paper was gaining more support all the time. By the time war broke out, people were eager for the Republican viewpoint. Subscriptions were up. Especially outside the city."

Karen stuffed her handkerchief back into her handbag. "It wasn't that. It was the advertising."

"Advertising!" Emily pointed a triumphant finger at her sister. "You mean the ads were being dropped?"

"Yes."

"And who do you think was behind that?"

Karen pointed a finger back at her. "Oh, no, you don't. We already went through this with Papa. Him and his crazy conspiracy theories. To hear him tell it, Malcolm Davenport was solely responsible for everything from the breakup of the Union to last year's bad tobacco crop."

"Well, who else would benefit from pulling advertising from the *Gazette?*"

"No one, but that doesn't make it so, Em."

"Fiddlesticks. Davenport's got his fingers stuck into dozens of pies. Don't you think that just a word from him would— "

"But he wasn't worried about the *Gazette,*" Karen argued. "It was just a little paper, certainly no competition for the *Herald.*"

"Not yet, maybe, but down the road it would have been."

Karen tossed both hands up. "I surrender. Think what you want. You're impossible to reason with."

Emily wrinkled her nose and turned her back to run a finger over the empty bed of a job press. "What is Mama planning to do with the equipment?"

"Sell it, of course."

"Sell it? But—"

"We need the money," Karen interrupted, anticipating Emily's knee-jerk opposition. "Papa didn't leave her a rich widow."

Emily hadn't thought about the financial straits her mother might be in now that her father was gone. "Are there any savings?"

"Some, but not a lot. Especially once the debts are paid. He wasn't much of a businessman, Em."

That was true. Nathaniel had always cared more about his principles than his profits. It was one of the traits Emily had always admired most. It was what had set him apart from men like Malcolm Davenport. Now, though, it seemed that Nathaniel's dedication to principle over the almighty dollar had left his widow with money problems. "I didn't consider that," Emily admitted. "How will she get by after the savings are gone?"

"Well, she has the house, and now that Papa's gone, it probably makes sense for Henry and me to stay on instead of finding a home of our own like we planned. His job at the mill should be enough to support all of us, but the lease on this shop expires at the end of next month. We've either got to move the stock and equipment out of here or sell it. There's no place to store it and no reason to try. What else do you propose we do?"

"Oh, drat." Emily moved to one of the desks and sank into a chair. "Things are a lot worse than I realized."

"We'll get by."

Emily sat forlornly for a moment before brightening. "Wait a minute."

No doubt Karen recognized her sister's tone from past experience. "Oh, no. Don't even start with one of your—"

Emily jumped to her feet. "What if we pick up where Papa left off? Why, we have everything we need and—"

"No, no, no, no." Karen shook her head vehemently.

"What's the matter?"

"What makes you think we could make a profit?"

"Papa always made a profit in the jobbing department. Is Jason Willoughby still around? And Billy O'Leary?"

Before Karen could reply, Emily plowed ahead. "You give me two good men like Jason and Billy, and I guarantee I could get this place up and running again. We'd be making a profit in no time."

"Oh, Em, it'll never work."

"Why?" Emily challenged her, confounded and annoyed that all the rest of the world seemed to see were storm clouds when it was so obvious to her that the sun was close behind.

"For one thing, who's going to bring their business to a print shop run by a woman?" Karen posed practically.

"But I just know I could run this place!"

"I don't doubt it, but how would you convince the rest of the business community of that?"

"Well, it might take some time to build the business back up to what it used to be, but . . ." Despite herself, Emily began to see the logic in Karen's argument.

"And how would you pay Jason and Billy in the meantime? They have families to support."

"Well, I'm not sure just yet, but—"

Karen drove home her final point in a gentler tone of voice. "And what happens to the business if you get married and have children?"

Emily turned away and folded her arms tight. That question, although tactfully posed, was like a stake to the heart. "Not much chance of that. Not around here. Who would have me?"

Karen's reply was soft but firm. "Any man would be lucky to have you."

"Spoken like the truly good-hearted sister of a fallen woman."

"Don't say things like that."

"People are talking again. I can see it in their faces."

"I doubt that, and even if they are, it'll pass."

"I'm sure it will. As soon as I go back to Baltimore."

Karen approached from behind and rested a hand on her shoulder. "I know Mama would love for you to stay, and so would I. Dorcas deserves to know her aunt Emily, but . . . "

"But?"

"If you decide to stay, you know it won't be easy. Given a choice, people will always believe the worst. It's human nature."

"Now you sound like Papa."

"Thank you."

Emily forced a deep breath, deliberately composing herself before she turned back to face her sister. She tried to smile. "You're welcome."

Karen didn't smile back. "And then there's the other thing."

"What other thing?"

"He's engaged to her, you know."

Another stake to the heart. Emily knew, of course, to whom her sister was referring.

At the funeral, as she had sat so stoically in that front pew, she'd wanted, more than anything, to be able to turn to the man she knew sat six pews behind her. She wanted to lose herself in Ross Gallagher's strong, competent arms. She wanted to cry on his shoulder, but that was impossible.

Ross was present in the church, barely ten feet

from where she sat, but the emotional distance between them could never be forded. They weren't children anymore, or even tentative adolescents, and their friendship was a thing of the past. He was a man, and he was sitting next to the woman who would soon be his wife. Johanna.

When Emily finally brought herself to reply to her sister's statement, she feigned casual disinterest. "Who is engaged to whom?"

Karen gave her a stern look. "Ross is engaged to Johanna Davenport."

"Johanna Butler, you mean," Emily corrected. Karen raised a skeptical eyebrow, but Emily turned her back to stroll around the shop. "Anyway, I'm happy for him."

"Oh, Emily." Karen's tone was reproachful.

Emily made a face as she ran a finger over the dusty surface of a worktable. "Well, he always wanted to marry into that stinking rich family of hers. I'm happy he's finally going to get his wish."

"What's that I hear? Jealousy?"

"Certainly not. It's just that I never quite understood how easy it was for him to trade loyalties."

"Loyalties? You can't mean when he left his old job here to go work for the *Herald*? That was years ago."

"Now that he's finally gotten himself engaged to Lady Johanna, I suppose he's right in line to become editor of the *Herald*."

"I don't doubt it. After those articles he wrote, he probably deserves it."

Emily looked around at Karen. "What articles?"

"He wrote a series on his experiences as a prisoner of war. He spent some time at Andersonville."

"Andersonville?" Emily repeated softly. "I didn't know. Everything I've heard about that place—"

"Yes. It must have been horrible. After he came back and wrote the articles, he showed them to Papa. The *Gazette* was no longer in business, but Papa wrote a letter to Mr. Greeley in New York and urged Ross to submit them. Mr. Greeley was impressed enough to run the whole series in the *Tribune*. After that, Malcolm snapped Ross up and put him on staff."

Emily frowned. "You mean, it's true that Ross didn't go to Davenport for the job? Davenport went to him?"

"That's the way I heard it. Now I understand he's working on a novel."

"A novel?" Emily flashed a smile despite herself. "That's wonderful. I always knew he could do it."

Karen gave her a sardonic look. "I'll just bet you did."

Emily almost retorted, then stopped herself. What was the point in trying to pretend with Karen? "All I meant was, he's a good writer."

"Mmm." Karen also looked as if she were about to say something more, but then changed her mind. She cleared her throat. "What do you say we get going to market?"

Emily turned away. "Do you think you could wait for me? I'll be out in a minute."

"You have a lot of memories to sift through, don't you?"

"Something like that."

"Fine. I need to get something at the dry goods store. I'll meet you there, but don't be long."

After the door closed behind her sister, Emily expelled a long sigh. It was much too warm and stuffy in here from being closed up for the past few weeks, but she could still detect a trace of those wonderful old smells underneath. Ink, turpentine, pipe tobacco. Memories. Of this place, Papa, and of so many other things.

## August 1855

*"It's beautiful, Em.* Exactly how I imagined that scene when I wrote it."

Emily beamed, pleased at Ross's compliment.

He hunkered down next to her on their picnic blanket by the creek, examining her sketch with an appreciative eye. "The bear looks so big next to poor little Matthew. And so ferocious. He doesn't know if he can really shoot that old grizzly." Ross looked up with a grin. "It's perfect."

Emily gave him a sly smile. "Flawless."

Ross raised an eyebrow, taking up her challenge. "Peerless, in fact."

"Impeccable."

"Supreme."

Emily's brain reached and stumbled. *Best?* No, any two-year-old knew that. "Uh, unequaled."

Ross's grin widened. He was sensing victory. "Consummate."

Good one, Emily thought grudgingly. "Matchless."

"Superlative."

*Superlative?* Jiminy pats. She'd have to look that one up when she got to the print shop. "Um . . ."

"Sublime," he said when she paused too long.

Emily wrinkled her nose. Who could beat a word like that? Mr. Ralph Waldo Emerson, *maybe.* She let out a bothered little sigh—her way of conceding defeat—before taking the sketchbook from him. "So, now that I've done such sublime work, does that mean you're finally going to let me read the end of the story? Does Matthew shoot the bear or not?"

Ross ran a hand through his tawny brown hair, clearing a stray lock from his forehead. It had lightened considerably over the summer. Streaks of gold ran wild all through it. "Next Saturday," he said, rising to his feet. "I'll let you read the end next Saturday."

Emily tore her gaze from his handsome face to look down at the sketchbook on her lap. Next Saturday. It would be their last Saturday before school started again. The summer was rapidly coming to an end.

"I don't know if I can wait that long," she said. "What if it rains and we can't meet, and then . . ."

It wasn't really the possibility of waiting two weeks to find out the end of the story that bothered her, it was the approaching end of summer. She had never had a summer as wonderful as this one, and that was because she had never had a friend as wonderful as Ross.

He was two years older, and he was a boy, but somehow that didn't matter. They thought the same thoughts, they shared the same dreams. Emily had other friends, friends that were girls, friends that she went to school with and played hopscotch with, but none of her other friendships had ever been like this. Secret and exciting.

She heard a sound—*dip-dop-dop-dop!*—and looked up to see Ross skipping rocks across the sparkling surface of the summer-shallow creek. He was tall and solid for a boy of thirteen and growing taller with each passing month. The sleeves of his homespun shirt—a shirt that had fit him perfectly in June—now barely reached his wrists. His denims were rolled up to his shins, disguising the fact that he was growing out of them, too.

As he stood before her, with the late morning sun behind him, Emily evaluated his barefooted, broad-shouldered frame with the keen eye of a budding young artist. Her fingers itched to capture him on paper. Just like he was now. She wanted to trap this moment forever.

Tired of skipping rocks, Ross returned to her side and dropped to his haunches. "School starts soon," he said, catching her gaze and holding it. "We'll be in the same schoolroom this year."

Emily didn't reply. Neither did she look away. What he said was true. Emily was moving to the upper level classroom. Ross was in his last year there before moving on to the boys' high school. For one year, they would share a teacher and a classroom.

"Between school and the shop, we'll be seeing a lot more of each other." He narrowed his eyes, trying to ascertain if she followed his line of reasoning.

Emily nodded. "I know what you're trying to say."

"You do?"

"We can't let anyone know."

Ross smiled and let out a heavy sigh of relief. "You do know what I'm talking about."

"No one would understand. They'd think—"

"Precisely. That's why we have to act as if—"

"We barely know each other."

"Or even as if we can barely stand each other, because—"

"The kids would never leave us alone about it," Emily finished.

"That's right." Ross cleared a stray lock from his forehead and gazed absently at the slow-moving creek. For a few minutes there was no sound, no sound but the trickle of creek water passing over rocks and the soft flutter of summer breezes stirring the oak branches overhead. When Ross looked back at her, his expression was sober. "We've got a secret to keep, and there's only one way I know to seal it forever."

Emily's eyes widened at the grim look on his face. "What?"

"We've got to seal it in blood."

"B-blood? How do we do that?"

"Well, it has to do with an old Indian ritual of becoming blood brothers. One blood brother can never betray the other."

"Indian ritual?" Emily was doubtful. Was Ross pulling her leg? "Can't we just swear on a Bible?"

"Not good enough."

"What's this old Indian ritual about?"

Ross didn't answer right away. Emily watched curiously as he rose to his feet and moved to the edge of the creek. Soon, he bent and pulled something from the mud. After swishing it around in the creek water, he held it up like a prize. "This will do."

As he approached, Emily squinted at the sliver of glass that glinted in the sun. Probably a shard from an old whiskey bottle. It looked wickedly sharp. "What are you going to do?" she asked, trying to keep the apprehension out of her voice.

Ross sank to his haunches again, his dark eyes searching her face for fear. Emily scowled, knowing that if he detected any misgivings, he would think her a weak-kneed female.

Ross waved the sliver of glass under her nose. "We've got to cut our palms. Just enough to make them bleed. Then we've got to mingle our blood."

Emily's nose wrinkled before she had a chance to stop herself.

"Well, if you're scared— "

"I'm not!" Emily denied quickly. "You go first."

Ross opened his left palm and examined it. "Since you're a girl, maybe we can just nick our fingers. How about that?"

"Fine. Just let me see you do it first."

He gave her a wily smile, and Emily got the feeling that he was teasing her just because she was a girl, but before she could say anything, he had the sharp edge of the glass shard pressed against the fleshy pad of his forefinger. She let out a gasp when he slashed it, drawing a swell of bright red blood.

"Oh!" Her eyes crossed as he offered his wound directly in front of her nose for inspection.

"Quick. Give me your finger."

Emily felt queasy. What was the matter with her? How many times had she tripped and fallen while running, skinning her knees or gashing her elbows? Plenty of times she'd bled. Plenty of times. Why did the prospect of it now suddenly seem so . . . ghastly?

"You aren't going to turn all yellow on me, are you?"

Emily forced herself to meet his expectant gaze. There was no sound but the call of a wood thrush and a barely discernible plop from the creek, a small fish or frog. She thrust out her hand, forefinger extended. It trembled some, but there wasn't much she could do to control that.

Ross took her hand in his. "This is it."

Emily closed her eyes and held her breath. She felt pressure, then a sharp sting. When she opened her eyes, she stared as one drop of blood billowed like a soap bubble on the tip of her finger.

Ross let go of her and threw down the glass shard. He held up his bloody finger. "Now, touch."

Feeling almost hypnotized by the sight of her own blood, Emily touched the tip of her forefinger to his. It was wet and slippery, but Ross grasped her wrist, holding her steady. A thin stream of blood ran down both their fingers, but by then she didn't mind so much anymore. She'd done it! And she hadn't even flinched!

"There," Ross said after a long, properly respectful moment. "Now your blood runs in my veins and my blood runs in yours. Thus we are joined forever."

When Emily raised her gaze to Ross's face, she saw that all signs of tomfoolery were gone. She had never seen him so serious. Their eyes held for a breathtaking moment before he continued, lowering his voice. "I'll never betray you, Emily. From this moment on, you're my blood sister and I'm your blood brother. I'll stand by you and I'll never lie to you. Forever and always. Now, you say it, Em."

Emily knew then that Ross Gallagher was not pulling her leg. He meant it. She nodded slowly, solemnly. "I promise," she whispered. "Forever and always."

## 1865

*Emily's attention caught* on something shiny and silver lying on a nearby table. As she moved closer, she saw it was a string of metal bells. Door bells. For as long as she could remember, those bells had hung from the front door of her father's shop, jangling noisily to announce arrivals and departures.

She picked them up, blew off a thin layer of dust, and gave them a gentle shake. The tinkling music seemed unfamiliar and oddly out of place in the quiet, and she frowned.

Ever since arriving home, she had assumed she would return to Baltimore. But why? What was she so afraid of? Memories? Wagging tongues? People?

It was true that her life in Baltimore was adequate. She enjoyed the lively company of her maiden aunt Essie, but both of them had always known what Emily was really doing there. She was hiding. And what kind of life was that?

Her real life was here. Here with her mother and her sister and a niece she had never had the chance to know. She would stay. She would stay for as long as it took to face down her past, and when that was done—In her mind, a stern voice interceded. *Hold those wild horses, Emily Elizabeth. Take it one step at a time.* Her father's words.

Crossing to the front of the shop, Emily stood on tiptoe to hang the string of silver bells from their hook on the door. When she was done, she brushed off her hands and appraised her work. A business had died here, but in her heart she knew that a new business could also be born here.

"There has to be a way," she said aloud.

But she was visited by no epiphany, no sudden flash of divine inspiration. One step at a time, she reminded herself. First, she would find a way to make this her home again.

# 6

*Ross followed Billy O'Leary* into the dining room of the Blue Swan Hotel. Ross had been coming here for breakfast and dinner all week, ever since he'd heard that Emily Winters was still in town.

Billy scanned the crowded dining room for an empty table. "There's one."

Ross noted that the table Billy had chosen was one of Emily's stations. "Lead the way, Big Bill."

It wasn't all due to altruism that Ross had invited his burly companion to share a midday meal. Although the man was now employed as a pressman at the *Herald*, Billy had formerly worked for the *Gazette*. Ross knew that Emily had always liked the gregarious Irishman. It would be impossible for her to continue to ignore him if Billy shared his table.

When the kitchen door swung open, Emily emerged carrying a water pitcher. As if by some sixth sense, her harried gaze immediately shifted to clash with Ross's. Then she looked to Billy, and Ross knew just by the apprehensive tightening of her mouth that his idea of inviting Billy along had been a good one.

The jovial Irishman waved as she wove a circuitous path around tables and gesturing patrons. "Well-and-a-day! There she be! Me sweet *mavourneen*, Em-il-ee!" Billy's booming voice reverberated throughout the dining room, turning more than a few heads.

Emily's already flushed cheeks were set to blazing as she hustled to get to them. "Hello, Billy," she greeted in a lowered voice. She poured them each a glass of water and set the pitcher down on the table. "How are you doing?"

"Why, I'm doing just fine, I am. But if you aren't a sight for sore eyes! I heard you went back to Baltimore."

Billy was wearing such a huge grin that it was impossible for Emily not to return at least a weak smile. "I decided to stay for a while. How are Lettie and the boys?"

"Why, they're better and better each and every day. Maybe you haven't heard, but Lettie's expecting again."

Emily's expression brightened. "That's wonderful. Congratulations."

Billy winked. "Well, we couldn't be happier, of course, but after four lads, I think Lettie's hoping for a lass to keep her company."

Emily actually laughed, and Ross couldn't help noticing how beautiful she was with an honest to goodness smile on her face. There had been a time, long past, when he had been able to make her laugh, too. God, how he missed those times, their special friendship, their unspoken camaraderie. He missed it so badly that it made his heart hurt to look at her.

"Well," she said, "what'll it be today, Billy?"

"Since Moneysacks Gallagher here is buying, I'll

order some of those chicken and dumplings with a nice thick slice of rhubarb pie for dessert."

Blowing an errant strand of hair from her face, Emily pulled an order pad from the pocket of her apron and took down Billy's order. For a week now, Ross had watched her scurry about, attempting to keep up with the midday crowds that swarmed the understaffed café. The owner, Jacob Groff, was a notorious penny-pincher. As long as business was brisk, he cared little that his waitresses were overworked.

"Chicken and dumplings and rhubarb pie." Emily bit her lip as she scribbled the order on her pad. From behind her, two or three impatient customers called out, "Waitress!" "Miss!" "Miss!"

Emily ignored them. "Will that be all, Billy?"

"I do believe so."

She didn't bother to look at Ross as her voice proceeded to turn flatter than a pancake. "And *you?*"

Ross didn't reply. Emily wore a smudged white apron over a black day dress, and after he allowed his gaze to slide down over the gentle curve of her bosom, he focused upon the waistband of that apron. With a sharp stab of guilt, he dropped his gaze to the table. But that proved it, didn't it? Her waist was still so narrow he could span it with his hands. The ugly rumors about her couldn't possibly be true. If Emily had ever borne a child, he'd forfeit seven months of Uncle Sam's back pay.

"Well?"

Ross looked up to see that she was waiting with one eyebrow arched stiffly. And there it was, the wall, the same impenetrable barrier she had erected between them at the funeral. It made Ross want to take her by the shoulders and shake her. Even if it was true that he'd had a hand in building that wall, he was more determined than ever to tear it down, brick by brick, if necessary, to find the old Emily.

"I'll have the same," he said.

"Fine." She started to turn away.

"Except—"

Irritated, she stopped and turned back. "Yes?"

"What kind of pie did you say you have today?"

"I didn't."

Ross gave her a cool smile. She wasn't going to get away from him so easily. Not today. If he couldn't make a dent in her damned wall with good intentions, then he'd be content to annoy her. Any emotion was better than none. "Could you list them for me, please?" he asked.

"Rhubarb, gooseberry, raisin, apple, shoofly—"

"Excuse me, but is that apple *schnitz* or fresh apple?"

Emily pursed her lips and raised her gaze to the ceiling, a sign of aggravation Ross remembered well. "*Schnitz.*"

"And would the raisin be fresh-baked?"

Emily's gaze refocused on him. Her eyes were very, very dark blue today. "Fresh-baked, Mr. Gallagher. Now, would you please—"

"I think a slice of shoofly pie will touch the spot."

Emily gave him a scathing look before marching back toward the kitchen. She ignored the many choruses of "Miss! Miss! Waitress!" that followed in her wake.

After she was gone, Billy leaned across the table. "What's that all about? I thought you were friends."

Ross picked up a butter knife. Very slowly, he

tapped out a beat of pure frustration on the tabletop. "That was a long time ago. Time changes all things, Billy."

Billy shook his head. "Not that much, boyo. Something's botherin' her, and that something has got to do with you."

"When did you get so smart?"

Billy's gray eyes twinkled. "Is that why you offered to pay for my food? Did you think maybe I could soften her up a bit?"

Ross gave a humorless laugh and tossed down the butter knife. "Let's just say I figured she wouldn't be able to look the other way so easily with you at the table."

Suddenly, an earsplitting crash came from the kitchen. From the sound of it, Ross estimated six or seven dinner plates had bit the dust. He had been in here every day for the past week, and only one meal had passed without some mishap taking place in the back.

He shook his head. "She was never intended to work anywhere near a kitchen."

"You can say that again," Billy agreed. "'Tis a pity the *Gazette* went out of business. Emily would have been a natural to take over for Nathaniel."

Ross smiled wistfully. "I used to think that girl had ink running in her veins. I'm almost surprised she hasn't tried to get it started again on her own. The paper, I mean."

"If the *Herald* weren't the only paper in town, maybe she could get work. I know she's a lass, but . . ."

Ross was about to muster a grunt of rueful agreement when the glimmer of an idea sparked in his mind.

". . . but lass or not, she had a flair for newspapering," Billy was saying. "You know, I never would have said it out loud, but I often thought that if Emily were running the paper it might not have gone adrift. She always had a—"

"Billy, you're brilliant."

"Am I, now?"

Wearing a broad grin, Ross rested both forearms on the table. "Absolutely, unequivocally brilliant."

"Well, then, how is it me wife's never noticed?"

"You said it yourself. She has a flair for the business, and the *Herald* is the only paper in town."

Billy's good humor vanished. "If you're saying what I think you're saying—"

"Jack Michaels is retiring next month, did you know that?"

"He's head of advertising, ain't he?"

"Right."

"But what's that got to do with . . . ?" Billy's eyes glowed with sudden insight, but then he shook his head. "Oh, no. I know what you're thinking."

"Michaels is going to retire, which means his assistant, Freddy Brubaker, will probably be moving up to take his job. That leaves Freddy's old job open."

Billy was not so easily persuaded. "You know Emily as well as I do, Ross. She would sooner eat dirt than work for Malcolm Davenport, and working in the advertising department would appeal to her about as much as—"

"But it's newspaper work, Billy."

Emily pushed through the kitchen door, balancing plates on a tray. Ross motioned to Billy to hush as she approached a trio of ladies seated at the table next to them. Ross recognized the patrons as seamstresses from the dress shop down the street.

After Emily set three plates of sauerkraut and pork before them and hurried back to the kitchen, the eldest, a woman with steel gray hair, spoke in a plaintive Pennsylvania German accent. "Well, if that don't beat all."

The second one in their party, a painfully thin, beak-nosed girl barely out of her teens, looked up, her fork poised over her plate. "What's that, Althea?"

"It wonders me why Jacob Groff don't know better than to hire a woman like that. Why, everybody knows about her. It's not like people are going to forget something as *schondfol* as that."

"Something as shameful as what?" Eyes big, the young one leaned over her dinner plate so far that her bodice nearly dipped into her sauerkraut.

"You don't know? Why, that's the Winters girl."

"Oh? You mean the same Winters who ran the newspaper?"

"That's the one. She had to leave town years ago. Everybody knew she was—Well, you know what condition I speak of."

"*Oy*, anyhow! You don't mean . . . ?"

"Don't say it!"

"I-to-goodness, no!"

"Up the stump and no daddy in sight," the third one, a pudgy-cheeked redhead, managed to add around a mouthful of food.

The elder one continued, "You're too young yet to remember, Ruth. It was just after the war started."

"I remember it," the redhead said, chewing with relish and buttering a biscuit. "Shocking, just shocking."

"I cannot for the life of me understand why Jacob would hire a girl like that," the elder one reiterated.

"What kind of reputation does he want? Soon respectable women will stop coming in here. Then you know what'll happen next, don't you?"

The young one's eyes widened. "No, what?"

"Why, just then this place will become no better than a *schondfol* saloon. Pass me the butter, Grace."

Ross met Billy's grim expression from across their table. "It's too bad they're women, isn't it?" he asked in a low voice. "If they were men, they'd be laid out on the floor about now."

Billy merely shook his head in disgust.

Ross continued, "I can tell them why Jacob Groff hired Emily. He knows the war's over, and there aren't many jobs for women. He knows he can get away with working her to death and paying her a pauper's wages."

Billy grunted. "Jacob Groff's so tight he would skin a louse for five cents."

"You know, I've heard some other bad talk since Emily came back to town. It's making me sick."

"Talk can be as hurtful as the cut of a knife," Billy observed gruffly. "I remember the rumors starting up when she left. Nathaniel never said a word about it to me, but I could tell it broke his heart. It had to be even worse for Mrs. Winters, but she held her head high, she did. Just as you would expect. She's a fine woman."

"That she is," Ross agreed. "And so is Emily. You still think she's better off working in a place like this than she is at the *Herald*?"

Billy's tone was doubtful. "Even if Mr. Davenport were willing to hire a lass, what makes you think he'll hire the daughter of his competitor?"

Ross spread his hands as if to explain the obvious.

"He hired us, didn't he? His main concern is making money, and that means putting out a good paper. To put out a good paper, he's got to hire good people. Malcolm knows that. And besides, you know how he's always put on a big show of harboring no ill will toward Nathaniel. To hear him tell it, it was always Nathaniel's hot temper that caused bad feelings between them. How better to prove it than to hire Emily? Hell, it would make him look like he's got a heart of gold."

"You might be able to convince me, Ross, and you might even be able to convince Mr. Davenport, seeing as how you're set to wed his one and only daughter, but I don't know how you'll ever convince *her*." Billy inclined his head, indicating to Ross that Emily was emerging again from the kitchen, her serving tray laden with new orders.

"I know you've always had a way with the lasses," Billy said, "but with that one, well . . ." He chuckled. "You're goin' to need all the luck o' the Irish and then some, Rossy, me boyo."

By the time the dinner rush was over and the kitchen was brought back into order, Emily's shift was done. She removed her soiled apron, folded it into a square, and tucked it under one arm as she grabbed her handbag. Tonight, as she had every night since taking this job, she would scrub her apron with lye in the kitchen sink at home and leave it to dry overnight in time for her shift to begin again at six the next morning. She called good-bye to the two waitresses who had arrived to take over, then headed through the nearly empty dining room to the hotel lobby that adjoined it.

As if she didn't have enough to worry about just

keeping up with the demands of her new job, Ross had taken to stopping into the café each morning for breakfast and noon for dinner. She wasn't fool enough to believe it was because of the food. He was trying to smooth things over between them, trying to pretend that everything was the same as always. Well, it wasn't the same as always, and Emily knew that the one thing she couldn't afford to do was allow herself to fall victim to his charm and dimpled smile. She had no intention of putting herself through that kind of misery again. He was set to marry Johanna in two months, and the best she could hope for was that after his wedding, he would keep to his side of town so she could keep to hers.

Emily nodded to the young clerk behind the hotel check-in desk as she rounded its corner to stand before a pine door designated *Manager*. After two brisk raps, she waited for her elderly employer's grumbling permission to enter.

"Mr. Groff," she said, closing the door behind her. "Mary's here, so I'm going home now."

The gaunt, bald man behind the cluttered desk peered up at her through gleaming spectacles. "What? Three o'clock already?" He pulled a pocket watch from his waistcoat and squinted at its face. "Oh. So it is, so it is." After replacing the watch, he dipped his pen into an inkwell and returned his attention to his accounts journal.

"Mr. Groff."

"Eh? What's that?" The man looked up, appearing annoyed that she hadn't somehow evaporated into the atmosphere to leave him in peace.

"It's payday, sir."

"Payday?" His mottled brow creased. "Already?"

He turned to squint at a railroad calendar on the wall behind his desk. "So it is, so it is." He arose from his creaking swivel chair and shuffled over to a cast-iron safe in the corner. Pausing, he threw a suspicious look over his shoulder.

Knowing his concern, Emily presented her back. Only then did he proceed to turn the dial on the combination lock. *Snick, snick, snick, snick . . . snick, snick, snick . . . snick.*

Hinges squealed in agony as the door swung open. Coins jingled. When she turned around, it was to see her miserly employer counting out the few bills and change that represented her weekly wages.

He was a skinflint, but at least he had given her a job. With the war winding down, there weren't that many openings for women, and what with the old rumors that had been stirred up with her arrival in town, Emily had seen more than a few noses turn up when she applied for various jobs. She knew that Jacob Groff had hired her more out of respect for her deceased father than anything else. He had been a loyal patron of Nathaniel's print shop since before Emily was born.

"Well, there you are, young lady." He pushed the small pile of currency across his desk. "One week's wages less fifty cents for those broken dishes we discussed."

As Emily reached for her earnings, something familiar on the corner of his desk caught her eye. "What's that?"

Mr. Groff perused the piles on his desk, squinting behind the thick lenses of his spectacles and pulling a handkerchief from his vest pocket. "What's what, young lady?"

# FOREVER AND ALWAYS    89

Knowing the man was half blind but loath to admit it, Emily pointed to the sheet of paper that had taken her attention. It was a menu, handwritten in Mr. Groff's illegible scrawl. Attached were instructions. Printing instructions. She had seen those hieroglyphics on Mr. Groff's print orders for many years.

Jacob Groff blew his bulbous nose and carelessly stuffed the handkerchief back into his trouser pocket. "New menus, young lady. New menus and order pads," he replied, sinking back down to his chair with a rheumatic grimace.

"Which printer are you using these days?" Emily tried to sound casual as she deposited her pay into her handbag.

"Denton's."

Emily pretended to be surprised. "Denton's? They're fairly expensive, aren't they?"

Mr. Groff snorted disdainfully. "*Sopperlut!* They're highway robbers, but it's them or Malcolm Davenport, and I wouldn't take my business to that old *glutzkupp* even if he managed to buy himself a seat at the right hand of God Almighty." With that proclamation, he picked up his pen, dipped it, and resumed scratching numbers in his account book.

Emily had to suppress a sly smile as an idea formulated in her mind. Her mother had already sold one job press to Mr. Denton, but Emily had pleaded with her to hold off on selling the second. Why she had bothered with this effort, she didn't really know. As Karen seemed so intent upon reminding her, she was only delaying the inevitable. The lease on the shop would be up in six weeks. Inevitable or not, though, all Emily knew was that she couldn't bear to see her father's business slip away from them piece by piece. Not just yet.

"I see your predicament," Emily said, starting to turn to leave, then stopping and turning back. "Mr. Groff, I just had a thought."

The old man looked up. "Eh?"

"I know my father's shop is out of business, but it just so happens we have plenty of paper and ink in stock, and Mother still hasn't sold the second job press." She tried to smile sweetly, even though she suspected such feminine wiles were wasted on this codger. His idea of supreme feminine beauty would be Miss Liberty on a ten-dollar gold piece.

"Well, it seems a shame for you to spend more than you have to for those menus when I could probably do it for, say . . ." Emily raised her gaze to the ceiling to calculate. She tallied a figure ten percent below her father's rates and twenty percent below what she knew Denton's would charge for the same order. This would leave her only a meager profit, but meager was better than nothing. And it was a start, wasn't it?

When she looked back at her irascible employer, her tone was flat and businesslike. "Three dollars, fifty cents."

Mr. Groff raised bushy eyebrows, recognizing a rock-bottom price when he heard it. "Three dollars, fifty cents, you say? Does that include order pads?"

"Certainly. It seems a shame to let all that equipment and paper go to waste when it could be put to good use while we're waiting to sell it, don't you agree? The price reflects little more than the cost of the paper and ink involved. The labor would come practically for free, but that's only because I know what a valuable customer you were to my father, Mr. Groff."

## FOREVER AND ALWAYS 91

"Hmm." The man blinked rapidly as he cogitated upon these cost savings to his pocketbook. "You know how to run a press, young lady? I won't stand for shoddy work. That wouldn't be worth the paper it's printed on."

"Mr. Groff, I assure you, I could run that job press in my sleep. If the quality of printing isn't just as fine as what my father would have delivered, I won't expect one penny in return."

"Not one penny, you say?" Jacob Groff thought about this seriously before his liver-hued lips rearranged themselves into an uncharacteristic but very shrewd little smile. "Young lady, you've struck yourself a deal."

# 7

*It was Saturday,* not her mother's usual washday, but ever since the funeral two weeks before, routine chores were lagging behind schedule. That was why, when the knock came at the front kitchen door of her family's rambling stone colonial home, Emily was in the summer kitchen, working up a sweat as she scrubbed petticoats over a corrugated board inside a washtub.

Knowing her mother would get the door, Emily reached for a dolly stick to transfer the soaking garments from the washtub into the rinse bucket. From there, they would go into the wringer, then out onto the wash line.

At the sound of her mother's voice drifting in from the front kitchen, Emily lifted her head, suddenly alert.

"Why, Ross Gallagher, forgive my manners. I'm just surprised to see you, that's all. Come in. Emily's in the back kitchen doing some, uh—Well! It's been quite some time since you've come to visit."

Emily stifled a squeal of dismay. What the devil

was Ross doing here? Horrified, she gaped down at her threadbare gingham housedress.

His relaxed voice carried to her ears. ". . . four years or more, I figure. It was a long war."

"Too long," Marguerite agreed. "What brings you by, Ross?"

The dolly stick clattered to the floor. Emily's hands flew to her hair to find that it was half up and half down, with wisps flying everywhere. She rubbed her cheek with the palm of her hand, noting that it came away smudged with coal dust she must have picked up while lighting the cookstove earlier.

". . . come to see Emily if she's home. I stopped by the hotel, but . . ."

Emily shot a glance around the room, her attention catching on the back door. Maybe she could slip out before—

"She's in the summer kitchen. Emily!"

Emily tried to think of a hiding place. *The root cellar!*

"Emily! Now, where in creation . . . ?" Her mother appeared in the open archway of the summer kitchen. "There you are. What happened? You lose your hearing?"

"I was busy," Emily muttered. Her gaze lifted to find Ross, who towered beside her petite mother. Carrying a black derby hat in one hand, he was dressed neatly, though casually by city standards. Beneath his short coat, Emily noted a crisp white collar and knotted necktie. She felt her cheeks warm as his sparkling dark gaze ran her over from top to toe, taking in her dishabille with maddening amusement.

"What's *he* doing here?" she demanded.

"Emily Elizabeth!" Her mother's tone was one

used all the world over to admonish obnoxious ten-year-olds.

Emily snatched a towel from the stone sink. "You have a reason for stopping by, Ross? Or is this strictly a social call?"

"I need to talk to you about something."

"Really?" Emily threw the towel back at the sink. "Something you neglected to mention at the café?"

Ross smiled, apparently undisturbed by her surly mood. "It's something that just came up."

"Uh-huh."

"Well, I'll leave you two alone," Marguerite said, but Emily didn't miss the be-polite look she shot her before returning to the front kitchen.

Emily placed a hand on each hip. "So, what's so all-fired important that it brings you out on a beautiful Saturday afternoon? I would have thought you'd be spending time with your lovely fiancée."

Ross didn't flinch at her mention of Johanna. "I'm meeting her later. I needed to talk to you first."

"Hmm. You sure don't waste any time, do you?"

"Waste time?"

"Back only three months and already you've gotten yourself ensconced at the *Herald* and all set to marry Lady Johanna." Emily's words came out more biting than she intended. "Well, I shouldn't be surprised. You always had ambition."

"Yes, I always had ambition. And so did you. What happened?"

Emily was struck by his bluntness. Perhaps she deserved it. She had blindly set out on the offensive, not expecting him to bite back. "What happened?" she echoed, her hands slipping from her hips to hang limp at her sides.

"You've been reduced to waiting tables in a hotel café. That's not what I would have imagined for you four years ago."

Emily paused a second to study him. He was strong, smart, confident, and heartbreakingly handsome. Success was written all over him. There could be no doubt about it, even if he weren't dressed in expensive city clothes. It was in his stance and in the way he carried himself. It was in that determined, get-out-of-my-way glint that came to his eye whenever he was frustrated at reaching some goal. She suddenly felt more slovenly than ever in his competent male presence. "Times are hard," she said. "Money is scarce. I do what I have to do to help my family get by."

"I'm not talking about money. I'm talking about you, Em. You had talent. When Karen told me you'd moved to Baltimore, I assumed that you were going to art school or that you were working for a paper."

"You assumed wrong."

"Then she implied that you were getting married."

"Wrong again."

"What were you doing in Baltimore for four years, Em?"

She held his penetrating gaze for as long as she could bear before looking away. "I did some volunteer work at the soldiers' hospital."

"You could have done volunteer work here. Why Baltimore? Was there a man?"

"I don't think that's any of your concern."

"No, I suppose not. I just can't make any sense out of your moving away."

*He knew.* The realization hit Emily like a slap in the face. It was difficult enough to brave the busybodies in town when she went to work. She hadn't considered how she would face Ross when someone inevitably told him of the rumors that had followed her departure four years before. Incredibly shortsighted of her.

She forced herself to return the silent challenge in his gaze. *Go ahead and ask, Ross. Ask me if what they're saying about me is true. But be forewarned, you might not like the answer.*

For a heart-stopping second, she was sure he would ask, but then something changed in his eyes, a shadow of indecision that was there, then just as quickly gone. Some essential part of him had backed down, and Emily understood then how it was with him. He didn't *want* to know. Not if the answer wasn't what he hoped.

"Well, I suppose you aren't obligated to tell me if you don't want to," he said.

"Darn tootin' I'm not." With an inner sigh of relief, Emily moved to grab two empty buckets from beside the back door. "You still haven't said why you've come."

Ross followed her out into the sunny backyard. "I've come to offer you a job. If you want it."

Emily stopped on the flagstone walk that led out to the pump shelter. "A what?"

"A job."

Emily eyed him suspiciously. "I already have a job."

He gave her an easy smile. It was the same smile that had been turning girlish hearts to mush since their schooldays. "If you want to call it that."

Emily bristled at this. "It pays enough. What kind of job would you have to offer, anyway?"

"Not the kind that involves waiting tables and washing dishes."

"Hmm. Like I said, I already have a job." Emily tried to quash her traitorous curiosity as she stomped down the walk.

"Oh, that's fine, then. I'll tell Malcolm he can put a sign in the window. I'm sure he'll have no shortage of applicants. Jobs are scarce these days."

Emily stopped again. "The opening is at the paper?"

"The ad department. I know it's not the most prestigious job, but a good worker could find herself promoted to something else in due time. Especially if she's a talented illustrator."

Emily could tell by his smug tone that he thought he knew what she was going to say. How annoying. "If you think I'd consider working for Davenport, you mustn't know me very well."

"Oh, I know you well enough, Em. I know you're miserable waiting tables at the Blue Swan. I know this job probably pays twice as much as what you're getting now, and I know you were born to newspaper work."

Emily scowled and moved to the water pump, setting her buckets down with a clank. Before she could proceed any further, Ross had donned his hat and was at her side, stepping up to snatch the tin pitcher of water that sat by the base of the pump. "Let me."

"You don't have to help."

"I know," he said, pouring water into the barrel of the pump to prime it for use. "But can't you just let a fella act like a gentleman every once in a while?"

Emily stood by helplessly as he set down the pitcher, then swept one of the buckets up, depositing it into the trough before working the pump handle.

"You'll get your clothes all wet." Her anger was beginning to dwindle despite her best efforts to hold onto it.

Ross grinned as the spout sputtered, burbled, then spat its first splash of clear, cool water into the bucket. "Since when did a little water hurt anyone? As I recall, neither one of us was ever scared of getting wet. You remember, Em?"

As Emily watched him stroke the old pump handle, memories rose up like warm, loving arms to embrace her. Memories of lazy summer afternoons spent in the wooded shade by a shimmering creek, her sketchpad on her lap, soft breezes caressing her face. And Ross would always be sitting somewhere nearby with his journal, scratching away with a pencil until the moment he would look up, wearing a bedeviling grin. *"Hey, Em, you wanna take a dip?"*

Ross stopped pumping, removed the full bucket from the trough, and replaced it with the second one. He looked at her, one hand resting on the handle. "You do remember, don't you?"

Emily imagined that she felt those dark brown eyes penetrating her soul, and she frowned, averting her gaze and pretending to swipe at a gnat. "I remember." Damn him. He thought he could get to her by reminding her of old times. Well, it wouldn't work.

When the second bucket was full, Ross picked up both of them to take into the house. "I assume you need these inside?"

"Rinse water," she said.

"Rinse water," he echoed, a subtle, knowing smile tugging at his mouth before he turned to take the flagstone walk back to the house. Emily's heart fluttered, and she gritted her teeth. No. It wouldn't work.

She stayed a few paces behind, noting that his shiny black boots were getting splashed with water. He didn't seem to mind. *Since when did a little water hurt anybody?*

When he came to the back door off the summer kitchen, he set the buckets down on the walk. Before he could reach for the door, though, his attention was caught by the sound of carriage wheels on the dirt drive around the side of the house. More callers?

Emily turned in time to see Karl Becker reining in a sporty runabout buggy. Karl? Here? Now? She had spoken to him briefly at her father's funeral, then again on the street when she had run into him coming out of David Stauffer's law office.

"What the hell is *he* doing here?"

At hearing the hostility in Ross's voice, Emily peered up at him, but his attention was riveted on Karl. Although Ross and Karl had been close friends while growing up, the year before war had broken out, they had once come to blows over a ridiculous misunderstanding. Ross had been under the mistaken impression that Emily, at the age of sixteen, had needed protection from Karl's lascivious advances. In truth, Karl's great sin had consisted of stealing one rather bland kiss behind a springhouse, and Emily hadn't felt herself in need of protection at all. She'd never been kissed before and was merely satisfying her own adolescent curiosity when Ross had charged in like a raging bull to save her virtue. The whole episode had been silly and more than a little annoying. She could take care of herself, and her virtue had never been in the least imperiled. But all that was in the past. Apparently Ross and Karl hadn't rectified their differences since returning home.

By now, Karl was crossing the side yard, relying on his cane. "Good afternoon, Miss Emily!"

"Good afternoon."

Karl nodded in Ross's direction. "So, Gallagher, we meet again. It seems as if you're everywhere these days."

"I could say the same for you."

"I'm surprised to see you here, though, Rossy. I could have sworn you were engaged to the other one. What was her name?"

Emily had to raise a hand to her mouth to stifle an unladylike guffaw. Perhaps it was a good thing that Karl had stopped by after all. Being from the "wrong" side of town, Karl had never cared much for society or how it judged him. Perhaps a touch of his irreverence was just the tonic Emily needed to cure her doldrums.

Ross, however, didn't seem at all amused by Karl's brand of humor. "I just stopped by to see how Emily was doing."

"Well, by the looks of her, I'd say she's doing quite well. Quite well indeed." Like Ross, Karl appeared dapper today, dressed in a top hat and tailored city clothes that enhanced his new aura of respectability. Karl had never been conventionally handsome, but there had always been something about him, something rakish and daring, that had never left him wanting for female companionship.

As his appreciative gaze swept over her, Emily was reminded that she looked a fright. "What brings you by, Karl?"

"I apologize for calling without advance notice,

Miss Emily," he began with mock formality, "but the day was so beautiful, I felt the urge to hitch up my new runabout and take her for a whirl around town. Would you care to join me?"

Emily was surprised by the question. It was the kind of question a man asked when he was interested in courting. They had begun a relationship, tentative though it was, years before, but, well, that was years before. And hadn't he heard the rumors?

Emily tried to smooth her disheveled hair. "Well, I, um, I was just helping my mother with the, um . . . "

Ross intervened. "Bad timing, Karl, old boy."

Emily glared at Ross, who was too busy gloating at Karl to notice. She remembered that he would be spending this afternoon with Johanna. A picture took form in her mind's eye—that of her wretched self bent over a steaming washtub, stirring heavy folds of laundry with a dolly stick while Johanna Davenport strolled about town on Ross's arm.

She faced Karl. "I can be ready in five minutes."

Karl's attention shifted from Ross back to her, and his expression of surprise was replaced by an engaging smile. "Wonderful, Miss Emily."

Emily addressed Ross. "Was there anything else you wanted?"

Ross set his jaw. There was a flash of something in his eyes. Jealousy? No, she corrected herself. Anger, of course; anger at being brushed aside.

"No, there was nothing else." His dark gaze flicked to Karl. "I suppose you two would like to be alone."

"Yes," Emily said, forcing a bright smile. "We would."

"Fine. Think hard about what I said. If you want the job, you'd better apply for it right away. It won't be open long." He nodded a curt farewell to Karl as he brushed past them. "See you around, Becker."

"I look forward to it." Karl tipped his hat and turned to watch Ross stride across the side yard. He didn't turn back until Ross had reached the road and disappeared from view. He raised an eyebrow at Emily. "A job?"

"Nothing important." Emily's gaze was still glued to the spot where Ross had vanished. "Nothing at all."

Ross had walked off most of his frustration by the time he reached Johanna's house. Or so he'd thought. Now, he snapped the reins of their buggy, urging one of Malcolm Davenport's prized bays to pick up its pace on the open road outside of town. Johanna, dressed in a white dress with pink ribbon trim, was perched by his side. A picnic basket, packed by the Davenport's cook, sat between them by their feet. But Ross's mind wasn't on Johanna or their afternoon outing to Rocky Springs. His thoughts kept returning to the fact that the rig he drove was a partially enclosed, more expensive version of the runabout Karl Becker had pulled into Emily's side yard this morning. He kept imagining Emily and Karl, sitting side by side and unchaperoned in Karl's little runabout, and the very thought made his blood boil.

"It's such a lovely day," Johanna was saying. "Thank goodness we had this planned, or I would have been stuck attending mother's tea for the ladies' auxiliary. Mercy, if I have to sit through even one more of those . . ."

Johanna was not an empty-headed woman. She had graduated from the Young Ladies' Seminary at

# FOREVER AND ALWAYS

the head of her class, but when she prattled on like this, Ross was hard-pressed to differentiate her from many of her inane social companions.

His thoughts turned back to Karl and Emily. What was Karl up to? Trying to pick up with Emily where he had left off before the war? In that case, Ross couldn't understand why Emily was even giving Karl the time of day. If the rumors were true— He checked himself. Of course the rumors weren't true.

But that didn't mean Karl was any good for Emily. Even though they had barely spoken in over four years, Ross knew Karl like a brother. When Ross had first met him, Karl was something of a street ruffian, but even with a drunken father to contend with, he always managed to make it to school. He was one of the first boys to befriend Ross after he came to Lancaster, and it wasn't long before Karl's two ready fists helped to even the odds when Ross tangled with John Butler and his friends.

Later, Ross and Karl had come of age together, puffing on their first cigars and suffering through their first whiskey hangovers. They'd even managed to shed their virginity on the same night out on the town. Certainly Ross knew his former friend better than anyone. Karl might have gotten himself a college education and a respectable suit of clothes to match, but he was still the same old rogue underneath. Unfortunately, Emily seemed incapable of seeing past his smooth-talking exterior.

"Oh, look!" Johanna interrupted his train of thought to point to a grassy area just off the side of the road ahead. "Let's stop and have our picnic there."

"I thought you wanted to wait until we got to Rocky Springs," Ross said.

"I did, but I'm famished." Johanna flashed him one of her come-hither smiles. "I just can't wait that long. Can you?"

Her eyes sparkled a devastating bright blue today. Her honey blond hair was tied back into a netted coil beneath her beribboned straw hat, but a few tendrils had come loose to frame her heart-shaped face with soft curls. That smile, that tone of voice. *I just can't wait that long. Can you?* A double entendre?

Ross tried to gauge her meaning from her expression but couldn't be sure. They had agreed to wait until marriage to consummate their relationship. Ross was content enough to bide his time since he now knew his chance would come to finally claim this elusive woman and all she stood for as his own. Now, though, the possibility of stealing a few kisses and perhaps a fondle or two was mighty appealing. It could be just the distraction he needed to get his mind off Emily and Karl.

He scanned the rural landscape. They were on a lonely stretch of road halfway between town and their destination. No other vehicles had passed for at least twenty minutes. Off to the right, behind the grassy area Johanna had indicated, were some weeping willows and a cluster of oaks. Not a soul for miles.

"Well, now that you mention it," he said, pulling in the reins to slow the buggy, "I'm hungry, too."

He urged the bay off the road and over to a nearby tree. After securing the reins, he helped Johanna down from the rig and snatched up their folded picnic blanket as well as the covered basket of food.

Johanna strolled over to the nearest weeping willow to pick her way around it delicately. Adjusting her bonnet, she stopped every so often to peer up and determine the angle of the sun. "Mercy, it's so bright today. I hope I don't get a burn."

Ross assumed it wasn't the pain of a burn she was concerned with so much as the scandal of a freckle, and so he sacrificed his own preference for sitting in the sunlight in favor of spreading their blanket in the shade.

"Oh, yes. This is a nice spot," Johanna concurred.

Ross didn't actually pull out his pocket watch to time her, but he figured it took at least four minutes for her to situate both herself and the myriad of folds, ruffles, hoops, and crinoline that comprised her afternoon attire. Once she was comfortable, she uncovered the basket and produced two plates, two immaculate linen napkins, a dish of cold fried chicken, and two slices of apple pie. She stopped and frowned down into the empty basket. "Oh, mercy. Cook forgot to pack the utensils."

"We don't need utensils." Ross doffed his derby, tossed it onto the blanket, and endeavored to move closer. It wasn't easy, considering the many layers of crisp white muslin that protected her as effectively as a stockade fence. "It's just chicken."

She wrinkled her nose, still peering into the basket. "But it's so greasy."

"We've got napkins." Ross took her by the chin and forced her to look at him. When he leaned forward to kiss her, he bumped his forehead against the brim of her bonnet.

"Oh, Ross, not here. We're in public."

Ross glanced over his shoulder to see that their "public" consisted of her father's prize bay, who seemed content to ignore them as he grazed. "I don't think Chester cares much if we steal a few kisses, Johanna."

"But anyone could come riding by, and what would they think?"

Ross was annoyed. Despite himself, he was imagining Karl and Emily in a hot, heaving embrace in Karl's runabout, and it just about snapped his patience. "They'd think we're engaged to be married soon, so what the hell difference does it make?"

Johanna nibbled her lower lip. Her gaze shifted to the empty road before moving back to Ross. "Well, I suppose just one little kiss won't hurt."

Forcing down all grating thoughts of Karl and Emily, Ross tugged on the bow to Johanna's bonnet. "That's right, it won't hurt at all." When he leaned toward her again, he pushed her bonnet back to tumble out of his way.

They kissed twice before her lips parted beneath his, then . . . nothing.

Puzzled by his own lack of response, Ross shifted position, pulled her closer, and deepened their kiss. She did all the right things. Her delicate tongue danced against his, she even brushed against him and made a tiny sound in her throat, yet Ross didn't feel the pleasurable rush of sexual arousal that he'd anticipated.

He pulled back to study her face. Her eyes were closed, her lovely pink lips still slightly parted. She was as beautiful as ever, the girl of his adolescent dreams. He should have been game. Hell, he should have been straining at the bit for her. But he wasn't. He didn't feel much of anything but a confused sense of frustration.

Johanna's long brown lashes fluttered open. Round blue eyes blinked at him, and he was absurdly reminded of the vacant, blown-glass gaze of a French fashion doll. "Is something wrong, Ross?"

Something. Yes. Perhaps he was just too distracted. He had a lot on his mind lately.

"Ross?"

"No," he said, forcing a weak smile. "There's nothing wrong."

"Good," she said, then flashed a dazzling smile of her own. "Shall we eat?"

# 8

*Perhaps it was true that* Ross still knew Emily a little better than she cared to admit. After she took a couple of days to think over his job offer, she came to the conclusion that not admitting this infuriating fact was hardly worth running herself ragged at the Blue Swan. Besides, she had begun to formulate plans of her own, plans that would be better served by swallowing her pride and applying to Malcolm Davenport for the job of advertising assistant.

Upon entering the building at nine-fifteen Monday morning, Emily was taken aback by the size and grandeur of the front business office. This was the first time she'd had occasion to set foot in enemy territory.

An immaculate waiting area with a marbled floor, cushioned armchairs, and potted ferns had been arranged before a long mahogany counter. The office area behind the counter boasted no fewer than four employees, all of whom seemed occupied with mountains of paperwork. Out of the three, Emily recognized only the business manager, a sharp-eyed,

German-born man named Oberholtzer. He had been with the *Herald* since before Malcolm Davenport had taken over from his father.

After stating her purpose, Emily crossed the mahogany barrier and followed a clerk through a rear doorway to a sizable job printing department. Here, she met with the sights, sounds, and smells she recognized and loved. Men in smudged aprons and rolled-up shirtsleeves. The creaks and groans and scrapes of wood working on metal. She counted five job presses, four of which were actively engaged.

Once ushered up a staircase to the second floor, she stepped into an open office area cluttered with flat-top desks and chairs, many of which were still empty, since the reporters and copyboys didn't begin their workday until nine-thirty.

As soon as the clerk announced her presence to Mr. Davenport, it became apparent to Emily that Ross had already laid the groundwork for her. Malcolm appeared not at all surprised by her visit. In fact, he welcomed her boisterously, offering—for the benefit of those few ears perked and present—his most sincere condolences on the recent passing of her father. Then he closed the door to his office and offered her a seat.

Malcolm was a big man, tall and square-shouldered, with a build more suited to the back-breaking labor of a miner or a farmer than that of an office-bound newspaper editor. As he stood behind his desk, Emily folded her hands in her lap and tried not to appear intimidated by his sheer size and bulk.

When she stated her purpose, she was dispirited to note that he didn't deign to sit. All the better to look down upon her with those penetrating steel gray eyes that so perfectly matched the flocculent set of side whiskers he'd cultivated for as long as she could remember.

"I don't normally hold with hiring women," he pronounced. "Their very presence tends to disrupt the smooth functioning of the staff."

Emily sat still as a lamppost, listening politely as Mr. Davenport discoursed upon the virtues of womanhood and the vices of man's workaday world. It was a mix that apparently gave him night sweats to even contemplate, yet after all was said and done, he condescended to grace her with a patriarchal smile. "However, due to my great respect for your lately departed father and your extensive background in newspapering, I'm inclined to make an exception in your case, Miss Winters. You may start tomorrow."

By the time Emily left Malcolm's office, the city room was filling with bearded, cigar-chomping reporters. Emily did her best to ignore the only clean-shaven one in the bunch, but it was fairly impossible, since his desk was so close to the managing editor's office.

"Good morning, Miss Winters."

"Good morning, Mr. Gallagher," she said, brushing by him with a glance and curt nod.

"See you tomorrow, Miss Winters."

Oh, but how Emily grated her teeth as she tramped down the narrow staircase that led to the ground floor. Humble pie had never been one of her favorite dishes.

Malcolm Davenport had spoken the truth when he'd told Emily that he was disinclined to hire women.

After reporting to work at eight-thirty the following morning and being given a brief tour, she began to suspect that she was the only representative of the fair sex in the entire building.

Her immediate supervisor, Freddy Brubaker, was not much older than she. Although he hadn't attended the same grammar school as Emily, she remembered seeing him about town. He had been a chubby, ordinary-looking boy with a mop of nut brown hair and a clubfoot that later limited him to serving in the Invalid Corps during the war. By now, he had grown from chubby to stocky and was attempting with little success to grow Davenportesque side whiskers.

Although Freddy, a mild-tempered sort, tried his best to be polite, Emily could tell by the pained, squinched-up expression on his face that he was less than enthusiastic about having a woman assist him at his new job as head of advertising.

When Emily finally sat down to work in the office across the hall from the city room, she resolved not to let such prejudice deter her. If there was one thing she knew, it was the newspaper business, and so she resolved to prove to every condescending male in the place that their unspoken biases were wrong. It was a resolution easier made than accomplished.

She'd written copy for ads before, but she'd never spent eight to ten hours a day immersed in the stuff. She sold dry goods and fancy goods, balmoral shoes and hoopskirts, waterproof shirtfronts, suspenders, and boots. She sold various and sundry items to ingest, inhale, imbibe, and apply, from Turkish smoking tobacco to Arctic Cream Soda to Dr. Starr's Chemical Hair Invigorator.

By the end of the week, her head was in a spin and

her vision was bleary from setting fine type. But she had accomplished her purpose, at least as far as Freddy was concerned. The pained, squinched-up look on his face was gone. Not only could his female assistant write advertising copy, she could set it as quickly and accurately as any of the men in the composing department.

When Freddy handed her the bank draft that represented her first week's pay, Emily felt a sense of satisfaction she hadn't experienced in a long time. Even if this wasn't the newspaper work that she loved, it was at least newspaper work.

Perhaps that was why she felt such a bothersome twinge of guilt as, at five o'clock on Friday, she pretended to be busy with last-minute details as Freddy put on his frock coat and called out that he would see her bright and early Monday morning.

Emily bid him a pleasant good evening as he hobbled out, then continued to shuffle some papers on her small desk as the rest of the second floor business office emptied. All but Mr. Oberholtzer.

The elderly office manager was notorious for working until all hours of the evening, but Freddy had told her that he made it a point to be home for supper every Friday. In fact, he hadn't missed a Friday night supper with his wife in twenty years.

Emily was counting on him not to break with tradition tonight.

When he finally pulled the venetian blinds in his private office and emerged wearing his top hat and carrying his cane, it was almost five-thirty.

"Still at work, Miss Winters?" He spoke with a thick German accent and peered down his hook nose at her through bifocals. There was something in those sharp, slate blue eyes that caused a shiver to trickle down Emily's spine. He was the type of fellow who would be suspicious of his own shadow, never mind the daughter of a man who was once a fierce competitor.

"Yes, Mr. Oberholtzer. I want to be sure to get a head start Monday morning."

"Commendable, Miss Winters, but you should not so unduly exhaust yourself. Your family expects you home, *ja?*"

She glanced at a square-faced wall clock and pretended surprise. "Oh, goodness. I hadn't realized how late it was. I'll be sure to finish up soon."

Oberholtzer glanced from the clock to her then back at the clock. He was torn. No doubt Mrs. Oberholtzer had pork and sauerkraut waiting. "*Ja.* Soon, then." Grudgingly, he turned to leave. "Be sure to lock the door behind you."

"I certainly will, Mr. Oberholtzer. Good evening."

When she was sure he was gone, Emily scurried to the door to see if anyone else still loitered in the hallway. It was empty.

In the city room across the hall, she knew that most of the reporters, including Ross, would still be at work. In the press room, the men would be busy until nine or ten tonight, printing tomorrow's first edition, but not one of them had reason to wander outside their own work area after hours. This was the chance she'd been waiting for all week.

She hurried back to her desk, donned her bonnet, snatched her handbag, and turned the lock on her way out the door. Once downstairs, she passed through the deserted job printing department. Unlike the busy pressroom upstairs, the jobbers went off shift with the office employees at five. When she reached the front business office, the blinds were pulled and the place was empty.

She made a beeline for one of the desks, the one where she knew the latest print orders would be waiting to be processed on Monday morning. Squinting in the shuttered light, she located the orders and began thumbing through them. There were many familiar names, some of them old customers of her father's. That was what she was looking for, someone who had been loyal to Nathaniel in the past.

She finally spotted an order for billheads. It was from Henry Wilkerson, who owned the hardware store on West King. A former customer of her father's, and, much like the crusty, opinionated Jacob Groff, a fellow who had never cared for Malcolm Davenport's business practices or politics. Judging by the estimate of charges, Emily surmised that Malcolm was offering a discount off his usual prices, no doubt in an effort to attract her father's customers away from the only other competition remaining in town, Denton's Printing. Shrewd, Emily thought. But not shrewd enough. Not if she had anything to say about it.

"What are you doing?"

Emily almost shot through the ceiling. Shoving the print orders back into place, she spun around to see Ross standing in the doorway to the job press room. He was dressed for the street, his frock coat buttoned, his tie knotted, his top hat in one hand, obviously leaving work early. He'd come up quiet as a cat. Lord, how long had he been standing there?

Emily tried to swallow past the lump in her throat. She'd done her best all week to avoid him and had been fairly successful. Now she couldn't decide if she should feel more guilty for her transgressions or angry with him for choosing this moment to sneak up on her.

"A . . . a handkerchief," she blurted. It was the first lie that popped into her head.

"What?"

"I . . . I was looking for my handkerchief." She lifted her handbag as if in proof. "There was, um, something in my eye, but it seems to be gone now." She squinted in what she hoped was a convincing manner.

Ross's discerning gaze narrowed, and she knew with conscience-stricken certainty that he sensed her fabrication. Reaching into his pocket, he produced a crisp white handkerchief and approached her. "Here."

Emily inched backward, away from the desk and toward the door. "Oh, no, thank you. As I said, it seems to be gone now."

"Uh-huh." His gaze flicked to the desk she'd been rifling through, then back to her. "Are you sure?"

"Quite." Emily retreated a few more steps toward the door. Unfortunately, she didn't know the layout of this office as well as she knew her father's. The heel of her shoe smacked into a brass cuspidor, shattering the stillness and making her wince.

"Emily . . ."

"I'm fine, Mr. Gallagher, just fine." Sidestepping the cuspidor, she pushed through the bat-wing doors to the waiting area. "I've got to be going."

In a blind rush, she went for the door.

*"Oh!"*

Before she could stop, Emily barreled out into the

street and straight into a bustling mass of yellow-checked gauze and crinoline. Bouncing blond ringlets and an overpowering whiff of eau du lilac confirmed that this could be nothing less than the climactic scene in a very bad dream.

"Johanna!" Emily gasped.

"Emily! Why, mercy!"

They blinked at each other in feminine horror then rapidly disengaged, stepping back to straighten their respective bonnets—Emily's a practical, black-banded straw bonnet, Johanna's an outlandish white horse-hair concoction trimmed with what seemed like yards of mauve ribbons and violets.

"Mercy, I was just reaching for the door when— "

"I'm sorry," Emily muttered. "I wasn't looking where I was going."

"That's quite all right, Emily, dear. I'm simply surprised, that's all."

The flamboyant, scooped neckline of Johanna's gown and the flash of diamond pendant earrings signaled that she was dressed for a night on the town. Emily glanced over Johanna's shoulder to see the Davenports' double brougham waiting by the curb. Well, at least now she knew why Ross was leaving work earlier than usual. No doubt an elegant restaurant dinner followed by a box seat for the new concert opening at Fulton Hall.

Ross's voice came from behind. "Everybody all right out here?"

"Everybody's fine," Emily muttered. "I've got to go."

She didn't spare a glance for either of them as she brushed by and hastened up the sidewalk. She didn't want to see the glint of triumph in Johanna's eyes when she took Ross's arm. She didn't want to see the admiration in Ross's gaze when he looked at Johanna.

"Good evening, Emily, dear!"

Johanna's parting words nipped at Emily's escaping heels, carrying with them an edge of gloating she recognized all too well from their spite-filled childhood.

Or perhaps, Emily reminded herself miserably, it was just her own childish resentment that transformed Johanna's innocent words into antagonistic preening.

When she reached the corner of King and Queen Streets, she stopped to catch her breath. She told herself she didn't care. She told herself not to look back. She had more important things to think about, but . . . Biting her lower lip, she turned around just in time to see Ross handing Johanna into her family's fine carriage. As he did so, Malcolm emerged from the newspaper office, and he too climbed into the carriage. Ross followed suit. The brougham moved off down the street.

Emily stood, unable to move as she watched the carriage disappear around a corner. If it had been anyone but Johanna, perhaps she could have brought herself to accept it.

She remembered the year after that first summer with Ross. Before school had started, she was excited and looking forward to moving to the upper grade classroom to be with him, but that first week had dashed all her expectations.

When she looked around the class, she discovered that very few of the other girls wore their hair plaited anymore. Most opted for curls tied in ribbons, and they had traded their knee-length dresses and frilled pantalets for colorful, ankle-length crinoline petticoats and skirts.

And it wasn't only the style of clothing that had changed. Most of the girls, even those Emily's age, were beginning to narrow in the waists, widen in the hips, and develop bosoms. It seemed that everyone was on the fast track to womanhood except Emily. Even her close friend Melissa Carpenter had betrayed her, leaving school the summer before flat as an unleavened biscuit only to return, much to Emily's chagrin, *buxom*.

Perhaps none of this would have bothered Emily so much if it weren't for Ross. He was well built, strapping, and growing handsomer every day. It was a sorry fact that when Miss Breckenridge presented her back to the class, most female heads invariably turned to gaze in Ross's direction. As for Ross, he never seemed to take notice of all this adoration. Like every other boy in their class, *his* head was turned in Johanna Davenport's direction.

Johanna, with her expensive silk dresses, her burgeoning young woman's figure, and her soft blond hair was everything Emily was not, and Emily had felt those first painful stabs of jealousy. Could it be that she had already begun to fall in love with Ross even then?

Emily closed her eyes at the thought. What good could come of all this dredging up of the past? Ross would soon marry Johanna and, in the process, gain all he'd ever aspired to. He would have a newspaper career, money, and a place of respect among the upper echelons of local society. Emily would do well to take a lesson from his pragmatic example. There was nothing she could do to change the past. She should concentrate on her own goals. Business. Deadlines.

Squaring her shoulders, she turned to cross the busy city street.

It was on a hot, lazy Saturday afternoon, over a week after Ross had caught her snooping through the *Herald*'s print orders, that Emily found herself trudging along the dusty road to the old Hockstetter place. She wasn't looking forward to the unpleasant task she'd set for herself today.

Just ahead, the sandstone farmhouse with its familiar tangle of evergreens and weeping willows came into view. Set against a blanket of corn and wheat fields, the house, with its whitewashed barn and other outbuildings was hard to miss. It was the only dwelling for almost a half mile in all directions.

Pressing a gloved hand to her middle, she forced herself to take deep breaths to calm her nervous stomach. She didn't like the idea of asking for money; she liked even less the idea of asking for money from Ross. Unfortunately, she was running out of time, and she could think of no other way to accomplish her goals. No reputable bank would grant her a loan, not without substantial assets to offer as collateral and certainly not for the purposes she had in mind. As she saw it, Ross wasn't just her best hope, he was her *only* hope.

Releasing a splintered wooden latch on the front gate, Emily took the front walk to the porch steps. She was surprised to see eye-catching splashes of yellow marigolds, white and pink poppies, and rainbows of pansies along the front of the house. The late Mrs.

Hockstetter's rosebushes were trimmed back and prepared to bloom. The grass in the yard was cut, and there was nary a weed in sight. Even the porch looked as if it had taken on a recent coat of whitewash.

Business, Emily reminded herself grimly as she climbed the steps to the front door. Flower gardens had nothing to do with why she was here. She had to keep her mind on business.

She rapped twice on the front door of the old house and waited. In her mind, she rehearsed her opening lines. She would bid Ross good day, he would invite her in, they would discuss the weather, and he would ask why she had come. Then she would make her brisk, very businesslike request for a loan. She would promise to make installment payments at a fair rate of interest.

Yes, that seemed reasonable.

Emily marked time for another minute or two before she realized Ross might not be home. But she'd spent half the night lying awake dreading this hideous, ignoble moment. How could he not be home?

It was then that she heard it, one muffled *thwack* followed by another and then another. It sounded like the familiar, steady beat of someone hard at work chopping wood.

Steeling her nerve again, Emily descended the wooden porch steps and rounded the corner of the house to the back. The startling sight that confronted her stopped her cold and erased every memorized opening line from her head.

With his back to her, Ross stood over a thick tree stump that served as a chopping block near the springhouse. Tall and magnificently broad-shouldered, shirtless and sweating in the early summer sun, he raised his ax to bring it whistling down into a section of cordwood, splitting it in half and sending it tumbling to the ground by his feet. Still unaware of her presence, he bent to pick up a second piece.

For a second, Emily considered fleeing before he had a chance to see her. To hell with all her mental rehearsals. The thought of facing him now, with her mouth gone all dry and her palms sweating buckets, was—

"Emily?"

He must have caught a glimpse of her. When he turned around, he appeared almost as surprised as she was. "I didn't see you there."

Even from where she stood, perhaps fifteen feet away, Emily saw a nasty pink and white slash of scar tissue below his collarbone. Her gaze dropped to fasten upon another scar, this one even worse, just below his rib cage.

Emily wasn't a nurse, but she'd volunteered enough at the military hospital in Baltimore to know that if that Confederate minié ball had penetrated one or two inches to the left, his injury would have been fatal.

Since she'd returned home and discovered that the report of his death had been a mistake, she'd forced herself to forget the heart-numbing despair she'd felt upon reading her sister's letter the year before. Now it came back to her with dreadful clarity. *Alma Brenner's daughter Lorraine came by to tell us her Mama got a letter yesterday. Ross Gallagher was reported killed on the first day of fighting at Wilderness in Virginia.*

Mere inches from death, Emily thought, staring at

that wretched scar. She had to take a deep breath before looking up.

His expression gave no indication that he sensed the direction of her thoughts. Quite the contrary. From the dry smile that curved his lips, it was apparent that he'd recovered from the surprise of discovering her in his backyard.

"So," he drawled, "to what do I owe the honor of this unsolicited visit, Miss Winters?"

At his sarcasm, Emily stiffened. "There's no need to be so formal. We're not at the paper."

"Oh?" Turning his back, he knocked the unsplit section of wood from the chopping block. Then he drove the head of his ax into the tree stump with such unnecessary force, it made Emily jump. She hadn't considered that he might be angered by her attempts to keep him at arm's length all these weeks. His next words left no doubt in her mind. "I was beginning to believe that you'd forgotten my first name."

As he bent to gather an armful of firewood, Emily took advantage of his diverted attention to refortify her resolve. His antagonism wouldn't make it any easier for her to humble herself and ask for a loan, but it sure helped to cure her maudlin mood. "Don't be ridiculous," she said, as he moved toward an open shed at the back of the house.

Disappearing inside, he disposed of his bounty quite noisily before emerging again and facing her, hands on hips. "So, what brings you all the way out here, Em? What do you want?"

"What makes you think I want something?"

"I've been persona non grata ever since you came home. Now you suddenly drop by for a visit. You obviously want something."

"Maybe I came out to thank you for recommending me for the job at the paper."

His eyebrows raised in smug amusement, but he said nothing.

Emily knew what he was waiting for. He was waiting for her to eat humble pie. "All right," she said, "so maybe I didn't come all the way out here just to thank you for the job, but that doesn't mean I don't—" She had to swallow down what felt like a shard of broken glass in her throat. Lord a'mighty but this pie was painful to swallow. "I mean, I do, uh, . . . appreciate it."

"You're welcome."

His words were simple and gracious, but those dark brown eyes shined like new pennies. They seemed to say, "Gotcha this time, didn't I, Em?" His self-satisfied expression made Emily want to fly into him. It made her want to stomp off in a huff and find some other way to raise the money she needed. More importantly, it made her wish he'd put on his damned shirt.

It was lucky that he chose that moment to change the subject. "Freddy Brubaker said you're doing a good job."

Cautiously, Emily relaxed her guard. "He did?"

Ross crossed the yard to the hand pump, where he snatched a cotton shirt from over the metal spigot. It was then that Emily noticed the white picket-fenced garden behind him. Like the rest of the yard, it was well tended, with six long rows of early vegetables beginning to sprout. Potatoes, peas, tomatoes, carrots, and what might have been pumpkin seedlings.

Ross put on his shirt. "Freddy's tickled pink that you already know how to set type. That takes a lot off his shoulders, considering he's trying to learn a new job, too."

Emily watched as long, capable fingers worked at each button, cutting off, one slow step at a time, all remaining glimpses of his bare chest. "Uh, well, I'm glad to hear it," she said, clearing her throat and focusing on his face. "He's actually been very helpful since I started."

"You sound surprised by that, Em. What's the matter? Did you think all Democrats breathe fire and sprout horns?"

At these fighting words, Emily struggled to maintain what tenuous poise remained. "Does that mean you've been converted?"

He folded his arms and smiled, apparently pleased that he'd piqued her ire. "No, but maybe I've learned to be a little more tolerant of other viewpoints."

"Tolerant? Is that what you call it?"

"Call what?"

"Keeping quiet about your opinions in print."

His smile faded, and a hint of annoyance sparked in his eyes. "I use discretion in choosing my battles."

"Really? What about Negro suffrage? Or better yet, how about women's suffrage? Now there's two worthy battles to cut your journalistic teeth on. Have you tried going up against Malcolm yet, or are you saving that for after the big wedding?"

"The *Herald* is a Democratic paper, Emily. It always has been. That's not going to change overnight. If it did, we'd lose a lot of subscribers. My purpose in joining the paper wasn't to put a muzzle on its viewpoint or to drive it out of business."

"Well, that's a moot point because Malcolm wouldn't allow you to. If you ever dared go against the Democratic party line, he'd kill your piece before it could go to press."

"The same could be said for most Republican papers."

"Not the *Penn Gazette*."

"The *Gazette* is dead."

At this blunt utterance of the truth, Emily couldn't do much more than glare at him. Where was the old Ross? Why couldn't he see that he was selling out on principles that mattered?

When she didn't reply, he spoke again. "Sometimes, Em, we have to compromise."

"Did you learn that in the war?"

"Yeah. It's called reality, and most of us have to face it when we grow up."

Emily clenched her hands. Inside her gloves, her palms were slick with sweat. The sun felt unbearably hot as it beat down on her shoulders. She was suffocating beneath the heavy material of her mourning dress, not to mention the distressingly familiar dark-eyed gaze that pinned her from three yards away. His intimation, that she still believed and acted like a child, stung more than she would ever admit. "I don't care much for your reality," she said.

"I know you don't. That's why we could go around in circles like this all afternoon and still not get anywhere."

Emily wondered where they'd gotten off track. In none of her imagined scenarios had she foreseen them arguing politics in his backyard. "I need a favor," she said.

He just looked at her, the expression on his face neutral. For one of the few times Emily could remember, she had no clue what he could be thinking. "Oh? What kind of favor?"

"I've come to request a loan."

Something flickered in those dark eyes, something like concern. "A loan? You mean, *money?*"

"What other kind of loan is there?"

He didn't react to her sarcasm. "What do you need it for?"

Emily tried in vain to recall how she'd decided ahead of time to handle this possible direction of inquiry. "Why . . . why do you need to know?"

"How much do you need?"

"A hundred dollars."

That got a rise out of him. His cautious, penetrating gaze vanished instantly, and his eyes widened. "A hundred dollars? What do you need a hundred dollars for?"

"Oh!" Emily's poise fled, and she turned her back. "I just knew you'd ask me that question."

"Well, of course I'm going to ask you that question!"

"Can't you just trust me?"

"Em, that's not the—"

"Stop calling me Em! I am *not* a letter of the alphabet!"

"Well, you never minded when we were kids."

"We're not kids anymore!" Emily hadn't meant to blurt this with such vehemence, and she wished that she could take it back now, but it was the truth. Ironically enough, it was probably at the root of all that had ever gone wrong between them.

There was a pause before she sensed his approach from behind. His manner had softened. "Emily, you aren't in some kind of trouble, are you?"

When she felt his warm, strong hand come to rest on her shoulder, she couldn't help it, she jerked away. Snatching up her skirt, she fled across the yard toward the front of the house. "Oh, never mind, never mind. I'll take care of it myself."

"Emily . . ."

"Just forget I was here!"

"Emily!"

As she scurried around the corner of the house, peripheral impressions of bright-colored flower beds were blurred in a threat of frustrated, angry tears. Ross's voice carried after her, but she could tell by the sound that he still stood where she'd left him.

Swearing at the stubborn fence gate, she finally shoved it open to escape. It was for the best that he'd chosen not to follow her. It had been stupid of her to come here in the first place. They weren't children anymore, and it had been a very long time since their friendship had meant anything to him. If, in her heart, she hadn't truly recognized this fact before, she was forced to recognize it now. Why, Ross had even done her the courtesy of putting a name to it. *Reality.*

She didn't care for it at all.

# 9

*Monday morning and she was late.* Drat, Emily thought as her heels snapped along the sidewalk toward the perennial bustle of Centre Square. She'd overslept and barely had time to swallow a few mouthfuls of lumpy oatmeal before flying out the door.

She could just imagine her chortling male coworkers. *Well, ain't it just like a woman? Barely a week on the job and already late!*

While it was true that Freddy Brubaker was now on her side, she didn't like the idea of adding ammunition to Malcolm Davenport's arsenal of prejudices against women in the workplace. If there was one thing she wanted to set straight before she could afford to quit his employment, it was that a woman could excel at newspaper work as well as a man.

It was a man that had caused her problems this morning. If she hadn't lost so much sleep the past weekend over that humiliating scene with Ross, she never would have overslept in the first place!

"Why, Miss Emily Winters. Is that you rushing by

like a fire carriage, or is it just me indulging in wishful thinking?"

At the sound of her name, Emily skidded to a stop, nearly colliding with a street lamp before spinning around to see Karl Becker sauntering behind her on the sidewalk with the aid of his cane. "I'm late."

"I gathered as much," he replied amiably, pausing beside her.

"I'm sorry, but I can't talk now, I've—"

"Tut, tut." He raised a long finger to touch her nose. "I can see you're in dire need of expert advice on the subject of employer-employee relations."

"What are you talking about?"

"You've worked mostly in a family-owned business in the past, so this sort of situation has never arisen before, has it?"

"What?"

"You must never go flying into the office all wild-eyed and with your tail feathers askew. It creates an incriminating impression of guilt."

"But I *am* guilty."

He shook his head disapprovingly. "Never say that aloud."

"I'm late."

"Nonsense. Your watch is just slow." He offered a devilish grin and held out his arm. "It so happens that my timepiece is also running slow this morning. May we at least walk together and commiserate over the shoddy workmanship of today's watchmakers?"

Emily hesitated for a moment at the prospect of taking his arm. Such an act might start tongues wagging. Then again, what could people possibly say about her that hadn't been said before? She would be hard-pressed to top herself.

She accepted Karl's gallant gesture, and they resumed their walk toward the center of town at a much saner pace. "You're incorrigible," she scolded good-naturedly.

"So I've been told."

"I'll bet you have. By more than one woman, too."

"You're right," he said with a rakish chuckle. "By more than two, too."

Emily rolled her eyes. "You haven't changed at all."

"Ah, but you have, Miss Emily. You've grown up very nicely indeed."

"Do you think so?"

"Oh, absolutely."

"Well, I suppose I'll have to admit that you did, too. How's the lawyering business treating you?"

"Very well, actually. David Stauffer has always had quite a brisk business in real estate and criminal defense, but along with collecting survivors' pensions, soldiers' bounties, and back pay, we've got more than we can handle."

"Do tell."

"In fact, Miss Emily, we've been so busy that we're considering hiring a secretary. We could use the organizational skills of an intelligent businesswoman such as yourself."

Emily looked at him incredulously. "Is that a job offer?"

Karl laughed. "I suppose it is."

"Well, I'm flattered, but I'm already employed." She focused her attention on the street ahead. She'd been right earlier. They were indeed drawing interested glances from passersby. Somehow, with Karl beside her, though, the thought of stirring up the old town didn't seem quite so bad.

"Already employed. Hmm, I see," Karl said. "Then the outlandish rumors I've heard about you are true?"

*"Rumors?"* Emily's head snapped up. "What rumors?"

"That you're working for Davenport's newspaper. Surely, it's just nasty, vile gossip."

"Oh, those rumors." She had to suck in a deep breath to regain her composure. She had become much too defensive lately. "It's true."

"I'm sure you have your reasons."

"I do."

"I suppose that was the job Gallagher was speaking of the day we went riding."

"It was." Emily frowned up at him. "You know, the two of you really should try to make amends. I remember when you were the best of friends."

For once, Karl's expression seemed to reflect something close to honest regret. "Yes, I remember, too, but some elements of the past are difficult to recapture."

So true, Emily thought glumly as they reached the two-story brick front where Karl was employed. Both city hall and, across from that, the Davenport building loomed on the square a mere block away.

Karl smiled down at her. "Well, it seems our morning stroll has come to an end all too soon."

"Yes."

"Perhaps we can get together and talk again sometime."

Emily hesitated. Was he asking permission to come call? She remembered a time over four years ago when he'd phrased almost the same question. He'd come calling on her after that. Karl was fun to be with, but no sparks of passion had ever kindled between them.

"I'm sure you have other lady friends to call on," she said carefully, "I wouldn't want you to waste your time."

The knowing expression in Karl's eyes told her he took her meaning. "Well, as it so happens, I'm free these days. It's a perfect time to renew old friendships."

"All right, then," Emily said, "perhaps we can get together to chat."

He smiled. "I'll look forward to it."

Emily tried to smile back, but the effort was weak. By now, she'd been accosted by the memory of old rumors and was reminded that it was perhaps Karl who'd been the most innocent victim of all. Even if he didn't know it.

He must have read something amiss in her expression because his bantering tone softened. "Emily, is there something wrong?"

She had to tell him. He was working hard to set up a respectable career in this town. "Karl, you need to know something."

"Yes?"

"I . . . that is, soon after you enlisted and left for the army . . . well, that's when I left to go live in Baltimore."

"Oh?"

Emily had to wet her lips. Her mouth felt as dry as old newsprint. "Well, if you remember, um, before that, you called on me a few times and, well, a while before that, there was that time at the chestnuting party. A lot of people saw us together there, and—"

"And Gallagher broke my nose," he interjected ruefully.

Emily bit her lip. "Oh, dear. I forgot about that."

Karl massaged the bridge of his nose. "I recall it vividly."

She winced. "It took weeks to heal, didn't it?"

"Six."

"I never did apologize, did I?"

"It wasn't you who threw the punch."

"I'm so sorry, Karl."

"That's all right. I've even had a few ladies tell me the new bump lends me something of an aristocratic air." He gave her his profile to demonstrate. "Do you agree?"

Emily had to close her eyes. "I'm sorry. It's very impressive, but it's not your nose bump I meant to discuss."

"Oh?"

"After I left for Baltimore, there were some rumors."

"Oh," he said disparagingly, "those."

Emily's eyes flew open. "You heard?"

He shrugged. "Of course, but what's new? If every rumor that's ever gone around about me in this town were true, I'd have sired half the illegitimate children in the county."

Emily gaped at him.

Karl bent down to look her in the eye. "I'm bad, Miss Emily, but I'm not *that* bad. Nobody's that bad, even if they aspire to be. So, tell me, what is it that's on your mind about it?"

"I just wanted to say that I'm sorry."

"You've done that already. For the nose. And you didn't have anything to do with that, either. Is there anything else you'd like to apologize for this morning? The Union defeats at Bull Run, perhaps?"

He was joking of course, trying to make light of

this horribly awkward moment, but Emily couldn't bring herself to smile for him. She felt instead an unexpected lump in her throat. At least one old burden had just been lifted from her shoulders, and she wondered how things might have turned out if she could have brought herself to fall in love with Karl all those years ago instead of—

Emily banished the thought. "I only take partial responsibility for Bull Run."

"Perhaps we can work on that over time," Karl said with a wink. "You have much too active a conscience, Miss Emily."

"Some might argue with you," she replied, remembering how Ross had caught her searching through Davenport's print orders.

"Well, good day for now." Karl tipped his hat. "Do keep in mind my job offer, and I hope you get your watch fixed."

Emily gave him a little smile. "Indeed, Mr. Becker. If I find a competent jeweler, I'll be sure to let you know."

Ross tugged at his collar, wishing he could loosen his tie just a bit. He was on his way to town, though, and it wouldn't do to show up at the paper looking as if he were ready to call it a day before the week even got started.

He turned off the dirt lane from the Hockstetter place and walked along the side of the pike. He had another mile ahead on foot, but he didn't mind. On a morning like this, with fields of young corn and tobacco spreading for as far as the eye could see, pleasant memories of past summers were strong and compelling. It was only his stiff collar and tailored trousers that reminded him that he was no longer the thirteen-year-old boy in worn denims and a homespun shirt who had knocked his way along this same road to school. He was a grown man with a responsible job, a bright future, and one very bloody war behind him.

The rattling sounds of a wagon approaching from behind didn't immediately take his attention. The pike was always busy at this time of day. Soon, the wagon drew even with him and groaned to a stop.

"Here now, Ross. Thought that was you. All fancied up like you are. Couldn't be anybody else. Need a ride to town?"

Ross's young landlord, Phares Hockstetter, leaned a brawny, suntanned forearm on one knee and peered down at him from beneath the brim of a broad straw hat. Only a few years older than Ross, Phares already wore the leathery sun-wrinkles of a man a decade his senior. If he was aware of them, though, he no doubt wore them with pride. Being one of the stoic, hardworking breed of Pennsylvania Germans that had built Lancaster County into one of the most productive agricultural areas in the nation, Phares made no secret that he considered Ross's choice to make a living with his pen rather than the strength of his back very peculiar.

Ross hesitated. "A ride?" He glanced in the direction of town where brick buildings huddled on the horizon and smoke stacks puffed steam into the sky.

On a morning like this, Ross preferred to walk. It was a simple pleasure, to bask in the openness and beauty of the farmland, to revel in the smell of newborn country air untainted by the stench of unwashed bodies and human disease. A simple pleasure. Like being able to eat his fill of golden roast chicken or loaf cake with apple butter and to feel his body growing strong and healthy again as each new day passed. A simple pleasure. Like lying between clean sheets at night and being able to close his eyes without worrying that another prisoner, one out of his mind with cold and starvation, might murder him in his sleep for a half ration of weevily cornmeal or the tattered remains of his blanket. These were simple pleasures Ross still savored and hoped he would never fail to appreciate again.

Remembering his manners, Ross offered Phares a smile, thanked him, and climbed up into the ladder wagon. He doubted the farmer would understand his very personal reasons for wanting to leg it to town, and it wouldn't do to spurn a neighborly offer.

Phares released the hand brake and snapped the reins, commanding his old mule, Wilma, into sluggardly forward motion once again. "Phoebe was by the house day before last. She sure does like what you done to the old place," Phares said.

"Well, it's not that much," Ross replied, "just some paint on the porch and a few flowers out front. The vegetable garden's coming along pretty well, though, and I finally got a chance to fix the door on the springhouse this past Saturday."

Phares nodded. "*Ach*, yes. The place started to run down soon after Mommy died. Kept after it best I could, but what with plantin' and Phoebe expectin' a new little one and all, I just couldn't keep it up."

Ross knew the story. When he answered the young farmer's advertisement for a tenant, he learned that the family farmhouse had been empty for months following Mrs. Hockstetter's death. Prior to that, the couple had sold off most of their farmland when Mr. Hockstetter grew too ill to work. As for Phares, he'd married the only child of a land-wealthy farm family and now owned a hundred-acre farm of his own.

"I expect to fix the handrail on the front staircase this week," Ross said.

"Ain't now? Well, that's good. Appreciate it."

As Wilma towed the clattering wagon along the rutted pike, they fell into a comfortable silence. Ross liked Phares. He was the kind of man one could sit with and not feel awkward as the quiet stretched out between them.

Ross also liked his weekends and evenings spent alone in the old stone farmhouse. While it was true that he would live and die by his pen, he took a certain visceral satisfaction from effecting routine repairs and restoring Mrs. Hockstetter's yard and gardens to their once well-tended state. He liked working with his hands. He liked seeing the results of his efforts, clear and unarguable and tangible.

"Still lookin' to sell, you know."

Ross looked up. "Sell what?"

"The house," Phares said, not taking his eyes from the road. "Ain't much land that comes along with it. Only the woodlot and that patch around back of the springhouse. No farmer will want it, but it sure does seem like just the thing for a man with a town job to support him."

Phares had made this offer once before, and Ross had been sorely tempted to take him up on it. "I'd like to, but Johanna has her heart set on living in town."

"Hmm. Miz Davenport."

"Uh, Butler, you mean."

Phares just chuckled. "Sorry. I keep forgettin' she married that fancy fella before the war."

Ross absorbed this dryly. He could think of a few other, much less flattering descriptions of Johanna's first husband. Setting aside his bitter past rivalry with the late John Butler, though, Ross decided that Phares Hockstetter's depiction was an understatement. John had been a bit more than some "fancy fella." His family owned one of the grain mills in town, not to mention a staggering amount of real estate. It was no wonder that Malcolm had cut off Johanna's early flirtations with Ross all those years ago when she had a suitor like John Butler waiting eagerly in the wings.

Phares left him off at the corner of King and Queen Streets with a half hour to spare. There was plenty of time to stop by the bank and take care of the problem that had nagged at him all weekend. Ever since Emily had stopped by the house.

Ross hurried past the Davenport building, then crossed the street to the national bank. As he waited for a teller, he had time to ponder the question Emily had asked him on Saturday. *Can't you just trust me?*

It was a question that had needled at his conscience all weekend. He had vowed to make amends for the past, to win back her friendship, and trust was an important element of that friendship.

Ten minutes later, when Ross entered the Davenport building, a banker's envelope plumped an inside pocket of his coat. The wall clock read nine-ten. Emily would already be at work in the second-floor business office.

Waving to one of the job pressmen, he passed through the printing department and took the stairs. The last thing he wanted was to run smack-dab into

Malcolm. His future father-in-law came barreling down the hall with all the delicacy of a charging bull.

"Ross!" he boomed, stopping to pluck a fat Corona Ducal cigar from his mouth. "I left this morning's wires on your desk. You can dole them out however you like, but Governor Curtin has the list of Pennsylvania soldiers who died at Andersonville. I thought you'd want to handle that one yourself."

Impatient to keep moving, Ross nodded. "Thanks, I do."

Malcolm pointed with his smoking cigar. "And there's that city council meeting this afternoon."

"Got it." Ross said, growing irritated. They both knew that as assistant editor it was Ross's responsibility to cover city government—even if he didn't like it. Most of the men on the city council were still old-style Democrats. Of all the subjects Ross had been assigned to cover since coming to work for the *Herald*, he found city council meetings not only the most dull but also the most difficult to write about without offending Malcolm's political sensibilities. His articles inevitably came out sounding like meeting minutes.

But that was beside the point. If it was his job, Ross would make sure it got done. He resented that Malcolm felt inclined to remind him of his duty as if he were an irresponsible six-year-old.

"I've got a meeting with my lawyer and some other business to attend to," Malcolm said, pulling out his pocket watch. "I'll be back after one. You can man the ship until then."

"Will do," Ross said.

As usual, Malcolm was too self-absorbed to take notice of a subordinate's discontent. He clapped Ross on the back. "Good! Looking forward to supper tonight!"

Supper. At that moment, Ross couldn't imagine a worse way to pass the evening. As he watched Malcolm vanish around the corner, Ross struggled against a flare of resentment.

More and more often, it seemed, he had to remind himself that it was Malcolm who held his future in the palm of his hand, that it was Malcolm who even now still dangled his lovely daughter like a carrot before Ross's hungry eyes.

"You will, of course, be married in the Episcopal church." Malcolm had said this two months ago, the evening Ross came to discuss the idea of marriage to his daughter.

"I see no problem with that," Ross replied, sitting forward in a richly upholstered wing chair. It was perhaps ironic that he'd survived hair-raising battles and the horrors of Andersonville only to be experiencing a rush of nerves at a time like this. It seemed incredible to him that he was sitting in Malcolm Davenport's plushly furnished study, that he was actually having this conversation with the man who, four years before, had unilaterally cut off his relationship with Johanna when it had threatened to become more than casual flirtation.

"Have you considered joining the congregation?"

Ross was caught off guard by this question. He'd assumed the religion issue had been dealt with. "What?"

"Ross, let me be candid." The older man rose from a leather armchair and moved to a side table to pour himself a second shot of bourbon. "You acquitted yourself well during the war, rising to the rank of sergeant in three years, and you already show exceptionally bright promise as a writer and a journalist. You're a fine young man with a bright future ahead, but,"—Malcolm turned to face him—"I won't stand for any grandchildren of mine being raised Catholic."

Ross didn't flinch beneath the older man's steel gaze, but he was nevertheless temporarily caught short of words. He hadn't set foot in a Catholic church in years, not since he'd left the orphanage in New York to come live with the Brenners, yet something inside him dug in its heels. He had to fight an almost overwhelming impulse to tell Malcolm Davenport that he could take his assistant editor's job and his beautiful daughter and go straight to hell.

"That will be . . . fine."

Malcolm's lips spread in a slow smile of satisfaction. He raised his glass. "Then an Episcopalian wedding it is."

Left alone in the hallway, Ross had to take a moment to rein in his prideful emotions, to call on his more pragmatic side to remind him that he was much too close to attaining his goals to chance messing things up now. How many years had he dreamed of success? Of gaining respect? Of possessing the elusive Johanna? Too long to throw it all away for the fleeting, admittedly sweet satisfaction of telling Malcolm what he could do with his job.

Ross reached up to massage the stress-corded muscles in the back of his neck. It wasn't even nine-thirty, and he wanted to go home. Ever since Emily had come back to town, it seemed he couldn't think straight anymore. He was being constantly bombarded by memories of the past, of where he'd come from rather than where he intended to go, and that was no good for his career. No good at all.

He took a deep breath. The sooner he took care of the money matter, the sooner he could get his head straight and get to work.

Continuing down the hall to the business office, he paused in the open archway to make sure old beak-nose Oberholtzer's office door was safely closed. The business manager had been vehemently opposed when Malcolm had hired Ross and still made no bones about his feelings on the subject.

Seeing that the coast was clear, Ross scanned the room. Like the clerks and the pressmen downstairs, the advertising and accounting department was busy. Emily sat at her desk writing copy, her head bent in concentration.

A shaft of morning sunlight played off the sleek ebony lines of her hair, and Ross found his eyes tracing not only the delicate, graceful line of her neck but also the soft, undeniably feminine nips and curves of breasts, waist, and hips beneath her clothing.

With a start, he jerked his attention back to her face. What was wrong with him? Hadn't he learned anything from the past? There was no surer way to get into trouble than to begin thinking of Emily as a woman. *Again.* Oh, hell . . .

Ross wasn't sure how long he stood immobile in the archway before realizing that Freddy or one of the other fellas was bound to look up and notice something was wrong.

Wrong? Ridiculous. Nothing was wrong.

He crossed the office and stood beside Emily's desk until she was forced to look up at him. Upon seeing who it was, she donned her usual expression of subtle annoyance.

"Here," he said, shoving the envelope into her hand before she could speak.

She looked astonished. "What . . . ?"

"The matter we spoke of on Saturday."

"I don't understand."

"The money," he said, lowering his voice.

She stared up at him.

Ross glanced over his shoulder to make sure no one was paying attention to their exchange. "Just take it."

"Ross, I . . . I mean, can you afford to—"

"I'm fine. I've already gotten some back pay, and there's still more coming. Besides, in another month, I'm—" He cut off. In another month he'd be marrying into the Davenport dynasty. Money would be the least of his worries.

Emily looked away, fingering the envelope indecisively, then she opened a desk drawer and extracted her handbag. "I'll pay you back," she said quietly, "with interest."

"I don't take interest from you. We'll talk later if you want."

She stuffed the envelope into her handbag and closed the desk drawer, still not meeting his gaze. "Why?"

"Because you were right. I should have trusted you. You wouldn't have asked if it wasn't important."

She looked up at him, and for the first time in a long while, the sweet, vulnerable spirit he remembered behind those magnificent sea blue eyes was left unguarded. "Thank you, Ross."

Ross. *Not* Mr. Gallagher.

"You're welcome." Sucking in his breath, he turned away. As he crossed the hall to the city room, his hands were clenched into fists.

He'd set out to make things right between them, to see her look at him with something other than distrust and disapproval, but now he wondered if he'd just opened both of them to consequences he hadn't foreseen. Was it wrong to try to rebuild bridges that he himself had burned long ago? He was no longer so sure of the answer.

# 10

*Friday came as a welcome relief.* Ross had suffered through not only one town council meeting, but three Davenport family meals. Consequently, he had found little time to work on house repairs or his novel. The few attempts he'd made to put words on paper had been hampered by thoughts of Emily.

He'd hoped that lending her the money would ease the tension between them, and it had. Some. Her wariness had diminished, but she hadn't explained what the money was for. Also, in contrast to her first two weeks on the job, she now seemed scattered and distracted. Every day, without fail, at barely one minute past five o'clock, she rushed from the office, buzzing down the hall like a bee on a mission.

Ross was worried. What could she need a hundred dollars for? Where was she rushing to after work? He was convinced that her sudden need for a loan and the dark circles under her eyes were connected. There were rumors that Emily and Karl Becker had been seen walking arm in arm down the street. Could her problem have something to do with Karl?

Ross had snapped more than one pencil at this possibility.

He glanced at the wall clock near his desk in the city room. Ten to five. Quickly, he put the finishing touches on an article for Saturday's first edition and signaled to one of the copyboys, a gangling adolescent named Ignatz Metzger.

"Take this to the composing room," he instructed. "Tell Mr. Davenport I'll be in tomorrow morning to sort through the wires. I'm leaving early tonight."

The boy's forehead wrinkled with concern. "Not feeling good?"

"Uh, that's right." Ross felt a twinge of guilt for lying to the lad. Iggy was earnest and hardworking as hell. He reminded Ross of the bugle boys in his regiment. He was too intense, too idealistic, and possessed with the same sort of burning, blind patriotism that had sent so many underage volunteers scurrying to swell the ranks of both armies.

"What is it?" Iggy persisted. "Not the ague, I hope?"

"Uh, no," Ross said, trying to put the boy's mind at ease. "Just some indigestion."

Iggy was not put at ease in the least. He looked horrified. "Stomach trouble! Flux! My uncle was down with it last week."

"It's not that bad." Ross glanced at the wall clock again and stood, reaching for the suit coat he'd draped over the back of his chair. Three minutes to five. He didn't want to miss Emily tonight. He was determined to find out what was going on.

"Don't go wastin' money on them pain and indigestion pills. Get yourself some of that ginseng tea. That's what my ma says. Ginseng tea for stomach distress."

# FOREVER AND ALWAYS 147

"I'll do that." Ross started across the city room, heading for the door.

"Ginseng plus black cherry plus yellowroot makes a good tonic," Iggy called after him. "'Specially when you add some whiskey. That's what my ma says."

"Thanks, Ig. See you tomorrow."

No sooner did Ross pull open the door than he caught a glimpse of Emily's dark skirt disappearing around the corner.

That was close. One more home remedy from Ignatz's mother and Ross would have missed her for sure. He waited for her to clear the stairs before following. Upon emerging on the street, he spotted her heading west toward home. Could he be wrong? All these evenings when she'd rushed from the office, was she simply eager to get home after a hard day's work? Then she entered Wilkerson's Hardware and Farm Implements Store. Hardware?

She emerged a few minutes later, crossing the street and heading back in the same direction from which she'd come. As Ross followed at a distance, she turned on the corner of Queen and headed north. But this wasn't the way home, this was the way to—

When she stopped at her father's old print shop, she pulled a key from her handbag and threw a quick glance over her shoulder. The furtiveness of this action, the implicit guilt, was not lost on Ross. Maybe that was because he knew her too well.

After the door closed behind her, Ross took up a post across the street, folding his arms and leaning up against the front of a furnishings store. Ten minutes passed before he pulled out his pocket watch. It was clear that whatever she was up to these days was happening inside that shop.

Stuffing his watch back into his pocket, Ross swore under his breath. The shade was still pulled on the door glass, and the window shutters remained closed. Of course, he could be wrong, but he was already getting a bad feeling, like maybe he knew exactly what she was up to but wished he hadn't poked his nose into it.

"Emily Elizabeth," he muttered, "for once, please prove me wrong."

He crossed the street and tried the front door. The knob turned easily and he stepped inside. An unnatural quiet greeted him when he closed the door.

Intellectually, he'd known what to expect, but emotions were not governed by intellect. Although Emily was nowhere in sight, she had pulled open the shutters in the back of the shop. There was enough light to illuminate a scene that instantly and profoundly depressed him.

With no windows open for ventilation, the heat and humidity was oppressive. The place smelled like an old attic. Some of the furniture and equipment had been moved out, and there was dust everywhere, thick coats of it on the empty desk tops. On the floor, a flurry of crisscrossing feminine footprints only served to accentuate an impression of abandonment.

No pulse, he thought as he started through the shop. He remembered what it was like when he worked here as an errand boy and much later, when he served his short stint as a reporter. He imagined the office as it had once been, teeming with conscientious employees. He could almost see Jason Willoughby standing before his composing desk, setting type and chatting with his coworkers. He could almost hear Billy O'Leary's barreling laugh over the scrape and groan of the double-cylinder press. He could imagine Nathaniel clenching his white meerschaum pipe in his teeth and crumpling a sheet of paper to send it hurtling into a wastebasket. And he saw Emily, nearly all grown up, ebony hair streaming smooth, dazzling lines down her back, a pencil tucked behind her ear, and her flounced skirt bouncing as she followed on her father's heels to his office. *Papa! If we order from out of town, we can save three percent. I have the figures right here, see?*

The shop had always had an urgent, thriving blood pulse of its own, a life force sparked and infused by Nathaniel's boundless spirit, his dogged adherence to principle, and the sheer, raw energy he brought to his work. Now it was gone. Almost.

As Ross approached the back of the shop he caught a whiff of a fresh and familiar odor—turpentine?—just before seeing that a desk, a worktable, and the job press were clean of dust. Stacks of paper, cut to different sizes, were bundled with twine. On a composing desk, two drawers of type were pulled open. A composing stick and a half-filled galley lay out on the sloped frame above it.

Work in progress?

Ross appraised the items on the worktable: billheads, circulars, business cards, and menus. A pile of print orders lay next to the stack. The date scrawled in the right hand corner of the first order was today, and the customer was Henry Wilkerson. Ross realized then why Emily had behaved so oddly the day he'd stumbled upon her in the front business office. He'd attributed her nervousness to defensiveness. Now he knew exactly what he'd read on her face. Guilt.

At the sound of rapid footsteps on the back stairs, Ross turned to see Emily in the open archway, clutching a thick batch of paper to her chest. Her face went white. "Ross."

"Emily."

She glanced about as if to be sure he hadn't brought an army of constables with him. "What are you doing here?"

"I followed you."

"Good heavens, why?"

"I was worried."

"You needn't be."

"Oh? I'm not so sure. What's this?" He pointed to the bundle of menus. "And this?" He snatched business cards that read *Karl Becker, Law office of David Stauffer, Atty.* and waggled them at her before throwing them down. "Don't even tell me."

At his tone, she lifted her chin. "All right. I won't."

"You're filling print orders."

"Obviously."

By now, she had recovered some of her composure. She moved to the worktable as if nothing were amiss.

"Is this what the money was for?" he demanded.

"Rent," she said, throwing down her supply of clean paper. "I'll need some time before I'll be able to turn a profit, and the lease was due to expire very soon."

"A profit? You really expect to make a profit? When? Next year? How are you going to keep this up till then?"

"I have to take this one day at a time, Ross, otherwise I'll defeat myself before I start." Brushing by him, she moved to the composing desk. "Don't worry. Whatever happens, I'll be sure to pay you back."

"I don't care about getting paid back! That's not my point."

"Well, then, what *is* your point?"

"All this . . . this . . ." Ross found himself at a loss for words, a rare condition he despised. He gestured to the print orders. "It's . . . it's unethical!"

The line of her jaw hardened as she picked up the composing stick and began plucking type from an open case. "What's unethical?"

"These are Davenport's customers. He's your employer. What you're doing amounts to stealing behind his back. Even you have to admit there's something not quite right about that."

"Ha!" Apparently he'd struck a nerve. Emily slammed down the composing stick and turned on him. "I'll tell you what's not quite right. I spoke to Henry Wilkerson and Jack Martin, who runs that little grocery on King. I also talked to David Stauffer, the lawyer Karl works for. Do you know what they all have in common?"

She didn't wait for a reply but plowed ahead, jabbing a finger at his chest. "I'll tell you what they have in common. They all rent their shop space from Malcolm Davenport or one of his partners, and they were all former advertisers with the *Penn Gazette*. They all ended up pulling their advertising from the *Gazette* shortly before it went out of business. You know why?"

Ross folded his arms. "No, why?"

"All three of them said that when it came time to negotiate new leases, they were shocked to learn that their rents would double. None of them wanted to move, but they couldn't afford that kind of increase."

"Well, that's a shame, Emily, but there's nothing very unusual about any of that."

"But that's not all. The upshot of the matter was that if they would agree to pull their advertising from the *Gazette*, then a more reasonable rate could be negotiated. One hand washes the other. That's what Malcolm's lawyer told David Stauffer."

"Are you sure about this?"

"Why would all three men lie? In fact, they're part of a minority who will even talk to me about it, so you can bet there are a lot more like them. That sure helps explain why the *Gazette*'s advertising revenues dipped so drastically almost overnight."

Ross dropped his arms. "Oh, damn."

"Eloquently put. My feelings exactly." Having finished presenting her case, Emily snatched up her composing stick and resumed work.

"I have a hard time believing that even Malcolm would sink that low."

"Why not? Papa's business was growing and his wasn't. He couldn't control all the new subscriptions that were pouring in from around the county, but he sure could affect a lot of the city businesses who advertised in the *Gazette*. Maybe now you can see why I'm not particularly concerned about the ethical ramifications of stealing back a few print customers from under that scoundrel's nose."

"I'm not sure that what he did justifies you sinking to his level."

Emily paused long enough to give him a withering look. "*Now* who's being unrealistic?"

That stung. "All right," Ross conceded, "but gaining a certain amount of spiteful satisfaction isn't worth putting your real job in jeopardy."

"My real job? What makes you think *this* isn't my real job?"

"Because you're not making any money at it. You can't seriously expect to make a go of this?"

"Why not? People start new businesses everyday."

"Not by themselves. Not without some financial backing, anyway, and certainly not when they're women."

Ross didn't miss the poisonous side glance she sent him. She had never taken well to being reminded of her gender's biological or social limitations. In fact, she had never taken well to being reminded of *any* limitations. It was just Ross's sorry luck that he'd always been the more practical-minded of the two and that it was often his unpleasant task to force her to face reality. He took up that task now, even if he understood why she was doing this. "It's crazy, Emily. You're tilting at windmills."

"You sound like Karen," she muttered. Her fingers moved quickly and artfully, plucking type and setting it, plucking and setting, without missing a beat.

"Maybe it's as hard for her as it is for me to stand by and watch you work yourself into the ground for nothing. You're heading for a big disappointment."

"Then don't watch. Leave."

Her dismissal couldn't have been more effective if she'd slapped his face. He knew he should follow her advice. He should leave, but his feet wouldn't move. "Come with me," he said.

"No."

"Emily, you can't do this alone."

She expelled an exasperated breath and faced him. "Then, for God's sake, Ross, why don't you help me?"

He felt as if she'd tossed a flaming cannonball into his lap. Help her? He glanced at the pile of print orders on the table. Only a handful, not more than an afternoon's work if she had a normal staff to support her. As it was, she'd probably be sweating it out here all night.

But he couldn't be the person to help her. And it wasn't only because he believed she was setting herself up for a fall. He had his own future to think about. He had no intention of telling Malcolm what he knew, and that was probably bad enough. To actually get involved with Emily's ill-fated scheme would be tantamount to professional betrayal.

"I can't."

She didn't flinch. She merely held his gaze a few seconds longer, then she turned back to her work. "I didn't think so."

Ross stood motionless for another long moment. "You can't expect me to help you dig this hole for yourself."

"Oh, I certainly wouldn't," she said with exaggerated sarcasm, plucking and setting, plucking and setting.

"Fine." He wanted to throttle her.

"Fine."

Ross strode to the door, yanked it open, and slammed it behind him. Stubborn! Stubborn and impulsive and reckless and stupid. If she wouldn't listen to reason, there was nothing he could do to help her.

He didn't pay attention to which direction he chose on the street. *Away.* Away from her was the only direction that counted. Good Lord, how could she ask him to help her when she knew very well what an awkward position it would put him in? Now, because of her and her unreasonable request, he felt like an unchivalrous lout, leaving her to sweat over a job press all night.

Damn her.

She'd deliberately put him in a no-win situation. If Malcolm found out that he was helping Emily steal print customers from him—and he would, sooner or later—how would that look?

He had too much time and effort invested into forging a promising future with the *Herald* to consider tossing it all to the wind. Why, just taking into account all the Davenport family meals he'd sat through, the price exacted in sheer blood-and-guts agony was running pretty damn high. Interminable, dreary affairs they were, with Malcolm presiding at the head of the table, pontificating upon whatever political or local issue had caught his interest that day, and Mrs. Davenport, sitting silent and faintly pretty at the other end. And then there was Johanna, who perched across the table from Ross, smiling coyly as she offered to pass the bread.

Why, just the previous evening, as Malcolm had droned on and Ross's annoyance had begun to build, he'd had to remind himself of his priorities. For the price of a few dull mealtimes, his future was assured. While it wasn't common knowledge, Ross knew that Malcolm had his eye on a state senate seat. If that came to pass, Ross might find himself sitting in the managing editor's desk sooner than he expected. That was tempting enough without taking into account that he would soon be claiming the lovely Johanna as his prize. It should have been enough to make any man willing to sit through a few boring meals.

But Ross's mind had kept wandering. He tried

casting his attention in Johanna's direction, allowing his gaze to settle on the lush swell of her breasts beneath the bodice of her evening dress. Every so often he even caught a gratifying glimpse of cleavage when she leaned forward to pass the salt. Of all things, the sight of Johanna's lovely feminine figure should have distracted him with fantasies of bounteous sex, but Ross found himself thinking of Emily instead. He imagined her riding with Karl Becker in his runabout, and it was unwelcome fantasies of Emily and Karl ripping off each other's clothes to roll naked and wild on a picnic blanket that ultimately caused Ross to lose his appetite—*all* of his appetites. He'd left the Davenport home with a pounding headache and a mutinous attitude.

Ross stopped cold at a busy intersection, breathing hard more from exasperation than exertion. He glared up at a street sign to see that he'd walked three-quarters of the way around the same block. "Damn her!"

Awash in guilt, he looked up the street in the direction of the print shop. Mutual agreement on all issues had never been characteristic of his relationship with Emily, so why should he expect it to be so now? She was wrong, but he was nevertheless assailed by images of her toiling over a heavy hand press. He was left with a bad taste in his mouth at the thought of leaving her to fight her hopeless battle all alone.

When she had asked him to help her, had it been some kind of test? If so, it was a test he'd managed to fail in a prompt and spectacular fashion.

"Damn," he swore again softly. "Emily, why do you have to make this so difficult?"

\* \* \*

They worked well into the evening by lamplight in the old print shop. When Ross had first returned with two covered dinner plates from the Blue Swan, Emily appeared surprised, but she didn't ask why he'd come back. Even as they partook of a hasty evening meal in near-silence, it was clear why he'd come back. He was capitulating. Well, perhaps that was too strong a word. He still made it clear that he didn't approve of what she was doing, but he pitched in, taking over operation of the press while Emily set type and arranged copy for the orders she had promised to deliver the following morning.

As they worked, they kept their distance, each tending to his or her tasks. Emily kept an uncharacteristically restrained silence while Ross was still too confused over his own motivations to put much into words. When they did speak, it was of neutral topics, those they could discuss without upsetting the apple cart—the weather, the Lincoln assassination trial, and Alma Brenner's state of health.

Only once were they forced to confront the alien tension that had grown between them. As they passed each other, he on his way to replenish his ink supply, she returning from delivering a full galley to his worktable, Emily's toe caught on the leg of a chair, shooting her forward and directly into Ross's stunned arms. His fingers instinctively wrapped around her waist, anchoring there, refusing to move. They stared at each other.

"You all right?"

"Yes."

Ross had almost forgotten what a woman felt like, what Emily felt like—so delicate and feather-light. Beneath the lining of her bodice and corset, she would be soft to the touch, fine and warm and smooth. They were both sweating in the abominable heat, but she smelled like rosewater. She must have washed her hair in it or something. He felt her hands on him where she'd caught him for balance. Her fingers gripped his forearms tightly beneath his rolled-up shirtsleeves.

"You sure you're all right?"

"Yes." Her death grip relaxed, then released.

Ross did likewise and stepped back. "I . . . uh . . ."

"Big feet," she said before he could finish making a complete jackass out of himself.

"What?"

"My big dumb feet," she said, then pushed past him to resume work.

By nine o'clock, Ross was exhausted, and he could tell Emily was in no better condition. "Let's call it a night," he suggested, pulling out the bed assembly of the press. He lifted the frisket and removed the last of a two-hundred-sheet handbill order.

Emily frowned, then moved to the worktable where the completed orders were ready to be bundled for delivery. "I've just got one more thing to do."

"Emily." His warning tone must have gotten her attention. When she turned, he inclined his head toward the wall clock. "Isn't your family going to worry?"

She blinked and pushed a stray lock of hair from her sweat-dampened forehead. The shadows that lurked beneath her eyes were clearly evident in the glow of a desk lamp. "Oh, I . . . I hadn't realized what time it was."

"As I said, time to call it a night."

"I'll just clean up here and—"

"Leave it for tomorrow," Ross interrupted. "Sit down. I'll clean the press, then I'll walk you home."

"Oh." But Emily didn't move. She seemed dazed with fatigue. Ross moved toward her, taking her by the elbow and leading her over to an empty desk to sit.

"I'll be through in a couple minutes."

For once, she didn't argue. Crossing her arms on the desk, she rested her head and closed her eyes. "Gotta get an early start in the morning," she mumbled.

"How long have you been at this?" he asked, disengaging the chase and lifting it from the bed of the press. "All week?"

She nodded without opening her eyes. "Mmm-hmm."

"Most of last week, too, I'll bet."

"Mmm-hmm."

"You can't go on like this." This was the first time since his earlier walkout that Ross had chosen to restate his argument.

She let out a long sigh. "Please. I'm too tired to fight you, Ross."

He didn't say anything more as he soaked some rags in turpentine and finished cleaning the type and the press's inking mechanism. When he was done, he moved to a washstand in the back of the room and proceeded to wash his hands of turpentine and printer's ink for the first time in years. He tried not to think about how good it had felt to get his hands dirty again.

When he was finished, he took a clean hand towel, wetted it from the pitcher, and moved to Emily's bent figure. "Here."

She opened her eyes, then sat up, accepting the towel and dabbing at her forehead to cool off. "Thank you."

Ross didn't reply. Taking a chair from a nearby desk, he turned it around and straddled it, resting his forearms on its back. The quiet seemed to swell as he watched her throw her head back and dab the wet cloth down the arched column of her neck.

Against his better judgment, his gaze dropped to her breasts, then rose again to linger on the pale, damp skin of her exposed throat. He felt an unbidden, unwanted sexual stirring that he had no business entertaining. It was an old battle that confused and angered him.

He spoke in even, clipped tones. "You plan to spend all day here tomorrow, too?"

"I can't. Maybe some of the morning, but I promised Mother I'd help her in the afternoon, and I'm not sure if I can come up with a plausible excuse to get out of the house after supper."

"So Marguerite doesn't know."

"No. Karen thinks I'm crazy, same as you, but I made her promise not to tell. If this doesn't work out, we can sell the equipment as easily in another couple months as now."

It was the first time he'd heard her voice the possibility of failure. Perhaps she was capable of facing reality, after all. "You can't keep this a secret for long," he said. "Not in this town. Soon Oberholtzer or Malcolm will find out, then it'll all be over."

She stopped dabbing and looked at him flatly. "But they won't learn it from you."

It was phrased as a statement, but Ross knew it was a question. A test. Too tired to fight him? Never. Not Emily.

"No," he said.

"Then I'll just have to deal with it when the time comes."

As Ross held the determined, dark blue gaze of those beautiful eyes he thought he knew so well, he realized that he didn't know her at all. She had kept her second job a secret—from both him and Marguerite—and he now wondered how many more secrets she kept.

*Karl's baby.* A child that was perhaps even now being brought up in the care of Emily's aunt Esther in Baltimore. Or perhaps given up long ago for adoption to a loving family. Now there was a secret, a humdinger of a secret, and the very possibility that the rumors could be true couldn't have been worse than a bayonet through the gut. God, he hated Karl when he thought about it, and maybe even Emily a little, too, but he didn't want to dwell on why it ate at him so.

He pushed up from the chair abruptly and moved to retrieve his coat and hat from a peg on the wall. "Time to go."

Emily said nothing but complied by rising from her seat. Ross waited for her to slip off her apron and get to the door before he extinguished the lamps.

The night was muggy, the streets quiet except for a lone constable that passed. They didn't talk at all during the long walk out of town. Emily seemed preoccupied with her own thoughts, while Ross was tormented by images of Emily and Karl.

When they reached the Winters home, they stood beneath a young chestnut tree inside the front gate. Ebony strands of hair wisped free about Emily's fine-featured face, and her ivory complexion shone pale and soft in the moonlight. When she looked up at him, Ross had to swallow hard to keep from asking the question that burned in his throat.

She must have seen the anger on his face because she looked concerned. "What's wrong, Ross?"

*Wrong?* What indeed was wrong? There was apparently plenty wrong, because instead of asking for the truth, he did what he'd promised himself he would never do again. He kissed her.

His fingers delved deep into the rich thickness of the hair behind her jaw, setting her chignon tumbling loose down her back. She let out a small sound of surprise when he pulled her to him, but she didn't resist. She clung to his coat when his mouth closed on hers, then her soft lips parted, and he tasted of memories so forbidden and sweet, they sent his rational mind into a spin. Wrong?

This was a mistake, a terrible mistake. What the hell was he doing?

He pulled back abruptly and released her. She jumped back, too, her eyes wide and blinking, one trembling hand rising to touch her lips as if she was in shock. "Oh, no," she whispered.

"I'm sorry. I—" He cut off, painfully reminded of a similar summer night four years before. What was the matter with him? Was he doomed to keep repeating the same mistake with her all over again?

"I'm sorry, Em," he began again. "I don't know what made me—"

"I've got to go in now."

Before he could say another word, she was hurrying up the flagstone path. She flung open the door and vanished into the house.

Stunned at his own reckless actions, Ross stood

in the dappled evening shade of the chestnut tree, staring after her. It all started with that question. What was her secret? Part of him yearned for an answer, part of him *demanded* to know, yet there was another part of him, a part that was just as insistent, that turned away. He was afraid of what her answer would be.

# 11

*"Emily, I wish you'd reconsider."*

Karen stood with her black veil folded back from her face, her hands on her burgeoning mother-to-be hips in sisterly disapproval.

Emily was not about to budge from her curled-up position on the brocade sitting room sofa. She wore a gray cotton housedress and no shoes, hardly an ensemble in which to gallivant about town. "Karen, I just don't feel like going out today."

Dorcas stood by her mother's side, her little forehead creased in puzzlement. She too was in full mourning black; however, she was anything but correspondingly somber. After all, today was Whit Monday. "But why, Aunt Emily? It's fun. Didn't you know? There's a circus in town. Don't you like the circus? Are you afraid of the elephant?"

Emily couldn't help but smile. If anyone could have convinced her to travel into town today to partake of Lancaster's annual Whit Monday festivities, it would have been her niece. Dorcas's attitude toward her had changed considerably—the result of a penciled portrait Emily had done for her. "Mammy, look!" she had cried. "Aunt Emily made a pretty picture of me!" And it *had* been a pretty picture, a beautiful picture, a picture of four-year-old innocence. Funny how that absently sketched portrait had transformed Dorcas's attitude from one of distrust to one of adoration.

"Afraid of the elephant?" Emily leaned forward, feigning insult that Dorcas would suggest such a thing. "Why, no. I positively love elephants, and elephants love me."

"Then why don't you want to come with us?"

"Oh, Dorcas, my dear, sweet baby— "

"I'm not a baby."

"Of course not." Emily tried to appear properly remorseful. "I'm sorry, but it's just that I'm tired today, and—"

"Tired is right," Karen interrupted sternly. "You look terrible. You've been working too hard, that's what's the matter. You need to get out and have some fun."

Emily was well aware of the fact that she looked terrible. She felt terrible. She'd gotten precious little sleep the past few nights, but working too hard was the least of her problems. Before she could offer any further argument, Henry stuck his head in the door. "Your mother's on the porch waiting, Karen."

"Just a minute," Karen said. "We've just about got Emily talked into going with us."

Henry, bless his practical heart, merely expelled a sigh of masculine impatience. "We'll miss the horsecar into town if we wait much longer."

"You'd better get going," Emily urged. "I'll be fine."

Karen looked from Emily to Henry then back to

Emily again, loath to relent. As for Dorcas, it might have been true that she now adored her aunt Emily, but there was a circus in town, and that was that. "No elephants for you!" she crooned, then bounded to her father.

Henry bent to catch her up in his arms. "If Emily wants to stay home, leave her be. Let's go." And then father and daughter were gone.

Emily had to admit that there were times when a male point of view was most welcome. This was one of those times. Karen was left without a leg to stand on.

"Oh, all right, all right." Bustling to the door, Karen adjusted her veil and shook a parting finger. "Next year, you're coming. Whether you like it or not."

The front door squealed on its hinges before swinging closed. Next year, Emily thought. Who said she would still be here next year?

She rose to cross the carpeted floor of the sitting room. Pushing aside a lacy window curtain, she peered outside until her family was well on its way down the dirt lane toward the busy pike. If they were lucky, the horsecar wouldn't be too full on its return circuit to town. From as early as daybreak, rural folks, both on foot and in all manner of conveyances, would be congesting the main roads. Whit Monday drew crowds from all around. It was a rollicking, late spring holiday marked by town fairs, parades, and often a traveling circus. For the children, it was an event preceded by as much breathless anticipation as the Fourth of July.

Emily dropped the curtain. She had told her sister the truth. She was tired, exhausted, in fact, but that wasn't all that kept her home today. There was too good a chance she would run into Ross and Johanna, and she didn't think she could bear that. After what happened the other night, she was left feeling much too vulnerable. Even now, if she allowed herself to stop for even a moment and remember, she would be able to feel Ross's lips pressed against hers, a peculiar, heady mix of warmth and raw passion, a mix that was purely Ross, a mix that she remembered all too vividly.

Emily moved to the sofa and sank back against the red velvet upholstery. Tucking her legs beneath her, she closed her eyes. That single, rushed kiss had shaken her down to her very foundations, but, in reality, it had meant nothing. They'd both been tired, and he'd been frustrated with her. She knew she couldn't read any more into it than that. She also knew that she couldn't afford to let him get to her emotionally. But he wasn't making it easy.

She remembered one time when they'd had an argument over something silly. How old had she been then? Thirteen? The argument had escalated, and soon she'd imparted her lofty opinion that Johanna Davenport was nothing but a shallow, two-faced snob and that any boy who couldn't see past Johanna's pretty face and blossoming figure to that plain truth was a bosom-faddled blockhead. Well, needless to say, that hadn't set very well with Ross. He'd been justifiably insulted, but very soon, Ross being Ross, his anger had cooled. Ironically enough, it was Emily who had stayed angry the longest, perhaps in an attempt to protect her own feelings. She'd hoped that if she managed to stay angry with him, then it wouldn't hurt so much if he ended their friendship. Better yet, if she managed to persuade herself to hate him, then the fact that he didn't care for her more than as a friend wouldn't hurt so much, either. It was very simple, really, except Ross had never been one to leave well enough alone.

A day or so after their argument, he'd approached her at the shop, asking if everything could be smoothed out between them again. They could forget all about what had happened. Why not? He could take a joke. That was what he said, then after no answer from her, he'd just shrugged and walked away. But not for long.

Emily soon learned that it was very difficult to stay angry with someone who insisted upon chatting with the back of her head every time he was in the vicinity or who offered to open the door every time she went to leave. The harder she tried to ignore him, the cheerier Ross got. Dad blast it, she'd thought. Why couldn't he just leave a girl stay mad if she wanted to stay mad? If it was better for the both of them if she just stayed mad forever?

Then, one afternoon, she'd arrived at the shop to discover a slim, rectangular parcel wrapped in newsprint and blue ribbon tucked into the pocket of her work apron. Ripping it open, she'd found a box of sixty-four assorted soft French pastel crayons, something she'd been saving her pennies toward for months, and a card that read, *It's lonely by the creek these days. I miss you. Can I have my illustrator back?*

Emily let out a bothered sigh and scowled. No, Ross had never been one to leave well enough alone.

A knock at the front door shattered her train of thought.

\* \* \*

Ross knocked on the front door of the Winters house for the second time and waited. He was relying on his instincts. Everybody was in town for Whit Monday festivities, but if Emily hadn't been sleeping any better than he had for the past few nights, there was a good chance she would be home. She wouldn't be in any more of a mood to celebrate than he was.

He knocked on the front door again and wondered if he might be wrong, after all. Hadn't he been thinking just the other night how very much he *didn't* know about Emily these days? Then, out of the corner of his eye, he caught the flutter of a curtain at the parlor window. Oh, she was home, all right. She just wasn't answering the door.

Confident once again, Ross pounded on the door hard enough to rattle the hinges. "Come on, Emily! Open up!"

Still, he waited another full minute before the door squeaked part way open. Emily stood in the narrow space, her hand still gripping the inside door knob. Her hair was down today, loose and fluid about her shoulders. She looked very pretty and very vulnerable, despite the guarded defiance in her eyes. "Hello, Ross."

"Good morning," he said, trying his best to sound amiable. He'd already vowed to remain coolheaded no matter how she acted. "It took you a while to answer, but I was pretty sure you would be home"

She didn't seem to fall for the false cheer in his tone. At least, she didn't smile. "Most people are in town," she said. "Why aren't you with Johanna?"

"She's gone out to Rocky Springs with her mother. I took the opportunity to get some work done at the office, then I thought I'd head back home to catch up on some writing."

"Hmm." She didn't say any more, she just looked at him.

Ross took a deep breath. "I thought we should talk. About what happened the other night, I mean."

"What's there to say?"

"I'm sorry. I was out of line, and I don't know why I—"

"I accept your apology," she interrupted, effectively cutting off all manner of speeches he'd planned. "It doesn't matter, anyway. We were both tired, right?"

Ross could feel his aggravation rising. It didn't matter? She was behaving as if nothing had happened while he'd lost three nights' sleep over it. "You sure don't make things easy, Em."

"Neither do you," she countered flatly.

He had no idea what she meant by that, but he managed to keep his voice even and controlled. "Well, since that's all cleared up, there was something else I wanted to talk to you about."

"Oh?"

"This idea you have about resurrecting the print shop."

She stiffened. "I'm not going to change my mind."

"Before you slam the door in my face, do you think you could at least hear me out?"

She frowned.

"Can I come in?"

"I don't know if that's a wise idea."

"Then why don't you come out here? It'll only take a minute."

Her gaze flicked away from him—to the porch

swing and the empty front yard behind him. She apparently detected no signs of impending rescue. "All right," she allowed grudgingly, "but just for a minute."

Ross congratulated himself on this infinitesimal victory as Emily pulled the door closed behind her, then stood a good yard and a half away from him with her arms folded. It was her battle stance. All shields in place.

He gestured toward the empty porch swing. "You want to sit?"

"No."

At this point, Ross had to remind himself of his vow to remain coolheaded. "I was thinking about your situation, and it occurred to me that if you could see some future for yourself at the *Herald,* maybe you'd give up this crazy idea of getting your father's business started again."

Even before he could finish, she dropped her arms and pulled herself up to full height. "It's not a crazy id—"

"Wait." Ross raised a hand. "Hear me out. This isn't common knowledge, but it's not a secret, either. Malcolm may throw his hat into the race for the state senate seat."

"And that's supposed to be good news? What's that got to do with me?"

"If he wins, it's likely I'll be taking over the managing editor's position."

"Good for you."

Ross ignored her sarcasm. "Listen to me. I know you're talented, not only as an illustrator, but you're a first-rate news reporter, too."

"Thank you. But what are you *really* trying to say?"

"I'm saying," he enunciated clearly, "that if you stay with the *Herald,* there's a good chance of being promoted out of advertising. That is, if you're interested."

Though her breathtaking sea blue eyes narrowed, and she tilted her head as if assessing his words, somehow Ross doubted she was truly considering his proposal. "And if Malcolm loses the election?"

"I'd still do my best to see that you're not overlooked when it comes time for a promotion."

Emily let out a snort, then laughed. "You're forgetting two things. First, you're forgetting that I'm a woman."

Never, Ross thought, struggling with his temper. He wished he *could* forget she was a woman. His life would be a hell of a lot simpler.

"Malcolm doesn't even like to hire women, much less promote them," Emily continued. "Second, you're forgetting that I would be compromising my principles if I were forced to write from a Democratic viewpoint."

Her principles. Well, why *not* throw her highfalutin principles into the argument? This was Emily, after all. "You wouldn't necessarily have to write from a Democratic viewpoint," he explained, trying not to grind his molars. "You would just have to exercise a certain amount of discretion."

"Discretion?" She repeated the word as if he'd asked her to drag her tongue through cow dirt.

"That's right, discretion. You *have* heard of it?"

"I suppose."

"Well, luckily, you may not have to worry about that. We've been thinking of adding a women's page to the Monday edition."

"A women's page? What could one possibly put on a women's page?"

# FOREVER AND ALWAYS

Ross shrugged. "I don't know. Nothing political. Fashion news, etiquette, recipes, things like that."

Emily rolled her eyes. "No, thank you."

"Why don't you just think about it?"

"Ross, I couldn't care less if hoopskirts grow or shrink. I certainly can't imagine wasting my time writing about it."

Ross sucked in a slow, deep breath and tried to remind himself that strangling her would serve no purpose. "You wouldn't have to write about it forever, just until—"

"No."

His temper snapped. "Why do you insist on being so damned mule-headed?"

Emily's eyes flashed. "I'm not! Maybe I just stick to my principles a little more tenaciously than *some* people."

Just that fast, all shields were down and swords were drawn. Ross didn't even care that they had careened off the subject at hand and were hurtling in what could be a very dangerous direction. His voice went cold. "Meaning me, I suppose."

"If the shoe fits."

"Sometimes, Emily, I don't even know why I bother to help you at all."

"I didn't ask for your help."

"No," he retorted, "you just asked for my money."

It was a low blow and Ross knew it. Still, it was the truth and he was gratified to see that prickly attitude of hers falter, if even for a split second. "I . . . I . . . well, I shouldn't have!"

"Yeah. Maybe you should have gone to Karl instead."

She gaped at him, again taken off balance. "Karl? What's Karl got to do with this?"

"Don't play innocent with me."

"What?"

"What's going on with you two, anyway?"

"Nothing!"

"And I'm supposed to believe that?"

"I don't care what you believe." She shot forward to come toe to toe with him. "And if I want to take up with Karl, I'll darn well do it without *your* permission!"

Ross gave a sarcastic laugh. "Oh. Here we go again. Cutting off your nose to spite your face. Very intelligent, Emily. Karl is a womanizer. You should know that better than anyone."

"Why?" she shot back. "*Why* should I know that better than anyone, Ross? Have you been hearing rumors?"

She'd obviously flung out the question without giving a thought to the consequences, but now the realization of what she'd done was beginning to dawn upon her. He could tell by the sudden drain of color from her cheeks. But she didn't flinch. No, not Emily. Maybe she hadn't meant to blurt the question, but it was done, and now she would never back down. She held his gaze, daring him to probe old hurts.

"I don't pay attention to rumors," he said evenly.

"Well, maybe you should. Maybe some of them are true."

Damn her. He'd given her an out and still she pushed him to go a step farther. What did she want from him? "All right," he said, his mouth going dry. "Then it's true that you left town four years ago."

"Yes."

"Why?"

"Why do you think?"

The rumors were true. They were true. He'd tried to convince himself they weren't, but Emily had now made that impossible. So, what was left? Ask her if it was Karl? Did he want to hear her answer if it was? And if it wasn't . . . ?

The question strained to pass through his clenched lips, but he didn't voice it. Instead, he said, "Emily, all I want is for things to be like they used to be between us."

He thought he saw a shadow of regret mix with the anger and hurt in her eyes, but then it was gone. Or maybe he'd imagined it. "I don't see how that's possible."

He held her gaze for a long, hard moment, then backed off. "Never mind."

"I'm—"

"Never mind." He turned and strode to the porch steps, feeling like a fool. "I shouldn't have come."

"Ross, I—"

He didn't hear the rest of whatever it was she had to say. He was already pushing his way through the front gate.

# 12

*After Ross returned home,* he tried to get some work done on his novel, but it was no use. He was too angry, and this time his anger had nothing to do with the hellhole at Andersonville. He was learning to deal with that. In fact, it was through rereading his own diaries and by transforming much of what he found there into thinly disguised fiction that he was beginning to make some manner of peace with it. No, this anger was different. It was more immediate and compelling, and the source was Emily. That stubborn, pigheaded little girl had grown into an even more stubborn, pigheaded woman.

He gave up on his writing, then paced the floor of his parlor, then banged around the kitchen, rustling up some eggs and fried potatoes for his midday meal. He went outside to see about repairing the front gate but soon learned he hadn't the patience for that either. He was too restless. He needed physical exertion. And lots of it. With an ax and saw in hand, he tromped out to the woodlot.

By four o'clock, he'd felled a dying oak and had

sectioned and transported some of it by wheelbarrow to his backyard, where he commenced to chop it into firewood. Hell, if Emily kept driving him to distraction much longer, he'd have the Hockstetter woodshed full and all set for winter by next week.

Using the back of his arm, Ross mopped the sweat from his forehead, then bent to hoist another chunk of wood onto the chopping block. He was bound and determined to exhaust himself. He meant to be flat on his back soon after sundown. Maybe then he wouldn't lie awake half the night, mentally rehashing each word they'd exchanged, each movement she'd made, each nuance of barely repressed emotion that had crossed her face.

Even now, despite his efforts to remain focused on his mind-numbing work, he found himself thinking back, trying to recall exactly when it was that Johanna said Emily left town. January of '62. That was when her last letter to him had been dated.

He remembered receiving it that month. At the time, his regiment was encamped on Port Royal Island following their first engagement with the enemy. Ross hadn't been so caught up in the thrill of victory, however, not to notice the distant, almost formal tone of her letter. It contained no hint of their special relationship. Ross knew then, with a sick, desperate feeling, that he'd lost her, but he was too far away to do anything about it. His next four letters had gone unanswered, and he'd given up. In fact, with the exception of two annual Christmas missives—one dutifully addressed to Alma Brenner and the other to Nathaniel at his shop—Ross had stopped writing home altogether. With Emily lost to him, what was left there for him to care about?

Parched and sweating, Ross took a break from his work to cross to the pump shelter where he ran a stream of blessedly cool water over his head, then he took a long drink from the dipper. Settling down on his haunches, he rested back against the stone slab and stared out at the neat rows of vegetables he'd planted in Mrs. Hockstetter's garden.

Emily had as good as admitted that she'd left town because she was pregnant. It was a truth that Ross was still having trouble coming to grips with. It was a truth that he'd worked hard to disbelieve ever since the day Johanna had told him of the rumors. It had turned his world upside down, so that now, no matter how much he wanted to deny it, he couldn't. Now he had to sort out the truth. Who was the father?

Ross had left to join the army late in September of '61. At the end of January, Emily left town carrying an unborn child. Ross counted back four months and wondered what had happened during that intervening time. Johanna had told him that Karl and Emily had been seen together during those months before Karl, too, had left for the war. Was it true? Had Karl and Emily been courting?

Ross had no way of being sure. The truth was, he didn't know what was going on in Emily's life at that time. Prior to the night he'd left for Camp Curtin to join his regiment, she hadn't spoken to him for almost three months, not since the beginning of the summer when he had resigned from the *Gazette* to go work for the *Herald*. Karl had been working his way through college by then, and Ross was immersed in his own new job. And even aside from the fact that their adult lives had taken different turns, Karl wasn't on speaking terms with Ross, either. They hadn't exchanged words since the night of that chestnuting party in Brenners' Woods.

Ross dropped his head and groaned aloud at the memory. What a calamity that had been. And in hindsight, disastrously prophetic. He'd had excellent reason to be in good spirits that night. After years of ups and downs in his quest for Johanna's attentions, she'd had a public tiff with his despised arch-rival, John Butler, squelching all rumors of an engagement announcement. Ross's path had seemed clear once again.

Johanna had happily accepted his invitation to the chestnuting party, and as they picked their way through Brenners' woods, collecting the fallen nuts in a basket, they'd taken their earliest opportunity to slip away from the group to steal a few kisses in private.

Later, when an early dusk had begun to settle over the autumn countryside and a bonfire was lit to call the remaining excursionists from the woods, Ross was in high spirits. That was, until he noticed Emily was missing.

He left an indignant Johanna perched on one of the logs around the bonfire as he set out to find Emily among the flirting young couples in their group. If it hadn't been for Karl's showing up at the party without a female companion, he might not have been so concerned, but he remembered Karl's earlier remarks upon spying Emily in the woods. "Is that little Emily Winters?" he had inquired slyly before letting out a long, low whistle. "Lordy, Lordy, but I almost didn't recognize her. That little spitfire has finally grown up and filled out, hasn't she?"

"She's only sixteen," Ross had replied tightly. "Leave her alone."

"Leave her alone?" Karl turned to Ross, feigning innocence. "That would be a flagrant waste, don't you think?"

Karl had sauntered away then, first in Emily's direction, then, with a teasing wink to Ross, changing course and heading instead toward a group of fellows. That had been the last Ross had seen of Karl, but that had been hours before. Ross's anxiety rose another notch when Emily's best friend, Melissa, told him that Emily and Karl had last been seen heading across the open meadow toward the Brenner homestead. Ostensibly, they'd gone to fetch some more apple cider for the group. A likely story.

Ross had barely kept his anger in check as he'd strode across the darkening meadow in the direction Melissa had indicated. It wasn't long before his suspicions were confirmed. A low murmur of voices drew him to a stone springhouse.

Reaching the side of the small outbuilding, Ross pressed back against the cold stone wall and listened. Emily's voice reached his ears.

"It's getting cold. They've probably got the bonfire going by now. We'd better get back."

"Forget the bonfire," Karl said. "There are other ways to warm up."

"Oh? And how is that?"

Karl chuckled. "Why, with a few kisses, of course."

"Kisses?" Emily repeated dubiously. "Are you trying to tell me that kissing generates heat?"

"You better believe it. If you've ever been kissed before, and it didn't warm you up some, then you haven't been very well kissed at all."

"You sound pretty sure of yourself."

"I am. You want to find out what I mean?"

Emily sounded coy. "Is that a challenge, Karl Becker?"

"That depends. Are you up to the challenge, Miss Emily?"

"What do you think?" she tossed back.

By then, Ross stood rigid, his jaw clenched as he tried to keep a tight rein on his skyrocketing temper. Listening to their ridiculous banter had been bad enough. Withstanding the lengthy silence that followed was worse. It was all Ross could do to keep from springing from his hiding place and yanking Karl away from her.

"There," Karl said finally, sounding like the conceited rogue that he was. "How was that? Warm you up any?"

Ross held his position by telling himself that Karl would soon get his comeuppance. Emily would put him in his place. Any second, Ross anticipated the satisfying sound of a resounding slap to Karl's cheek.

"I liked it," Emily said brightly. "Let's do it again."

She *liked* it? Ross was too stunned, too infuriated to move. *Let's do it again?*

Karl chuckled at his victory. "All right, Miss Emily, this time I'll give you an advanced lesson."

That was it. Ross's paralysis fled. His temper exploded. He bolted from his hiding place and did what he should have done before. He grabbed his debauched friend by the back of his collar and yanked him off balance. During the scuffle that followed, Ross's fist shot straight out to connect with Karl's nose. That rash act had promptly ended whatever was left of their boyhood friendship, but even that, as it turned out, was not to be the end of the evening's folly.

After Karl had stormed off, nursing his bleeding nose with a handkerchief, Ross had been left to face Emily, who had remained behind. She stood with her back against the springhouse wall, her dark hair disheveled, her arms at her sides, palms pressed flat back against the stone. She stared at Ross, saying nothing.

"Are you all right?" he asked anxiously. In the deepening shadows of dusk, he couldn't read her expression.

"No," she said.

At the odd flatness in her tone, something twisted in Ross's gut. He grasped her by the shoulders, pulling her to him. "Did he hurt you? Did he touch you? By God, if he—"

"No," she repeated, "I am *not* all right. I am mortified."

"What?" Then he felt something in his gut again, only this time it felt more like a breath-stealing sucker punch to the solar plexus.

Probably because that was exactly what it was.

He released his hold on her to gape downward. Emily's small fist was still clenched and drawing back for a second blow.

"Whoa!" He jumped back and threw out a hand to deflect a second attack. He jerked his head up just in time to catch the warning flash of hellfire in her eyes.

"Blast you, Ross! What are you doing, following me around like that? Who do you think you are? What business is it of yours who I choose to be friends with?"

This barrage of questions came in a flurry of flying fists, first from the left, coming up for his jaw, which he sidestepped neatly, then from the right, which he managed to duck before he would have gotten clipped in the ear. Hell! What was the matter with her?

"Do you enjoy embarrassing me?" She swung out again, wildly this time, missing him by a foot and nearly tossing herself off balance.

"Stop it!" Ross commanded, finding his voice along with a fortifying shot of indignation. He'd rescued her. She should be grateful, damn it. He caught her forearm on a new backswing. "Emily, stop this! You're hysterical!"

"Hysterical? I'll show you hysterical!"

Ross caught her other wrist before she could do any damage and ran her arms back up against the springhouse wall. "What's the matter with you?"

"What's the matter with *me*?" She let out a yelp and tried to free herself. "*Me*?"

Realizing that she was capable of bringing a knee up to wreak havoc with his personals, Ross closed the slight distance between them, sandwiching her to the wall to hold her still. They were uncomfortably close.

"What's the matter with *you*?" she demanded, pushing back with all her might.

Too damn close, Ross thought, breaking into a sweat. He imagined that he could feel every distressing detail of her plump young breasts against his chest, yet he couldn't think of any way to disengage from their indecent clinch without getting himself nailed silly.

"Why can't you mind your own business?" she yelled.

"I saved you!" he shouted back. "What did you think you were doing, going off with a fella like Karl? You want to ruin your reputation?"

"My reputation is none of your business!"

"It sure as hell *is* my business! Where's your common sense? You want to get yourself in trouble?"

"Trouble? Ha! You should talk! Where do you spend your Saturday nights, Ross? In the taverns with fancy women?"

"That's different!"

"How?"

Ross opened his mouth, ready to give her an earful, then clamped it shut when an earful failed to occur to him. He still felt a little crazy with the anger and whatever else it was that had driven him to follow her and then flatten Karl with a vengeance that far outweighed the provocation. He knew this, and yet he was helpless to control it or identify it.

"How is it different?" Emily repeated, tilting her chin up so that her mouth came dangerously close to his own.

"It . . . it just *is*, that's all! I'm a man, for one thing, and you're a—" He shut his mouth again. Woman. He was going to say woman, but she *wasn't* a woman. Not yet. Neither was she a child. This was a fact that was becoming impossible for Ross to ignore. As they pressed too close, Ross felt the heat of his own anger rapidly changing to something else.

He realized too late that his hot young blood cared not to differentiate between platonic female curves and those of a more available nature. The warm flush that spread from his loins to the singing nerves of his very fingertips was distracting enough to make him nearly forget the self-disgust he *should* have felt at his inappropriate reaction to a girl who had always been like a sister to him.

But not quite.

Releasing her, he backed away, putting distance

between them. This was Emily, he reminded himself. *Emily.* His boss's daughter and his closest friend. Who else could she trust with her virtue if not Ross? Even just thinking of her the wrong way made him want to burn in hell.

"I was just trying to help," he said, trying to mask his own bewilderment and dismay at what had just happened.

"Then stop treating me like a child!"

He wondered for a panicked second if maybe she had felt something, too. Breathless from her struggles and with her shining ebony hair streaming over her shoulders, she leaned back against the wall as if she needed it for support.

"I don't treat you like a child," he denied.

"If I want to take Karl as my beau, then I'll darn well do it! There's nothing you can do to stop me."

Ross could think of no coherent reply. Take Karl as her beau? *Karl?* Was she out of her mind?

"Go back to your precious Johanna. That's where you belong, isn't it?"

Ross had just stared at her, trying to sort through his maddening confusion, then he'd turned away. He didn't have an answer to her question. With his tumultuous emotions still running high, he'd left her behind at the springhouse.

After that, things had never quite returned to normal between them, even as they'd worked together at her father's shop during the months that followed. They made up and became friends again, certainly, but something had changed.

Emily turned seventeen that year, and Ross became much too uncomfortably aware that she was now a young woman. He went out of his way to make sure that he didn't touch her or end up alone with her for any length of time. Above all, he didn't want to experience a repeat of the inappropriate emotions that had taken him by such bewildering surprise behind the springhouse. It didn't help, either, that Emily despised that Ross was still vying with John Butler for Johanna Davenport, or that Ross bristled whenever he thought of Emily continuing to be friends with Karl. Then, of course, at the beginning of the summer, when Ross had quit the *Gazette* to go work for the *Herald,* Emily had considered his move nothing less than high treason. They'd stopped speaking altogether. That was, until one night in September, the night before Ross left for the war.

Now, as he leaned his head back against the pump shelter behind the Hockstetter's farmhouse, Ross stared up at the cloudless summer sky and recalled Emily's heated declaration the night of the chestnuting party: *If I want to take Karl as my beau, then I'll darn well do it! There's nothing you can do to stop me.*

No, there wasn't anything he could have done to stop her. Not back then and not now. There wasn't a damn thing he could do about it if Emily had, in fact, turned to Karl Becker for comfort after Ross left for the army. Simple arithmetic dictated that it was very possible that Karl could have fathered Emily's child. But there was another possibility Ross was forced to consider, too, a possibility that he hadn't been able to bring himself to believe until now because—

"She would have told me," he said aloud, still contemplating the wide, empty sky overhead. They'd never lied to each other before. Damn it, she *would* have told him.

Wouldn't she?

# 13

*Ross should have seen trouble coming,* but he didn't. It had been a long day at the newspaper, and he was too caught up in his own miseries to think much about the predatory glint in Oberholtzer's wrinkled, beady eyes as he shuffled past Ross's paper-strewn desk and disappeared into Malcolm's office.

Two days had passed since Ross's Whit Monday confrontation with Emily. Now, it was *he* who ignored *her* for a change. If they passed each other in the lobby or met in the corridor, he was the first to brush by and bid her a chilly "Good day, Miss Winters." More than once she tried to stop him to say something. He thought for a moment that he saw an apology in her eyes, but he ignored her anyway. He was through with shouldering more than his share of the burden for rebuilding their relationship, through with trying to help her when all he got in return were scathing rebukes and painful reminders of his own guilt.

*All I want is for things to be like they used to be between us.*

*I don't see how that's possible.*

Ross recalled those words with stinging clarity. An ironic role reversal had taken place. It was she who had finally forced him to face reality. To try to recreate the past was impossible. It seemed that his reckless, adoring childhood friend had been replaced by a proud and willful woman who would never accept him as he was now.

*"Gallagher!"*

Malcolm's enraged bellow reverberated throughout the city newsroom, causing heads to jerk up and silence to descend like the abrupt snap of a guillotine. Ross hadn't heard his name so sharply enunciated since those days when he'd worked here as a fledgling reporter.

Ross had changed since then, though, grown a lot and seen a lot, and so he didn't rattle as easily. He raised his head very slowly to observe his managing editor's broad figure framed in the open doorway to his office. Chewing on the remains of a smoldering Corona, Malcolm's face was mottled pink with anger. His steel gray eyes were hot.

"In my office!" Without waiting for a response, Malcolm vanished in a swirl of cigar smoke back into the recesses of his holy den.

Ross didn't acknowledge the raised eyebrows or curious stares that followed at his back. When he closed the office door behind him, his attention was drawn to Oberholtzer's sly, gloating demeanor. The old man sat before Malcolm's desk, his skinny elbows resting on the arms of his chair, his long, bony fingers steepled before him. Ross shifted his attention to the furious figure who towered behind the desk.

"You called?"

"Damn right I called! What do you know about *this*?" For the first time, Ross noticed the sheet of paper Malcolm had crumpled in one huge fist. It came at him in a wad, tossed across the desk.

Even before Ross reached down to smooth it out and pick it up, he knew what all this had to be about.

"You recognize it?" Malcolm demanded.

It was a playbill for Fulton Hall. In one corner, Ross noted a whimsical woodcut illustration featuring a cello and a musical note that, to his practiced eye, had "Emily" written all over it. Keeping his expression neutral, Ross looked up. "I see that the Holman Opera Troupe is opening at the Fulton on Monday."

The expression on Malcolm's jowly, whiskered face brought to mind a snarling mastiff. "*We* used to do the playbills for the Fulton. You know who's printing them now?"

"Not us?"

"Damn right, not us! Your friend, Miss Winters, has been stealing our customers!"

Ross shot a measuring look at Oberholtzer to see that the man was practically preening. Emily's secret was out, and the old geezer was all too happy to be the bearer of ill tidings. "That's absurd," Ross replied. "Emily works for us."

"She *used* to work for us."

"She quit?"

"No," Malcolm said, his voice lowering menacingly as he leaned forward over his desk. "*You* are going to fire her."

"Me? Why me?"

"Because you're the one who recommended her in the first place."

"You have any proof of these allegations?"

Oberholtzer interjected in a calm tone. "After this matter was brought to my attention early this afternoon, I took the liberty of investigating further. Miss Winters has been quite busy these past few weeks, severely undercutting our rates in order to lure our patrons away."

Ross fought to quell his mounting annoyance. Annoyance with Oberholtzer for being such a persistent, nosy bastard and annoyance with Emily for landing him between this particular rock and hard place. "Well, that's the nature of healthy competition, isn't it?"

"I knew I shouldn't have hired a woman," Malcolm growled, sending up sparks as he stabbed the butt of his cigar into a brass ashtray.

"I doubt her gender has a whole lot to do with this," Ross reminded him. "She did a good job while she was here."

"A good job of making fool jackasses out of us! Her daddy must be howling in his grave."

"All right," Ross said, wanting to end it. "I'll talk to her." He turned to leave.

*"Wait."*

His hand on the doorknob, Ross silently cursed Malcolm, Emily, and Oberholtzer.

"I asked you what you knew about this. You didn't answer me."

Setting his teeth, Ross turned to face his managing editor. "What do you think? That I knew what she planned to do when I recommended her for the job?"

Malcolm's gray eyes narrowed on him. "You've known her for a long time. You went to school with her. You worked with her when you were with the old *Gazette*."

"Are you questioning my loyalty?"

Malcolm didn't look away, but Ross noted that his assessing gaze cooled somewhat as he pondered whether or not to call his future son-in-law's bluff. At this point, even Ross wasn't sure if he would utter an outright lie to save his job as well as his impending nuptials.

"It wouldn't be very smart to cross me now, Ross."

"No one ever accused me of being stupid, Malcolm."

At this, Oberholtzer moved for the first time, dropping his steepled fingers and shifting his weight in his seat with great dignity. "I am sure, Mr. Gallagher, that if you will see to ending the young lady's employment, we may return to business as usual, *ja*?"

When the old man tilted his head to peer up at Ross, the light caught and flashed off his bifocals. The smug curve of his lips told Ross that he was well satisfied with the results of his good works for today, but that Ross should continue to watch his own back in the future.

"Fine," Ross replied tightly, then looked back at Malcolm. "Is that all?"

Malcolm studied him for another moment before deciding to let the question of Ross's loyalties drop. "Find out what we owe her for the week. Mr. Oberholtzer will draw up a check. I don't want her to set foot in this building again, understood?"

"Understood." Ross yanked open the door.

"She's too much like her father," Malcolm added, causing Ross to pause and tense in the archway. "He was so busy building castles in the air, he couldn't recognize his own defeat until it was too late. He had to learn the hard way. You tell her, Ross. If she wants a fight on competitive pricing, we can teach her the hard way, too. We'll run her little makeshift business right into the ground."

Emily removed her hat, hung it on a peg on the wall, then slipped a work apron over her head and tied the strings behind her waist. As she moved through the print shop, opening the rear windows to let in some fresh air and light, she couldn't resist pausing over her desk to admire her own handiwork on the Fulton Hall playbill.

She always retained at least one copy of every print order. It came in handy if a customer returned with requests for similar jobs. This time, though, she was especially proud of the illustration she'd created for the concert announcement. It had taken extra time to do the woodcut, time she didn't really have to spend on any one job, but she knew it was worth it when she delivered the order yesterday morning and saw the light of approval on her customer's face. He would be back again.

Moving to the composition desk, she rolled up her sleeves and pulled open a drawer of type. Without missing a beat, she picked up a composing stick and resumed setting a half-finished print order for billheads. After taking a light supper at the Blue Swan, she had a pile of work, enough to keep her here past midnight if she had the freedom to do so. Unfortunately, she'd told her mother that she was visiting with her old friend Melissa Carpenter these evenings. Emily would be hard put to explain what topics of conversation kept them engrossed until after midnight.

A loud knock on the door almost made her drop her stick. The door shade was still drawn, and as far as most of the public was concerned, this was still an empty building.

The doorknob rattled, followed by an insistent tapping on the glass. She'd started to lock the door ever since Ross had walked in on her.

"Emily! Open up. It's Ross."

Emily hesitated. Ever since their conversation on her porch, he'd grown cool and unapproachable. It seemed that she'd gotten her wish. He'd finally backed off. But instead of being relieved, Emily was left feeling abandoned and unsure of herself. She hadn't meant to throw those old rumors in his face, and not for the first time, she cursed her impulsive temper. She had tried to apologize when she saw him at the office, but he cut her off, leaving her standing alone in an empty hallway. The smiling Irish eyes she loved so well had brushed over her and then coldly dismissed her. The effect was as stunning and hurtful as a kick in the teeth.

Emily set down the composing stick and moved toward the door. Her knees were wobbling and her heart pounded crazily in the hope that he'd come to make up. Just like always.

Of course. That was it. He'd been angry with her. Who wouldn't be after the way she'd acted on Monday? But he'd said a few harsh words, too. If they'd both lost their tempers, that was nothing new. He'd had some time to cool off, and now he'd come bearing his customary olive branch. When she opened that door, he'd be leaning against the door frame with his arms folded. He'd be wearing that crooked, dimpled smile. Those dark eyes would wash over her, warm and familiar and safe, and everything would be all right again.

Emily wiped a sweating palm on her apron, took a deep breath, then unlocked the door and opened it.

Ross was not smiling. And the expression in his eyes wasn't very warm, familiar, or, least of all, safe. "I need to talk to you."

Emily tried to ignore a painful wrench of disappointment. She had been foolish to expect things to be the same as they used to be. When would she learn that? "Well, I'm busy right now," she began.

"That's what I hear." He brushed by her to enter the shop. "This won't take long."

Emily opened her mouth to protest, but glancing back to see a curious middle-aged couple passing on the street, she decided against it and hastily closed the door. "Is something wrong?"

In reply, Ross reached inside his coat, pulled out a piece of paper and tossed it down onto the nearest desktop. Even before Emily got close enough to read it, she recognized the musical illustration and stopped. "Where did you get that?"

"Malcolm's office."

"Oh."

An envelope landed next to the crumpled concert bill.

"What's that?"

"Your pay for the week. You're fired."

"I see." Emily looked up to see no softening in his expression, no signs of sympathy.

"Well, you asked for it," he said.

"Yes."

"He's very angry. I don't think there's much I can do to smooth things over for you this time."

"It's not your responsibility to smooth things over."

"No. It's not."

It was all she could do not to look away from that detached, yet condemning, gaze. The stakes had just risen. Her attempt to resurrect her father's business would no longer be a secret. Now, her success or failure would be played out in public for all to see. Feeling a little stunned, she turned and went back to the composing desk.

Ross thought she was a fool to try to make a go of this business. Karen thought so, too, and if her mother had any idea of what she was doing, she would try to discourage Emily also. It was only her deceased father's reaction Emily was suddenly unsure of. What would he say? She didn't know, and perhaps that was part of what scared her the most. Now, without Ross's support, grudging though it had been, and what she imagined would have been her father's tacit approval, she felt as if both legs had just been slashed out from beneath her.

Not knowing what else to do, she took up the composing stick. She still owed Ross an apology. "I'm sorry for how I behaved the other day. Sometimes I say things I don't mean."

"Oh, you meant it, and you were right. There's no way to go back to the way things used to be, and I think we both know the reason for that."

"I don't know what you're talking about." She tried to hide the trembling in her hands, but she was afraid that he wasn't talking about the printing business anymore. She set an *a* instead of an *e* and cursed silently as she corrected the error.

"I think you know exactly what I'm talking about."

Ross's statement hung in the air between them like an overripe apricot, quivering on its stem, ready to burst. Her heart started to pound.

He continued. "Maybe it's time we get some things out in the open. Like the truth."

Emily's fingers stopped their mindless work. She stared blankly at the tiny compartments of Caslon type, suddenly unable to recall which letters were stored where. Her pulse was so rapid it seemed to thunder in her ears. "What truth?"

"Like the truth that you were . . . what?" He let a paralyzing silence pass before she sensed his slow approach from across the room. "What would you have been, Emily? About four months pregnant when you left town?"

Emily could do nothing but squeeze her eyes shut and shake her head.

"That child was mine, wasn't it?"

# 14

**September 1861**

*Except for the soft glow of* the coal oil street lamps, it was dark. The air was early autumn cool, chilling Emily's arms and the exposed skin above the dipped neckline of her yellow silk taffeta evening dress. Fumbling nervously, she missed the keyhole on her first try to unlock the door of the print shop.

She was taking an awful chance. Her father would be furious with her when he returned from his three-day meeting with a group of editors from other Republican newspapers. But this was a matter of principle, and wasn't it Nathaniel himself who had taught her that principles were worth fighting for? This was the premise of the argument Emily planned to use when her father returned home and discovered what she was about to do.

"Blast it," she muttered as she jiggled the key in the lock. It finally turned, and she slipped inside the darkened shop. It was Saturday night, the only night when the *Penn Gazette* offices were empty. There was no

Sunday edition to put out, so the staff wouldn't return until Monday morning.

As she groped in the dark for a desk lamp, she thought about the article she'd written two weeks before. Its subject was an out-of-state rally in which Miss Susan Anthony had addressed the issue of women's rights. This was a cause that Emily identified with, perhaps even more so since she'd discovered that her own father was entrenched in the enemy camp.

"Women's rights?" he had inquired with amusement when she'd presented him with the article. "Emily Elizabeth, oh beloved, mule-headed daughter of mine, what can I expect from you next? Bloomers?"

How could a man who so passionately advocated abolishing slavery of another race fail to comprehend the societal shackles that just as effectively enslaved an entire gender?

"Is there something wrong with the writing?" she asked, infuriated by the patronizing twinkle in her father's eyes.

"Not that I can see."

"Well, then, when will it run?"

"Soon," he'd said, then set it aside without initialing it to indicate approval for publication.

Soon.

It was the sort of answer one offered to pacify a whining child. After another week had passed, Nathaniel finally initialed the article, but now it still sat on his desk, going nowhere. It wasn't in the two-day backlog of editorial pieces he'd left for his assistant editor to print in his absence. Emily knew this because she'd checked before leaving the shop earlier today.

# FOREVER AND ALWAYS 199

Her father's slight had eaten at her all evening, stirring up a new storm of righteous indignation all through dinner and well into the concert she had attended with Melissa Carpenter and Melissa's mother at Fulton Hall. Finally, just after intermission, Emily whispered to her friend that she had a dreadful headache and needed to see about catching the horsecar to go home early.

But she hadn't gone home. She'd come here to take a stand for what she believed in. She intended to take her article from her father's desk and place it with the other editorial pieces to be printed. It was bold and maybe a tad underhanded, but he *had* cleared it for publication. What was the harm in nudging it along? Ironically enough, maybe her father would be proud of her.

After he had about a year to cool off.

Taking a lit desk lamp in hand, Emily crossed the room toward her father's office.


Ross had to squint, then blink twice to assure himself that it wasn't the whiskey playing tricks with his eyes. From his position across the street, he had a clear view of the *Penn Gazette* building. Except for the frilly dress, the young woman who had just slipped inside the deserted shop looked like Emily.

What was she doing sneaking around at this hour?

Ross had no idea exactly how long he'd been sitting on the curb, sullenly nursing a pint of whiskey in the shadows. He'd started out headed for the south side of town, determined to get drunk and find a girl at one of the roadside taverns with whom to spend his last night in town. Instead, he took a roundabout route and ended up here to brood. He couldn't wait to get this lousy town far behind him, but there was still one regret on his conscience.

He hated that Emily was still angry with him for leaving the *Gazette* to go work for the *Herald*. He didn't necessarily regret that decision; it had been logical at the time. Even Nathaniel seemed to understand that Ross couldn't afford to stay with the *Gazette* when his chances of advancement were so slim. If he were to ever make a successful career of newspapering, he would need the experience of working for a larger paper. The fact that Ross had every intention of marrying the publisher's daughter didn't even enter into it. No, that wasn't part of the logic, but it *had* been part of Ross's long-standing dream. Now, though, that dream was crushed, ground into the dirt by Malcolm Davenport himself.

"We can't see each other anymore." Johanna had appeared sincerely distressed as she'd made this tearful declaration two nights ago. "It's my father. Now that I'm done with school, he says it's time to choose a suitable husband."

That neat and tidy word, "suitable," had sliced into Ross's pride with the cold, impersonal efficiency of a surgeon's scalpel. "What's wrong with me?" he demanded. "I'm as suitable as anybody. Damn more suitable than John Butler."

"Oh, Ross, Papa likes you, he really does. He says you're smart and that you're a hard worker and that you'll do well, but you're not . . . "

Johanna hadn't finished the sentence. What was the point? Ross didn't have any family clout or money behind him, and he was Irish besides. How *unsuitable* could a fella get?

# FOREVER AND ALWAYS

A muted glow of lamplight spilled through the closed window blinds of the print shop, then abruptly dimmed, as if moving toward the back of the shop. What the hell was Emily doing?

Ross took one last scorching swig from his bottle, then corked it and rose to unsteady feet. Perhaps it was fate that had brought him here tonight, fate that had brought Emily to cross his path. Perhaps this was his last chance to make things right between them. Slipping the pint bottle into his coat pocket, he started across the street.

"Oh! My lights and stars!"

Spinning around, Emily nearly knocked the lamp from her father's desk. There, leaning in the open doorway to her father's office was the last person on earth she expected to be confronted with this night. "Ross!"

"Working late?" he inquired calmly, too calmly. There was something different about him, something about his oddly subdued tone, something about the brooding, unfamiliar cast in his eyes that was wrong. Or maybe her powers of observation were skewed by the low light as well as the effects of near heart failure.

"You scared the living daylights out of me. What are you doing here?"

"I should be asking you that question," he countered. "It has to be at least ten o'clock."

Emily raised a hand to her heart in a vain effort to calm its thundering beat. Her voice quavered regardless. "It's no business of yours. You don't work here anymore."

"And you'll never forgive me for that, will you?"

His suit coat was rumpled, he wore no tie. His hair was mussed, and his jawline was shadowed. He could obviously use a shave. Very out of character for Ross, who was always so fastidious about his personal appearance. He still hadn't moved from his much-too-relaxed stance in the open archway.

"What do you want?" Emily demanded.

"I want to talk. I want to get this thing straightened out between us. It's gone on for long enough."

It was then that Emily caught a whiff of alcohol and realized what was wrong. He'd been drinking. When he pushed off from the doorjamb and moved toward her, she almost retreated in sudden confusion.

"So, what are you all prettied up for? Your beau, Karl?" He stopped only inches away to stand over her. His gaze dropped and lingered on the low-cut neckline of her evening dress before climbing to meet her own, and Emily felt a matching flush of heat rise to her cheeks. He'd never looked at her like that before.

"What do you care?" she asked.

"Did he stand you up? Karl does that sometimes, you know. When he gets tired of a girl. He conveniently forgets to show for an engagement, then she never hears from him again."

Emily didn't bother to tell him that she hadn't planned to see Karl tonight. In fact, she rarely saw Karl unless he was between paramours, which was just fine with her.

"You're drunk," she said.

Ross merely offered a crooked half smile. "You gonna hold that against me, too?"

"Why are you here?"

His smile faded. "I told you. I want to set things straight."

"They are straight. You chose to go work for the *Herald*."

"You make it sound so simple, so cut and dried. I told you months ago why I quit. There were two men ahead of me in seniority. I could be bouncing grandchildren on my knee before I'd be up for assistant editor."

"I heard you then, and I hear you now," she said, averting her gaze to stare at his chest. It seemed safer than looking into his eyes, and she sure wasn't going to give him the satisfaction of backing away.

"You hear," he said, "but you don't try to understand."

"I understand just fine. You could have found a way to further your career without working for Malcolm Davenport."

"Davenport owns the biggest paper in town. It would be stupid to ignore that. What do you expect from me?"

"I don't expect anything from you. Not anymore."

"Reasoning with you is like trying to get a toehold in a brick wall."

Indignant, Emily dared to look up at him. "Why? Because I don't see things the way you do?"

"No, because you won't even try."

"Then go about your business and leave me alone."

"All this is pointless. I quit my job at the *Herald* this morning."

As the meaning of his words sank in, Emily felt a dazzling shot of hope. She opened her mouth to ask why, then cut off. She knew why. The same reason he reeked of alcohol. One way or another, everything

Ross did boiled down to his obsession with Johanna. Emily had heard about her engagement to John Butler. Now, Ross was on a bender and feeling sorry for himself.

She reformed her original question to lash out and bait him. "Why? Because Johanna finally decided to throw you over?"

Emily had said things she regretted in the past—too many to count—but she'd never intentionally set out to wound before. The flash of pain in Ross's eyes was immediate and appalling.

"I'm sorry," she said before he could reply, then pride compelled her to turn away. She clasped her hands together to stop their sudden trembling. "But I never liked her. You know that. You were bound to get hurt." *Like me,* she added silently. He'd been hurting her for a long time now, though he didn't know it. How could he? She'd been in love with him for years, but he'd never seemed able to see her as a grown woman.

"Johanna didn't have anything to do with it," he said.

Even if she didn't know better, the repressed anger in his denial would have been enough to convince her that it was a sham.

"I enlisted," he said when she didn't answer. "I leave for Camp Curtin in the morning."

*Enlisted?* Emily could only pray that she'd heard wrong. "What?" she whispered.

"I said, I'll be leaving in the morning."

She swung around to stare at him. "No."

"They need volunteers."

"You're a fool!" she blurted. "You're going to run away and get yourself killed because of Johanna!"

"This doesn't have anything to do with Johanna. It has to do with what's right and what's wrong and whether I have the guts to fight for my own beliefs."

What he said was true. They were going to war, and it was impossible to conceive that Ross's conscience would allow him to ignore President Lincoln's call for volunteers. Sooner or later he would enlist, Johanna or no Johanna, but Emily had hoped it would be later. She wouldn't permit herself to think about it until the time came, but here it was; the time was *now*.

She turned away again, balling her hands into fists. Even after the Union fiasco at Bull Run, there were many who said the war would be over quickly. Emily wasn't so sure. She might be young, but she was smart enough to know that no war could end soon enough, never before spilling a frightening amount of blood on both sides.

Ross gripped her shoulders from behind. His voice was low. "Emily, I don't want to leave without setting things right between us."

"No," she said again, not really hearing him. She was overcome with a smothering sense of panic. Her mind filled with terrifying images of him lying bloody and dead on some faraway, body-riddled battlefield.

"I don't care what anyone thinks of me, Em. I don't care about Johanna or her father or anyone else in this town, only you. I can't leave with you hating me."

She turned to face him. "What do you want me to do? Send you off with a smile and a soul-stirring rendition of 'Yankee Doodle'? If that's the case, then you'd do better to look elsewhere. If you get yourself killed—"

"I won't get myself killed."

There were tears in her eyes, something Ross couldn't remember ever seeing before. Immediately, his frustration with her fled, and he reached to take her in his arms.

She came much too easily and naturally, resting her cheek against his shoulder as if she'd been made to fit there. A feminine floral scent rose from her hair, and he suddenly knew the real reason he'd set out to find the dubious comfort of a warm and willing female during his last hours in town. The resentment he felt over Johanna's rejection was only part of it.

He believed in the Union cause and he was primed for the fight, but there was also a part of him that was fearful and uncertain. He'd pushed a plow and he'd wielded a pen, but he'd never shouldered a musket meant to kill another human being. When it came right down to it, would he be able to pull the trigger? Would he have the courage to stand and fight when the bullets were flying and he came face to face with the deadly end of bayonet? And, of course, there was the very real possibility that Emily's fears were well founded. He might not come back. At nineteen, this wasn't an easy concept to grapple with.

Emily pulled away just enough to look up at him, and the shimmering, vibrant blue of her eyes reminded him of a little boy's idea of natural beauty in its purest form. He remembered a summer afternoon when the sea breezes caressed his cheeks and the sun's warmth kissed the crown of his head. He'd held his mother's gloved hand as they looked out over the awe-inspiring expanse of the New York harbor, and he'd felt assured and content. It was one of the few happy memories he still clung to from his early childhood.

"Don't go," she said, her voice barely a whisper.

"I have to go."

"But not so soon."

"Yes."

"Then make love to me."

He should have been shocked or surprised or, at the very least, mildly taken aback by what she'd said, but he wasn't. It occurred to him that it must have been the alcohol that numbed his brain. The trouble was, he didn't feel numb; he was acutely aware of his surroundings. He was aware of the fickle, muted lamplight that could play such mesmerizing tricks with the color of a young woman's eyes, of the unnatural stillness of Nathaniel's office, and of Emily, especially Emily. She looked very different to him tonight, with her raven hair pulled back in a loose chignon and her pale skin glowing like gold against the yellow silk of her evening dress. All grown up and pretty enough to make any fellow proud to escort her on his arm.

"Six years ago, we made a promise to each other, Ross. Do you remember?"

"Yes."

"I meant it."

"So did I."

"We sealed it with our blood."

"We were kids then," he reminded her.

"But we're not kids now."

Emily didn't care that she could be laying her heart out for the slaughter. The possibility that she might never see him again made her reckless. She tilted her face up, and he bent his head, and their lips met for the first time. It was just a whisper of a kiss, feather light and utterly exquisite; then they drew apart.

"Did you ever wonder what it would be like?" he whispered.

"Yes," she said.

He couldn't know how very long she had wondered, how many times she had dreamed of what his kiss would be like, of what it would be like for him to look at her the way he was looking at her now. But even her dreams hadn't begun to match reality. Her heart pounded in her throat, her knees felt as if they might buckle beneath her.

Cupping the back of her head with one hand, Ross kissed her again, harder and longer, so that when she felt the first invasion of his hot, whiskey-sweet tongue in her mouth, her fingers clutched at the rough material of his suit coat to keep her upright and steady on her feet. The sneaking, tingling heat, however, the heat that seemed to coalesce in her middle before slowly uncurling and radiating to the very tips of her extremities didn't come as a surprise at all; she had felt it before, many times, at night when she was alone and thought of what it might be like to make love with Ross.

For Ross, that second kiss turned from sweet to hot with stunning swiftness. There was still a part of him, a lingering shade of rationality, that clung to the knowledge that what they were doing was somehow not right, but it was dim and unconvincing and too easily ignored. When Emily pressed up against him, pliable and eager, with her sweet lips parted and questing beneath his own, she didn't feel like a best friend, nor anything remotely related to a sister.

He pulled back and mumbled, "This isn't the time or place."

"Ross, after tomorrow, there may never be time. I want you to be my first."

"Your husband should be your first."

"No, Ross, you. It's always been you. Didn't you know that?" She tilted her lips up, and they kissed again. Ross forgot all about trying to reason with her. Or himself. She felt good and she tasted sweet, which was exactly what he needed right now.

She pulled away and grasped his hand to move toward a closed door in the back of the office. He knew it was the room where Nathaniel kept a cot.

When they stepped over the threshold, the wavering yellow light from the outer office dimmed, leaving them bathed in shadows. She faced him and let go of his hand, and, without saying a word, reached up to undo the loose knot of hair at the base of her neck. The movement caused the silk fabric of her bodice to tighten, accentuating the appeal of corseted young breasts, and Ross knew that making love to her was going to be much too easy.

He took off his suit coat and threw it over a chair. As she reached back to undo the fastenings on her dress, he moved toward her. "I'll do it."

His voice had come out sounding much calmer and surer than he felt. Taking her by one arm, he gently turned her around so her back was to him. Likewise, his hands proved surprisingly steady as he undid first one hook, then another and another, until the back of her dress gaped open. This isn't just any girl, he reminded himself as he loosened the ties of her corset and unbuttoned her petticoat. This was Emily.

This was crazy.

But he pushed aside a silken curtain of raven hair and pressed his lips to the soft skin at the base of her neck. He inhaled her scent. He felt her trembling by the time he made his way up to her ear. "Do you know what you're asking for, Em?"

"Yes."

"It's not pretty or gentle or delicate. It's not like in poetry and sonnets."

"I . . . I know."

But he was afraid that she didn't know. Pushing the short sleeves of her evening dress down her arms, he let the garment drop away to the floor. Her corset was next, collapsing onto the pile of silk at her feet. Clad only in a camisole and drawers, she moved to step out of her clothes, but he caught her up short about the waist from behind and pulled her hard back up against him so there could be no mistaking what he meant. No matter how naive she might be, she couldn't mistake a full male erection pressing up against the soft curve of her buttocks.

Emily was seventeen and, up until a few moments before, kissed only once by Karl Becker that night behind the Brenners' springhouse. But she'd deduced enough concerning what went on between the sexes to comprehend the source of that daunting pressure behind her. It was not that she wasn't scared; she was— and literally shaking with it right down to her toes—but that didn't mean she wouldn't follow through with what they'd started. And Ross was wrong to think she held false expectations of what was to come. In fact, she didn't want to be treated delicately at all.

One of Ross's hands slid down over the slight curve of her abdomen, urging her still more firmly back against him, and his other hand slid up to cup her breast through the flimsy material of her camisole. Emily emitted a small sound that could have only been a cross between surprise and delight.

His mouth moved against her ear, his fingers spread to span her belly, and his thumb brushed over the peak of her breast. "You tell me to stop, Em," he whispered, "just tell me to stop, and I will."

Emily wasn't listening. The sensual tingling she had felt earlier didn't even compare to the urgent, unidentified yearnings that washed over her now. Biting her lower lip hard, she reached blindly and clasped his upper arms tight, marveling at the thick, solid feel of lean muscle beneath the linen material of his shirt. He'd always been much bigger and stronger than her, of course, but he was of modest build compared to some men. His slender frame was deceiving, she thought when he took her by the shoulders and turned her to face him.

His kiss was hard and hungry, and Emily returned it with equal passion. Throwing her arms around his neck, she pressed close, wanting nothing more than to somehow fuse with him, to become one in the physical sense as well as the spiritual. And there was nothing gentle or pretty about it. Thrilling and glorious and terrifying, yes, but not gentle, nothing even resembling that.

*I love you, Ross,* she thought. She'd always loved him. But she didn't speak it aloud, even when they drew apart, and she looked up at him.

"Stop?" he whispered. The rhythm of his breathing had quickened, almost matching the crazed staccato of her own heart. In the waxing and waning shadows, his eyes remained fixed on hers, waiting for an answer.

# 15

*Stop? Emily thought.* There would be no stopping this night. She'd waited too long to turn back now.

Piece by piece, their clothing fell to the floor, and as Ross pressed her, naked and shivering, down onto the soft cot beneath him, there was no doubt left in her mind that he loved her, too. Even if he might not know it yet. How else to explain the way he touched her, everywhere it seemed, with his hands and his mouth, somehow knowing even before she did what it was she wanted? Very soon, she felt as if every inch of skin on her body had been kissed and caressed to the point where she would go crazy for sure.

When he moved over her, fitting the length of his strong, hard body flush against hers, Emily willingly opened to him, knowing that this was what she'd waited for. Then, with one thrust and in one blinding instant, Ross was buried deep inside her, and it hurt. Exquisitely so. But Emily was glad for the pain. No true life's passage could be well marked without it, and as she held onto him and he began to move within her to find his own release, it drove home all the more eloquently that he was her first—her first and only—and nothing would ever change that.

Afterward, when her heart began to slow and her breathing began to approach a normal cadence, she curled up against him, basking in how wonderful it felt to be held in his arms. She listened to the strong beat of his heart and closed her eyes and tried not to think about him leaving in the morning.

As for Ross, the sex was done and the alcohol was diluting in his system. It was as good an excuse as any to explain why he was only now beginning to realize the full implications of what he'd just done.

This was Emily he held so intimately against him. It was Emily's warm, naked limbs that intertwined with his own; Emily's long, soft sighs that fanned across his chest, and Emily's silken hair that he sifted through his fingers. Emily. His childhood friend and Nathaniel's daughter . . .

Nathaniel's *daughter,* for God's sake. The man had been more of a father to him than anyone, and Ross had just repaid him by seducing his little girl in the very office where they'd worked together for so many years. He respected Nathaniel Winters and cared too much about Emily as a friend to have treated her no better than one of the tavern girls he—

No, no, it wasn't like that. He was horrified at his own mental comparison. It hadn't been like that at all, but the end result was still the same, and he couldn't shirk his responsibility for it. Emily would not be returning home a virgin this night, and he was leaving town the next morning.

"It's late," he said. "You should get home."

Disentangling himself from her embrace and

sweating from more than spent passion, he sat up. The aftereffects of the whiskey were already setting in, and the beginnings of a headache pounded at his temples. He deserved much worse than that.

Emily moved behind him, and her hands came to a gentle rest on his shoulders. He felt the sensual fullness of her breasts as she leaned against him from behind. "I don't want to leave. I don't want tomorrow to come."

Then her hands moved, her fingers spreading to caress down along his chest, and he tensed against the unwanted sexual reaction that was bound to ensue. He stopped her by reaching up to grasp one of her hands and bringing it to his lips. "There's nothing we can do to keep the sun from rising. If you don't get home soon, your family is going to worry."

He hoped there was enough truth in that to explain why he pulled away from her so quickly and crossed the short distance to where their clothing lay in a tangled pile on the floor. It didn't take long for him to sort it out, tossing her underclothes and stockings to her as he donned his own clothes. When she pulled her hair aside and turned her back so he could help lace up her corset, he realized that his hands were shaking. Too bad he hadn't had the good sense to develop an inhibiting attack of nerves *before* he'd ruined her.

"I'm sorry if I hurt you," he said, his voice catching so he had to swallow hard and clear his throat.

Unfortunately, by now, his eyes had adjusted much too well to the dim lamp light that filtered in from the adjoining room. When she turned to look up at him, he could clearly perceive the warm, trusting glow in those beautiful blue eyes. "You didn't hurt me. I feel wonderful."

He didn't have an answer for that; he felt too much like dirt. Sensing that she was about to touch him again, he moved, bending to retrieve her petticoat and dress. "We've got to go."

As she attached the crinoline underskirt, then slipped into her dress, he put on his suit coat. Preferring not to assist this time as she struggled to hook up her bodice, he instead dropped to his haunches and felt around the floor for her hairpins. He soon located five, having no idea if that was how many she'd dropped or not. What would Nathaniel think if he discovered hairpins on the floor? Horrified at the thought, Ross stood and his gaze was drawn to the rumpled cot where they'd—

*No.* It was dark in the room, but not dark enough. The stains on the bed sheet could only be— "Damn," he mumbled before he could stop himself. He shouldn't have been so shocked. Virgins were supposed to bleed the first time. It was one way a doubtful groom could assure himself of his bride's unblemished past. Thanks to Ross, Emily would exhibit no such proof on her wedding night.

"Oh!"

At her soft exclamation, Ross realized that she must have followed his gaze to see what he was staring at.

"It's all right, it's all right," she said hurriedly. She moved to the cot to tear off the sheets. "There are more linens in the chest. I can take care of these in the morning. I'll . . . I'll get rid of them or something."

Ross couldn't stand it anymore. He had to leave the room as she scurried frantically to dispose of all evidence of their indiscretion. Unfortunately, she could do nothing to remedy his aching conscience.

When she emerged into the outer office, she was breathless. Her cheeks were flushed, and her hair spilled wildly about her shoulders. In all her dishabille, Ross thought she looked younger and more innocent than ever.

Fighting another ludicrous urge to apologize, he gave her the hairpins, then waited for her to repair her chignon before taking the desk lamp and leading them to the front of the shop. After extinguishing the lamp, they stepped out into the bracing, head-clearing night air.

By then, Emily knew something was terribly wrong. The warm afterglow of contentment was gone only to be replaced by a cold, tightening knot in her stomach. She had never seen Ross so distant. Did he already regret what had happened? Had he been thinking of Johanna only to be rudely disappointed when he'd had to face Emily afterward?

Knowing that they shouldn't be seen together at this hour, they took a back alley. When they emerged into the open street at the edge of town, Ross broke the brittle silence. "You didn't mention what you were doing at the shop so late."

"I don't think you want to know," Emily said, trying to sound as if everything were normal. "Actually, you probably saved me from getting into big trouble."

She hadn't meant her reply to be double-edged, but when he said nothing, a side glance confirmed that Ross's jaw had hardened. His gaze remained fixed on the empty street ahead.

"When do you leave tomorrow?" she asked.

"The train pulls out at eight-fifteen."

"I could come and—"

"No," he said sharply. Glancing at her, his tone

softened. "I mean, I don't want any long, drawn out good-byes. I'll be back soon enough."

By now, they had reached the moonlit road outside of town. Emily could smell dew in the air. The fireflies were gone for the year, but as far as the crickets were concerned, this was still the tail end of summer. Their shrill chirps echoed in the darkened fields that lined the road. A dog barked in the distance. An occasional rustling from the dried cornstalks told Emily that a mouse or other small night creature deemed their approaching footsteps good reason for flight.

These were all small sounds she was so accustomed to, she rarely paid them any attention, but tonight they seemed to mock the awkward silence between her and Ross. There had never been such silence before, not in over six years of friendship and conflict. *It was Johanna he wanted, not you.* This stark realization turned around and around in her mind like some cloying music box refrain that refused to die down.

When they came to the edge of her front yard, they stopped, and Ross was forced to face her for the first time since they'd left the shop. What she saw in his eyes made her mouth go dry and a lump form in her throat. It was true.

"Emily, I—"

"Don't say it."

Wearing a pained look, he paused and shifted his gaze to something over her shoulder. As he gathered his thoughts, his attention seemed drawn to the soft glow of lamplight that came from the sitting room window behind her. Emily knew that her mother would be waiting up, perched on the brocade sofa, sewing a sampler or perhaps knitting.

"We made a mistake," he said softly.

"No." The soreness she felt between her thighs bore testament to the truth that he'd made love to her. That was no mistake, and for as long as it took her body to heal, Emily was determined to hold onto that.

"You're right," he corrected and started again. "I'm the one who made the mistake, and—"

"No." Emily shook her head fiercely and looked away from him so that she stared at a blurred, shimmering version of the darkened country road from where they'd come. She was horrified to realize that it was tears that distorted her vision.

"Em," he said, taking her face in his hands, forcing her to look up him. "I'm sorry."

"Don't say that."

Bending his head, he kissed her on the mouth. It was soft and lingering and sweet. "I'm sorry," he whispered, then he let her go and turned away. "Always remember that I love you, Em."

## 1865

*It seemed to Ross a long* time before Emily finally lifted her head to answer his question. "Yes," she said softly. "The child was yours."

Even though he'd braced himself, Ross had difficulty comprehending her words. He'd felt something like this before. An initial impact followed by the flash and burn of ball and buck as it ripped through his body. As his weapon flew from his hands and his head struck the battle ground, there followed a numbness and the slow, dizzy, disbelieving realization that he'd been hit.

Right now, his mouth was so dry, the words felt like clogged sand in his throat. "You were pregnant. Why didn't you tell me?"

"How could I?"

"How could you? *How?*" His hands clenched into fists. "You could have answered my letters! You never answered my damned letters!"

"I answered the first one," she countered. Her tone was dull and emotionless but somehow accusing just the same. "You remember that letter, don't you? That was the one where you apologized over and over, the one where you reminded me that what happened between us was a mistake. The one where you said we should forget it, that we should pretend it never happened, that we should try to go on with things as they were before."

Ross remembered the letter. He remembered how long he had labored over it, trying to get the words right, hoping to ease his wretched conscience but not succeeding. Nothing could rectify the mistake he'd made that night. "You still should have told me. We never lied to each other before."

"I didn't lie to you," she said, her chin lifting slightly in defiance.

"Not telling me was the same as lying, Emily. You should have told me the truth."

"I didn't know how to do that."

"You should have found a way."

"You weren't ready to hear it."

"Maybe not, but I had a right to know. I could have gotten leave. I could have come home and married you. Ours wouldn't have been the first seven-month baby born in this town."

"Yes. I know."

"Then, for God's sake, what were you thinking?"

"I didn't want a reluctant husband."

"So it was your pride." Ross kept his voice even, but he was still angry with her, more angry than he'd ever been before.

"My pride?" Something flashed in her eyes, perhaps some of her own anger. "I didn't want a husband who didn't love me. Or a husband who would forever regret the day he shackled himself to me in a shotgun marriage. Especially a husband who was in love with another woman. Not then, not now, not ever. If you call that pride, then think what you want."

"You denied your child a father and a home because of pride."

A shadow of uncertainty crossed her face. Her gaze seemed to lose focus. She shook her head. "No, I wouldn't have denied him a home. His home would have been with me."

"Him." Ross pounced on the word. "It was a boy."

Emily couldn't react at first. A boy. She didn't like to remember, not now when sometimes whole hours went by without thinking about it. Whole hours, but not whole days. Not yet. Never a whole day because there were always those moments when she extinguished the lamp by her bedside, those moments when the room fell dark and she was left in the quiet and all alone. "Yes," she replied, "it was a boy."

"Where is he?"

"What?"

"Where is my son, Emily?"

She was having a difficult time concentrating on his words long enough to understand the questions. No, she didn't like to remember, but even when she wasn't remembering, it was with her just the same, as

# FOREVER AND ALWAYS

if there had never been a time when it wasn't. Perhaps that's why she was so bewildered that Ross should ask where his son was when it should have been self-evident.

Before she knew what was happening, Ross had her by the shoulders, his face only inches from hers. He enunciated each syllable as if it were a dagger pressed to her throat. *"Where is my son?"*

"He died."

Shock drained all color from his face. He let go of her. "What?"

"It was an accident. He was too little. That's what the doctor said. He should have had more time to grow, but there was the accident, and—" Ross's look of confusion told her that she wasn't making any sense.

Turning her back, she took in a long breath. "When I went to stay with Aunt Essie, I wanted to get a job to help with the expenses. She teaches school and does fine, but I didn't like the idea of depending on anyone for my keep. I tried to get a job, but even in wartime folks aren't too enthused about hiring a woman who is with child. I ended up volunteering at the soldier's hospital. At least it kept me busy during the day."

Ross didn't say anything, but she could feel his gaze boring into the space between her shoulder blades.

"At the end of each day I walked back to our apartment, but after a few months, it got to be tiring, and so Aunt Essie suggested that I take a horsecab. I thought maybe she was right. I thought it was the best thing for the baby, but that's not how it turned out. The day of the accident, something spooked the horses just as I was stepping up into the carriage. I lost my balance and fell from the mounting stone."

Emily's voice, so even and controlled, finally broke. She tried to fill her lungs with air, but they felt as tight and hard as two blocks of ice. It sounded so trivial. *I lost my balance and fell.* So stupid it was almost laughable. It shouldn't have been anything, just some bruises. She should have been able to get right up from the street, brush the dust off her skirt, and forget about it. Except that wasn't how it turned out in the end.

She'd hit the ground belly first and sensed immediately that something was wrong. There was no excruciating pain, just a sudden, sharp twist that caused her to sit up and cradle the infant inside her with both hands. But the baby had begun to move quite vigorously, signaling, she thought, that all was well.

"The fall hurt the baby," Ross said, breaking into her thoughts.

"Not at first, but by later that night, it brought on my labor." Her terse explanation did little justice to the memories she kept locked inside.

The coach driver had been effusively apologetic, helping her into the horsecab and settling her himself. By then, though, she was beginning to cramp, which didn't seem normal, and it scared her. By the time she reached her aunt's apartment, there was no doubt that she was in trouble. She was bleeding, and the cramps had become much more painful.

Aunt Essie had sent for the doctor.

Her memories became disjointed and muddled after that. The cramps were in fact the first premature contractions of her womb. Later that night, all the while she labored, the doctor had babbled words like *trauma* and *placenta* and *abruption,* but by then she was too delirious with pain and loss of blood to understand any of it. All she knew was that, in the end, it had added up to a tiny, unmoving bundle in a bloodstained sheet. She'd been able to lift her head to see that much before finally losing consciousness. When she awoke, the tiny bundle was gone, spirited away by order of her attending physician.

Emily gathered what composure she could, then forced herself to face Ross, but his back was to her and his head was bent.

"Ross?"

"You should have told me."

"But I didn't know . . . how."

"No, no, I can't accept that."

"I'm sorry," she said, not sure whether she referred to a past neither of them had the power to change or a belated, confused regret for her own decisions.

After a moment, he lifted his head. "I have to think."

Emily didn't know what else to say. She felt drained and numb.

"I have to think," he repeated, more to himself than to her. He moved to the door, leaving her alone when it slammed closed behind him.

# 16

*Reality.* It was a word that Ross was fond of and one that Emily cringed from. Usually, it was because people used it to discourage new ideas or to dwell upon the dark side of life, but after her latest confrontation with Ross, Emily was forced to do some hard thinking. She had shed more than a few long overdue tears, too.

She'd had almost four years to deal with the loss of her baby, but she'd done a very poor job of it. Trying to pretend that she'd accepted it and had moved on was a lie. The guilt was still there, the hurt was still there, and the anger burned brighter than ever.

Looking back, if she had set aside her pride and told Ross that she was pregnant, he would have married her. She never would have been forced to leave town. She never would have tried to board that horsecab in Baltimore. And their son would be almost four years old now.

*Matthew.* It was the name she'd chosen for a boy. He might have had her dark hair, Ross's laughing brown eyes, and a dimple when he smiled. It didn't matter that his conception had been the cause of her flight from home and that she would never have been able to return. From the very first flutter of life within her womb, she'd wanted that baby. He was a part of her and a part of Ross. She'd already purchased a cradle and begun to fashion tiny garments with her meager sewing talents when she had the accident. Aunt Essie had tactfully removed those items from their apartment soon afterward, and now Emily believed that might have been when she had first started trying to pretend that everything was all right.

This morning, however, as she proceeded down King Street, she was intent upon dealing with another sort of reality, one not nearly so complicated, irreversible, or painful. Her fledgling printing business was doing as well as could be expected, but she wouldn't be able to make a livable profit for some time yet. She needed to supplement her income. That was where Karl Becker might be able to help.

She stopped and checked the angle of her prim, dark-veiled hat before climbing the front steps to enter the red brick building where Karl worked. She hoped that he hadn't been merely toying with her the other day when he'd mentioned a job.

She stepped into a dimly lit vestibule with a row of black mailboxes on the wall to her right. Lifting her veil, she noted the brass nameplate that hung above the one marked 2-B. *David Stauffer, Attorney at Law.* Someday, after Karl completed his two-year clerkship and passed an examination to be admitted to the bar, that nameplate might read, *Stauffer & Becker*. After his underprivileged childhood, Emily was glad that Karl had done well with his life.

She had visited here once before to discreetly

solicit some print orders from Karl, so she had no trouble locating him. The office he shared with his mentor was a three-room suite furnished with ponderous black walnut furniture, heavy draperies, and tall shelves crammed with leather-bound volumes.

Emily was glad to find Karl alone, perusing one of the bookshelves when she stepped through the door. "Why, Emily Winters!" he exclaimed, turning to greet her with a welcoming grin. "What brings you by today?"

"Business," she said. "I hope I'm not interrupting."

"Not at all," he assured her. "I was just doing some research, but that can wait." He inclined his golden blond head in the direction of his private office. "Would you like to have a seat?"

"Thank you."

When Emily followed him into the small room, she noticed that the mountain of paperwork on his desk hadn't diminished one bit since her last visit. It looked to be as thoroughly disorganized as ever.

"Oh, Karl, really. This is abominable," she said, tidying a pile of loose papers and files that threatened to spill over the side of his desk. "What do your clients have to say about this catastrophe of yours?"

Demonstrating remarkably quick reflexes for a man with a bad leg, Karl stooped to catch a stray sheet before it could flutter to the floor. "They don't say much of anything. David handles the real estate and bounty claims. I've taken on most of the paperwork for the criminal defense cases. Many of my esteemed clients are quite satisfied if I can manage to keep them out of county jail."

"You know, you really should try paper fasteners," Emily suggested.

"Paper fasteners?"

"Yes, they're the newest thing. Haven't you seen them advertised? Little metal clips. I use them at the shop to keep my orders together."

Karl appeared impressed. "Paper fasteners." He picked a pen from out of the conglomeration atop his desk and moved as if to jot the name down, then stopped and frowned upon finding his pen dry of ink. He scanned his desktop, only to discover that his inkwell was buried, too.

"Never mind," Emily said, taking a seat and pulling off her black kid gloves. "I'll try to remember to pick up a box of them for you at the drugstore."

"Oh, thank you. I'll certainly give them a try." Shifting his cane to his other hand, he sat in a leather upholstered chair. "So what brings you by today? Trying to drum up more business?"

"Not precisely."

"Well, what could it be, then? Since you're not working for the *Herald* anymore, I thought you'd be spending your days down at the shop."

Emily winced. She'd been fired on Wednesday. Today was Friday. News traveled fast. "So you've heard."

"Everybody's heard. In fact, this morning I ran into your old friend, um, oh . . . what was her name, the preacher's daughter?"

"Melissa Carpenter," Emily supplied.

Karl snapped his fingers. "Yes! That's it. Melissa Carpenter." He paused and looked thoughtful. "You know, I didn't recognize her right off. She wears her hair different, and she's thinned out some. I thought her eyes used to be brown, but today they looked more like—"

"You were saying?" Emily prompted, impatient to learn the gossip that was already making its rounds.

"Oh, yes. Well, at any rate, at the vestry meeting just last evening, Malcolm Davenport was apparently quite vocal about what transpired between the two of you. According to him, you accepted his charitable offer of employment, then turned around and stole his print customers right out from under his nose." Karl grinned and shook a finger at her. "Very naughty, Miss Emily. I'm proud of you."

She made a wry face. "I don't suppose he remembered to mention that he sabotaged the *Penn Gazette* before it went out of business, did he?"

"No, I don't believe Miss Carpenter said he mentioned anything about that." Karl's grin faded, and he leaned forward over his desk, suddenly intent. "It is still *Miss* Carpenter, isn't it?"

"Yes," Emily said, "but that's not why I'm here. Malcolm Davenport is the least of my worries."

"Oh? Something I can help you with?"

"I need a job."

"But what about the printing business? Don't tell me you're giving up on it so soon?"

"No, not at all, but it's going to take more time until I can turn enough profit to hire some help. Until then, I need a temporary job to earn some outside income to purchase new inventory and—" She stumbled at the thought of Ross, then cleared her throat to finish. "And to pay back, uh, some loans as well as other expenses."

"But how are you going to hold down two jobs? Since your secret's out, you'll have to open your doors for business, am I right? You can't be in two places at the same time."

"That's true," she admitted. "I can't be in two places at once, but luckily I've got some help."

"Who?"

"My mother and sister."

Karl's eyebrows shot up. "Oh? Then, I take it you've finally told your mother what you've been up to these past few weeks?"

"I didn't have much choice. The news was out. She was bound to learn of it from someone. I preferred that someone to be me."

"Very wise. When the jig is up, it's always best to come clean and beg forgiveness."

"Actually, she took it very well. In fact, she didn't even seem very surprised."

Karl chuckled. "Perhaps she knows her daughter better than you thought. What did she say?"

"'In for a penny, in for a pound.'"

"What?"

Emily let out a resigned sigh. "She said that if I was so dead set on trying to make a go of this business that I've been working myself ragged and sneaking around like a Confederate spy, then we might as well follow through and see what happens."

Karl sat back in his seat and interlaced his fingers around his middle. "I always did like your mother."

"The point is, until my sister's new baby makes its appearance a few months hence, both she and my mother will be able to help watch the shop during the day. They can take orders and organize deliveries and tally up accounts." Emily leaned forward and tapped a finger on the desktop for emphasis. "The important thing is, come hell or high water, our doors will be open for business from nine in the morning until five at night. Whether Mr. Davenport knows it or not, he's going to get a good run for his money."

Karl laughed heartily at this. "Damn the torpedoes, full speed ahead! Now, that's the spirit!"

Emily gave him a shrewd little smile. "So, what do you say?"

"About what?"

"About that job you mentioned to me a while back. It's obvious that you need someone to help get you organized."

"Is it?" he quipped with an amused grin.

"The question is, are you and Mr. Stauffer willing to pay for it, and if so, are you up to placing your trust in a woman to help whip this place into shape?"

Karl's eyes sparkled with old devilment. "Why, Miss Emily, when you put it that way, how can I possibly resist?"

When Ross came out of the Davenport building, the sweltering summer heat rose like a rude slap to greet him. Jamming his watch into his pocket, he muttered a string of invectives as he crossed the busy square to city hall. It was only ten-thirty on Friday, and he already had a raging headache. Virgil Davis, the local intelligence reporter, hadn't shown up for work. This wasn't the first time Ross had covered for him. Although he liked Virgil, the man's fondness for whiskey was a problem.

The police station and lockup were located in the basement of the city hall building. When Ross entered the small, windowless office, he found one of the constables, Lionell Smith, eating an early box dinner at his desk. Lionell was in his midtwenties, but his fair, wispy hair was already thin on top and he carried about a dozen unnecessary inches around the waistline. As far as Ross was concerned, Lionell was a perfect example of how badly the war had depleted the labor force during the past four years.

"Mornin', Ross," Lionell called as he set aside a half-consumed sandwich and pulled a sheet of paper from his cluttered desk. "Where's Virgil?"

"Sick," Ross replied. He already had his pencil and notepad ready by the time Lionell moseyed over to the oak counter near the door.

"Old Virge hitting the bottle too hard again, eh?" The young constable smirked knowingly as he presented the police log sheet to Ross. He was in the mood to gossip.

"Couldn't say for sure, Lionell." Taking the sheet, Ross caught whiffs of sweat and pickle juice as he scanned the first items on the police log. They were a burglary, a petty theft, a lost boy, and a drunk and disorderly. "So, how have you been?"

"Can't complain," Lionell said with a huge yawn. "You?"

"Fine."

Ross knew his reply was ludicrous. Ever since Emily had told him the truth, he'd been feeling anything but fine. Still, he managed to force a tight smile before he began jotting down the particulars for the following morning's local intelligence column.

"The little boy have a name?" Ross asked as he scribbled.

"What? Huh?"

"The little boy they found wandering in Duke Street."

"Uh, yeah, right there. Michael. Can't ya read?"

In fact, Ross couldn't read much of Lionell's chicken scratch, and his spelling was atrocious. "Michael," Ross repeated. "I see they took him over to the Home for Friendless Children. How old is he?"

"About three. Ain't old enough to tell us for sure."

Ross moved to the next item. A stolen awning rope from Mr. Stahl's store on Orange Street. "Didn't we just do a write-up about his awning rope being stolen last week?"

"Yup."

"Twice now," Ross mused as he wrote. "I imagine old Mr. Stahl's getting pretty steamed."

"Said he was gonna sit up all night with a loaded shotgun to catch the rascals, but the chief talked him out of it."

"Hmm." Ross stopped writing upon spotting an eye-catching name on the next line. He looked up. "Arnold Gibson? Holy smokes, that can't be the city councilman's son, can it?"

"Yep. It can and it is." Lionell's eyes sparkled with juicy knowledge.

This could be big. Ross knew he was going to have to satisfy Lionell's need to feel important. "I see what's down on paper here, Lionell, but I'm sure there's more to the story than that. Were you here? Do you know the details?"

"Well, as a matter of fact, I was here. And you're right. The story is a little more complicated than just what's on the sheet."

Ross leaned on the counter as if to get closer. He lowered his voice. "Why don't you tell me the real story, then?"

Ross's avid interest seemed to satisfy Lionell for the moment. "Well, you see, a fella from Marietta came in early yesterday evening saying he picked up a lady all bruised and bleeding by the side of the road outside town."

"What happened?"

"According to the little lady, she agreed to go for a ride with Arnie Gibson, but once they got out of town, he turned mean. She managed to get away from him and run back to the road where this fella happened to be going by and picked her up."

"She hurt bad?"

"Considering Arnie's size and temper and all, I'd say she got off pretty light." Lionell paused to extract a wrinkled handkerchief from a trouser pocket. He mopped beads of sweat from his forehead as he continued, "You know, that boy ain't been quite right in the head ever since he got back from the war."

"Is the lady going to be all right?"

"Her face was bruised up some, she had a knife gash on her arm, and her dress was torn. We sent her to see Doc Weaver in case she needed to be stitched up. You'd have to check with him."

"I don't see here that any charges were filed," Ross said. "Why not?"

Lionell offered an I've-seen-it-all chuckle as he jammed his soiled handkerchief back home. "Well, now, you know as well as I do, Ross, Arnie's daddy has lots of pull in this town. The chief brought Arnie down for questioning, but the councilman came charging in after him, mad as a hornet. Got a lawyer with him and everything. Can't tell you one way or another whether there'll be charges filed or not."

"But what about the lady's family?" Ross pressed. "Why aren't they up in arms?"

"The *lady?*" Lionell drawled the word dubiously.

"Well, now, you see, there's the other part of the problem."

"No," Ross said, "I don't see."

"The *lady* in question ain't exactly a *lady* if you get my meanin'."

"Why? Who is she?"

"Her name is Miss Stacy Bliss."

Ross frowned. "That name sounds familiar."

The constable leaned his pudgy forearms on the oak counter and gave Ross a lascivious wink. "So, you know her, do you? Ain't surprisin'. Most fellas 'round here do."

It was then that Ross put his finger on it. Stacy Bliss. A pretty, if not terribly bright, farm girl who had left school in the eighth grade. "I knew her when we were kids. She was a nice girl."

Lionell snorted. "Yeah, *real* nice. She's working down at the Bull Tavern these days, if you get a hankerin' to catch up on old times."

What the man was saying, plain and simple, was that Stacy was a prostitute. Considering what he remembered of the girl's worn-out shoes and poor clothes, this didn't come to Ross as a big surprise, but it was sad just the same. He'd meant it when he'd said Stacy was a nice girl. At least when Ross had known her. That was a long time ago now.

Ignoring Lionell's snide comment, Ross pressed him. "So, what you mean is, since the lady hasn't got anyone to take up her side in this matter, it's likely to be forgotten. Is that about the size of it?"

At this, the rotund constable's dull eyes lit with something akin to wary comprehension. He pushed up from the counter and straightened. "Well, her family ain't had nothing to do with her for years now. Just what're you gettin' at, Ross?"

"It looks like Arnie Gibson will get away with it."

The look of defensiveness faded, and Lionell shrugged. "Maybe. This time, anyway, and maybe again and again, too. At least until he slaps around the wrong daddy's little girl."

Ross read over the police log again. Stacy's injuries might have been relatively minor, but her dress had been torn. He wondered if she'd been assaulted in a sexual manner as well. Just because she hadn't reported it didn't preclude the possibility.

"This sorta thing ain't the chief's fault, you know."

Ross looked up to see Lionell mopping his forehead dry again. "I didn't say it was."

But Lionell continued as if Ross hadn't spoken. "If he decides to take it to a hearing, it probably won't even be bound over for trial, and even if it is, chances are no jury is going to give Arnie more than a fine or a couple days in the lockup."

"Maybe that's better than nothing. Maybe it'll get his attention."

"I doubt it," Lionell said.

"But it's worth a try," Ross argued. "What if the lady in question were your sister or your aunt?"

"Look, Ross, if you ask me, it wouldn't be no big loss to this community if Arnie was to be locked up for a while. Like I said, he has a rafter or two missing. But Stacy ain't nobody's sister or aunt. Not anymore. These girls ask for trouble, and when it finds them, there ain't many folks ready to offer sympathy. Now, them's the facts of life."

"It shouldn't matter who the victim is. Justice is supposed to be blind."

"Yeah, well, you can't change the world, Ross."

If that were true, Ross thought, then they'd just

fought one of the bloodiest wars in history for nothing. "I don't agree, Lionell. Maybe if we make an effort, we can change our little corner of it."

"Well, you do what you have to. If the chief feels he's got popular support on this, then maybe something will come of it. Otherwise, I wouldn't hold my breath."

Tucking his notebook back into his coat pocket, Ross prepared to leave. "Oh, I intend to do more than hold my breath, Lionell. I'm going to be out of town tomorrow on a story, but I'll be back to see you early next week."

"Take it easy, Ross."

Ross didn't intend to take it easy. His original notion was to drop his police log notes on another reporter's desk to do the write-up for tomorrow's edition, but he'd just changed his mind. This particular item he would compose himself. Right now, the identity of the victim wouldn't be an issue. Because of newspaper policy and his belief that Stacy needed to be protected from public scrutiny, her name wouldn't be published. But Arnold Gibson's would. If public pressure would help move this case into the court system, then that's what Ross intended to deliver.

# 17

*Malcolm was out of the office* until Saturday, which gave Ross editorial control. He took advantage of this authority by writing the local intelligence column himself. Late Friday afternoon, he sent his copy to the composing room to be set for the following day's first edition.

The next morning, Ross took a train to Gettysburg, where ceremonies were planned to accompany the laying of a cornerstone of a national monument. He intended to cover the story for the paper, but he also had personal reasons for wanting this assignment. His old regiment had been ordered to represent the infantry of the army. Many of the soldiers in the Fiftieth were veteran volunteers, his old comrades, and he looked forward to seeing them again before they were mustered out of service.

When the ceremony was done, Ross took a hotel room to stay the night. He hoped that spending time with his old friends might help distract him from his present troubles.

It did. For a while. They reminisced over camp life,

squad drills, guard duty, and hardtack. They recalled the battles they'd fought, the acts of gallantry they'd witnessed, and afterward, as one of the men accompanied them on the harmonica, they sang a few verses of "When This Cruel War is Over."

In the quiet that followed, they remembered their slain friends, and Ross was pressed to describe his experiences after being wounded and captured at Wilderness. He did his best to oblige, even though he didn't normally like to talk about it.

His stay at Libby Prison in Richmond had been brief, and he'd been in such pain and delirium from his wounds that he remembered little of it. By then, Libby was being used as a temporary holding facility for new prisoners, thus, its notoriously poor conditions had improved. Ross was lucky to end up in the care of a surgeon who seemed concerned about the patients' welfare.

After he was judged fit to travel, Ross and some other prisoners were transported south by boxcar to one of the new prison pens in Georgia—Camp Sumter, Andersonville. If there was a hell on earth, Ross knew the moment he stepped inside that stockade gate that he'd have to travel not one step further to find it.

It was fifteen acres of fenced-in ground with a swampy, diseased stream running through it and twenty thousand ragged, starving Yank prisoners. Only some of them were lucky enough to be sheltered by makeshift shebangs fashioned out of scraps of wood and blankets. When Ross arrived, men were already going about the gruesome business of dying at a rate of eighty a day.

No, his stay at Andersonville wasn't something he

liked to talk about, but he could write about it. At the time of his imprisonment, the chances of a letter reaching home were almost nonexistent, so Ross kept a diary. By the time he was moved to the prison at Florence and later released, he had two journals from which to draw the series of exposé articles he would later write, as well as the novel he was at work on now.

Sunday morning, Ross boarded a train to return to Lancaster. He used the travel time to compose his article on the monument ceremony, so that, once home, he was free to pull out the unfinished manuscript of his novel. It was still early afternoon when he sat down to work in the parlor, and it wasn't long before the words began to flow.

When a sharp knock sounded at his front door, he was surprised to see that the hands of the tall case clock had crept past six o'clock. A second rap brought him to his feet. When he opened the door, he found Emily on his front porch.

Dressed in black, she held a folded *Herald* newspaper to her chest as if it were a shield. It was of no matter that she didn't smile when he opened the door. This was the first time he'd seen her since their argument. An unexpected wave of relief washed through him, and he was surprised to realize that his anger toward her had all but vanished.

Although he still believed she should have told him about the baby, he knew she wasn't the only one who'd made mistakes four years ago. The possibility that he could have gotten her pregnant had occurred to him, but he also knew that the odds were slim. What hadn't occurred to him was the possibility that she wouldn't tell him if she were in trouble. When she hadn't answered his letters, he'd assumed the whole question was by then moot. Looking back now, of course, he'd behaved irresponsibly.

"Don't worry," she said, apparently misinterpreting his quizzical expression to mean that he was sorry she had come. "I know we have some problems, but I'm not here about that. I'm here on business. May I come in?"

Business. Well, naturally, Ross thought. Why else would the mother of his illegitimate child come by? Business. It was absurd, but he knew better than anyone that Emily had a streak of pride a mile wide. She would get around to the real reason for her visit in her own time. He opened the door wider. "Of course you can come in."

"Thank you." She brushed by him, leaving a head-swimming scent of rosewater in her wake.

Ross led her into the parlor, indicating with a nod that she should take a seat. "Make yourself comfortable."

She perused the small room, taking in the modest but cozy furnishings the Hockstetter family had left behind, including a writing desk, a patchwork haircloth sofa, and a colorful hooked rug that covered most of the hardwood floor. The only items missing to make this a real home were knitted tidies and family portraits.

"No, thank you," she said, clearing her throat and facing him. "I won't be long."

Ross took this to mean that she was primed for battle. If so, she was to be disappointed. He wasn't in the mood to fight with her. "What is it you want, Em?"

"I read your piece on Arnold Gibson."

# FOREVER AND ALWAYS

When she didn't continue, he prompted, "And?"

"How *could* you?" It was an accusation, an accusation that left him at a loss to respond.

"How could I what?"

"How could you write such a thing when you know very well that a woman was injured?"

Ross couldn't understand her indignation. All he'd done was write up the facts in the police log, then he'd called for a more thorough investigation of the incident. What could she find wrong with that?

"What are you talking about?" he asked.

"This!" She shoved the folded newspaper at him. "I always thought I knew you, Ross, but after reading this and talking to Lionell Smith, I don't know what to think anymore."

When Ross unfolded the paper, he saw that it was a Sunday edition. The column he'd written should have appeared in Saturday's paper. Then his eye fell on Gibson's surname, and he read aloud:

> Another Side to that Questionable Affair. In yesterday's first edition, we gave what was furnished by police officials as a factual account of an assault committed upon a woman. Since then, City Councilman Floyd Gibson, the father of the man said to have perpetrated the assault, has requested that his son's side of the story be told. He acknowledges that his son drove a young lady of questionable reputation two miles into the country but denies that he stabbed her. He states that his son put her out of the buggy and left her behind in punishment for insulting him. How are we to decide which

statement is truthful? The woman was rescued near the woods with a flesh wound in her side and bruises on her person. Councilman Gibson admits that his son was intoxicated and might have scuffled with her, but it was the lady who became hostile and initiated the unruly proceedings. Any harm that may have been inflicted was done in the name of self-defense. We would not knowingly misrepresent any citizen of this city and thus cheerfully give the councilman and his son the benefit of their version of the matter.

Ross concluded the lengthy account and looked at Emily. "I didn't write this."

"What?"

"I didn't write this."

"But I spoke with Lionell Smith after church and he said—"

"I did speak with Lionell, but that was on Friday. My article was the original account in Saturday's edition. I was out of town yesterday, Em. I only got back this afternoon."

"Well, then, that means—"

"This is someone else's doing." Ross folded the paper and set it down on the lamp table. "I'll find out what happened tomorrow, but I think it's rather obvious."

"What's obvious?"

"Arnold Gibson's father has pull in this town." Reading the flare of rebellion in her eyes, he held up a hand before she could voice it. "Those are Lionell's words, not mine, and it only follows that Floyd Gibson is using his political and financial influence to get this thing buried."

"That's not fair! What about the woman's family? You could go to them, and—"

"No. The woman doesn't have any family. At least none that will acknowledge her."

"What do you mean?"

"The woman who was attacked is Stacy Bliss."

"Stacy . . . Bliss?" She appeared to search her memory for the name.

"Maybe you remember her from school," Ross supplied. "Farm girl? Blond hair? She was in my class."

Emily nodded then. "Oh, yes. I do remember her. She quit school in the eighth grade."

"That's her. Stacy is now a waitress at one of the south side taverns," he said, wondering if Emily would grasp what that occupation entailed. "Her family disowned her a long time ago."

Emily's cheeks suddenly turned pink, which told Ross that she did understand his intimation, but her chin rose a notch out of pure stubbornness. "I see."

"So, that puts a different light on the subject."

"It most certainly does *not*."

"It does *not*?"

"That's right. It doesn't matter who the victim is. The point here is that a woman was attacked, and it appears that no one is willing to do anything about it."

He raised a finger. "That's not necessarily true. With a little prodding, we might be able to—"

"That's my point!" she interrupted, gesturing angrily. "It shouldn't take any prodding! Women weren't put on this earth to be well treated or shabbily treated at the discretion of whatever man she happens to be shackled to at the moment. How many women do you know in this community who have to face the backside of their husband's hand if they dare speak against him? It's high time judges and juries stopped winking and looking the other way. You can be sure things would be different if women had the vote. In fact—"

"Hold it," Ross stopped her. "We just jumped from Arnold Gibson and Stacy Bliss to women's suffrage. One issue at a time, would you, please?"

By now, she'd lost her breath as well as her composure. "It's all connected, Ross, and you know it! Sometimes I get so mad, I could—"

"But you don't," he counseled. "Instead, as a clear-thinking, mature woman, you remain calm and address each case as it comes in as practical a fashion as possible."

"Practical." She picked up on his choice of words in a disparaging tone. "One of your favorite words, I'll bet."

"You'd win that bet. Now, let me check into this when I get to the office tomorrow. I'll tell you what I find out. No matter what you might think of me, Em, I'm on your side in this case. I intend to do whatever I can to make sure it gets prosecuted."

His statement seemed to mollify her somewhat. "All right. Uh, fine. That should do for now, but don't think I won't see this through. Stacy Bliss may not be a prominent citizen in this town, but that doesn't mean she deserves to be manhandled by the likes of Arnold Gibson. He's clearly a menace to women. He should be put behind bars as an example to others like him."

"I agree."

"Fine, then, we, um . . . agree."

They stood for an awkward moment before Emily

reached into a side pocket of her skirt. "I have something for you."

Before he could ask what it was, he saw greenbacks and frowned. "What's that?"

"Your money. Well, part of it, anyway. I've worked out a payment schedule that should—"

"I don't want the money."

"It was a loan."

"Consider it a gift," he said impatiently.

"But this is business."

"Fine, then. If it's business, then put on your business hat. You can't afford it right now, can you?"

She hedged. "Well, no, I suppose not, but as I was trying to say, I've worked out a payment schedule that I should be able to keep now that I'm working at Karl Becker's office."

Ross's complaisant mood fled. "Karl?" His voice rose to accompany his temper. "You're working for *Karl*?"

"Well, technically I'm working for Mr. Stauffer," she corrected, not seeming to notice his discontent, "but only until the print shop gets up and going, then—"

"Ah, jeez, Emily!" Ross started pacing the room in frustration. "Karl! Of all people!"

"Oh, for heaven's sake." Emily planted her hands on her hips as she tracked his infuriated movements. "Why are you still so angry with him? That stupid fight you two had was years ago. I just know that if you made the first move, Karl would swallow his overblown male pride and follow suit."

"I can't stand him!"

"That's ridiculous. You used to be the best of friends."

"But he always annoyed the hell out of me!"

"Only some of the time," Emily pointed out, "and, besides, he can't help but be annoying. It's an intrinsic part of his personality."

"Personality?" Ross echoed incredulously. He stopped and faced her. "He's a conceited toad!"

"Yes," Emily agreed again, "but he means well."

"He's self-centered."

"Yes."

"And wise-mouthed," Ross added.

Emily nodded, but her eyes shined with amusement. "Yes."

"And unconscionable when it comes to pursuing women."

"Yes. And loyal and intelligent and ambitious and hardworking and charming and witty."

Ross glared at her, wondering at what point he'd turned into the illogical, mule-headed party in this conversation. "I always hated that the most."

"Of course you did." Her lips curved in a knowing smile. "But that doesn't mean you can't be friends again."

Seeing Emily's heartwarming expression nearly undid him. She looked so pretty when she smiled all for him, but he'd done very little lately to deserve that pleasure. It took a moment for him to tamp down his zigzagging emotions. He had to take a deep, logic-gathering breath before replying. "I'll think about it."

Her smile widened, lighting up her face. "I knew you would."

"Maybe," he added to keep hold of some remnants of his pride. Pretty? Had he thought pretty? She was beautiful when she smiled. His palms were sweating and his heart was pounding. One little smile and—what was wrong with him?

After a moment, though, her smile faded and she looked down at her hands, one of which still clutched a fistful of greenbacks. "Um, as I was saying," she began.

"I told you, I don't want it."

She looked up with a frown. "I don't care if you don't want it." She thrust the money at him. "It's yours."

Ross raised his hands. "This is silly."

"Why? Because you don't think I can make a go of this business?"

"No," Ross said, gritting his teeth at her single-mindedness. "This doesn't have anything to do with business. This is about you and me. Money shouldn't matter between friends." He paused at seeing the uncertainty on her face. "Or lovers," he finished and waited to see what would happen.

The color seemed to drain from her cheeks. It was almost as bad as the first day she'd come back, the day he'd happened upon her peering through the print shop window. But she thankfully remained on her feet this time.

Very slowly, Ross lowered his hands. "We need to talk about what happened that night."

She shook her head. "It was a mistake."

At hearing her use the same words he'd used himself, Ross realized how empty they sounded. He reached out to take her by the shoulders. "Maybe it wasn't a mistake. Maybe I was wrong. Maybe I never should have thought it, much less said it."

"But that's how you felt," she said. "You can't change how you felt."

"I didn't know what I felt. I was confused that night. I was afraid that we'd ruined our friendship by—" He cut off and closed his eyes. "I never should have written that stupid letter. I just wanted things to go back to the way they used to be between us, but maybe that's where I made the biggest mistake."

"You're not making sense," she said softly.

When he opened his eyes, he knew from her pained, puzzled expression that she was trying to understand, but how could she understand if he wasn't even sure of what he was trying to say himself? For five days he'd had time to sort through his tangled feelings about what had happened that night and afterward, but it was only now that he was with her that a resolution seemed within grasp.

He could remember as clearly as if it were yesterday those balmy summer afternoons spent by the creek, writing and sketching, then lying on their backs in the grass to make up stories to go with the cloud pictures that formed overhead. Those memories were precious and close to his heart, the lingerings of childhood when the future seemed boundless. Their relationship had begun to change after that, slowly and subtly, until finally, instead of the assumed trust and easy understanding that had always existed between them, there was only conflict and awkwardness and confusion.

It had culminated when he left the *Gazette* to go work for the *Herald*. They had come very close to losing everything then, but they hadn't. Even after months of estrangement, he and Emily had found a way back to the perfect, unspoken, eloquent understanding which had bound them together as children.

But only once. One night. Looking back, perhaps the odds were not so stacked against conceiving a new child on that particular night.

"It wasn't a mistake," Ross said again.

"How can you say that after all that's happened?"

She had such beautiful, long-lashed, sea blue eyes. When had he noticed how breathtaking they were? Was it that first day he'd confronted her by the creek? Ross was remembering more than their childhood at this moment, he was remembering making love to her. He'd never been able to forget it, not one second of it, even when he'd wished he could bury it along with all the guilt it caused, but the truth was, it had been only after the fact that the guilt had set in.

The act of making love to Emily had been sweet, almost painful in its perfection. He recalled the purely female, satin softness of her thighs, her belly, her breasts. He remembered the rosewater fragrance of her hair, the succulent taste of her mouth and her skin, and the hot, wet welcome of her body when he entered her. He could remember the instinctive raising of her hips with each of his thrusts, the soft, quickened sounds of her breathing, and the explosive, joyous release that had seemed, just for those fleeting seconds, to set his troubled spirit free. There had been no fear of dying in battle, no guilt, no second thoughts, no agony of regret or self-recrimination. Nothing but the two of them, kindred spirits, bound and joined as they were perhaps meant to be.

"Maybe we were too young," Ross allowed. "Maybe the war pushed us to act too quickly. Neither of us was prepared to handle the consequences at the time, but I have a feeling it would have happened sooner or later, regardless."

Emily shook her head. "You can't know that."

But no matter how hard she tried, she couldn't seem to look away from him. She couldn't keep from trying to understand what was in his heart. What he said didn't make any sense. He had been the one to see the truth first—that it had been a mistake. It had taken her months, no, *years* to accept that truth, and now he claimed to see it differently? Perhaps she should have been angry. That was certainly preferable to the mind-numbing spin of emotions that she was experiencing now.

"I know it was probably meant to happen between us sooner or later," he said, "because I remember how right it felt when it was happening."

He touched her jaw with one finger, then traced it down beneath her chin and bent his head closer. She knew that she should break away, but she didn't. The frightening truth was, she still craved him.

It was a gentle kiss, a teasing, mere brushing of his lips over hers, but it hurtled Emily back to that night four years ago, before the rejection and hurt, to that first exhilarating rush of hope and anticipation.

He ended the kiss and whispered against her mouth, "You remember, too, don't you?"

Of course she remembered. It was *he* who had been so hell-bent on forgetting. This thought, one last, pitifully weak flash of rebellion, flitted through her mind, but she didn't act on it because he was already pulling her tight against the full length of him. He kissed her again, deeper this time, moving his warm, seeking mouth over hers so that her lips instantly parted.

A tingling warmth spread to weaken her limbs and speed up her heart, and she knew that time and experience had not changed her feelings for him at all. When she reached up to lock her arms around his neck, the money she'd brought with her, the money meant to symbolize a final break from him, fluttered to the parlor floor.

# 18

*Making love with Ross* on a hooked rug in the late afternoon was not what Emily had envisioned for them in any of the forbidden fantasies she had concocted over the years. In those fantasies, they had coupled a thousand times in natural settings, usually by the creek on a blanket warmed by the sun or beneath the old oak tree they had climbed as children. But, as it had been that night four years before, reality proved no less magnificent than any exotic fantasy she could have created in her own mind.

When their clothes were shed, there was no place to hide and no secrets left to keep. The late afternoon sun's rays slanted through the cozy parlor's venetian blinds, casting their sensual encounter in an ethereal golden glow. Emily finally allowed her curiosity free reign to touch him as he had touched her that night so long ago.

She marveled at the stark beauty of his male body unclad, so hard and lean where she was soft and round. She ran her fingertips over the beard-roughened contours of his face, the gentle curve of his mouth, the sharp angle of his jaw, and the splendid expanse of his chest. All the while, he watched her and waited as she tested the taut curves of lean muscle in his arms and shoulders and trailed a gentle exploration along the wretched scars left behind by the war.

When he brought them both down to their knees on the floor, she even dared to touch the part of him that made him male, tentatively closing her hand around the hardened shaft that seemed a wondrous combination of steel and silk. It didn't take long, though, for him to cut short her explorations.

Pulling her into a tight embrace, he urged her down onto her back on the floor. He kissed her and touched every part of her that ached to be touched. He caressed her breasts, her belly, her thighs, and where his fingers grazed, his mouth soon followed. And when he finally took her in one smooth, breath-stealing stroke, there was no pain, only a stunning sense of fulfillment that was followed by an urgency that narrowed her consciousness down to the point of their physical joining and nothing else.

Emily threw her head back and clung to him, every muscle in her body tensing, her breath coming in harsh gasps as she strained to match his quickening rhythm. Her release, when it came, came as a dazzling surprise, all at once and in a spiraling, wit-scattering rush of pure sensual delight.

Later, when they were both sated, a sweet exhaustion stole over Emily, she lay very still, her arms slackening around Ross's neck, her eyes closed, her lips curved in a secret smile. She imagined that she was lying in the warm, wet grass by the creek after being sprinkled by a cool summer rain. If she opened her eyes, iridescent shafts of sunlight would be shooting through the breaking clouds overhead.

She felt Ross's mouth brush over hers. "Em?"

"Hmm?"

"Emily," he murmured again, and she forced her eyes open to see that he was watching her. His hair was tousled and tumbled over his forehead. Except for withdrawing from inside of her and pushing up onto his elbows, he hadn't moved. They were still in an intimate embrace, both of them slick with sweat, her knees straddling him from below, hugging his waist.

Emily felt a warmth wash over her cheeks. Considering what they had just done, it seemed ironic that he could elicit such a maidenly reaction with just one look. Then again, they had known each other for a very long time in almost every way, but not like this. That night four years ago notwithstanding, physical intimacy was very new.

"Ross, why are you watching me like that?"

He gave her a slow smile. "I'm trying to remember what you looked like in braids."

If she'd had any strength left at all, she would have swatted him for having the audacity to tease her. Instead, she wrinkled her nose. "And are you having any success?"

"None." Shifting his weight slightly, he reached with one hand to touch a tendril of hair that trailed over her shoulder. Her hairpins had been lost among their clothing, which lay scattered like autumn leaves all over the floor.

"I feel as if I'm meeting someone new for the very first time," he said, echoing her previous line of thought. His gaze dropped to follow the slow, tickling path his fingers took. Down, down along her neck and her shoulder only to pause and linger at the rise of her breast.

Emily caught her breath. His touch, so very light and subtle, seemed to stir up new bone-melting sensations. "I feel that way, too," she said.

"I've only grown older, Em. So have you, but there are some things that never change."

"Like what?"

He gave a shrug, then smiled, his expression lighting with the same sort of adolescent devilment she remembered. "Like . . . how many ways can you say . . ." He paused to bend his head and kiss the damp skin between her breasts. "Delicious?"

Emily's eyes widened. "What?"

"Delicious," he repeated, trailing his tongue up to run a tantalizing circle around her nipple.

Emily squeezed her eyes shut when his mouth closed upon the aroused peak. "I, uh, um . . ."

"Scrumptious," he murmured, leisurely shifting position to trail a line of warm, tickling kisses down to her navel.

"Tasty," she said breathlessly, biting down hard on her lower lip as he played his mouth over her abdomen.

"Luscious."

"Um, savory."

"Delectable."

He was cheating, Emily thought, as he slid one hand very slowly up and down the inside of her thigh. "Flavorful," she managed, but the word came out a weak and ineffectual squeak. Once again, she felt her body heating like a pot set to boil over a high flame.

"Mouthwatering."

"Um, um, um . . ." Her vocabulary was shrinking by the second, and she didn't care. He was nibbling at the inside of her knee. Who on God's green earth would have thought a knee could be so sensitive?

"Succulent," he muttered, and now he was working a slow path up her thigh. Up, up . . .

Everywhere he touched, with his mouth or his hands, he seemed to stir lush, toe-curling responses. Part of it, of course, had to do with the fact that it was Ross. Even when she was angry with him, he could turn her heart into a limp egg noodle with one crooked smile. It only followed that his touch would be ten times as devastating, but how could he possibly know so much more about her own body's responses than she herself? How could he . . . ? Emily's eyes fluttered open.

*Practice.*

The answer came like an onslaught of cold spring water. She stiffened. Just who had he been practicing with all these years? Women like that Stacy Bliss? And what about . . . Johanna?

Ross had always been a quick study. As he learned every inch of Emily's lithe and lovely body, he was keenly attentive to how she reacted to each touch and each kiss. This sudden tensing of her muscles was not in tune with what he had already come to expect.

Very cautiously, he lifted his head to see that she was, at the same time, propping up onto her elbows to fix him with a narrow-eyed glare. While he had spoken the truth earlier—he truly couldn't picture her in braids anymore—he did indeed recognize that look. He was in trouble for something. Bad timing, though. With all that shining ebony hair spilling about her shoulders and those pretty breasts rising and falling with each breath, Ross was primed to tumble her all over again.

"Ticklish?" he inquired sheepishly.

"You swine."

"What?"

Her voice was low, barely controlled. "Johanna."

"Who?" The inane question popped out of his mouth before the obvious slapped him in the face. *Johanna?*

Good God, Johanna.

"Your fiancée!" To punctuate her anger, she wrested her right leg from his grasp. The next thing he knew, in trying to scramble away, she inadvertently blindsided him on the head with her knee, knocking him off balance to land on his back on the floor.

"Merciful heavens!" Emily railed from somewhere above. "I must be a fool! Twice a fool!"

Ross raised a hand to his throbbing temple. Johanna. He hadn't thought of her in over two days. He probably should have called at her house when he arrived home from Gettysburg, but she'd completely slipped his mind.

"And this time you're betrothed to another woman!" Emily shrieked, apparently not noticing or caring that she'd practically knocked him senseless in her hurry to get away.

Ross turned his head to squint up at her as she muttered and ranted and struggled into her drawers. Betrothed. He didn't feel betrothed. Especially not now as he took note of how nicely rounded the feminine hips and buttocks were that she was unfortunately encasing in white cotton, and how if she turned just a few degrees to the right he might steal yet one more gratifying glimpse of lovely, nubile breasts before she managed to locate her chemise.

She was right. He *was* a swine.

"Wait," he said, pushing up to a sitting position, then up to his feet. "We should talk about this."

"Talk about it? Talk about it?" Emily refused to look at him as she pulled her chemise over her head and tied it closed with hurrying fingers. "It's a bit late to discuss our options."

"You seem to be under the impression that—"

"A mistake is a mistake whether we rehash it or not," she muttered, searching out her stockings, then balancing on one foot as she maneuvered to get one on.

"It wasn't a mistake." He was trying not to lose patience with her, but this was a sorry finish to the splendid encounter that had just taken place between them. Hadn't he made himself clear earlier?

"It wasn't a mistake," he repeated, "not then and not now."

But she wasn't listening as she scurried about in an effort to get dressed.

"Damn it, Emily! Stop that and look at me!"

But she wouldn't stop and she wouldn't look, and Ross was left to stand bare-assed naked in the middle of his own parlor, wondering what it was he could say or do to make it clear to her that what had happened between them had nothing at all to do with Johanna or his blasted engagement.

Oh, hell. Maybe it was just better to let her calm down before expecting her to listen to anything he had to say. He cursed under his breath and tried to hold to that thought as he searched about for his own clothes, then dressed in sullen silence. By the time he pulled on his trousers and shirt, she seemed much calmer. Maybe too calm. When she spoke, her tone was so low and soft he barely heard the words.

"I never should have come."

Ross turned to see her sitting on the sofa, bent at the waist as she fastened a shoe. Her hair was still loose, falling like a dark curtain to hide her profile. He had the terrible, panicked feeling that she was about to cry. Except for the night before he'd left for the army and the day she'd returned to Lancaster, he'd never seen Emily cry. He hated that he was the cause of it.

"You're right," he said. "You shouldn't have had to come here today. After the other night, I should have come to you."

She didn't reply. Instead, she stood and, keeping her back to him, reached with unsteady hands to gather her hair and twist it into a knot at the nape of her neck.

Bending down, Ross retrieved the few hairpins still on the floor, then closed the distance between them. "Look, I'm sorry, Em. I shouldn't have barged out of the shop and left you like that. I was just surprised and confused and—"

"Don't be so hard on yourself." She surprised him with how steady she sounded. "I've had four years to adjust to the idea of losing a child, you've had less than a week."

When she finally turned around to face him, he saw that she wasn't crying, but the bleakness in her expression couldn't have been more devastating than if tears had been streaming down her face. "You were right. I should have found a way to tell you about the baby. Maybe things would have turned out differently if I had."

Ross didn't have an answer for that. They looked at each other for a long moment, long enough for him to wonder how things might have turned out if either of them had made different choices—if she had chosen to tell him the truth or if he had chosen to face the consequences of his rash behavior rather than try to pretend nothing had ever happened.

Feeling useless, he offered her the hairpins. She took them without comment. He knew it was pointless to speculate on what might have been. They had to concentrate on the present. Unfortunately, it was a present which, thanks to today, had turned into a complicated, tangled mess of its own.

---

Despite Emily's vehement protests that she could see herself home, Ross insisted on accompanying her. Except for that fateful night four years ago, it seemed the longest walk of his life.

The sun was setting, casting a wildfire glow from behind the hills on the western horizon. Cornfields lined the quiet dirt road along most of their route. The fertile countryside was quiet, undeniably calming and peaceful, but Ross could find little peace within himself. His mental burdens had increased a hundredfold from that morning.

What insanity had possessed him to touch her again? The last time it had ended their friendship and resulted in disaster. This time seemed destined to end no better. As they walked in heavy silence, she didn't so much as glance at him. He could only assume that she still regretted the moment of recklessness that had caused her to succumb to his ill-timed seduction.

He waited until they'd covered nearly a quarter of a mile to attempt some sort of awkward repentance. "I'm not in love with Johanna."

Emily threw him a questioning glance, as if surprised by this declaration—though no more than he now that he'd actually spoken it aloud—but then she set her chin and focused again on the road. "Don't be absurd. You've always been in love with her."

Ross opened his mouth to refute this, but then closed it again. He hadn't always been in love with Johanna. Had he? Or had he ever been in love with her at all? Attracted by her beauty, yes. Enticed by her inaccessibility, perhaps, but was that love? Looking back now at all the time he'd spent competing for her against John Butler, it seemed as if he'd never gotten the chance to know her very well before her father had demanded she break off with him to marry John. Then Ross had left for the war and all but forgotten his adolescent obsession with her.

It wasn't until he'd returned home to find the *Penn Gazette* shut down and Emily living in Baltimore that his interest in Johanna had been rekindled. Ironically enough, it had been Malcolm himself who had set those old fires burning again. After Ross's articles were published in the New York *Tribune,* Malcolm had approached him with an offer to work for the *Herald* again, and not merely as a reporter but as assistant editor. To sweeten the pie, he'd even invited Ross to dinner, and Johanna had appeared at the table looking more sumptuous than the broiled steaks and hot buttered rolls that were being served.

It had seemed as if Malcolm were dangling in front

of him all that he'd ever hungered for as a youth—money, a successful career as a writer, and unconditional acceptance in established society. That was what Johanna had really represented to Ross that night, and crass as it seemed, Ross had a gut feeling Malcolm knew it.

Things had changed from four years before. Ross had acquitted himself well in the war and recently published in one of the most prestigious newspapers in the country. Irish Catholic or not, he was a journalist with his star on the rise. Malcolm had no sons of his own, and he needed a son-in-law capable of taking the helm of his precious family newspaper.

If Ross had learned anything during his time in hell at Andersonville, it was that life often took everything a man had but rarely gave anything back. If this was his chance to take what he wanted, then what kind of fool would he have been to refuse?

"No further," Emily said, breaking into his thoughts.

Ross realized that she'd come to a full stop a few steps behind him. They'd reached the mouth of the covered bridge. Once on the other side, her family's gray stone colonial would become visible in the distance. With an aggravated sigh, he turned back to her. "Em, I said I would see you home, and that's what I intend—"

"You don't understand," she said. "I told my family that I was going into town for a few hours. I can handle Henry and Mother's questions, but if Karen sees me coming from this direction with you, I'll never hear the end of it."

Ross studied her impassive expression in the fading light. Had he imagined a trace of anxiety in her voice? "Why?" he asked. "Does Karen know the truth about us?"

Emily's detached expression didn't flinch, but she averted her eyes. "Yes, but I made her promise not to tell anyone."

Suddenly, Karen's cold manner and early attempts to keep him and Emily apart when he'd first returned from the war made perfect sense to Ross. How else could she be expected to behave toward the man who had left her younger sister alone and pregnant? In that light, it didn't even matter that Ross hadn't known the truth. Emily had been hurt, and Ross was the one who'd hurt her, even if he hadn't meant to. Blood was thicker than water.

"What about your mother?" he asked.

Emily shook her head, still not looking at him. "No."

"Your father?"

This time she did look at him and all pretenses of composure vanished. "Of course not! Good heavens, how could I? Papa would have never understood!"

Now that the subject had been raised, Ross knew she was right. He was brought up short, however, by the humbling realization that he'd been so caught up in absorbing the knowledge that he'd both sired and lost a son that he'd failed to consider how it might have affected Emily's relationship with her family. No father would take well to the idea that his daughter had been compromised, but how much worse would it be if that very same daughter refused to name the man responsible?

He hated to think what Emily's refusal to betray him had done to the special relationship she'd had with the father she had idolized. The fact that it had actually taken his death to bring her home four years later said it all.

"Emily, if I could change the past, I would."

"Yes, Ross, I know. It was a mistake. You've made that perfectly clear from the begi—"

"I would have come back so that we could have faced your family together."

It took a few seconds for his meaning to sink in, but sink in it did. Her wary gaze seemed to probe his, to test his sincerity, but to his further frustration, he saw no acceptance. She didn't believe him. She wouldn't allow herself. Not yet. But he could sense that some part of her *wanted* to believe him, and that surely counted for something.

He despised feeling so impotent, but there was nothing more he could say now to change her mind, so he changed the subject. "When I get to the office tomorrow, I'll check into that write-up about Arnold Gibson. I'll let you know if there are any new developments, all right?"

"Fine. I'll be at the shop every afternoon and most evenings."

"Don't worry, Em," he said, turning to leave. "I'll find you."

# 19

*The following morning,* Ross was loaded for bear and ready to confront Malcolm over the Arnold Gibson affair, but his managing editor was nowhere to be found. The local intelligence reporter, Virgil Davis, as red-eyed and blossom-nosed as ever, informed Ross that Malcolm wasn't expected in the office until noon.

After questioning Virgil more carefully, Ross discovered that his hunch was correct. Floyd Gibson had come by Saturday morning to speak with Malcolm, after which the two men had spent a good thirty minutes behind closed doors. Ross knew that the city councilman wasn't only a business acquaintance of Malcolm's, he also had a tremendous amount of influence within local political circles. It was Malcolm himself who had penned the second write-up.

Ross soon dispensed with the items that had piled up on his desk in his absence, delegating most of them to other reporters, before settling down to write an editorial piece rebutting Sunday's "cheerful" acceptance of Councilman Gibson's version of the matter.

With all of his emotions running so close to the surface, perhaps his pen was a bit more vituperative than normal, but when he finished and read his own blistering words, he felt a prime sense of satisfaction. It was a feeling that had become more and more rare since he'd taken his position at the *Herald*. It was the feeling that he could make a difference.

At eleven-thirty, Malcolm burst into the busy city room in a cloud of cigar smoke, barking orders at two startled reporters as he doffed his top hat and stalked past them to his office. His thunderous expression and curt manner was not unusual. It merely meant that he was ready to get down to business. So was Ross.

Taking his editorial in hand, Ross followed the managing editor to find him chomping on his huge Corona cigar and hanging his coat on a rack just inside the open doorway. "What is it? It better be important."

"It is." Ross closed the door behind him and threw the lock for good measure. He wanted no untimely interruptions.

"How'd the Gettysburg trip go?" Malcolm rounded the corner of his desk and began shuffling through a mound of papers.

Ross knew he wasn't concerned with the weather or his comfort on the train. "I turned in my copy this morning. About half a column. The laying of the cornerstone from a veteran's point of view."

Malcolm grunted his approval as he sank into his seat. "Sounds good. That all?"

"No." Stepping forward, Ross held out the editorial.

"What's that?"

"Read it."

The older man grunted again, this time in annoyance, but he took the paper. Within seconds, he tossed it down and extracted the cigar from his mouth. "This matter is closed."

"Not in my opinion."

Malcolm resumed shuffling through the papers on his desk. A cue that Ross was being dismissed. "It's clear that you've been misinformed about the facts in this case."

"Not so. I got my facts from the police log."

Malcolm stopped shuffling and glared at him. "Not all the facts were in the police log. I thought that was made abundantly clear yesterday."

"Perhaps they would have been if the councilman and his lawyer would have allowed the chief to question Arnold properly."

"The boy was in no condition to be questioned at the time."

"Why? Was he drunk?"

Malcolm waved a hand through the air. "That's neither here nor there. I'll grant you, Floyd's son may not be a model citizen, but the girl is nothing more than common trash."

"The girl has a name. Stacy Bliss."

"Sounds like you know her."

"Somewhat."

"Uh-huh." All at once, a sly understanding crept over Malcolm's bulldog face. He grounded the cigar out in his brass ash tray. "So *that's* how it is."

"That's how *what* is?"

"Let's be frank, Ross. A man's private business is his own affair, but you'll be marrying my daughter in less than two weeks. If you feel the need to dip your wick elsewhere from time to time, that's no concern of mine, but you damn well better take your business out of town and keep it quiet." He paused, then leaned forward, lowering his voice and pinning Ross with a steel-eyed warning. "If it ever comes back to me that you're dallying too close to home, I'll make sure you regret it. Is that clear?"

For a moment, Ross couldn't bring himself to react. He'd just received Malcolm's approval to cheat, albeit discreetly, on Johanna. How much could the man care for his own daughter?

"I said, is that clear?"

"Very. But that's not what this is about."

Malcolm sat back in his chair and let out a cynical chuckle. "Oh. Well, then, what *is* this about?"

"Justice. It's about justice. In this case, it's clear that we have a difference of opinion. When I agreed to write for the *Herald* you said I would have freedom to express my own views. You never mentioned that those views had to coincide with yours."

"We have a certain philosophy that we adhere to at this paper. You know that as well as I do."

"I understand that, but this has nothing to do with political philosophy. This is a case of public safety. More importantly, this is a case of right versus wrong. Stacy Bliss was cut with a jackknife and beaten black and blue. Those are the facts. To my mind, it doesn't seem unlikely that she might have been raped, too."

Instead of being moved by the savagery of Arnold Gibson's acts, Malcolm snorted as if Ross had made a bad joke. "Raped? Be realistic. We're talking about a girl who spreads her legs every night of the week for the price of a cheap hat. Flip her a couple gold eagles and she'll be more than happy to call it even."

Ross had never liked Malcolm Davenport or his political leanings, but he'd always respected the man's hard-edged knowledge of the newspaper business. Because of that and his engagement to Johanna, Ross had resigned himself to enduring his unpalatable opinions. The raw contempt that rose up inside him now, however, made him feel sick with self-loathing. At what point did his decision to remain open-minded translate to hypocrisy?

Ross had to take a deep breath to control his mounting anger. "I want the piece to run."

"No." All traces of tolerance vanished from Malcolm's fierce countenance. Resting both hands on his desk, he rose to his full height. "When it comes out that the victim is a two-bit whore, we'll look like fools."

Ross wanted to state the truth. He wanted to say it so badly that he could taste the words. Malcolm was more worried about offending Floyd Gibson than about looking foolish for daring to champion the rights of an undesirable. Ross managed to hold his tongue, but just barely. "I don't think it will make us look foolish."

"Let it go," Malcolm ordered.

"No. This is important. Either run it as is or—"

Malcolm's voice lowered. "Or what?"

There was a knock at the door. Neither of them moved. There came another knock, then the doorknob jiggled. This was followed by a high-pitched, feminine voice. "Daddy? Are you in there? Mercy! Whatever can be wrong with this door?"

"Just a minute, Johanna."

Malcolm hadn't raised his voice, but each word weighed with authority. He was not a man accustomed to having his decisions questioned, and that was exactly what Ross was doing now.

"Mercy," they heard Johanna quibble from behind the door. "I'll be late for my fitting."

"Or what?" Malcolm pressed Ross again.

"You can put my name to the piece," Ross said, ignoring the challenge. "Add a disclaimer if you want. I don't care. Just so it runs complete as I've written it."

Once again, Malcolm's eyes narrowed on him. He was assessing how far Ross would go. Ross merely held the older man's hard gaze and waited. He was a little surprised that he felt no compunction at posing the threat his wordless stance conveyed, but he'd offered the only concession he was willing to give. Now it was up to Malcolm.

"Why is this so important to you?"

Ross had to consider his reply. He knew that there were other factors running through Malcolm's mind aside from gambling on a walkout by his assistant editor. For example, did he have anything at all to gain by running the piece? And exactly how much did he stand to lose if Councilman Gibson withdrew his personal political support?

Ross reminded himself that the most important issue here was that a crime be brought to trial, not that he emerge the victor in a power struggle with his editor. He decided to break the impasse. "Maybe I should mention that Emily Winters has picked up on this incident as some sort of female crusade. She doesn't have a newspaper to publish her views, but you know she'll find some way of stirring things up."

## FOREVER AND ALWAYS

Malcolm scowled at this, but the tension in his broad shoulders seemed to lessen, taking the pressure off both of them. "Emily Winters," he muttered and flopped back down into his chair. "A troublemaker. Just like her father."

Ross resisted an urge to smile his satisfaction. Emily would be delighted to learn that the mighty Malcolm Davenport had flinched at the mere mention of her name. "You know she won't give up easily," he added. "In fact, it's already too late to ignore this thing. It won't go away simply because we refuse to print it. Our readers will wonder why we had our heads buried in the sand on this one."

"They're like warts," Malcolm grumbled as if he hadn't heard a word Ross said. "No sooner do you get rid of one than there's another growing in its place. Run the damn piece."

Ross had to be sure he'd heard right. "Did you say, run it?"

"Yes, I said run it, but it's going to be your name on it. I'm sure as hell not taking the backlash for this when it comes out who the 'lady' is, you hear me?"

"I hear."

A renewed flutter of feminine knocking came at the door. "Daddy! I won't wait one more minute!"

Before Malcolm could change his mind, Ross took the editorial from his desk, tucked it into his coat pocket, and reached for the door.

"Why, Ross!" Johanna exclaimed, sweeping into the office. "What a delightful surprise! I didn't know you were back! Daddy, why didn't you tell me Ross was back?"

She was dressed in a fluffy beige-and-brown day dress with a matching feathered hat. Her bright blue eyes sparkled and her pink lips curved in a beguiling smile. Delicate, feminine perfume invaded the room with her, chasing away all remnants of her father's cigar smoke. She clutched a leather portfolio to her bosom.

"I only got in a few minutes ago myself," Malcolm responded, not bothering to rise from his seat. "You've brought my portfolio, I see."

"Oh, yes." She set it on his desk. "Mama said you'd be fit to be tied when you realized you'd left it behind."

"Your mother was correct. Extend my thanks to her when you return home."

"I will when I get there," Johanna said lightly, then turned to Ross again.

She was utterly breathtaking in appearance, but Ross could no longer bring himself to feel anything for her. Instead, his mind flashed upon stormy blue eyes, silky raven hair, and feminine underclothing scattered upon the floor of his parlor. He should have felt guilt, but he didn't. He felt nothing at all as Johanna linked her arm through his. "I'm on my way to the dress shop for my final fitting."

By her impish expression, he discerned that he was supposed to pick up on some undercurrent of meaning. "A final fitting?"

She laughed, obviously taking his ignorance for male obtuseness. "Why, for my wedding dress, silly."

"Oh. Of course." It suddenly felt as if live fish were swimming circles in the pit of his stomach. The sense of victory he'd experienced a few moments ago had vanished. He was a man good and well trapped in a snare of his own making.

"Why don't you take your dinner break, Ross, and

walk her to the shop? I'm sure there's much for you two to catch up on."

Malcolm's tone was flat, but full of implied meaning. Ross looked to see the man still seated behind his desk. He had relaxed back into his chair, his hands clasped around his middle in a casual pose. His hard gray eyes, though, were anything but casual. They were fixed on Ross as if seeing into his thoughts.

*I don't love your daughter.* It seemed to Ross that the truth had to be plain on his face.

*Love,* those cold gray eyes seemed to reply, *has nothing to do with it.* Ross had already pushed him. He was not a man who would take well to being crossed.

"Oh, Daddy, what a wonderful idea!" Johanna was saying. "Say you'll walk along with me, Ross. So much has happened since you've been gone. Why, I'm fairly bursting with it all."

"Go on, Ross," Malcolm said in that same flat monotone, "You've accomplished more than enough here for one morning, don't you think?"

"Fine," Ross said, tearing his gaze from Malcolm. He tried to muster a smile for Johanna's sake. "Let's go."

As he led her through the city room, he reminded himself that it wasn't Johanna's fault that he'd fallen in love with another woman. It was Emily he wanted, but after all that had gone wrong between them, would she ever be able to trust him? Unfortunately, there was only one way to learn the answer to that question. He would have to jilt Johanna and bring Malcolm Davenport's wrath down upon his head. He would have to throw his future away.

He had some hard thinking to do.

\* \* \*

"Merciful heavens, Emily, it's hard to believe it's her, isn't it?" Melissa Carpenter whispered. She leaned to one side to cast a discreet glance at the garishly dressed, disheveled blond who was puzzling her way through the latest edition of *Godey's Lady's Book* in the cluttered front parlor of Miss Beatrice Ellinger's Boardinghouse for Young Ladies. "She's changed so much, I wouldn't have recognized her. She looks so . . . so . . ."

"Old," Emily supplied, casting a pitying look over her shoulder at Stacy Bliss.

Emily had been shocked, too, when Karl had brought Stacy by the print shop that afternoon. After listening to Emily complain all morning about the injustices of the court system toward women, he'd suggested that perhaps they should try to do something about it. First, though, they needed to talk to the victim in person. Would she be willing to testify if they could pressure the police chief into bringing charges against Gibson?

Karl had taken it upon himself to seek Stacy out and had had little trouble locating her. Emily had barely been able to reconcile her memory of the fourteen-year-old farm girl of their schooldays with the brassy-looking woman who stood in the print shop. It was clear that Stacy had been leading a hard life. She was only a few years older than Emily herself, yet she looked like a worn-out woman in her thirties. The cheerful sparkle Emily remembered in this young woman's eyes had been replaced by a cynical glint that suggested the vivid bruises still marring her neck and cheekbones were not the first she'd encountered at the hands of a disgruntled "suitor."

"She says she'll testify against Gibson," Emily continued, "but we still have a problem."

"What problem is that?" Melissa asked.

Stacy wasn't the only one who had changed over the years. It was no wonder that Karl had not immediately recognized Melissa Carpenter upon running into her on the street. The redheaded duckling had transformed into a graceful swan. Having outgrown the pudginess that had marked her childhood and adolescence, the minister's daughter had thinned out everywhere except for her hips and well-developed bosom. Her high cheekbones accentuated large, long-lashed, golden brown eyes, and soft auburn curls escaped her black net snood to frame an elegant, classically beautiful face.

Knowing Melissa, however, Emily suspected that her friend remained blissfully unaware of the enhanced feminine attributes with which maturity had graced her. Having obtained her teaching certification three years before, she had surprised her family by turning down a proposal of marriage from her steady beau, Elwood Beamsdorfer, before moving into Miss Bea's Boardinghouse for Young Ladies. Since then, she had dedicated herself to her job and her volunteer work at the Home for Friendless Children.

Taking her old friend by the arm, Emily led her down a carpeted corridor to the kitchen where an enticing aroma of boiled ham and sweet apple *schnitz* wafted from a covered kettle on a cast-iron range. They had excused themselves from Stacy on the pretense of pouring some iced tea.

"We need to clean her up," Emily said, "get her settled in some decent surroundings, and find her a respectable job."

"You mean, she's not going back to . . ." Melissa reddened at the idea of Stacy's occupation. "You know what I mean."

"She told Karl that she doesn't want that kind of life anymore, but she doesn't know how to get away from it."

Melissa frowned, then moved to take three drinking glasses down from a cupboard and set them on an oak table. "Maybe she should just move away from here. People aren't likely to forget what she's done. You know that better than—" Melissa cut off, clearly horrified at her own slip. "Oh, dear. I didn't mean that how it sounded. I just meant—"

"I understand." Emily knew her friend better than that. Over the past four years, they had exchanged occasional letters and never once had Melissa referred to the rumors about Emily or asked if they were true. Instead, she'd kept her missives cheerful, writing mostly about the children she taught at school and at the home.

"You only speak the truth," Emily said. "I *do* know from experience that most people aren't quick to forget the past. Maybe you're right that it would be best for Stacy to move away eventually, but first she needs a hand up. She needs friends. Remember, she's not blessed with a family who will stand behind her in times of adversity."

Melissa let out a sympathetic sigh as she moved to the range and tested a brass teakettle to see if had cooled. "That poor girl. What a terrible shame."

Sensing that she was gaining headway, Emily pressed on. "First and foremost, she needs a place to live and a job. I'd give her a job myself except I can't afford to pay any help yet, and since it's clear that her family won't help her, that's where you come in."

Melissa turned to Emily with wide eyes. "Me?"

"Well, you and Miss Bea, that is."

"Miss Bea?"

"You mentioned at the funeral that a room would be vacant at the end of the month. One of Miss Bea's tenants was leaving to get married. Is that room still available?"

"Well, yes, but I thought at the time that you might want to move in. I'm not sure how Miss Bea will react to having a—" Melissa reddened again and turned away, quickly retrieving an ice pick and a bowl from a second cupboard. "Well, what I mean to say is, we need to maintain a certain level of propriety for the sake of the other ladies' reputations, if not for our own."

Emily waved this concern away. "Bea Ellinger has a heart bigger than the Susquehanna River. I'll bet there are ten stray cats on your back porch waiting for their dinner as we speak."

"More like a dozen," Melissa admitted.

"And what about that time she let Old Quint Stehman stay in her garden house when he was drying out from the rum?" Emily pressed. "Nobody else in town believed that man was worth a dime and now, because of Miss Bea, he's got a job at the mill and has reconciled with his grandchildren. The woman's a saint, I tell you, and she's got the spunk of twelve men to boot. She's never backed down from a fight just because of what people might think, and she won't turn Stacy away, either. Not if you tell her that Stacy wants to repent from the sordid life she's been living."

"You may be right about Miss Bea's soft heart,"

Melissa said, moving to the icebox, "but what if Stacy doesn't really mean it about wanting to change? What if she turns right back around and resumes that sordid life of hers even after Miss Bea and I decide to take a chance and help her?"

Emily had known Melissa Carpenter since they were toddlers and had never once failed to talk the pleasant-natured minister's daughter into anything Emily had set her mind on. She sensed now, however, that a coup de grace was in order.

"I was thinking the very same thing as we were on our way over here," Emily said, squelching the twinge of conscience that would have nipped this white lie in the bud, "but you know what I thought of then?"

"What?" Melissa asked as she chipped some small chunks from a block of ice in the top compartment of the cabinet.

"I thought about what the Good Book says in cases just such as this."

All at once, Melissa stopped chipping. There was no sound in the kitchen aside from the simmering kettle on the range.

Emily let out what she hoped sounded like a heartfelt and penitent sigh. "'He that is without sin among you, let him first cast a stone at her.'"

Melissa showed no signs of responding, so Emily continued, "Whether Stacy is sincere at heart, I certainly cannot know, but how many times are we called to forgive? Is it seven?"

Ice pick and bowl in hand, Melissa turned around to assess Emily. "You know, I always hate it when you quote Scripture."

Emily tried to look innocent. "I can't imagine why."

"It won't work."

"What won't work?"

"You can't make me feel guilty by quoting Scripture, and that's that."

"Good heavens, why would I want to make you feel guilty? You certainly have nothing to feel guilty about, do you?"

"I should say not."

"Well, good. That's a burden off our shoulders."

Melissa frowned hesitantly, then turned back to the icebox to finish her task. When she was done she crossed to the table and set the bowl of ice down with a clunk. For a moment, she didn't move.

Emily held her breath.

"Seventy times seven," Melissa muttered.

Emily's heart leapt. "What did you say?"

"Seventy times seven," Melissa repeated, her attention stubbornly trained on the ice bowl. "That's how many times we are called to forgive. If Miss Bea gives permission for Stacy to stay here, then maybe I can get her a job doing laundry at the Home."

Emily felt an almost overwhelming urge to embrace her dear old friend, but she managed to hold herself in check. "I just knew you would help. Miss Bea isn't the only one with a heart as big as the Susquehanna."

When Melissa raised her head, Emily was glad to see a knowing smile. "Emily Winters, I do love you, and I am happy you're finally home where you belong, but why do I get the feeling that my quiet and peaceful life is about to change?"

"Don't be silly!"

But when Melissa turned her back to retrieve the teakettle from the stove, Emily couldn't fight a sly smile of her own. Karl Becker's interest in the "new" Melissa had not escaped her notice. He had sown his wild oats in the past, but that was no drawback as far as Emily was concerned. When he was ready to settle down—and she sensed that the time was about to come—he would settle down very well for the right woman. Perhaps Melissa's life was about to change, after all.

# 20

*It was two days later* when a knock came at the print shop door. Emily looked up from her account book to the wall clock in her father's office. It was already past six P.M. Earlier that day, she'd promised her mother and Karen that she would be home for supper. She would have some explaining to do.

At a second knock, Emily set down her pen, capped her inkwell, and pushed up from her chair. She was officially closed for the day, but she would be happy to accept any customer with an order. Malcolm Davenport had lowered his rates, and it was already having an effect on her business. One look at her account books had confirmed the worst.

Despite her morning job with Karl and her family's help, she was barely making a profit. Also, she was still without credit to borrow money for more supplies. She needed hard cash to get through the next couple of months—cash she didn't have. The only thing that might save her now would be a timely increase in work orders, but that wasn't likely to happen. Not with Malcolm Davenport's ruthless price-cutting to thwart her.

When she opened the door, she found a friend instead of a customer. Leaning on his cane, Karl Becker tipped his stovepipe hat and grinned. "I thought you'd still be working, Miss Emily. I have good news. May I come in?"

"Good news?" Emily tried not to sound as defeated as she felt as she gestured for him to enter. "I hope that means you've brought some business."

"In fact, I have." He reached into his coat pocket and extracted a folded sheet of paper. "David has decided to pull all of his printing business from Denton's."

She unfolded it to see that it was a blank sheet of Mr. Stauffer's business stationery. "What's this?"

"If you can duplicate the letterhead, we can start with a five-hundred-sheet order."

Emily felt a lump rise in her throat. "Oh, Karl . . ."

"Now, don't go all maudlin on me, Miss Emily. This is just business, after all."

"But I do appreciate—"

Karl held up a hand. "I'm only the messenger. You did such fine-quality work on my business cards, he was happy to place a new order."

"Thank you," she said, adding the stationery to a stack of other orders on a nearby desk. "I'll have it ready by early next week if that will do."

"That will do just fine," he assured her, "but that's not the reason I came. I assume you saw Gallagher's article in yesterday's *Herald*?"

At his unexpected mention of Ross, Emily had to force down certain scintillating memories of that past Sunday afternoon. The mere thought made her blush like an overripe peach, and Karl was too astute to miss such a reaction. "The article about Arnold Gibson, you mean. Um, yes. Yes, I did. I was very impressed."

"Impressed?" Karl raised an eyebrow. "I was more surprised by his uncensored candor than impressed, but now that you mention it, I suppose he did make a somewhat stirring presentation."

"That's high praise coming from you." Emily turned away and headed for the job press to clean up for the night. She wasn't doing a very good job of repressing unchaste thoughts. Her cheeks were burning even as they spoke.

"Apparently Ross's article is already garnering some results. I had to speak with the chief of police on some other business this afternoon, and I mentioned it to him. He's heard from a few other people about that article, too. It seems that, after reading about the incident in the paper and seeing Stacy's injuries for themselves, Miss Bea's whole quilting circle is in a righteous flurry."

Emily was unable to repress a laugh as she soaked a rag in turpentine and set to work wiping down the inking mechanism. "Now, that surprises me. Then again, Miss Bea has been known to work miracles."

"She's apparently taken Stacy under her wing, which puts a whole new light on the subject. With upstanding citizens like Miss Bea and Melissa Carpenter seeing to her welfare, not to mention Gallagher's article, Stacy's case now has all the makings of a soul-stirring social cause for the church ladies. What's come out of all this is that the chief asked me to bring Stacy down to speak to him a couple of hours ago. He's ready to press charges against

Gibson. If all goes smoothly, he'll appear before Alderman Chase tomorrow morning."

Upon hearing this, the glimmer of an outrageous idea formed in the back of Emily's mind. Perhaps the timing of Arnold Gibson's court appearance could work to her advantage. Then again, she could be grasping at straws. "Tomorrow morning, you say?"

"Yes. After escorting Stacy and Miss Carpenter home myself, I couldn't resist coming by to share the good news with you."

"I'm glad you did. I needed some good news about now."

"Why? Things not going well?"

Emily shrugged as she removed the last traces of ink from her equipment. She didn't want to get onto the depressing subject of her business troubles. "Nothing that I can't take care of myself."

"Say, do you need any help with that? You look busy. Have you had supper yet?"

She laughed. "No, you'll get your clothes dirty. Yes, I am busy, and no, I haven't had supper yet." She dropped her soiled cleaning rag into an empty coffee tin at her feet and began removing the metal chase from the bed of the press. "I was just about ready to clean up and head home when you knocked."

"Then perhaps we can grab a bite at the Railroad Eating House. There's another matter I'd like to discuss with you."

"Oh? Sounds mysterious. Don't keep me on pins and needles."

"Well, it's about Miss . . . uh, Melissa Carpenter."

"Melissa? How is she?"

"She appears to be quite well."

"What's on your mind?"

"I asked her to go riding with me this weekend."

Emily smiled to herself as she carried the chase over to a table. "And what did she say?"

"She said no."

"Hmm." Emily worked quickly to disassemble the metal frame and reveal the pages she'd set and printed earlier.

"She said she was far too busy with her work to be pointlessly gallivanting around town."

"Oh."

"Does she have a beau?" Karl blurted.

"Not at the moment."

"Well, then, it doesn't make sense."

"What doesn't make sense?"

"That she declined my offer. What could she possibly be thinking?"

Emily rolled her eyes at Karl's high opinion of his masculine charm. "Perhaps she's not interested in being trifled with."

"Trifled with?" He sounded surprised. "What's that supposed to mean?"

Emily took a font case from one of the composing desks and moved back to the worktable. "Your reputation is . . . how shall I say it? Slightly blemished from an overabundance of frivolity when it comes to women?"

"It is?"

"Yes."

"Oh. Well, what do you think I should do about Melissa?"

Emily's fingers moved swiftly to replace the used type, plucking and dropping each letter, space marker, and symbol into its proper compartment.

"What have you done when this sort of thing has happened in the past?"

"What sort of thing?"

"When a woman said no to you."

"No woman ever has."

She stopped and stared at him. "What do you mean, 'no woman ever has'?"

Karl shrugged. "Just what I said. No woman has ever said no to me."

"That's preposterous."

"It's the truth."

Emily studied him critically before returning to her task. He was going to need more work than she'd thought. "Well, all right, then. Use your imagination. What do you think you would have done if a woman ever *had* said no?"

"I imagine I would have cut my losses and moved on to the next one."

"The next woman who caught your fancy?"

"Yes."

"Well, then, why not try that?"

"But I—" He paused and Emily sensed him stewing for a moment before he finished. "Well, I don't think I want to move on just yet."

"I see." She let him stew a little more before offering a new solution. "Well, if you're determined to win Melissa, perhaps you should leave off with your usual sweet talk or whatever it is you do, and instead go straight to the heart of the matter."

"Which is?"

Emily looked to see that Karl was bent forward, waiting intently for her answer. "Show her that you've changed, that you've become responsible and dependable."

He just stared at her.

"Show her that you're serious," Emily clarified.

"Serious?"

"You *are* serious, aren't you?"

"Well . . . yes," he said, straightening with a thoughtful frown. "I suppose so. Why wouldn't I be?"

"Indeed?" she asked back. "Perhaps you should consider volunteering at the Home for Friendless Children. I'm sure they could use your legal advice with adoptions. That might convince Melissa that you've left the irresponsibility of youth behind."

Before Karl could reply, there came another knock at the front door. He cocked his head and arched an eyebrow. "Busy at this time of the evening, aren't you?"

"Not normally, but I'll take any business I can get. Could you see who it is? Tell them I'll be with them in a second. I've got my hands full of turpentine and ink."

"My pleasure."

As Karl went for the door, Emily crossed to the back of the shop and disappeared around the corner of a storage cabinet. Pausing over the washstand, she poured some fresh water into the porcelain basin, then began scrubbing at her stained fingers with a bar of soap. Upon hearing Karl greet her latest visitor, however, she froze in midstroke.

"Well, well, speak of the devil. Mr. Gallagher himself."

Oh, no, Emily thought. She couldn't bear to face him. Not after what had happened Sunday.

"What the hell are you doing here?" she heard Ross demand indignantly.

"I might ask the same of you, Gallagher," Karl

replied. "I know for a fact that you're supposed to be engaged to the other one, but you just keep insisting on buzzing around *this* one."

Losing track of the exchange, Emily squeezed her eyes shut and willed her galloping heart to slow. As was its habit of late, however, her body paid no heed whatsoever to her mind's commands. Her face was growing so hot, it felt as if she'd taken fever, and her hands were shaking. Damn Ross Gallagher. What did he want now? He'd told her that he didn't love Johanna, yet she had heard that he'd turned up at the Fulton House with the Davenport family just last night. Either he'd lied to her or he felt that love had little to do with marriage. Either way, Emily was furious with him. He was playing her for a fool. Even worse, she was furious with herself for losing all common sense and succumbing to temptation a second time. Good Lord, she could barely think.

". . . a word with her in private, if you don't mind," Ross was saying. The tension in his voice suggested that Karl was about sixty seconds away from having his nose broken again.

"Why, I don't mind at all," Karl said flippantly, "but I'm not the one to ask." He raised his voice. "Miss Emily? Gallagher claims he wants a word with you in private. I told him that we're on our way to supper and that if he wishes to confer with you, perhaps he should endeavor to come by during normal business hours. What do you think of that?"

Knowing that she either had to face Ross or flee rabbitlike out the back door, Emily wetted a clean towel and pressed it to her cheeks. "I'll be there in a moment."

After tucking away some stray hairs, she removed

her apron, smoothed her skirt, and told herself to be calm. A moment later, she was stepping out from behind the cabinet. She rolled down her dress sleeves in a casual manner and wore what she hoped was a serene and unruffled expression. "Good evening, Ross."

Ross stood just inside the front door, glowering at Karl and carrying a parcel wrapped in newsprint and twine in one hand. The instant his gaze shifted to her, however, Emily felt another blush creep over her cheeks. She spoke quickly to squelch it. "What brings you by after hours?"

"I have something for you." He shot another glare at Karl. "But I wasn't planning on an audience."

Karl merely smiled and touched the brim of his hat. "I can wait for you outside, Miss Emily." He paused significantly. "If that's what you want?"

That was not what she wanted, but she'd have to face Ross some time. Better now in private than accidentally on the street with Johanna on his arm. "That will be fine, Karl. Thank you."

Ross waited for the door to close behind Karl before he turned back to Emily. His tawny brown hair was combed back, but, as always, stubborn wisps had broken free to fall over his forehead. The cut of his jaw was squared, the shape of his handsome mouth distressingly reminiscent of sensual delights. He had no business looking so darned good to her at the end of a workday.

"It appears that the police will be pressing charges against Arnold Gibson," he said.

"I heard."

Emily knew he hadn't come by just to tell her about Gibson's troubles, so she folded her arms and waited until he spoke again.

"I have a favor to ask."

"Oh?"

He held out the wrapped parcel. "This is the first half of my manuscript."

Emily stared at the parcel. Even when they were children, Ross had never allowed anyone, not even her, to read his work before he deemed it finished. "I don't understand."

"I want you to illustrate for me."

Emily was left without words. Why was he coming to her with this now? Then, she remembered another parcel wrapped in newsprint, one with a blue ribbon tied around it. A box of soft French pastel crayons and a card that read, *It's lonely by the creek these days. I miss you. Can I have my illustrator back?* Guilt. Ross felt guilty about what had happened in his parlor, and this was his way of smoothing things over. Well, it wouldn't work. Not this time. "Perhaps you should seek a professional artist."

"I don't want a professional. I want you."

"I don't have the training. I doubt I could do it justice."

"On the contrary," he said, taking a step toward her. "You're the only one I know who could do it justice. I don't care about formal training. No one will see this book the way you'll see it. When we were kids, you could always read beyond the words I'd put on paper. You could envision exactly what I imagined."

For one terrible moment, Emily wavered. There was truth in what he said, but he was also very clever at using their past to play on her emotions—emotions that now pulled her in two directions. She understood his need to salvage whatever they could of their damaged relationship. In fact, she shared that need. Childhood bonds such as theirs were not easily severed. Never mind that she couldn't make him love her the way she wanted him to, she could hardly bear to imagine going through life without his friendship. During her time spent volunteering at the soldier's hospital in Baltimore, she had seen the tragic results of countless amputations. Arms. Legs. Vital parts. But no part as vital as a heart.

"I know what you're trying to do," she said, "and it's not going to work."

"What's not going to work?" Ross took another step toward her, and Emily felt the urge to step back, but she resisted it. "What do you think I'm trying to do?" he asked.

"You're trying to make up for . . . for what happened the other day, but it's not necessary."

"What are you saying?"

"I'm saying, it was a mistake. People make mistakes all the time. We're perfect examples of that. We made the same mistake twice, but it won't happen again."

"It didn't feel like a mistake to me."

"Johanna might not agree."

"I told you, I don't love Johanna. I'm *not* going to marry her."

"Oh? Does that mean you've broken your engagement?"

Ross was caught short. She'd maneuvered him right into a corner, and he felt like punching a wall. No, he hadn't broken his engagement. Despite his efforts to get Johanna alone, he'd been circumvented at every turn. The day before last, as he'd walked her to the dress shop, she had been so gushing and happy about preparations for the wedding, he hadn't found the heart to tell her the truth right there on the street. Later, he'd gotten tied up at the newspaper office until nine o'clock. Last evening, he'd fully intended to get it over with, but was chagrined to discover upon arriving on her doorstep that Mrs. Davenport had planned for all of them to go to the theater. He couldn't end his engagement while in public and in the company of Johanna's parents as well as two prominent businessmen and their wives.

"No, I haven't broken my engagement," he admitted. "Not yet, but I'm going to."

"When? At the altar?"

The anger in those stormy blue eyes was lethal, but Ross was feeling a bit short-tempered, too. He'd finally been able to talk himself into believing that his jealousy over Karl was ill-founded, only to come face to face with him upon arriving here tonight. Not only was Emily working for Karl every morning, now they were spending time alone after hours and planning to share meals in public.

"If I say I'm going to break the engagement, I'm going to break the engagement," he said through set teeth, "but maybe you should explain exactly what's going on with you and Karl."

Emily's eyes narrowed as if trying to read his mind, then she shook her head and jabbed a finger at him. "Oh, no you don't. You can't change the subject. I'm not going to answer that."

"Fine," he said, slapping his manuscript down onto a table. "Don't answer it!"

"No!" Dashing to the table, she snatched the parcel and shoved it at him. "Don't leave it. I can't illustrate for you."

"Why?"

"Because we can't see each other any more. We can't be lovers and we can't be friends. We can't even speak on the street. Otherwise, it hurts too much. It gets too complicated. For both of our sakes, there has to be a clean end to it."

Ross didn't move. She'd said a lot of things in the heat of anger before, but she'd never said anything like that. "You don't mean it."

"Yes." Again, she shoved the manuscript at him. "Yes, I do. Take it."

He looked down to see that her hands were shaking. Whether she meant what she said or not he wasn't sure, but right now, it was obvious that she believed it. Cautiously, he spoke. "Too complicated, you said. A long time ago, we promised to stick by each other forever. Not just until things got complicated. We were only kids then, but I thought you meant it. Maybe it would have been easier for you if I'd stayed dead. If I hadn't come back at all."

At his harsh words, her face paled. "How can you say such a terrible thing?"

"Promises are easy to keep when we're kids and things are going smoothly. It's when we grow up and things begin to get a little complicated that it really counts."

She stared at him.

He took a step back, preparing to leave. "Just do this one thing for me, Em. Read it. Then if you still don't think you can illustrate for me, I won't ask anything else of you again."

Ross didn't give her another chance to protest. Instead, he turned and left the shop. When he closed the door behind him, though, he had to stop to get his bearings. He could feel his heart knocking in his chest like he'd just finished a hundred yard sprint.

For the briefest of seconds, he'd seen in her eyes what he'd hoped to see—that she still cared for him—but it was a mixed blessing. Emily never did anything halfway. When she believed in something, she believed one hundred percent. If she fought, she fought hard; if she loved, she loved forever. Yet that sort of single-minded commitment was fraught with risks. If she was hurt, the wound cut deep. Convincing her that he could be trusted not to hurt her again wouldn't be easy. It had been a mistake to come here before he'd had a chance to end his relationship with Johanna.

"Judging by the look on your face, I assume you two haven't managed to settle anything."

Ross had forgotten about Karl. He stood less than five feet away, leaning back against the brick front. He appeared to be observing the traffic on the street as he cupped his hand to light a cigar.

"And I suppose that's just fine with you," Ross said.

Karl's tone was matter-of-fact. "Not at all. Your concern that I'm stealing away your woman is ridiculous. It's ridiculous now, and it was ridiculous all those years ago. She's always been yours, even if you were too busy chasing after Johanna Davenport to see it."

"I never said I thought you were stealing her."

"No, you didn't, but it's as plain as the nose on your face." Karl gave him a smirk. "Or perhaps I should rephrase that to say it's as plain as the nose on *my* face."

For a long moment, Ross eyed the telltale bump

that marred Karl's profile. His anger with his boyhood friend had been misplaced from the beginning, and deep down, he'd known that all along. "I suppose I should say I'm sorry."

"That would be a good start."

Ross walked over to lean back against the building next to Karl. He shoved his hands into his trouser pockets and let out a rueful sigh. "I never should have hit you."

Karl blew a frothy smoke ring. "Agreed."

"I've been acting like a jackass."

"Double agreed. Would you care for a smoke?"

"No, thanks. I'm on my way to see Johanna."

"She's not a good match for you, old pal. She may be delicious to look at, enough to get any man's pecker up, but marriage . . . that's going a bit far, if you ask me."

"Boy, do I know it, but it seemed like the right thing to do a few months ago."

"Before Emily came back to town, you mean."

"Yes. Now, I can't think of anything worse. How did I get myself into such a mess?"

"Sex."

Ross frowned.

"Not sex?" Karl asked when he didn't reply.

"To be honest," Ross said, "I was trying to be practical."

"Practical? Are you sure it wasn't sex?"

Ross thought about his surprising lack of reaction when he'd kissed Johanna during their picnic. "Yeah, I'm sure, but that's beside the point. I've recently come to the conclusion that there's more to all this man-woman stuff than a good roll in the hay anyway."

"Really? Are you positive?"

Ross let out a dry laugh. "You just wait, old pal of mine. One of these days, you'll wake up to find that some woman has gotten ahold of your heart so tight, you won't be able to think straight. You won't be able to eat. You won't be able to sleep. It'll be pure hell."

Karl squinted at him doubtfully, then shook his head and took a puff from his cigar. "It sounds like pure hell, but it'll never happen."

"We'll see," Ross said, taking his hands from his pockets and straightening.

"Where are you going?"

Ross felt satisfied that he had finally taken care of unfinished business with his friend. Now, though, he had much more unpleasant business to take care of.

"I'm going to see Johanna," he said. "Wish me luck."

# 21

*Ross's confrontation with Johanna* went even worse than he anticipated. It was clear by her surprised expression when she came to the door that she hadn't been expecting him, but she recovered quickly, donning her brightest smile and society-hostess manners.

Her poise and etiquette were probably the most valuable skills she'd learned from her otherwise ineffectual mother, Ross thought as he led her to the front porch swing. That poise, however, utterly disintegrated when he told her he wanted to break their engagement.

"No," she gasped, "I just can't believe it. I won't!"

"Johanna, I'm sorry," he said. And he meant it as he placed a hand on her arm. "I honestly believed that our getting married was the right thing to do, but I see now that we don't belong together. We never did."

"No!" she repeated, yanking her arm away. "This simply cannot be! The wedding is little more than a week away! Do you know how many people we've invited? I'll be humiliated!"

"It's better to break off now than to find out later that we made a mistake."

Johanna shot up from the porch swing. Even though she had not been expecting company, she wore an elaborate yellow dress trimmed with purple ribbon. It was a frock Ross didn't remember seeing before. He watched the hem of her hoopskirt bob angrily as she paced the length of the wooden porch.

"I simply won't have it! I won't!" She stamped her foot, then whipped around to pin him with a savage glare. "It's another woman, isn't it? Isn't it?"

Ross almost denied it, then stopped. Now was not the time to embark on a whole new run of lies. "Yes," he said carefully, "but she's not the reason you and I don't belong together."

"Pah! Not the reason? How can you sit there and tell me that you've been consorting with another woman and that she isn't the reason you're breaking off our engagement? That's the most ludicrous—"

Ross stood. "If you'd listen to yourself, you would realize exactly why we don't belong together. You're more concerned about being embarrassed than you are about ending our relationship. You're not in love with me any more than I'm in love with you."

"Love?" She stared at him as if he'd lost his senses. "What's love? Something silly that wears off in six months, that's what! Love isn't the reason people get married, people get married to make good matches! They get married to have well-bred children! They get married to secure a good future!"

"I used to think that, too," Ross said, "but I've changed my mind."

"Because of that trollop!" Johanna strode the short distance between them to face him. "You fool! You're throwing away your future because of some dirty little—"

"That's enough, Johanna." Out of the corner of his eye, Ross saw a parlor curtain flutter from behind a closed window. Either the maid or Johanna's mother had apparently sensed trouble in paradise, but he knew neither would be bold enough to intrude. As for Malcolm, he wasn't home. That was just as well. Ross preferred to deal with him separately.

"Who is she?" Johanna demanded.

"That's not important."

Her lower lip quivered. "You unspeakable cad."

"You have a right to be angry," he began, "but after you've had a chance to calm down and think about it—"

He saw her move, maybe even in time to stop what was coming, but he didn't try. He absorbed the sting of her slap with thinly held restraint.

By now, her features were contorted with rage, and Ross thought that if his adolescent fantasies of her hadn't been dashed before this, they surely would have been now. "After all I've done for you! And now this! Papa was right about you from the beginning, but I wouldn't believe him. When you came back from the war, I told him you'd changed. I told him about the articles you published. It was me who got you your job at the paper. Me! If it weren't for me, you'd still be nothing but a—"

"A low-class Irish hack?"

She drew back, looking horrified. "I never said any such thing!"

"No, but you were thinking it. You've always thought it. Why don't you do us both a service and consider yourself excused from doing me any more favors?" He turned to leave, glad to be done with the biggest mistake of his life, but she caught him by the sleeve.

"Wait! Ross, you don't understand. Wait. Please."

Just that fast, her tone had gone from bitching shrill to soft and pleading. Reluctantly, he paused.

"Is it . . . is it because we haven't—" She cut off and began again. "Has that woman allowed you intimate favors? Is that how she lured you away from me? Because if it is, our waiting will soon be over. I only wanted our coming together to be special."

Ross looked back at her. "No, Johanna, it's not that."

Her expression had undergone a drastic change to match her manner. Vanished was the shrew, and in her place was the heartbroken fiancée. Her round blue eyes were wide and shimmering with welling tears. "But I love you, Ross. We'll have beautiful children together."

"No," Ross said. She'd changed tactics so quickly and deftly, he was amazed. It was a formidable skill, one she'd no doubt developed while trying to manipulate her tough-as-nails father all these years. But part of her ploy was working. Ross felt new pangs of guilt that kept his feet planted where they were. He doubted that Johanna had any idea what real love was, and that made him feel sorry for her.

She stared up at him for a long moment, absorbing his blunt rejection. He thought she might burst into tears, but then those shimmering blue eyes turned cold once again. "It's Emily Winters."

"Leave Emily out of this." He realized he had spoken too quickly and cursed himself for being so transparent.

"It *is* her, isn't it? I knew it! You haven't been the same since she came back home!"

Her hand moved again, but this time Ross caught her wrist a split second before she could make contact. "Sorry, Johanna. You only get one shot."

"You fornicating liar," she said from between clenched teeth. "If you marry that hussy, I'll sue for breach of promise, and, as for her, I'll—"

"You'll do nothing." He'd had all he was going to take. She had a right to be angry with him, to hate him, perhaps, but Emily was another matter.

Lowering his voice, he leaned in so close they were nose to nose. "As it stands now, you can say anything you want about our broken engagement. You can tell your friends that you were the one to change your mind. That should save you heaps of embarrassment, and I won't say anything to contradict it, but if I hear one nasty rumor about Emily . . ." He paused, not needing to finish his threat to expose the truth, that he had indeed broken off with her in favor of another woman. He knew that Johanna's vanity would make it difficult for her to publicly admit such a thing, much less bring a messy legal action against him. "Do you understand?"

Her lips thinned and her eyes narrowed. She yanked free from his grasp. "Yes! But you'll regret this."

Oh, she was sorely wrong about that. Ross turned his back on her for the last time.

"When my father finds out what you've done, you'll never get a decent job in this town again! Do you hear me? You'll regret the day they ever let you out of that rotten prison!"

Dusk was falling as Ross slammed the Davenports'

iron gate closed behind him. He didn't reply to Johanna's enraged threats. He was well aware of the consequences for his actions this evening. Tomorrow he would face Malcolm.

As the clock on the parlor mantel chimed midnight, Emily finally laid Ross's manuscript on the lamp table. Her eyes burned and her neck ached. She should have been in bed long ago—she had big plans for tomorrow—but she hadn't been able to put Ross's manuscript down until now.

The novel revolved around Andrew Flannery, a twenty-two-year-old private in the Fiftieth Pennsylvania regiment, and his sidekick from home, Gregory Lewis. Flannery's name and rank came from Ross's imagination, and Emily wasn't sure about Lewis, but she sensed that the rest was real. Andrew Flannery was Ross. Some other names might have been changed, too, but the events must have taken place in one form or another.

The writing was vivid, much too vivid for Emily to remain detached as she read. She saw what Flannery saw: starving men skirmishing over bits of tainted meat; panicked teenage guards shooting men who crossed the "dead line" for nothing more than a taste of clean water; renegade prisoners murdering bewildered newcomers for their scanty possessions. She envisioned the frightening Captain Wirz, the one they called the Flying Dutchman. He rode a pale horse and presided over the filthy prison stockade like the Grim Reaper personified.

But even as Emily smelled the death and disease and tasted the poisoned water that killed thousands, in those pages she found hope, too. Few of the men would leave their wretched conditions when the enemy came recruiting, and there were always plans in the making for escape. When Flannery closed his eyes at night, he comforted himself with memories of home, particularly childhood memories of times spent playing by a creek in the woods with Lewis and Lewis's younger sister, Eleanor.

Eleanor.

Emily frowned. With the exception of the fictional Lewis, Flannery's memories bore a striking resemblance to . . .

"Oh, good heavens. Look at you, still awake at this hour." Wearing a white cotton nightdress and nightcap, Marguerite stood in the doorway of the parlor holding a bedroom candlestick.

"I'm sorry. Did my light wake you?"

"No," her mother said, entering and setting the candleholder down on the lamp table next to Emily. "I had a frightening dream in which my daughter was working herself to a frazzle. That's what awakened me. Now I see it wasn't a dream, after all."

"I was just getting ready to come to bed."

"Of course you were," Marguerite said doubtfully as she took a seat opposite her. She nodded to the manuscript. "Is that what's been keeping you awake half the night?"

"It's Ross Gallagher's novel."

"Oh?"

"It's about his prison experiences. It's very good."

"Well, I'm not surprised. Your father always said he was a talented writer."

At the mention of her father, Emily couldn't help a twinge of guilt. "Ross asked me to illustrate for him."

Marguerite raised an eyebrow. "Did he, now?"

Emily frowned, wary of the knowing expression on her mother's face. "Well, I'm not going to do it."

"Indeed? And why not?"

"Well, because . . . because I can't. He's marrying Johanna Davenport and—well, I just don't have the time."

"Hmm. I see your point. Not having the time, I mean. As for Johanna, I'll believe that when I see it."

Emily cursed the part of her that wouldn't allow this cryptic comment to pass. It was the same part that had held out hope Ross would break off his engagement after what had happened in his parlor. "Why do you say that?" she asked. "Their wedding is the Saturday after next, and if what I've heard is correct, half the town is invited."

"Call it motherly intuition."

"I would, except you're not Ross's mother."

Marguerite smiled. "True, but I'm yours."

"That hardly answers the question."

Marguerite's smile faded. She seemed to search Emily's face for something before speaking again. "Have you had a chance to tell him about the baby?"

Emily was stunned by the question. It wasn't only that they'd managed to tiptoe around the subject for years now, but there was something in her mother's dead-on, level expression that intimated she knew full well that Ross had fathered Emily's child. But how could she know? Unless Karen had divulged her secret, but that was unlikely. Karen had never gone back on a promise before.

"Why . . . why would I—" Emily had to swallow hard to get the words out. "Why would I tell him such a thing?"

"Well, the child was his, wasn't it?"

Emily tried to take a deep breath, but it suddenly felt as if a brick had lodged in her chest. She wiped sweating palms on her skirt. "How did you know?"

"I didn't. Not for certain. But I suspected from the beginning."

"Oh, dear," Emily muttered, closing her eyes. All at once, she felt a little dizzy. "Did you tell Papa?"

"No, I did not tell Papa."

Emily forced her eyes open to face her mother. "But why not? He was so angry when I wouldn't tell him."

"Yes, he was, but it wasn't my place to speak up. You needed to make that decision for yourself."

Emily couldn't help but remember how shocked and angry her father had been when he'd learned his youngest daughter was expecting a child. When he'd demanded that she tell him who the boy was, she had refused, stating only that it was not Karl Becker. In truth, she hadn't intended to blurt out even that much, but her father had been in such an agitated state she feared he might go after poor Karl and force him to the altar. Now, she shuddered at the memory. The whole household had been in an uproar. What a dreadful time that had been.

"I couldn't tell him about Ross," she explained. "He wouldn't have understood."

"Perhaps not. At least, not then."

"And now he's gone." Something stuck in Emily's throat so that tears threatened at the corners of her eyes. She blinked them back. "It's too late, and he never forgave me, did he?"

At this, Marguerite frowned. She rose from her seat to sit next to Emily on the sofa. "Perhaps it's too late to tell him about Ross, my dear, but you mustn't think that he never forgave you for making a mistake. Why, nothing could be further from the truth. Good heavens, you haven't been laboring under that ridiculous misapprehension all this time, have you?"

In fact, she had. Because she knew it was true. During the four years that she had lived with her aunt Essie, Marguerite had come to visit a number of times, and Karen had sometimes come along. Nathaniel, however, had accompanied her only three times. They were awkward visits, too, with Marguerite and her sister Essie keeping up the small talk while both Emily and Nathaniel had perched like two stiff, uncomfortable bumps at opposite ends of the dining table.

When Emily didn't reply, Marguerite put an arm around her shoulders and hugged her tightly. "Of course he forgave you. He loved you. You were his special little girl, didn't you know that?"

Emily stared down at her lap. "But he never said—"

"No, I don't suppose that he did." Straightening, Marguerite took Emily by the chin and forced her to look up. "I thought you knew him better than that. Your father was a wizard with words when it came to expressing his political views in print, but I'm afraid he fell drastically short when it came to personal matters. How many times do you remember him telling you that he loved you while you were growing up?"

Emily blinked. Her vision was still blurry from pent-up tears, and, looking into her mother's dry-eyed, patiently lecturing expression, she suddenly felt all of ten years old. "I can't—I don't remember," she began, but then she started to really think back. "Never?"

"And so what did you make of that?"

"I don't understand."

"Perhaps you thought he didn't care for you at all."

"No!" Emily was insulted that her mother would even say such a thing. "Of course he cared! Why else would he have let me hang around the print shop all those years? Why would he have shown me how to run the presses and write copy and carve illustrations and—" She stopped.

With a little nod, Marguerite let go of Emily's chin and folded her hands in her lap. "And why else would he have been so upset when he learned that his little girl was suddenly a woman and facing a situation no woman should have to face alone? Why would he have felt so angry and frustrated and helpless when his little girl refused to confide in him? Why do you suppose that was, Emily Elizabeth?"

"Because he loved me."

"Yes, and because he loved you, he wanted to make things all better. By grabbing some boy by the scruff of the neck and marching him down the aisle, he would have been able to do that, but you wouldn't let him, would you?"

Emily pursed her lips and frowned. "It wouldn't have fixed anything."

Marguerite gave a little shrug that indicated she didn't necessarily agree. "All that's in the past. The point is, your father loved you and he forgave you, even if he never did quite figure out how to deal with the willful woman you grew up to be. Perhaps the two of you were just too much alike." She stood and adjusted her nightcap. "Mule-headed."

Emily's spine stiffened. "Why does everyone call me that? I am *not* mule-headed."

"Oh, of course not. That's why you're so bound and determined to keep that blasted print business going. Believe me, your father, wherever he may be at this moment, is tickled pink over the whole idea."

"Darn right. That's because it's a *good* idea."

Marguerite laughed as she reached for her bedroom candle. "What was that military saying you mentioned Karl Becker was so fond of? Full steam in the sails and . . . ?"

"Damn the torpedoes, full steam ahead," Emily supplied. Amazing, but she now felt rejuvenated, not tired at all. "I believe he was quoting Vice Admiral Farragut."

"Oh, yes." Marguerite moved to the doorway and paused. "Your father would have liked that one, don't you think?" She gave a conspiratorial wink before disappearing into the darkened hallway. "Do get some sleep, dear. We've got a big day tomorrow."

# 22

*The sky was clear,* the fields a deep green. A soft summer breeze ruffled the cornstalks, offsetting the growing heat of a new morning. A fine day to get the boot, Ross thought as he reached the edge of town. He felt light on his feet today, which was miraculous, considering he still had Malcolm to face. Then Emily.

He figured he was as prepared as he would ever be to face Malcolm Davenport; it was Emily he was unsure of. He worried that his decision to end his engagement and his career at the *Herald* might have come too late.

Offering Emily his manuscript had been a last-ditch effort to appeal to her emotions. It was a low blow, but if it affected her the way he hoped, then the hell with playing fair. Besides, he hadn't lied. He did want her to illustrate that book. It was a part of him, and she was the only one who had ever been able to see into his heart.

When he came within sight of Centre Square, he saw that the sidewalks seemed more crowded than usual for a weekday morning. Was there something happening that he'd forgotten?

A disgruntled group of bearded, broad-bellied tradesmen and a sizable group of well-dressed women stood in front of the city hall building. Hand-painted placards mounted on wooden stakes waved above the women's heads. JUSTICE FOR OUR DOWNTRODDEN SISTER! proclaimed one facing in Ross's direction.

The militant sign-bearer was Miss Beatrice Ellinger, a petite, bespectacled boardinghouse proprietress well known to possess the temperament of a bulldog once she latched onto a devout cause. Ross thought that the lively little spinster had to be almost seventy by now. Many of the others he recognized to be active Episcopal churchwomen. And could that be the shy, soft-spoken Melissa Carpenter who stood with her chin tilted at such a determined angle by Miss Bea's side?

Oddly enough, these two core groups—the ill-humored, cigar-chomping men and the irate, fire-eyed church ladies—appeared to be engaged in a shouting match. It was no wonder that they had already attracted a crowd of curious onlookers.

"You ought to be ashamed of yourselves! Respectable women marching about in public like a bunch of rabble-rousing suffragists!" shouted a man Ross didn't recognize. "Get you home where you belong!"

"Respectable women do not turn their eyes away from the wrongs of this world!" returned a hefty-bosomed, middle-aged lady in a huge feathered hat. "If we are to be the keepers of morals in this society, then it is our duty to ferret out injustice and expose it for the world to see!"

Ross approached the gathering nearest the ladies to see Karl Becker leaning on his cane. His attention seemed fixed on the proceedings. Judging by the broad grin on his face, he found the unfolding events immensely amusing.

Elbowing his way through the crowd, Ross nudged him. "What's going on?"

Karl glanced over his shoulder. "Oh, it's you. For a newspaperman, you're certainly behind on current events, aren't you, Rossy?"

"It's a little early in the morning for your sarcasm, Karl."

He chuckled. "Gibson's hearing started fifteen minutes ago. I was going to attend, but then the ladies showed up with their signs. That only added fuel to the fire."

"What fire?"

"Oh, you missed that, too." Karl handed him a folded handbill. "That little woman of yours is a real firebrand."

Ross unfolded the handbill and saw what Karl meant. In bold letters across the top was printed: *Local Woman Beaten. Villain Walks Free. Is this Justice?*

"Oh, hell," Ross muttered as he scanned the words that followed. It was a scathing editorial blasting the injustices of the court system with regard to women's rights. The author felt that when females finally won the vote and could sit on juries, such vulgar inequities would begin to be addressed.

Firebrand was right. Even though the editorial was officially unsigned, it was obvious who was behind it. Emily must have had a full head of steam when she'd penned this one, but not so much that she'd lost sight of a business opportunity. Near the bottom of the handbill she'd inserted a flamboyant advertisement: *Job Printing Done in the Highest Style of the Art!*

In honor of the grand reopening of the Winters Print Shop, the ad said, the first twenty customers would receive a twenty-five percent discount. Ross suspected that twenty-five percent off a sizable print order just might make even the most politically conservative businessman think twice before turning down her offer.

"Where is she?" Ross asked, surveying the group of women. His protective instincts were stirred. He believed in Emily's right to speak out, but he certainly didn't intend to stand by and allow her to be verbally attacked in public.

"She distributed about a hundred of those things, then went inside with Stacy for Gibson's hearing," Karl responded, not shifting his attention from the women. He paused, then shook his head in wonderment. "Damn, but she's magnificent, isn't she?"

"Sure she is," Ross said. "Who else would have the harebrained gumption to write such a thing, then attach an advertisement to stir up business?"

"Not Emily. Melissa."

"Who?"

Karl pointed. "Melissa Carpenter. Look at her! She's right in the thick of it. Why, who would have ever suspected such a lovely, peaceful creature to be full of such fire and passion? By George, I love a woman with fire and passion, don't you?"

Before Ross could respond, a beefy man in shirtsleeves shook a fist and bellowed over the grumblings of his comrades. Ross recognized him as Charles McMinn, owner of a tavern near the cotton mill.

Charlie and Miss Bea were old antagonists. Miss Bea's active involvement in various temperance societies had pitted them head-to-head on many occasions.

"The laws are designed to protect the fair and weak among us!" shouted Charlie. "Not to condone the shameless behavior of trollops!"

"Shame on *you*, Mr. McMinn!" Miss Bea jabbed a bony finger at him. Her piercing voice rose so that it carried clear across the street and then some. "Shame, shame, thou hypocrite! Thou dispenser of spirits! First cast the beam out of thine own eye and then shalt thou see clearly to cast the mote out of thy sister's eye!"

"Beatrice Ellinger, don't you be spewin' Bible talk at me, you dried-up old bat!"

Miss Bea's icy blue eyes sparked as she moved forward to address her attacker. She brandished her placard like a medieval war weapon. "Why, you crusty old drunken coot! I oughta—"

Melissa snagged her elbow in the nick of time. "Miss Bea! Remember our mission! We are soldiers of the Lord!"

The older woman's wrinkled cheeks flushed scarlet. It was clear that she was still as furious as a bee trapped in a bottle, but she halted her advance. "Onward, Christian soldiers!" she shrilled, then began leading her little group in a march around the square.

"We might have a little bit too much fire and passion today," Ross observed dryly. He held up Emily's handbill. "Do you mind if I keep this?"

"Not at all. You going to do a story on it?"

"Not in the *Herald*, I'm not."

"What's that supposed to mean?"

"I'll explain later." Ross slipped the sheet of paper into his coat pocket as he turned away. "I've got to go."

As the shouting in front of city hall had grown more pronounced, so too the throng of curiosity-seekers had thickened. As Ross negotiated his way through the crowd, he took notice that many were passing around the already notorious handbill and commenting upon its contents. Surprisingly enough, not everyone seemed to find it offensive. Many of the men were plainly amused by Emily's ideas concerning petticoat government, and he even caught a few references to the late Nathaniel Winters's infamous penchant for playing devil's advocate.

Ross pulled open the door to the Davenport building and nodded to two clerks who had been observing the city hall fiasco from the front window. Their shocked expressions upon seeing him spoke volumes. The news of his broken engagement had already spread.

When he entered the city room, the copyboys were busy and most of the reporters were already at their desks.

"What? Gee whillikins! Mr. Gallagher! What are you doing here?"

"Good morning, Iggy." Ross spared the slack-jawed youth a smile in passing. "How's your mother?"

"My ma? Uh, my ma's just fine . . . "

"Morning, Virge," Ross said as he approached his own desk.

A grizzled Virgil Davis sat at his neighboring desk, pen held frozen in midstroke. "Ross, what the hell are you—I mean, we didn't expect—"

"Quite a spectacle taking place across the street," Ross commented, "I hope someone is covering it." A quick scan of his desktop revealed that it was conspicuously empty of Associated Press telegraph sheets, a sure sign that something was amiss. His first priority each morning was to go through the national news dispatches and assign write-ups.

Pulling open his top drawer, Ross located his favorite pen and a pair of cuff links. Slipping both into his side pocket, he moved on to a side drawer to find a fresh shirt collar, a folded handkerchief and a half-full drugstore bottle labeled *Swayne's Compound of Wild Cherry*, a sore throat remedy Iggy's mother had recommended. So much for personal effects. Perhaps he had never settled in here as comfortably as he'd once believed.

*"Gallagher!"*

Ross decided to take the shirt collar and handkerchief and leave the Compound of Wild Cherry. Perhaps Malcolm could use it after he was through bellowing his lungs out.

"Gallagher!" Malcolm yelled, clearly in a fury at being ignored. "In my office! Now!"

"Time to get hauled over the coals," Ross muttered to himself, then gave Virgil a crooked smile and a careless shrug before turning and taking the long walk. As was getting to be habit of late, all eyes in the city room followed his progress until he closed Malcolm's office door behind him.

"You sure got a lot of sand in your craw to come here today, you know that, Gallagher?"

Ross met Malcolm's burning gaze. The older man hadn't taken a seat but stood behind his desk, feet planted wide apart, his big hands clenched into fists.

The barely controlled fury on his jowled face might have been deadly if he were a man prone to physical violence.

"What did you expect?" Ross asked. "I thought it would be a good idea to clear the air between us."

"Clear the air?" he repeated. "You humiliate my daughter and make a fool out of me, and you thought it might be a good idea to clear the air?"

"It was never my intention to hurt Johanna. I thought we could make a good marriage, but I was wrong. She deserves a man who will care for her like a husband should. That man isn't me."

"Oh, you were wrong, all right. Wrong to underestimate my tolerance for traitors. How long have you been in cahoots with Emily Winters?"

Ross sighed. "Let's leave Emily out of this."

"I suppose you found it amusing that she took advantage of her position here to try to rob me blind?"

"No, I didn't, but I also couldn't blame her. She had reason to believe that you were responsible for forcing the *Gazette* out of business."

Something in Malcolm's expression faltered as he absorbed this information, then he smiled thinly and narrowed his eyes at Ross. "Did she? Well, we all know how a woman's imagination can be driven by her emotions."

"Not in this case. She has sources to verify that you and your partners applied financial pressure to the *Gazette*'s advertisers to drop their ads with Nathaniel. Is that true?"

"What if it is? There's nothing illegal about it. Business is business. That was something poor Nathaniel never quite grasped. Now it's too late for him, isn't it?"

"Maybe so, but his daughter certainly seems to be quick to learn." Reaching into his side pocket, Ross withdrew Emily's handbill and tossed it onto Malcolm's desk.

He gave Ross a wary look before picking it up to scan its contents. A brief frown creased his brow as he took in the advertisement, but then he crumpled the paper and threw it down with a dismissive snort. "Doesn't matter. We'll drop our rates to match hers."

"But not before she gets her twenty orders today."

"Maybe not, but we'll keep them down until she folds. She can't possibly outlast us."

"I wouldn't be so sure," Ross said. "She can be very tenacious once she gets fixed on something. Have you taken a look out your window this morning?"

Malcolm grunted in disgust. "It'll blow over."

"Only time will tell. Maybe you should have stuck to sound business tactics to deal with Nathaniel Winters from the beginning. Like trying to put out a better paper." Ross moved to leave. He'd said all he'd come to say, but Malcolm wasn't about to allow him the last word.

"Take a good, long look around before you leave, Ross. I told you that you were wrong to underestimate my tolerance for traitors. I intend to see that this is the last newspaper you ever work on."

"Do your worst," Ross muttered, then yanked open the door. This time the city room was quiet as a cemetery as he strode through. Poor Iggy stared, looking almost on the verge of tears. Ross offered him a wink and a quick two-fingered salute on his way out. There was no turning back now.

\* \* \*

The war wasn't over, but the first battle was won. Unless he changed his mind and pled guilty, Arnold Gibson would go to trial in a few weeks. Of course Emily was happy as she and a conservatively dressed Stacy came out of the city hall building. She accepted Melissa's warm hug and Miss Bea's fond pinch on the cheek. It was with a certain sense of accomplishment that she watched a new, more confident Stacy Bliss leave under the wings of Miss Bea and her do-or-die quilting circle. And she also had a very good feeling about Melissa and Karl. When Karl took Melissa aside to confer on the corner of the square, she paused to watch them with a somewhat wistful sense of completion. Neither of them seemed to know it yet, but she predicted a wedding before the end of the summer.

It was certainly a day for celebration, Emily thought as she strolled back to the print shop, yet she wondered why these victories tasted so bittersweet and why she was suddenly left feeling so curiously empty inside.

When she entered the shop, Dorcas came scurrying up to her before the door bells could stop jangling. "Aunt Emily, look! We got orders! A hundred of 'em!"

"Twelve," Karen corrected with a smile from behind one of the front desks. She waved a handful of order sheets. "I meant to get your office floor mopped, but it's been so busy, I haven't had a chance to get back there all morning."

"Which is for the best," Marguerite interrupted sternly, coming forward with a huge feather duster in hand. She addressed Emily. "I told her she wasn't to do any heavy work today. Her ankles are swelling up like pumpkins."

# FOREVER AND ALWAYS

Karen rolled her eyes in aggravation. "Mama, I can't just sit here like a crystal statuette. What good is that?"

"Plenty good," Emily cut in, eyeing her sister's very pregnant middle. "You're here to take print orders. You needn't worry about cleaning. I'll take care of that later."

"When 'later?'" Karen demanded, again waving the print orders at her. "You're going to be a very busy lady."

"What have we got?" Emily asked.

"Three hundred business cards, fifty raffle tickets, one hundred programs . . . "

Emily nodded. This was all well and good. What she'd been hoping for in offering a temporary discount was an order large enough to help offset her immediate cash problem. "Anything big?" she asked hopefully.

Karen gave her a sly smile. "How about five thousand carton labels and two thousand billheads?"

Emily's eyes grew wide. "All in one order?"

Grinning, Karen nodded. "You're lucky that Mr. Bertram Douglas happened to be in town this morning on business and that he knows a bargain when he sees one."

Emily didn't wait for her sister to elaborate. It was common knowledge that Mr. Douglas owned, among many other business enterprises, an iron foundry in nearby Sadsbury Township. She snatched the print orders and shuffled through them. There it was, in black and white, with Mr. Douglas's spidery signature to verify it. With an order that size, there would be room for a small profit despite her discount. Better yet, if she could impress the man with the quality of her work, there might be more orders from him in the future.

"Well, it looks like we'll be in business for another month," Emily said, looking up to meet her family's beaming faces. "We may make a go of this yet."

"Isn't that what you've been saying all along?" Marguerite inquired teasingly.

Dorcas didn't give Emily a chance to respond. "I want to help! I want to do letters!"

"Letters?" Emily repeated, puzzled.

"She wants to set type," Marguerite clarified. "All of four years old and she wants to be a printer like her pappy and aunt Emily. Remind you of anyone?"

Emily laughed and knelt down to look her niece in the eye. "When you learn your alphabet, you can help me put the type in their proper compartments, all right?"

"And I want to run the press!"

"Not just yet," Emily said. "Right now, Mammy needs your help and your mama needs to rest, so why don't you help dust, then I'll let you help me load paper into the press."

Dorcas frowned at this less-than-exciting proposition but agreed. "Oh, all right."

Emily stood. "Good girl."

Just then, the door bells jangled, and Emily turned in time to see Melissa sweep inside. Out of breath and with her bonnet slightly askew, her friend appeared flushed and windswept.

"Good morning, Mrs. Winters. Karen. Dorcas." Melissa nodded at each of them hurriedly, then crooked a gloved finger at Emily. "I need to talk to you about something."

"Let's go to my office," Emily said, handing Karen

the print orders and leading the way as her mother took Dorcas's hand and they set to work. "You look like it's something important."

"It is," Melissa responded. "Quite urgent."

"What is it?" Emily asked as she closed the office door behind them.

Melissa nibbled her lower lip and fumbled with the strings of her handbag. "I spoke with Karl Becker."

"Yes, I saw," Emily said, leaning back against her desk and folding her arms. "What did he want?"

"He asked if he could come call, and he also asked me to go to the Fourth of July celebration with him in a couple of weeks. This is the second time he's approached me. I turned him down about going riding in his buggy once before. He has such a rakish reputation, you know, but now I . . . I just don't know what to do."

"Well, do you want to go?"

"I didn't believe so at first, but then he said something that left me, um, rather unsettled."

"And what was that?"

Even though they were alone in the room, Melissa leaned close in a confidential pose and whispered, "He said that his loins *burn* for me."

Emily stared at her. It was a struggle not to laugh out loud. "Really? He actually said that right out on the street?"

"Yes," Melissa confirmed seriously, "according to him, they're virtually afire every minute of the day."

"Good heavens. I imagine that must be terribly uncomfortable."

"He said he can barely sleep at night, and that amorous thoughts of me are interfering with his work," she added, her cheeks glowing bright red by now.

"And what did you say?"

Melissa fluttered a nervous hand through the air. "Well, I didn't know *what* to say! I was aghast. None of my beaux ever said such shocking things to me before."

"Well, perhaps they were just too bashful to speak of it aloud," Emily offered, trying to be practical.

Melissa frowned. "I tend to think not. I never gave Elwood's loins much thought, mind you, but its rather hard to imagine them afire under any circumstances whatsoever."

Emily thought back to what she could remember of her friend's former beau, a bespectacled college student, and had to concur. "You're right. Elwood seemed much more passionate about his studies than womanhood in general, I think."

"Yes, but that certainly doesn't seem to be true with Karl."

"No," Emily agreed, "it certainly does not."

"What do you think I should do?"

"I don't see any harm in allowing him to pay a few visits, and why not accompany him on the Fourth? One thing is certain, you won't be bored, and you might even have some fun."

"Fun?" Melissa blinked at her as if the very concept were unheard of.

"Yes, fun."

"But he's so bold and . . . and *dangerous*."

Emily raised a skeptical eyebrow. "That didn't seem to bother you before. If I remember correctly, you had a bit of a crush on him when we were twelve."

Melissa colored again. "But we were just children. All children want what they can't have, and Karl was

# FOREVER AND ALWAYS

exactly that. The one boy I could never have. What did I know of love then?"

What do any of us know of love? Emily thought. She was the wrong person for Melissa to turn to for advice. The only man she had ever loved was due to walk down the aisle with another woman in less than a week. She didn't voice these doubts but instead pointed out, "You could have had Elwood or any of the other fellows you wrote to me about, yet you didn't marry any of them because you didn't truly love them. That's what you said in your letters, right?"

"Yes, but I don't understand what that has to do with this."

"Well, it may be that you will finally have your chance with Karl. How does that make you feel?"

Melissa frowned. "Very unsure and, to be honest, a little afraid."

"Afraid of what?"

Melissa let out a sigh and looked at the floor. "Afraid that if I allow myself to fall in love with him, he'll up and leave me for another woman. He has such a wicked reputation that way. I don't think I could bear that. Why take the chance?"

"Because perhaps Karl has finally grown up," Emily offered. "He's got a very good job, and he seems serious about making a success of it. Perhaps the love of a good woman is the final ingredient he needs to help plant his feet firmly on the ground."

"The love of a good woman?" Melissa's head popped up and she appeared to consider this. "Do you think so?"

"Well, there are no guarantees, of course."

"Fun," Melissa whispered. Her eyes seemed to lose focus as she pondered her options, but then she brightened and smiled. "Perhaps it's time to take a chance, after all."

# 23

*It was almost an hour* after his confrontation with Malcolm when Ross arrived at the Winters Print Shop. He would have come directly, but he'd had one stop to make first. He wasn't about to make another mistake; he'd come prepared this time.

"Ross!" Emily's sister appeared shocked from where she sat behind a receiving desk near the door.

"Good morning, Karen," he said as he surveyed the shop. "You look radiant, if you don't mind my saying so."

Today this place was a far cry from the deserted shell he'd found the night he'd followed Emily from the *Herald* office. Sunlight streamed in through the open windows to reflect off immaculate wood and metal surfaces. A summer breeze wafted through the shop, but not even that could completely eradicate an underlying odor of turpentine and wood polish. Marguerite Winters and Karen's young daughter Dorcas hadn't yet noticed his presence. They were busy chatting as they cleaned two tables in the back.

There was life and movement and vitality here

once again. A pulse. But this time it was Emily's spirit and determination that drove it.

"Do you want to place an order?"

Ross forced his attention back to Karen. She'd recovered from her initial surprise. With her lips pursed, she cocked an eyebrow and regarded him as if he were a cow patty on her parlor carpet. "Engraved wedding invitations, perhaps?"

"Very perceptive of you," Ross replied. He knew he would have to make his peace with Karen over time. He just hoped Emily would give him that time. "Keep an order sheet ready. Where's your sister?"

"She's not—"

"I'm right here."

Ross looked up to find Emily standing by the foot of the stairs with an unopened crate in her arms. She wore a soiled printer's apron over her dark dress, her sleeves were rolled up, and her hair was half up and half down. There was a huge ink smudge on her nose, and she was sweating. She looked beautiful.

"What do you want?"

"I came to get a job."

"You came to get a *what?*"

"I quit the *Herald*." He shrugged. "Or I was fired. I suppose it depends on whose viewpoint you take."

Emily stared at him.

Taking advantage of catching her off guard, Ross approached. "Malcolm's not real pleased with me right now. It might have something to do with the fact that I broke my engagement with his daughter, but that's all water under the bridge. Now it looks like I'll be needing a new job."

Ross stopped and took the crate from her. She was still watching him, assessing his words, and by now, he sensed both Marguerite and Dorcas as well as Karen were assessing him, too. The place had grown unnaturally quiet and expectant.

"You see, I need a job real soon," he continued, "because I intend to make a down payment on Phares Hockstetter's place. After all, a man can't propose to the woman he loves unless he knows he can provide a decent home for her." He paused and nodded to the crate he held. "Where do you want this?"

"Over there," Emily said, pointing to a worktable.

Ross took it over to the table she indicated. He smiled and nodded at Marguerite and Dorcas, who stood observing the proceedings with respective ill-concealed amusement and childish curiosity.

"Good morning, Mrs. Winters."

"Good morning, Ross."

"Good morning, little Miss Miller."

"'Morning, sir."

"Well, you can't possibly think you're going to get a job here!" Emily blurted.

Ross turned to face her. "Why not? The way I see it, I've got some money invested in this place. That means I have a direct interest in its success."

"You certainly do *not* have money invested in this business."

"Oh, I most certainly do. Or are you forgetting that hundred-dollar loan I made a while back?"

"And that's *all* it was!" She jabbed a finger at him. "A loan. I'll pay you back in full."

"Oh, no you won't."

"Oh, yes I will!" With a defiant toss of her head, she spun around and headed for the job press.

Ross followed her. "No, you won't."

"Oh, ho, ho! I most certainly will!"

"Won't."

"Will!"

"Children," Marguerite interrupted gently, "please think of the example you're setting."

Both Ross and Emily turned to see little Dorcas following their exchange with round, eager eyes. "Sorry," Ross said.

Emily was less contrite. She waggled a finger at her niece. "Mind you, Dorcas, men operate under the misguided assumption that they are always right. It is our God-given duty as women to point out to them that this is rarely the case."

She gave Ross a pointed look, then turned her back to cross to the nearest composing desk. She pulled out a drawer of type. "You seem to have forgotten, Mr. Gallagher, that I already made one payment on that loan."

"Ah, yes," Ross said, reaching into his pocket, "glad you reminded me. I've been meaning to return this ever since you dropped it on my floor the other day before we—"

"*Stop!*" Emily's cheeks flamed scarlet as she charged the short distance between them to snatch the greenbacks he produced. Stuffing the bills into an apron pocket, she lowered her voice to a frantic whisper. "Are you out of your mind? My family is listening!"

"What's the matter? Afraid they'll force us to marry if they find out we—"

"Stop!" Emily clapped a hand over his mouth.

"Then marry me," Ross said, though the words were muffled beyond recognition into her palm.

"Outside," Emily said from between set teeth. Her tone was dead serious, but any authority she hoped to display was ruined by the huge ink spot on her nose. "We will continue this discussion outside." She removed her hand from his mouth.

"Em, you've got a—"

"Outside!" she insisted. Turning, she struggled to untie her apron strings as she moved toward the back door.

Ross followed, wincing when she tried to tear the uncooperative garment off over her head but got it stuck on her elbow. She yanked and muttered something unintelligible as it tangled in her hair, then she flung it backward to smack him in the face.

The door creaked open then slammed hard enough to rattle the washstand mirror on the wall next to it.

Ross pulled the apron off his head and grinned at Marguerite. "I really love it when she gets like this. I'm probably the only one, though, right?"

"Yes," she replied, "you probably are."

Ross winked and tossed the apron to Dorcas, who caught it with a giggle. He went outside to find himself standing in a small courtyard that separated the print shop from the rear of a three-story brick hotel.

"Over here!"

Ross looked to see Emily waiting with folded arms by the corner of the building. A second later, she vanished into the narrow alley off to the side. He followed her.

"What are you trying to do?" she demanded when he appeared around the corner. Her skirmish with the apron had loosened her chignon completely, leaving most of her hair streaming down her back and over her shoulders.

Ross smiled. "I told you. I came for a job."

"Do you find this humorous?"

"Not at all. I'm very serious. I quit my job. I also broke my engagement. I want you to marry me."

"Just like that?"

Ross shrugged. "Well . . . yes."

She poked a finger at his chest. "You break off with Johanna one minute, then traipse over here and propose to me the very next. How convenient. Have you checked on whether Father Carpenter is still available next Saturday?"

"No, I haven't," he replied, reaching up to capture her hand before she could pull it away, "but that's an excellent idea."

"Very funny."

"I don't mean it to be funny. I want to marry you, Em. It's been a long time in coming, and I don't see the point in wasting any more precious time, do you?"

"Yes!" she replied, trying to yank her captive hand free. "I mean, *no!* I won't do it. Who's to say you won't change your mind again? You did once before. Then what?"

"I won't change my mind," he assured her, wrapping his free arm around her waist and bringing her hard up against him. She wasn't happy about it, as evidenced by the riotous look in her eyes, but she sure felt good to him just the same. "And if you need proof," he added, "try this."

Oh, she wanted to kiss him, all right. Ross could tell by her surprised little gasp and the instant, almost imperceptible relaxing of her body against his, but she sure as hell wasn't about to admit it. A split second after his mouth came down on hers, she clamped her lips together. Tight.

He tried coaxing and probing with the utmost of patience, but to no avail. He whispered against her stubbornly sealed mouth. "Come on, Em. One kiss, that's all. Just one. You know you want it."

"No, I don—"

That was all he needed. He captured her parted lips, molding them to his own in a long, sensual kiss that elicited exquisite, intertwined memories of one reckless night's lovemaking on the eve of war and one Sunday afternoon's playful abandon on a parlor floor. If Ross had his way, he would have more of the same, much more, enough to fuel a lifetime's worth of memories for them both.

A frustrated moan came from deep within her throat before she turned her head away. "No."

"Yes," Ross said, skimming his lips across her jaw and down her neck.

"Let go."

Reluctantly, he did as she asked, but not, apparently, what she expected. When he let go, she stumbled back a few steps to smack into the brick wall behind her. "Oh! Jiminy pats!" she exclaimed, clapping a hand over her mouth. He hadn't heard her use that expression in years. "Curse my traitorous mouth!"

"While you're at it, you'd better curse every other part of your body that wants more of the same, Em."

"Stop doing this to me!"

"I never want to stop. I want to kiss you again and again and again. I want peel off all your clothes and touch every part of you. I want to take you to bed every night of the week and make love to you until you scream with delight. I want—"

Emily shook her head and covered her ears. "Go away!"

Ross took her by the wrists, pulling her hands from

her ears. "Hear this. I'm *not* going away. Maybe I need to state the obvious. There's a chance you could already be pregnant again."

"What? You think I haven't thought of that?"

"You're not behaving as if you have. One thing's for sure, though, you're stuck with me this time. I'm not leaving. Not ever again."

She pulled free. "Well, if you won't go away, then I will."

"Where?"

Turning away, she made a dash for the Queen Street end of the alley. "Someplace where I can think in peace!"

"All right! Fine!" he called after her. "But you should know that you've got a big ink spot on your—"

But she'd already disappeared around the corner and out onto the busy sidewalk.

"—nose," he finished and let out an aggravated sigh. He knew where he would find her. But that was for later. Now, he would go back inside that print shop, roll up his sleeves, and set to work. He'd promised her he wouldn't go away, and he intended to start making good on that promise today.

---

There hadn't been a good soaking rain for over a week. The grass was dry, prickling the back of Emily's neck and itching against her bare ankles and heels. The sun's rays dried the few drops of warm water that remained from when she'd splashed at the edge of the creek a few minutes ago.

Hot. Oh, yes, it was hot, and as she lay on her back with her eyes closed, soaking up the heat and sun, listening to the soft buzz and hum of insects, she was sweating clear through many layers of clothes. But that was good. Summer was supposed to be hot. It even smelled hot, like parched grass and stagnating, muddy water. Hot and lazy. Empty of worries and troubles.

A flutter of activity in the oak tree branches to her left made her crack one eye open to spy a pair of bluebirds perched on a low-hanging limb. They were side by side, the one a vivid blue with a burnished red breast and the other a shade lighter. A male and a female, taking a break from the serious business of food gathering and nest building to experience a few moments of quiet companionship. Emily closed her eyes again. For them, it was simple. Not so for her.

She tried to clear her mind, but it didn't work. Instead, she thought back to the very beginning, to the day Ross showed up at her father's shop looking for a job.

"Wish that boy would go away," she whispered to herself. "If Papa won't make him, then I will."

And she'd almost succeeded, except for the fact that the boy, in his own quiet way, had proven to be almost as stubborn as she was. She wondered how differently her life would have turned out if, all those years ago, Ross had gone away like she'd wanted. Very differently, she knew, and she found that despite all their tribulations, she didn't care for that idea at all.

There was a rustling sound far off to her right. She wasn't alone. Someone was making his way down the steep, wooded embankment. "Whoa! Whoops! Look out!"

At his warning call, Emily pushed up onto her elbows to shade her eyes. Ross was scrambling down the little hill, sending a shower of loose pebbles and puffs of dry dirt ahead of him. It was an incongruous sight, Ross in his city clothes and shiny black shoes, trying to negotiate in bucolic surroundings, surroundings Emily associated with their barefooted childhood. Yet no more incongruous than she herself—a full-grown woman dressed in mourning black, shoeless, lying flat on her back in the grass.

"What are you doing here?" she asked.

Wearing a familiar grin, Ross brushed himself off and approached. "Nice place. Come here often?"

Ah, so he wanted to play games. That was fine. In fact, that suited Emily's mood perfectly. Taking a deep breath, she lowered her voice and narrowed her gaze. "Go away."

Ross hunkered down before her. "Does your pa know you come here every Saturday?"

"Sure he knows. What business is it of yours?"

"It's my business because I know it's been you pulling those tricks on me at the shop."

Emily wrinkled her nose, then lay back down again, closing her eyes and folding her arms across her chest. "You don't have any proof of that."

"I don't need any. Your pa knows, too."

"Did he say so?"

"Nope, but he knows just the same."

"You're lying. If he knew, he would have given me the dickens for it."

"I hope he does."

Emily lay silent for a moment, then smiled in satisfaction. "But he never did, you know. He never said one word about it."

"That's because he left us to work it out on our own. He was a smart man, your pa."

Emily pushed up onto her elbows again. "Sure he was. And he had a smart daughter, too."

Ross had settled down to sit beside her. He picked at some grass blades as he spoke. "Don't I know it. Smart enough to revive his business and make a success of it. You know who stopped by after you left?"

"Who?"

"Old Jacob Groff. He plunked down his money and made your twentieth order for the day. He also said he'd take out a regular ad if you ever decide to start up the *Gazette* again. He doesn't hold with your crazy notions about women getting the vote, but he thinks you have a knack for getting people's attention. Everybody's talking about that handbill."

"Good," Emily said.

"Maybe we could even try it."

"Try what?"

"Start up the old *Gazette* again. I mean, after the job printing begins to earn a profit. Why not? We could start out as a weekly, and—"

"Wait a minute. What's this 'we' stuff?"

"You and me." Ross reached out to take her chin in his hand. "You and me. Married. With kids. And a house. And a business. And—"

Emily pushed his hand away and sat up. "I didn't say I'd marry you. There are things to consider first."

"Like what? I love you, and I think you feel the same about me. What else is there to consider?"

"Last week you were going to marry Johanna. This week you say you want to marry me." Emily paused. Her next question didn't come easy, but she had to pose it again and hope that he would tell her the truth this time. "Who will it be next week, Ross?"

"You," he said seriously. "Johanna doesn't mean anything to me."

"How can you be so sure?"

"Because I haven't felt anything for her for a long time. At least, no more than as a means to some pathetic idea I once had of success. Maybe I didn't know it at the time, maybe my pride was still hurting, but if I ever really felt anything for her, it was finished the night before I left for the war."

Emily frowned. The memory of that night was still very profound. And painful.

Seeing her expression, he pressed, "It wasn't Johanna I thought about those long nights when I was a prisoner, and it wasn't Johanna I came home for. It was you."

"Me?" Emily looked into his eyes to see if she could read any insincerity there. She saw none. "You came home for me?"

"I believed I had a mistake to make amends for. I thought we ruined our friendship by becoming lovers that night. I couldn't live with that. I wanted my best friend back. Now, though, I suspect that our mistake wasn't in crossing the line between friends and lovers but in trying to go back again. We can't ever go back again."

"No," Emily agreed cautiously. To her, this simple truth had always been evident.

Ross smiled. "But that's fine with me because I don't want to go back anymore. I still want my best friend, mind you, but I want my lover, too. In fact, I find it terribly intriguing that both happen to be the same woman."

"I could have told you that long ago," she said.

"I think you did." Ross leaned forward to toy with

a loose strand of her hair. "Except maybe not with words . . ."

The playful glint in his eyes stirred a warm tickle in Emily's stomach. To squelch it, she looked away and pretended to observe the antics of a squirrel by the foot of a sycamore. Clearing her throat, she changed the subject. "So, what happens to Eleanor?"

"Eleanor?"

"In your novel," she said, watching the squirrel dart up the tree trunk and disappear into a green scrub of leaves.

"Ah, so you read it. I knew you would."

"You haven't answered the question."

"That's because I haven't finished the book."

"Oh."

"Except . . ."

Emily gave him a cautious sideways glance. "Except?"

"Except maybe you can help me with the ending."

"Oh?"

"When Andrew left for the war, you see, Eleanor was still very young. Even though she was growing into a beautiful young woman, Andrew had trouble seeing that clearly. He preferred to keep thinking of her as his best friend's little sister. It was safer that way."

"Hmm."

"When Andrew returns from the war, both he and Eleanor have changed, and he realizes that she is indeed a very beautiful young woman and he falls madly in love."

"That makes perfectly good sense to me," Emily said. "He was an imbecile for not realizing it from the beginning."

"Well, yes," Ross said, "I think we've established that. The question is, what does Eleanor say when he asks her to wed?"

Emily pondered this as she stared at the sycamore tree. It seemed forever until Ross finally broke the silence.

"I meant to tell you earlier. You have an ink spot on your nose."

"What?" Emily looked around. "What?"

"An ink spot. Right . . ." Ross indicated the tip of her nose with his forefinger. "There."

"Oh!" Emily rubbed at it with her hand, then looked to see a smudge of black on her fingers. "Darn it."

"I know what'll help fix that. A dip."

Emily turned to see Ross removing his shoes and socks. "What?"

"A swim," he clarified, rising to his feet and shedding his suit coat.

Emily glanced at the slow-moving creek. "We'll ruin our clothes."

Ross yanked his necktie loose and flung it to the ground. "Not if we leave them here."

Emily just blinked at him.

Ross began unbuttoning his shirt and grinned. "We used to do it all the time when we were kids."

That was true. They'd often stripped down to their underclothing to swim. It was a common practice among country children, but they weren't children anymore. To anyone who might happen by, they would appear ridiculous if not downright scandalous. She moistened her lips. "But what if someone—"

"No one ever has before." Ross's voice became muffled as he pulled his shirt off over his head. He cocked an eyebrow when he tossed it down. "What's the matter? Scared?"

*Scared?* Like clockwork, Emily's pride kicked in. "Of course I'm not scared."

Ross didn't reply. He merely offered an enigmatic smile as he stripped down to his drawers, then left her to sit motionless and sweating under the merciless hot sun.

"Of course I'm not scared!" Emily called.

"Then come on in!"

He'd already disappeared over the small embankment. All Emily could see were smooth, muscular shoulders and the back of his head. Suddenly, she couldn't even see that much as he vanished beneath the water.

"Scared . . . I'll show him scared," Emily said under her breath as she began to unfasten the front buttons of her dress.

Resurfacing with a splash and a hearty whoop, Ross shook his head, spraying droplets in all directions. "Whoa! Exhilarating!" Then, he vanished again.

"Anything he can do, I can do, too," Emily muttered as she wiggled out of her dress and petticoat, and rose to her knees to wrestle with her corset. When she came to her feet, flinging the bothersome garment down onto the wrinkled pile in the grass, she wore a mightily determined expression and not much else.

Reaching the dried mud embankment, she stood in her chemise and drawers, watching as Ross rose from a sitting position to stand. The water level always dropped during the hottest, driest months of the year. If this were spring, it would have easily reached his chest. Today, however, the cloudy creek current only brushed his upper thighs. Water drops sparkled like liquid diamonds against the rich summer tan of his skin, and Emily's eyebrows rose with interest upon noticing that his thoroughly soaked white cotton drawers clung to his splendid male anatomy in a most detailed manner.

He taunted her, "Having second thoughts?"

"You mustn't know me very well." She made her way down the short slope until her toes sank in mud and water. It felt cool and squashy, like soft, wet clay, and she laughed. Two seconds later, the water was up to her knees.

"Come on," Ross urged.

Keeping her eyes locked with his, Emily forged ahead, fighting a delicious shiver that was only partly due to the cold water that lapped at her knees and thighs. She let out a delighted gasp when he reached out, catching her by the waist and bringing her flush up against him.

Wearing a sly little smile, he dropped his head, and she lifted her face, angling her chin so their mouths were only a tantalizing inch apart. She closed her eyes, and—

"Get wet," he said.

"Huh?" But his foot had already come around behind her ankle. A split second later, she landed with a splash on her rump, soaked to the skin and up to her neck in swirling muddy creek water.

"Ross!" She shook her head furiously, spat out some water, and blinked to clear her blurred vision. "That was a dirty trick!"

"Yup. Next time, watch out who you call an imbecile."

"You'll pay," she said. The cold water had been a shock at first, but it already felt good. She wasn't about to say it, though. She kept her eyes on him as he dropped to his knees and took her by one wrist.

"Of that I have no doubt," he said, then grinned as he pulled her up onto her knees to face him. "In fact, I can't wait, but now I want to tell you how the book ends."

"How?" But as he dropped her wrist to move closer and enfold her in his arms, her mind was not upon her own sweet revenge or his novel. It was upon finishing what they'd started.

Their kiss was slow and deep, as earthy and sensual as their surroundings. A new warmth that had nothing at all to do with the sun overhead blossomed in Emily's middle to spread like a long, lazy sigh through her limbs. If she hadn't been able to see the truth in his eyes earlier, she would have known it now. He did love her. He loved her the way a man was supposed to love a woman.

When they parted, Ross didn't release her but instead held her firmly pressed against the length of him. "When Andrew asks Eleanor to marry him, she says . . ."

"Yes." With her arms still locked around his neck, Emily closed her eyes and rested her head against his shoulder. As far she was concerned, they could stay like this. On their knees and in each others' arms. Summertime forever. "Yes, yes, yes, yes."

But Ross chose that moment to let go. Emily's head popped up. "You're not going to dunk me again, are you?"

He didn't reply as he brought his left hand from around her back and opened it to reveal a fragile golden circlet. Emily's lips parted slightly in awe as it caught the light and flashed dazzling white. A marriage ring. And he'd had it all this time.

"Forever and always, Em." Gently, he took her left hand and slid the gleaming gold circle very slowly down the length of her ring finger. "Now you say it."

"Forever and always," she whispered, for that was all she could manage. Her voice had deserted her. She lifted her gaze to his and smiled. As with the promises they'd made to each other so many years before, this one, too, they'd keep.

# AUTHOR'S NOTE

To avoid offending Civil War historians who know better and misinforming those readers who may not, I confess here to shuffling some dates in order to fit more smoothly into Ross and Emily's story. The cornerstone for the national monument at Gettysburg was laid on July 4, 1865, not in early June as it appears here.

And with regard to my home county of Lancaster, Pennsylvania, many of the businesses, streets, and local landmarks mentioned in this text are authentic. Some are not. While the Columbia Pike did indeed run west of the city, most other landmarks mentioned outside city limits are figments of my imagination—the Brenners' Woods and Mowrer's Creek, unfortunately, included. I would like to think, though, that there are countless very special places along our many lazy, winding streams where two children like Ross and Emily could have played in the woods. In fact, I know there are.

# *Let HarperMonogram Sweep You Away*

### MRS. MIRACLE by Debbie Macomber
**Bestselling Author**
Seth Webster, a widower with two young children, finds the answer to his prayers when a very special housekeeper arrives. Her wisdom is priceless, but it is the woman she finds for Seth who is truly heaven sent.

### DESTINY'S EMBRACE by Suzanne Elizabeth
**Award-winning Time Travel Series**
Winsome criminal Lacey Garder faces imprisonment, until her guardian angel sends her back in time to 1879. Rugged Marshal Matthew Brady is the law in Tranquility, Washington Territory, and he soon finds Lacey guilty of love in the first degree.

### SECOND CHANCES by Sharon Sala
*Romantic Times* **Award-winning Author**
Matt Holt had disappeared out of Billie Jean Walker's life once before, but fate has brought them together again. Now Matt is determined to grab a second chance at love—especially the kind that comes once in lifetime.

### FOREVER AND ALWAYS by Donna Grove
Emily Winters must enlist the help of handsome reporter Ross Gallagher to rebuild her father's Pennsylvania printing business after the Civil War. But will working closely with the man she's always loved distract her from her goals?

## *And in case you missed last month's selections...*

### DANCING MOON by Barbara Samuel
Fleeing from her cruel husband, Tess Fallon finds herself on the Santa Fe trail and at the mercy of Joaquin Morales. He brands her with his kiss, but they must conquer the threats of the past before embracing the paradise found in each other's arms.

## BURNING LOVE by Nan Ryan
**Winner of the *Romantic Times* Lifetime Achievement Award**
While traveling across the Arabian desert, American socialite Temple Longworth is captured by a handsome sheik. Imprisoned in *El Süf*'s lush oasis, Temple struggles not to lose her heart to a man whose touch promises ecstasy.

## A LITTLE PEACE AND QUIET by Modean Moon
**Bestselling Author**
A handsome stranger is drawn to a Victorian house—and the attractive woman who is restoring it. When an evil presence is unleashed, David and Anne risk falling under its spell unless they can join together to create a powerful love.

## ALMOST A LADY by Barbara Ankrum
Lawman Luke Turner is caught in the middle of a Colorado snowstorm, handcuffed to beautiful pickpocket Maddy Barnes. While stranded in a hostile town, the unlikely couple discovers more trouble than they ever bargained for—and heavenly pleasures neither can deny.

*Harper Monogram*

---

MAIL TO: **HarperCollins Publishers**
P.O. Box 588 Dunmore, PA 18512-0588

**Yes, please send me the books I have checked:**

- ❏ *Mrs. Miracle* by Debbie Macomber 108346-1 .................. $5.99 U.S./$7.99 Can.
- ❏ *Destiny's Embrace* by Suzanne Elizabeth 108341-0 ............ $5.50 U.S./$7.50 Can.
- ❏ *Second Chances* by Sharon Sala 108327-5 .................... $4.99 U.S./$5.99 Can.
- ❏ *Forever and Always* by Donna Grove 108404-2 ................ $4.99 U.S./$5.99 Can.
- ❏ *Burning Love* by Nan Ryan 108417-4 ......................... $5.99 U.S./$7.99 Can.
- ❏ *A Little Peace and Quiet* by Modean Moon 108315-1 .......... $5.50 U.S./$7.50 Can.
- ❏ *Almost a Lady* by Barbara Ankrum 108449-2 .................. $4.99 U.S./$5.99 Can.
- ❏ *Dancing Moon* by Barbara Samuel 108363-1 ................... $4.99 U.S./$5.99 Can.

SUBTOTAL ............................................................$_____
POSTAGE & HANDLING ..................................................$_____
SALES TAX (Add applicable sales tax) .................................$_____
TOTAL ...............................................................$_____

Name _____
Address _____
City _____ State _____ Zip _____

Order 4 or more titles and postage & handling is **FREE!** For orders of fewer than 4 books, please include $2.00 postage & handling. Allow up to 6 weeks for delivery. Remit in U.S. funds. Do not send cash. Valid in U.S. & Canada. Prices subject to change.  http://www.harpercollins.com/paperbacks  M038

**Visa & MasterCard holders—call 1-800-331-3761**

**ATTENTION: ORGANIZATIONS AND CORPORATIONS**

Most HarperPaperbacks are available at special quantity discounts for bulk purchases for sales promotions, premiums, or fund-raising. For information, please call or write:
**Special Markets Department, HarperCollins Publishers,
10 East 53rd Street, New York, N.Y. 10022.
Telephone: (212) 207-7528. Fax: (212) 207-7222.**